Shatterbreath

Evan M. Burgess

Book One

*For my family and friends, who, whether they liked it
or not, stayed with me every step of the way.
And to my brother, Jeremy.
Thanks, guys.*

Prologue

A faint glow illuminated the cave, emanating from deep within the jaws of the great beast. If it hadn't been before, the fear was a tangible presence among the soldiers, growing thicker with the smoke, suffocating the small cavern.

The captain sensed this and fought to protest it. "Archers, fire!"

Dozens of arrows raced towards the orange glow, but before they struck, the sinister glow receded into the billowing smoke. Silence overwhelmed the soldiers again—until the moment was broken by the crackling sound of arrows skidding across the stone floor, tossed back to them out of the ominous gray.

Again: smoke, silence.

The footmen began to draw their weapons—swords, hammers and poleaxes—but suddenly the dragon came charging. Many of the men stood still, stunned by the fact it was much larger than the average house. With a single swipe of its talons, the soldiers up front were thrown aside, crippled and moaning.

Some behind the front line chose to flee. Those braver—those searching for pride and glory—lunged out viciously with their weapons, which only scraped meekly against the dragon's thick storm-blue hide.

Infuriated, it opened its jagged maw revealing the source of the glow; it boiled up of the gullet of the beast and with a thrust of its head, it sent the scorching fluid forward, hissing as it washed over the screams of the soldiers.

The fire did not discriminate; it burned greedily through the flesh of both the cowardly and brave and the echoes of their torment were twisted into a cruel symphony in the acoustics of the cave.

Those yet unscathed turned back to escape through the opening of the cave. The captain grabbed one of the fleeing men and pushed him back. "Stand your ground, cowards! The king wants this beast dead and I fully intend..." his voice was silenced by a massive glowing rock, plucked from the ceiling and sent barrelling by the dragon's tail, carving a jagged and bloody line through the battalion.

Delvidar stood his ground as the dragon charged into the divide created by the stone. It reared with a serpentine motion, pausing for a grisly moment before it belched forth more fire over the soldiers to one side of the divide—Delvidar thanked the gods he wasn't on that side.

Cautious of its flailing tail, Delvidar joined his comrades as they attacked it from behind, working around to its sides to try and to reach its vulnerable underbelly. The dragon sensed the attack and it swung around, lashing with deadly talons, forcing Delvidar to dive to the ground in defence.

However, as he stood back up he was struck from behind by the dragon's tail. He experienced a moment of strange weightlessness before colliding painfully with a stalactite and crumpling. Dazed, he turned onto his belly and saw a light far away; he confusedly deciphered it to be the entrance of the cave. In an instant, his instinctual pull of self-preservation decided for him that he'd rather be outside and he started shuffling towards the light.

As he crawled away, he could hear snarls mixing with wrenching metal and snapping bones, ever highlighted by the with the agonizing cries of desperation The ground itself rumbled as the massive dragon went about the cave hunting down every last man.

Then, suddenly, everything went quiet. Delvidar laid where he was, petrified and wreathed in the hot blood of his comrades. There was a *huff* and a rush of warm air from behind pushed the hair over his face.

Shaking uncontrollably, he rolled onto his back to come face-to-snout with the dragon. Holding back sobs, he tried to scoot back, pushing with aching arms, moving only inches at a time. He tried to move slowly, for the dragon bared its teeth with every noticeable jerk his body made. It took heavy steps as he moved backwards, keeping the tip of its scaly snout only a foot away from his face.

His back hit the wall of the cave with small and horrible *clink*. With a cringe, he forced himself to look into the eyes of the great beast. It was then he knew he would die. Sharp, heartless, cold—they were eyes of a predator; a ruthless killer.

Then, strangely, he went still. Though his heart still pounded in his chest, he had lost complete control over the motions of his body.

But as the dragon drew even closer, he managed to find his voice hiding deep within the confines of his chest. "P—Please..." he stammered. "Please...no." He knew pleading with the monster was futile. It didn't understand words. It was just an animal; a predator. He couldn't help himself.

Images raced through his mind; of his family, his home and the beloved city he had left behind. The son he wouldn't be able to raise; the wife he would no longer be able to hold.

"I'm sorry," he said, speaking to the lingering images of his small family. The memory of his young child's soft touch enveloped his final thoughts. "I'm sorry I can't be there for you. I'm sorry, young Kael..."

Chapter 1

The blunt sound of thunder penetrated the deep night. The cool waves could be heard beating against the shoreline off in the distance and the spray of the ocean kissed against the cloaked figure. The dark form paused for a moment to make sure the coast was clear. This mission he was on it was of the upmost importance. Even more importantly, he must not be seen. After all was said and done, it would be like this never happened.

The cloaked figure spurred his horse forward, swivelling his body around on the back of the beast to get a view of his surroundings, as unexciting and colourless as they were. Far to the east, there was a faint glow. A kingdom aglow with sentries' torches, more than a single day's journey away. The light seemed called to him, telling him to get out of the frigid seaside air and into a warm chair beside a glowing fire.

But he couldn't, this was much more important.

Earlier, to escape detection, he had chosen the most foolish few sentries of a particular stretch of gate, enticed them with lavishing words and intoxicated them with highly expensive wine. They were women—as were all the guards—and did not take kindly towards his words at first, but he had a silver tongue and in the end his beguile prevailed. With the guard passed out, he had slipped out of the walls of the glorious city and out onto the farmland. He had to take such lengths to avoid arousing suspicion. A person of his...status leaving the city in the middle of the night was a curious thing. And rumours spread like weeds in his kingdom. The last thing he need were more false stories about him floating around.

It had been a short distance to walk, but it seemed to take an eternity before he had finally reached the farmhouse where he had hid his black stallion the previous day. He had found an old barn that had been abandoned long ago. It had been rank and rotten, but it had served its purpose. After he had fetched his horse, it was simply a matter of staying awake for the day and a half ride to the coast while riding along scarcely-used roads as to avoid human contact.

The pebbles popped and crunched under the horse's hooves as he rode it onto the sandy shore of the beach. The rancid stench of rotting seaweed covered this area of the beach and rough shrubs groped up at him. A slight fog hung in the air, adding to the lonely atmosphere. Shivering, he frowned, curling his nose to it all. He really should have chosen a better location. But, unfortunately, this was the best place to meet.

Stopping his horse at the edge of the water, he peered around, feeling tense. His horse kneaded the sand and chewed on its bit, throwing its great head back. He tugged on the reigns, cursing the horse under his breath for making so much noise. But yet, nothing stirred within the dark. Notwithstanding the reassuring stillness, he couldn't shake the ominous feeling in his gut...as if somebody were out there, watching him.

Ignoring the sensation, he turned his attention to the darkened ocean. A white sliver splashed over the waves—the eerie light of the moon reflecting on the waves. Somewhere out there was what he had come for...

Dismounting his horse, he paused once more, looking in all directions to make sure he was still alone. He pulled a tinderbox from a pocket and set to work building a fire after collecting a small pile of driftwood. After a few strikes of metal against flint, a crackling fire danced in front of his feet. It was small, but more than enough light to send his message.

A new source of light appeared over the waves, a tiny, flickering dot far off in the distance. The light of an oil lamp. Once again his thoughts turned to the city he had left behind and the warm castle within it.

The torch waved for a moment, suspended perhaps fifty feet above the water. It flickered out of existence a few moments later. Now he would have to wait, something that he hardly had the patience for anymore.

The supple sound of rowing oars drifted across the water. Even in the scant light, a boat appeared not far off in the distance. It was just a rowboat, filled with only three people. But the man on the beach new there was another, larger craft out there somewhere. Two of the men on the rowboat were rowing, and one stood with a leg on the bow confidently. All three figures were robed in black as well.

The small row boat pulled up onto the shore. Before it had even stopped, the man on the bow hopped off and began to walk towards the awaiting figure in one graceful movement. The other passengers pulled the boat up onto the beach and stood beside the boat with their arms crossed. The one who had alighted first walked up to the awaiting man and stopped a sword's reach away. He stood proud and erect in the posture of a strong military leader. His face was hidden by a dark shroud and the shadows of the night. The awaiting man reached forth his hand in a formal gesture. The newcomer did not return the handshake, but shifted his weight from one foot to the other impatiently, causing sand to crunch underfoot.

"Greetings," said the first man in a raspy voice, through his teeth. He cleared his throat, changing his tone to hide his impatience. "Did you have a nice trip?"

"Humph," the strange man growled, his tone was intolerant yet powerful, "hardly."

There was a slight pause, and then the first man spoke, crossing his arms across his chest. "Do you have the payment?"

There was a rustling as the stranger pulled out a blue silk bag out of his cloak. He hefted it in his hand for a moment, as if considering what was inside was worth the bargain he was striking. The silk bag gleamed beautifully in the moonlight, the finest silk one could buy. "So you're still in then? No second-thoughts? You won't try and double-cross us will you?"

The first man shook his head. "No, we would never consider..."

"Good," the newcomer interjected, "I hate traitors. Besides, it would be a waste of all our time if you decided to change your mind this far into the deal. And foolish. Such a...rash action would be unwise indeed, and dishonourable. There would be terrible ramifications for you."

"We take your advice graciously. As I was saying, we would never go back on our word. Our promise is good, as long as you and your kind keep your word as well. It is not a question of honour on our part, but a query of the same on yours."

"Well met," the newcomer said. His tone was neutral. "It is settled then. Our agreement will continue forth as planned." The newcomer balanced the bag in his hand one more time. He cocked his head under his guise. "Here is our next regular payment, as promised. And as usual, tell your investor that this is only a taste of the feast to come, as promised."

The first figure took the bag, unfurled the top and reached into it. He pulled out the content, a large diamond as large as his fist and glimmering under the light of the moon. With a nod, he placed the diamond back into the bag as if it was nothing special. "It is done then."

The stranger nodded as well. "That it is." Turning on his heels and disturbing the sand, the stranger turned back to his vessel. The boat and its passengers soon slipped back into the ocean, heading off towards the larger ship off in the distance that was hidden by the night.

Alone with his horse, the man waited awhile, feeling the diamond grow heavy in his arms. The deal was done; there was no reason to tarry any longer. He moved to get back onto his horse, placing the bag and the diamond into a pack on the saddle. There came a conflagration of thunder one more time, yet this booming noise sounded unlike any thunder a normal storm would carry. Night was turned to day as a great light erupted from a hill not far away. The dark figure spotted the disturbance, shielding his eyes from a direct view of the source.

A massive jet of flame spewed into the air. The heat was so intense he could feel it from where he stood. The hideously bright flame illuminated the cloaked man, sending deep shadows sprawling across his body. Pale, jutting cheekbones, a thin, curled lip and a pair leering purple eyes were the only things that could be seen through his hood. Those purple eyes scowled at the source of the flame. What was *it* doing here?

The source of his distress, and also the source of the flame, was a massive dragon. The large beast finished its exhalation, and a deep rush of air could be heard as it took a breath. It turned its great head distinctly towards him and even from where he stood he could see its eyes narrowed to slits.

They stared each other down. This was bad, this was terrible. The dragon knew about their meeting. This compromised everything!

But wait...what could it do? It was just a stupid beast, no smarter than the horse he was sitting on. Assuming the creature could even pull together a cohesive thought, whether or not it knew the full plan in action was irrelevant. It could do nothing to stop them and there was no way it could tell anybody. Who would listen or help it anyway?

The man continued to stare at the dragon, but the creature returned his cold gaze with an even sharper one. He quickly covered his face and cowered over his horse. He may have lost the dragon's challenge, but if he kept the visual contact any longer, he might have agitated it. Dragon's were like dogs in that way, look into their eyes too long and they'll pounce. Saying a silent prayer to ward off the dragon, he turned his horse towards home, hoping the dragon wouldn't follow.

There was a booming *whoosh* as the dragon took off from the rock it had been sitting on, his horse shied and he patted its neck in reassurance. The next time the cloaked figure looked up, the giant dragon was gone, like a spectre in the night. No matter. Although its knowledge of their meeting was distressing, he pushed the nuisance of a thought aside. The plan was perfect. It was like a charging bull, and with the momentum it had gathered thus far, nothing could stop it.

The sun was beginning to peek up over the horizon, the faintest glow illuminating the horizon to the west. Time was of the essence. He could not be detected. He flicked the reigns and kicked his steed in the side. The horse rose on two legs, brayed in protest and then set out in a full dash back towards the kingdom.

9

Chapter 2

It was a fine day. Finer than most. Kael paused for a moment, wiping the sweat from his brow with his forearm and standing up straight. He gazed around in bliss at the waves of wheat around him. It was such a green contrast to the sky, it was almost breathtaking. He quickly set back to work. There was a lot to do and no time to rest, especially at this time of year.

He tended to the wheat in a familiar fashion, the same exact thing he had been doing for several hours now. Every once and awhile he would pause again to look around at the beautiful colours of early summer. The sun was shining bright, the wheat rustled serenely from the soft whisper of wind, and there was nary a cloud in the sky to shy away the soft blanket of blue overhead. Although it could get rather boring, he enjoyed working the earth and tending to the crops, especially on days like this surrounded by other people.

Craning his neck, he caught glimpses at the other people working. There were four girls in his near vicinity out in the field, as well as a few older women here and there. They all had the same tanned skin as he and worn similar, if not more modest work clothing. He had dark, nearly black hair and brown, passionate eyes. He was stronger than any of them, and harder working because tending the crops was only one of his many jobs, and he had built up an impressive amount of muscle on his limbs from years of hard work. But by no means were these women weak.

He passed his hand through his dark brown hair. He had caught no end of lip from his friends for letting his hair grow out so long, but he liked it long. He was tall for his age and stood a head higher than most women in the city, which made it easier for him to find his way through crowds. His skin was tanned from all the days working out in the fields, which was often a sign of poverty. His body was moulded and strong from all his various jobs. He flexed his arm, and his bicep protruded impressively. It surprised him, he hadn't looked in a mirror in a long time and he had changed since he had.

The sound of the others could be heard over the rustle of the wheat as the women and he worked speechlessly. They were late on planting this year, due to a rigorous winter and biting frost. Hopefully they could pick enough to last them for another...

Kael looked up at the sky again. He was checking to see what time it was. According to the sun's position in the sky, it was nearly time to leave. Just a couple more minutes.

After doing some more hoeing, Kael threw the tool over his shoulder and began to strut back towards the large city to the east. Some of the women perked up as he took his leave.

"Leaving already?" a lady remarked, "see you later Kael!"

Another piped up. "Have a good day!"

Kael said his farewells to each in turn as he walked through the fields, smiling warmly. Many of the younger girls had been stealing looks at him throughout the day. One younger girl had even stopped working and had just stared in wonder when he took off his shirt due to the early morning heat. He didn't really like that blonde-haired girl, so he had put his shirt back on after fifteen minutes. She wasn't too bright.

The rest of the women continued to work, even after he had left the premise of the field. They would be working there for several more hours. But he was needed elsewhere at the blacksmith.

He walked along the familiar, ox-trodden road that snaked its way up to the city, wiggling his toes in his boots to see if it was time to purchase a new pair from the marketplace. The soles where worn out and it almost felt as if he wasn't wearing footwear at all. His thoughts were interrupted as a cart carrying a large batch of plums came up from behind. Turning his attention to the driver, he smiled and waved.

The woman driving the cart returned his jovial smile and threw a shiny plum at him. He caught it. "Kael," she called, stopping the cart beside him. The ox grunted throatily and Kael took a tentative step away from it. "How are you, my boy?"

Kael shrugged. "I'm doing well, Helena. Beautiful day, isn't it?"

The woman squinted, shielding her eyes from the sunlight. "A little too bright for my tastes, but otherwise it is very fine indeed."

Kael chuckled. Helena always had something to complain about, even if it was the perfect day according to her taste. It was almost a little game they had between each other. Kael bit into the plum Helena had given him, grateful for its sweet flavour.

"Where are you off to then?" she asked.

"You know," he said through a mouthful of juice, "to the blacksmiths. It's Monday, remember?"

She feigned surprise. "Really now? Where have I been for the last few days then? Come on then, boy, don't get sarcastic with me, I know what day it is. It's that blasted schedule of yours that I have a hard time keeping track of."

Kael shifted his weight onto his other foot. Helena pushed a strand of hair away from her face. She looked nice that day, with her brown hair pinned under her bandana. Why was she dressed differently? Usually she wore her hair wild and sprawled around her head like a bird's nest. "What can I say, I'm an important person!" he said, throwing up his arms jovially, "if it wasn't for me—"

"Hey, that's enough there," she interrupted, matching his joking tone. "So do you need a ride, mister so-important, or would you rather keep walking in those pathetic boots of yours?"

Kael nodded and hopped aboard on the edge of the cart. It rocked from the extra weight, but kept balanced. Helena flicked the reigns and the ox started forward. He was certain now; it was time to get new boots.

The cart creaked and swayed on the rugged road, but it was better than walking. They went through the easternmost entrance to the city. Kael then hopped off, waving to Helena. He set off at a quick pace, eager to get to work.

Making his way through the crowds, Kael ignored the usual looks from all the women walking past. He was walking on the main street of the city, which was formed in a general circle around the castle. He was heading through the market, towards the blacksmith's stocky building, but first he was going to make a few pit-stops.

Everywhere Kael looked in the market, there were women doing men's jobs. At the fish monger's, a short, pale woman was chopping the heads off the fish and removing the entrails, while yet another older woman was attempting to sell a high-quality tunic to another rather pompous looking lady over at a merchant's hut. But this didn't bother Kael, not one bit. This was the norm in Vallenfend. There weren't many men at all in the city, compared to the woman at least. Most of the males were either children under the age of fifteen, or older gentlemen pitted with deep wrinkles, neither of which were near suitable for battle. There were men older than teenagers, but it was rare to meet any of them.

As such, it was imperative that the women of the city fulfill the jobs that the men were supposed to work. Things definitely ran different in Vallenfend. And because the women worked these hard, laborious jobs, they were rougher, cruder and more weather-beaten than regular women. And vicious. It was a continuous hunt for them to find a proper suitor in this city. It was no surprise that a vast majority of the women were single, and perhaps would be for their whole lives. It was also no surprise that he, Kael Rundown, was much sought after by the girls around his age group. Ordinarily, he supposed that wouldn't be a bad thing, but again, they could get violent.

Luckily, Kael was kept safe by their grasping hands and voraciousness over him by his friend, Laura. It wasn't that he and Laura were a couple, they had just been best friends for their whole lives, and she made sure that he was protected. Although some girls just didn't care if he appeared taken already.

Thank Laura's heart. What a good friend she was.

"Oi, Kael!" A voice called over to him from the throng of people crowding. Kael pushed his way through a gaggle of girls to find Bunda standing outside her store, which was one of the only enclosed shops on this street. She beckoned him to come inside. "Do you have a moment?"

"Sure," Kael said. He still had several minutes before he was due in at the blacksmiths. He followed the large woman into her butcher shop. As long ago as he could recall, Bunda had always had this butcher shop. The walls were made of wood, with pitch filling the spaces in between. It was a solid building, and hard to break into. Bunda had never once been stolen from. There was a counter taking

13

up most of the room they stood in, with a door leading to the back. Her house was built straight into the building.

He liked Bunda. She was a wonderful woman, somewhat oversized with blotchy skin and a bush-like eruption of orange hair atop her head. She liked to talk using her arms, ensuring it was always an adventure to talk to her. Zealous and bubbly, Bunda had never failed to cheer him up on a sad or rainy day by cracking a rough joke. Just listening to her ecstatic rants was just enough to make him smile. She always loved to jest, and Kael appreciated someone with humour.

Bunda hobbled over behind her counter and pulled up her wooden stool her husband had made her when he was still alive. She paused and stared at the smoothed-out, knotted wood for a moment. She did that often, as if she could still feel his rough hands. He had been a butcher for trade, but had really wanted to be a woodworker. That stool was one of the only results of his hidden passion, as well as an oak chest in the back of Bunda's house.

"How old are you now, Kael?" she asked, sitting down on the stool. Her voice easily filled the room. "I heard that your birthday was a few days ago."

"Oh, yeah, it was. I'm...sixteen now." He had forgotten that he had had his birthday. It wasn't something he was as concerned about anymore. It just passed unceremoniously. It felt like an eternity ago already.

"Sixteen!" Bunda's eyes went wide in shock. She held a hand to her breast as if suffering from a heart attack. "How old my aching heart seems! Sixteen already! You're growing up to be quite the man, Kael."

He beamed. "Thanks, Bunda!"

"I suppose girls are starting to look quite appealing to your eyes now, aren't they?" she teased, slapping the counter.

Kael blushed. "This again? There are plenty of them around. It's kind of hard to ignore them."

Bunda burst out in laughter. "Well met!" Her face suddenly turned grave. "You should count yourself lucky then, Kael. Few boys become men in this city thanks to that cursed king of ours. That man has taken three of my boys already. I would hate to see you go as well."

Kael nodded, reflecting how truly lucky he was. Bunda was referring to the current king's decree. The king had declared that almost all able-bodied men were required to join the army. His law took effect once a boy had hit age sixteen, unless something exempted him from doing so. Some men were let to stay out of the military due to their vital role in the kingdom's economy, being a blacksmith, like Kael's boss for example. Others still were lucky—in a strange way—to have a crippling disease or ailment that left them unable and unworthy to enter combat. In Kael's case, he had been promised by a dear friend of his mother's that he would not be enlisted in the military ever. It was her last dying wish, and her friend in mention had been sealed to his oath. Kael's father, however... was not as lucky. Kael had only been five when his father left.

But the city still thrived. There were enough men to keep the city alive. Many men were let to pair off and have a few children before they were sent to fight, as was the case with his father. Most of those men stuck to their tradition and only married one spouse. Unfortunately, many others married more than one woman. It was generally frowned upon, but necessary to keep up the population.

It was impossible to determine whether or not someone when or if someone was to be enlisted. There seemed to be no pattern to the whole thing. Many men had tried to figure out the system, whether it be alphabetical, by birthdates or of any other similar fashion. Their effort had been in vain.

Kael shook his head, leaning on the counter. "Don't worry about me Bunda, I've been promised that I will never be drafted. You should be worried about Faerd if anything. He's been lucky so far, but..."

Bunda leaned back on her stool. Her eyes scanned over the arrays of meat hanging near the window and she breathed deeply. Kael mimicked her, smelling the thick, salty aroma of freshly cut and wrapped meat. "I wish my boys would have had the same liberties as you, Kael," she said, breaking the silence. "Perhaps I would have more help around the home and in work. My bones ache for rest. And I long to hold my boys again..." Her eyes faded over, as if she was looking in the distance, but she shook herself. "Bah, never you mind about my laments. You are sixteen! What a fine age to reach! By the way, I have a gift for you, my boy."

Kael frowned. "No, Bunda, I don't need anything, really. You keep it."

Bunda also frowned as she stood up off her chair. "What? You would rather play polite then have a nice meal? My word, boy, it's no wonder you're so thin."

Kael hesitated, allured by the prospect of a good meal. "Well, maybe I could accept a gift after all, if you insist anyway."

Bunda laughed heartily. "Oh, if you say so. Wait here." She disappeared into the back, leaving Kael to his thoughts.

Not long after she left, two soldiers entered the building. They were young, maybe only a year or two older than Kael, but they were still no less intimidating in their leather armour. One of them held a spear in loosely in his grip, the other a sheathed sword strapped to his back. Kael wondered at their weapons. It was surprising that they were garbed with their weapons, let alone the fact that they were outside the confines of the military training camp inside the castle walls. Their eyes flickered back and forth, as if they were scared of something or looking for somebody.

Kael didn't recognize either of them. It was rare that he didn't know a male's face in this city. There was so few of them and most got along quite well together. But these two didn't weren't familiar. One was a shorter boy, with a smooth face and delicate blond hair. The other was rougher around the edges, with dark hair. He was muttering curses under his breath. The one with dark hair used to be a farmer before he became a soldier, judging by his tanned skin.

"You there," the blond boy said, nodding towards Kael, "do you work here?"

"No," Kael replied, "but the lady who does is in the back right now. She will be back in a moment."

The dark haired boy cursed, looking out the window cautiously. "Thanks," the blonde boy said to Kael, patting his friend on the shoulder to try and reassure him.

They stood awkwardly in the room, neither the soldiers nor Kael saying anything. By the way they jittered at every noise outside, Kael could tell that these boys were in some sort of trouble.

Finally, Bunda came back holding a large sack. She paused when she saw the young men and placed it under the counter. "Hello, fellows, how may I help you?"

The blond boy stepped forward. "Yes, we need food."

Bunda shrugged, she wasn't using her usual jocular tone. She didn't trust these boys anymore than Kael did. "Alright then, anything in specific? Don't ask for vegetables though, remember this is a butcher's shop."

"What?" the boy shouted, his voice rising higher than was necessary. "Are you getting smart at me? I have orders from the captain of the king's army. We have come to acquire some provisions for the week."

Bunda crossed her arms over her breast. "Pardon me? I was cracking a joke, son. Humour is something you understand right?" Kael covered his face with his hand, pretending to scratch his nose. He knew Bunda well, and he also knew that you never, ever strike an argument with her. She was passionate with her beliefs, even more so when it was concerning the king. "First of all, the Royal Military buys its provisions from a different supplier, that includes meat, poultry, vegetables, everything. Second of all, if that accursed *king* came in here himself, I would refuse to serve him anything. So you two aren't going to buy so much as a steak bone from me."

The darker boy tried to interject, but Bunda beat him to it. "Now leave me be, go to some other shop that needs your attention more, or else exit and come back in and we'll try this again."

The blonde boy lifted a finger to say something, but Bunda simply raised her eyebrow, ready to argue. The boys said nothing. Giving her one last dirty look, they slipped out of the store and disappeared into the crowds thrumming by.

"What do you think of that?" she said.

17

Kael shrugged. "I doubt they were sent to get meat from you. They looked like they were in trouble or running from something."

"King's soldiers indeed, I doubt that's the last we'll see of them, good or bad," she huffed. "Curse King *Murderdale*, and curse his shadowed advisor. Those two are ill will for this city."

Kael winced as if hit in the gut. "Bunda, don't say that name! You know what the punishment is if you do!" It was well known that there were heavy consequences for calling the king that name.

Kael had to admit through, King Morrindale was rightfully called *Murderdale*. After a few years of the king's new policy, he quickly gained the title Murderdale. Outraged, he had made a decree stating that anybody caught saying that name would be immediately ejected from the city and forced to go fight the dragon alone without any weapons. Whether or not the people who were sentenced to this actually went to fight, or if they tried to escape to a different city was unknown. Either way, they weren't allowed to re-enter the kingdom, and either way, they would die.

The large woman huffed again. "I don't care anymore Kael, I loathe that man so much, yet I am stuck here hopeless. Bah, I put a downer on your day, my boy. But getting back to before..."

Bunda reached under the counter and produced the sack Kael had seen earlier. She untied the top to reveal a hefty stack of meat. "This is for you," she said lovingly, "consider it a payment for your years of friendship. Happy Birthday!"

Kael smiled. "You're far too kind, Bunda, thank you!" She nodded in reply. "Can I come get this later?"

"Of course."

Saying his goodbyes and thanks a few more times, Kael exited Bunda's humble store. He looked up at the sky through the grey rooftops of the merchant's huts. He cursed. He was very late! Kael set off at in a sprint.

Korjan, the blacksmith, was not very angry. There was little that could get that stocky man fuming. When Kael arrived, flustered, he pardoned Kael's tardiness and told him to stay a few minutes after his shift to make up for it.

Korjan was a big, brawny man, moulded from all his years as a professional blacksmith. His eyes were set deep in his heavy brow and his lips were positioned in a permanent frown. He was intimidating indeed, but Kael knew him to be a patient, if not somewhat of a rough person. Whatever negative things Korjan said, he never meant at all.

As Kael worked, pounding hot metal flat to make weapons, he considered how truly blessed he was, reflecting on Bunda's words. Joining the military was frightening, but that alone posed little true danger. It was the enemy which Vallenfend raged war with, which King Morrindale raged against. That was the real threat.

Vallenfend was a medium-sized city placed fairly close to the ocean, which gave them a moderate climate all year round. To the far west was the sea, but to the east there resided a large spine of mountain ranges that stretch north to south several hundred miles. Up on the closest mountain to the city, near the top, there rested a cave set deep into the mountain's side. It was in that cave where the sworn enemy of the kingdom lived. The one, lone enemy.

Kael shuddered as he thought about the cave. On particularly sunny days, when the eternal fog around the mountain subsided, one could clearly see the dark shadow that was the cave. Kael had once seen it, that dark pit surrounded by an unnatural cold blue. He had had nightmares that night.

Trying to push away the thoughts, Kael made a resolution to try and enjoy the rest of his day without thinking of the cave, what lived inside, or the army. He turned to the blacksmith.

"So, Korjan, is there anything new with you?" Kael asked. He paused his pounding. The huge blacksmith faced him as he poured some liquid metal into a mould.

"Nothing much," Korjan grumbled, turning back to his work. He shovelled some coal into the furnace, while mumbling something else.

"What was that?"

Korjan gave him an impatient look over his shoulder. "Nothing, Kael."

19

Undeterred, Kael tried again. "No, you said something just then, what was it?"

"Hmm. You're a persistence fellow, aren't you?"

Kael shrugged. "Always have been."

Korjan leaned up against a blackened counter. He wiped his brow with a dirty rag, then his bare chest. He had taken off his shirt long ago, which held its dangers. Korjan didn't seem to mind if he got burnt. "I said that Helena asked me to dinner yesterday."

"Really?" This was huge news! Anytime a woman attempted to court a man, or vice versa, it was quickly spread throughout the neighbourhood. Sometimes it was a deterrent though, as the news wasn't always positive and it spread ill feelings for others who had their eyes on a certain man. That explained why Helena was dressed nicely.

"I denied her request. She insisted on dinner tonight, but I'm not going."

"What?" Kael scoffed. "Why would you do that?"

"I have my reasons, boy, now get to work." This time, Korjan meant it. Kael set to work. He knew better than to cross the burly man.

Korjan had a secret hidden in his past that he had never told anybody, a dark deed committed that he wanted to hide at all costs. Not once had he ever mentioned anything from his past, or talked about old memories. It seemed as though when he worked, he did it to bring himself away from those memories, to tear himself away from his troubling thoughts. Maybe it was for that reason that Korjan was the best blacksmith the kingdom had.

Kael left him alone as he set back to work.

Kael left the blacksmith's in a hurry once his work was over, eager to get to his next job. Dogs barked in the background somewhere, and in the distance, birds could be heard singing cheery songs in the trees of the gardens. The sun shone happily from overhead, and indeed, every person Kael passed seemed to be wearing a smile. The wondrous day was beginning to trouble him. Still staring at the sky, he gulped. Sometimes a day as fair as this was a forbearing of a something terrible. A day like this hung on Kael's shoulders like a curse. It was on a day like this his mother had died and on a similar day that his father had been drafted. He had high hopes on those days too, that by some cosmic chance, neither of them would have to leave.

Kael turned his focus away from himself and to his attention towards hurrying to the granary south of the castle where he worked. They had been shifting the grain to make more room for the next season's batch. He liked the job because it passed quickly and the people who worked there weren't interested in talking. It gave him time to think. The only downfall is that it let out close to dinner, and he was starving already!

He was even hungrier by the time he finished, but that was alright because he was going to Laura's for dinner that night. They would have a glorious meal prepared.

Kael arrived at Laura's humble house in no time. It was only a few blocks from his house, and not too far from where he did his last job. He had set up all his jobs like that on purpose. Nothing was too far for Kael to get to. He supposed that was a blessing in his life as well. He would hate to have to run across the kingdom to get to something, and then rush all the way back.

Laura's mother was waiting outside when he arrived. She was a kind woman, but could get very stern. She was short and somewhat squat, with the same thin blonde hair as her daughter. She insisted that Laura do as little physical work as possible, saying that women weren't supposed to be so strong. She liked to hold onto dwindling traditions. Even so, it was inevitable that she and her daughter both had to get employed. Her job was far more demanding, whereas Laura's was not.

"Hello, Mrs. Stockwin," Kael chirped as he ran up. He paused to catch his breath. "How are you doing?" The sweet aroma of a succulent dinner flowed out of the humble house.

"Kael, I'm doing good, thank you," she replied courteously, the same stern edge in her voice as always. She considered Kael as one of her own, so she was never hesitant to treat him as such. To Kael, she was like his adoptive mother, and he greatly appreciated her influence. Her tone seemed to say, *dear heavens, child, where have you been, why are you so late?* "Come on inside," she said, herding him with her arm.

Kael followed her inside. There, surrounding a wooden table, sat Kael's closest friends. Nearest to him was Laura, with her long, almost white blonde hair flowing gently past her shoulders. She was a modest kind of beautiful, with delicate features and pale skin. Kael had always been impressed that she never seemed to get all caught up in looking her best to impress everybody. Kael had met her at an early age, and they had been the best of friends ever since. They were almost inseparable in their friendship.

Sitting on the other end of the table was Faerd, one of his best male friends. He was a flirtatious boy, and was often seen swooning over more than one girl at once, with them swooning right back. Despite his other priorities, he stayed ever-loyal to his number one friends. He flicked his head, sending his thin, blonde hair waving for a moment as he turned to look at the newcomer. His skin was also dark from working out in the sun. Scars lined his face, making him look older than he was and there was an underlying edge to the stare in his blue eyes, like tempered steel.

"Kael, welcome!" Laura said, placing her fork back down on the table. They had started eating without him.

"Hi, Laura, hello, Faerd," Kael replied, sitting down as Laura's mother placed a plate of roast duck and mashed potatoes in front of him. She then sat down herself. "Glad to see you waited for me."

Faerd laughed, gulping some water from a goblet. "Yeah right, you were as slow as a turtle today, Kael. Why's that? I thought you'd be quick to come for your own birthday meal."

Kael struggled to speak through a mouthful of food. He quickly swallowed and said, "I was late at the smith's because I visited Bunda. Korjan made me stay longer because of it. Same at the granary. I came as quickly as I could, give me a break."

"Why did Bunda stop you?" Laura asked, pushing a tendril of hair away from her eyes.

"Just to give me some meat for my birthday." Kael hesitated, remembering the soldiers. He didn't say anything about them, but opened his mouth to speak again. "You know Helena, the plum lady?"

"Yeah," Faerd scoffed, "everybody knows her and her crow's nest of hair."

Sometimes Kael wanted to punch his scarred face, but not today. Besides, Faerd had gotten into so many fights, he could knock Kael clean unconscious with two strikes. "She tried to court Korjan."

"Really?" Laura's mother interrupted. "That's interesting."

Kael wished he hadn't of said anything concerning that news. Mrs. Stockwin was a fierce gossiper. Any news passed onto her would spread like wine poured into water. He hoped the blacksmith would forgive him for this.

"Uh, yeah." Kael wished there was some way to unsay what he had just blurted out. "But he refused her offer."

Faerd spoke up through a bite of meat. "I don't understand that man, why doesn't he just choose a woman all ready, and stop prolonging this nonsense!"

"I could say the same to you." Laura's calm voice cut the air around the dinner table like a knife. She and Faerd had been quarrelling again. Laura wasn't happy with his flirtations again. Quite frankly, Kael didn't mind what Faerd was doing in his spare time, unless it involved danger or something stupid.

The dinner table stayed quiet for a moment, only the sounds of the clicking metal utensils penetrating the air. Kael could still remember when he had made these forks for them a few years back when he had been practicing his smith work. Finally, Faerd interrupted the awkward quiet. "I hear they're recruiting again."

"Blast that man," Mrs. Stockwin cursed, her eyes darting around the room in anger. Like most mothers she too had lost her boy to the king's army. But it was more than that. All the women were reluctant to give up their sons, but Mrs. Stockwin had been outright defiant. Some soldiers had come and ransacked her house. Her older daughter had tried to fight off the soldiers, but they had killed her without hesitation to get her out of the way. By force, they took her

23

son, burnt her first house down and nearly killed Faerd, who had also stood up to them. Faerd's face still held the scars from that terrible night. And although Mrs. Stockwin didn't have any physical scars, she was wounded inside. That's why she was so concerned with her only daughter and treated Kael and Faerd as her own. The two boys were orphans and she had found it her duty to look after them.

The mood around the table changed from awkward to glum at the mention of such dark news. Kael poked at the food on his plate. Suddenly, he wasn't so hungry anymore. He put his utensils down and picked up his plate. "Thanks for dinner," he said, heading for the kitchen, "I'll see you guys later, alright?"

He cleaned off his plate and walked outside, but Laura stopped him on the street before he could get very far. She embraced him, something she didn't do often. Kael wrapped his arms back around her. The moon shone down on them, glowing bright, undaunted by any overlaying clouds. The world seemed to slow down.

"I'm so glad you're protected from being drafted," she whispered. "You and Faerd are the only men I have left in my life, and Faerd is not as lucky as you, Kael, he's not protected by the king's scholar."

Kael nodded slowly. "I know."

"Don't ever leave."

He nodded again. The sentence struck him against his face for some reason and a chill ran up his spine. He suddenly felt cold. The words he then spoke seemed to come out hollow and empty. "I won't." It felt like he was telling a lie. It tasted dirty. He cringed for some reason.

He was an extremely readable person. There was hardly ever a time when Laura couldn't understand what Kael was feeling just by reading his expression. He didn't like that. Sometimes, he had wished that he could be a secretive, cunning individual, but change didn't come to his personality with ease. For the most part, he liked the way he was.

Laura let go of him, giving him a curious look, reading the same doubt Kael could feel in his chest. Kael bode her goodnight and turned around. Slow at first, he began to walk away. He could feel her watching him.

A few streets later, somewhere out in the distance, a wolf howled. It began low, then grew to an eerie, baleful pitch that echoed long after the animal's cry had ceased. Kael quickened his pace, shivers running the length of his spine. Something felt...off tonight. Another sound pierced the night, distinct from the one before. A loud, piercing clap of thunder resonated from somewhere to the north. It swept through the city, as if trying to drown out the still-echoing howl of the wolf. The two sounds seemed in competition with each other, but the thunder snuffed out the howl and remained ringing in Kael's ears long after it had departed. Kael quickened his pace to a light jog.

He was about halfway back now. Shadows played off all the buildings. Day had become night swiftly. Everybody in the neighbourhood was fast asleep by now. Why was he still awake? Why had he stayed so long at Laura's? He should have been in his bed, sleeping by then.

Kael scolded himself for being late; he should have foreseen the fact that he would have to walk home in the dark. He hated the kingdom in the night. He hated imagining all the things that could be lurking in the shadows. He wasn't afraid of the dark, he never had been. It was what could be hiding *in* the dark that frightened him.

Kael was just a few blocks away from his house, which was a sweet little two-room building that was just a bedroom with a small closet and a kitchen. Just as well though, he hardly ever spent any of his time in it anyway. He didn't have reason to.

The feeling of dark foreboding intensified. Kael slowed his pace to a crawl, carefully making his way towards home. A cat screeched as he approached and ran away into the shadows. He hated that cat. The edge of his house appeared into view. It looked dark and ominous in the fading light. Kael's eyes scanned the familiar features of his house. His breath caught in his throat as he spotted something flat and white lying on the front stairs to his door. With utter fear, he recognized what it was.

He slipped up to the stoop of his house and bent over the plain, white letter. Hands shaking, breath shallow, he scooped up the plain, folded piece of parchment. A cold sweat broke out on the nape of his neck and seemed to make that moment more real than it was. His blood thrummed far too loud in his ears. All he could see what the pure white of the parchment, all he could feel was the soft touch of the paper to his fingers, all he could hear was the rustle as he opened it numbly. The taste of bile filled his mouth.

He held the parchment at a hand's length away, now fully opened. He slumped down over the steps of his balcony in despair. No, this couldn't be. He had been promised... This wasn't supposed to happen. He had protection from this. Kael ached to crumple up the paper, to throw it away and forget what it said, but terrible things happened to people who refused to accept its calling.

For on the note was written, large and ominous: *You have been drafted.*

Chapter 3

Kael read and reread the letter long after he had planned to go to sleep. It stated that his enlistment would begin immediately the very next day in the afternoon, giving him just barely enough time for him to say his goodbyes and solve any unresolved ties. He was surprised by the vagueness of the letter, as if it was a death sentence.

Kael didn't want to die.

The very prospect of his doomed future had kept him up most of the night. When he did get some sleep, he dreamed of dark caves that spewed fire and giant talons tearing men to pieces. He had jolted awake several times in the night, sweating and breathing haggardly.

The reason joining the army meant certain death was a well-known fact in Vallenfend. It was the very reason there were scant amounts of men in the kingdom. Just about thirty-five years ago, the king of the city—and still current king—decreed that the colossal dragon to the east, the very one that lived in the cave cut into the mountainside, was a threat to their peace. How old the dragon was, nobody knew exactly, but by the size of the beast, it could very well have been centuries old. As far as Kael knew, dragons never ceased to grow. That single dragon alone was the cause for the under-population of males in Vallenfend. Legions upon legions of men had fallen and died under its savage might. Despite the overwhelming loss, King Morrindale had refused to let up on his campaign. From then on in, most boys, when they reached the age of sixteen faced mandatory enlistment and thereafter death. His father had been lucky to pair off with his mother, but he too, had to face the enlistment when he was in his late twenties.

Kael had lived his life as best he could, and he had been happy with the knowledge he would be one of the few to not have to suffer a short-lived existence. Malaricus had promised him this. Had it been the old scholar that had betrayed him, or had something arisen that compromised that promise? Either way, Kael was going to talk with the scholar.

27

Kael left his house glumly, packing his necessities inside a small backpack. He didn't bother to lock the door behind him. He had everything he needed in the small bag. Today was dark and cloudy, perfectly matching the dark troubles that Kael carried with him. It was early still, so there was nobody out yet to daunt his path.

He weaved through the kingdom's empty streets until he came upon his destination. Malaricus lived in the Royal Athenaeum, the kingdom's library. It was there where he served as the king's scholar. It was said that he was the best scholar the kingdom had ever seen in its history, and as such, he was appropriately named "Malaricus the Wise". To Kael, he was more than that. He was Kael's friend, and he had been his mother's best friend and comforter when her husband had died. Malaricus, along with Laura, were the only two people in the kingdom Kael trusted with his life. It was only natural, then, that Kael felt shattered by his betrayal.

Reflecting this, a tear came to Kael's eye as he climbed the spiral staircase up to Malaricus's study. Kael was raised as an honest boy, with clean standards and beliefs. Even after his mother's death, and his father's enlistment, he had kept these standards. When Kael chose friends, he did it according to their standards as well. Usually if they held the same beliefs as he did, he became very bonded to those people. That was one of the main reasons Laura and Kael got along so well. It upset Kael to think that Malaricus went back on a promise that he had made to a dying widow.

Finally, Kael reached Malaricus's study. He threw open the door without knocking. Of course, Malaricus was already awake, with his sharp nose planted in a book he was studying. The scholar stood up. His glasses feel to his chest, attached by a gold chain wrapped around his neck.

Being the king's personal scholar, Malaricus was always richly attired. Today, he wore his favourite ruby-red robe, which was the same colour and intensity as a roaring fire. Intricate lacings rimmed the edges of the cloak and it made a soft *whoosh* as he spun around to face Kael.

"Kael, how do you fare today?" he asked politely. Kael had been set on yelling a curse at Malaricus, but he bit his tongue. By the tone of the middle-aged man's voice, it sounded as if he had no idea of his enlistment. Kael quietly cursed himself for jumping to false accusations. But if Malaricus didn't betray him, why was that letter on his doorstep?

"Not so good," Kael wheezed, realizing how tired he was. Dropping the angry expression he had been wearing, he slumped down on a fluffy armchair next to a large globe situated in the middle of the library. The room was stacked to the ceiling with ancient, dusty books—Malaricus's personal collection, as well as the books needing repair. The library itself was just below the scholar's study. But Kael had never found it very exciting. He preferred Malaricus's room.

The smell of paper filled the study, summoning sweet memories of Kael sitting in this very room years ago, reading from some of the bigger books. He hadn't known how to read at the time, but would just marvel at the intricate little drawings that were so vivid, they seemed to dance on the page. When he was older, Malaricus had taught Kael how to read, and even though the books in there weren't especially interesting, Kael had been eager to read anything. He used to love to read. Now there was no time. Oh, how he wished those better days would come back.

"Malaricus, I've been drafted," he managed to say after several minutes of silence.

The scholar winced, shutting the book he had been studying from with shaking, ink-stained hands. "Excuse me?"

"I got this letter last night." Kael pulled out the letter. Malaricus reached out and took the letter, his mouth agape. Kael stared at the heavenly paintings in the ceiling as he read it. They were all so peaceful, depicting gods and angels frolicking in the heavens. Yet his heart was wracked with turmoil. How could something be so calm at a time of such agony?

Malaricus removed his reading glasses after he was finished looking the note over several times. He blinked, sighed, and rubbed his nose, at a loss. He looked sideways at Kael, who returned his gaze blankly. Malaricus put his glasses back on and scanned the paper one more time.

"I was up staring at that all night," Kael said wearily, his voice spilling out grainy from despair. "It's as clear as day."

Malaricus placed the paper down on the table, placing his fingers on top. He frowned, scowling at nothing in particular.

"I didn't... I didn't authorize this Kael," Malaricus stated despondently. Kael was surprised to find that he was at a loss for the right words. Malaricus always knew what to say. "I assure, you, I had no involvement in this at all. I told the king specifically that you were exempt from his order, you're name was put on a list." Malaricus struck the table with his fist. His voice was growing. "You *are* on the list of those who are to never join the army. This is an outrage!"

Kael still stared at the ceiling, but he had gone out of focus, and everything had become blurry. Deep thoughts of fire, caves and dragons wove through his mind, replacing the heavenly beings above him. An urge to pinch himself to wake him of this nightmare struck him, but he refused. This was no dream, and if it was, it was far more vivid and terrible than he had ever experienced before.

Malaricus stayed quiet for a long time. He stared at the letter and searched the surrounding bookshelves, looking for a solution. None of the books produced an answer, so Malaricus leaned forward on his chair. Kael stayed deathly quiet and still, his mind drawing blank.

"I shall talk to the king himself about this Kael," the scholar said resolutely.

Kael shook his head. A sense of helplessness was flowing into him. It made him feel as though nothing in the world could save him now, even if the dragon died that night in its sleep. Trying to shake his dreadful mood, he cracked a dry smile towards the scholar.

"I appreciate it, Malaricus."

The scholar nodded, stood up and placed a hand on Kael's shoulder. "It might take a while before I can convince the king, but I promise you, I will do everything in my power to save you, Kael. Who knows, perhaps you can get some basic sword training out of this before you're withdrawn."

Malaricus was, of course, referring to the month of hard training and practise that the military issued before sending its men off to die.

It was said that the training was brutal, but lacking, and hardly taught you how to fight against a dragon at all.

Waiting for a reply, Malaricus hesitated. But none was forthcoming, so he spoke again. "Be not dismayed, young Kael, I have an intuitive feeling that all will turn out well."

"How can you be so sure?" Kael cried. As soon as he did, he felt remorseful for being so impatient towards his old friend. Malaricus removed his hand from Kael's shoulder, a patient expression spread across his face. He suddenly looked so old. Kael raised a hand apologetically. "I'm sorry, friend. This bad news has made me irritable today. I should leave."

Kael stood up. He took one more glance back at Malaricus's study before exiting through the same doorway he had entered. The study was beautiful. The sun was rising finally, and its early rays were shining through the stained-glass windows, sending a kaleidoscope of colour washing over the already vibrantly adorned room. Would this be the last time he ever set eyes on this place? He sighed, drinking in the experience of it all. Malaricus watched him patiently. Malaricus had hopes that he would succeed in Kael's withdrawal, but behind his hopeful smile, there was a flicker of doubt, a falter in his smiling lips that bode a sense of loss.

Kael tore himself away from the study. There were more people he had to visit today. Today, his last day before the journey began.

Something caught Kael's eye as he exited the library, a poster plastered to a pillar of a large building across the street. Strange, he hadn't it before. He walked up to the poster. On the piece of paper were details describing where and when the new recruits for the army were to go—just past noon, at the courtyard of the south gates. The king held regular public meetings to rally the loyalty of his subjects, and to reassure them that their sons and brothers were dying for a worthy and noble cause. Oh, how he wanted to tear down that poster.

He ignored the poster, and instead walked along his way. He had a lot to do today, so many people to say goodbye to...

He started to make his way to Laura's house but after some consideration, turned a different way. No, he couldn't face Laura

31

yet. The very thought of saying goodbye to his best friend was something that he could not stomach so early. That would be the last thing he would do.

So he headed in the direction of the blacksmiths. As he walked dismally onward, the streets began to fill up as the light of the sun beckoned the people outside. It wasn't the rush of the afternoon, but the steady throng of people comforted Kael. He had thought that he would want solitude, but having others around him made him feel at ease and he almost forgot the seriousness of his dilemma.

A young group of boys ran directly in front of him, cutting him off. If it had been another day, he may have been angry at them or more likely, he would have laughed, but today, his face remained stern. He watched them go with longing. Childhood had been a haven for him, when everything was safe, and the world was right. But then, his father had disappeared, and his mother had died some time later. What did fate hold for these boys? How many of them would live past twenty? How many more would die under the king's ridiculous conscription?

The boys soon disappeared into the mass of bodies, but their loud, happy voices could still be heard over the din and motley smells of the streets. This was the busiest part of the city, the market, but Kael had always liked the urban, rushed hubbub of it all. It made him feel important to be a steady contributor to the society. But now he felt small and an inner anger made him want to yell and scream.

Before he could realize it, he had arrived at the blacksmiths. With fists clenched, Kael stood just outside the stuffy black tent. He listened to the pounding of a hammer against hot metal on an anvil— he would miss that noise. Would Korjan hire a new apprentice once Kael was gone?

Kael entered and found Korjan pounding on an axe. The blacksmith discontinued his work for a moment. He rubbed a large scar on his right arm in the same way he usually did, squinting through the steamy air at Kael. "Good morning, Kael," he said deeply.

"Good morning," responded Kael with less enthusiasm.

"You're here early."

Kael avoided the blacksmith's eyes. Here came the lies. He had decided to save his friends the grief, he would lie to them. He would tell them that he was going to go work on a farm far outside the kingdom and that he would be gone for several months. It was a despicable thing to do—Kael hated to lie—but he had decided it necessary to do so, to avoid the anguish that would arise. He remembered the pain that came when someone close had to leave. It was unbearable.

"I just came to say..." Kael swallowed. It felt like his pride was stuck in the back of his throat. "I'm going to be...away for awhile. Do you think you can get somebody else to cover for me?"

Korjan sighed. "Probably, but where are you going Kael? Nobody else knows how to manipulate metal with the same skill as you."

"I'm going to go work in the fields for awhile, there's a shortage of workers in the potato fields." It stung like a wasp's bite on his tongue to utter those words, how did others do it?

"Oh, that's unfortunate, what happened?"

Kael faltered. "What?"

"There have always been enough workers to tend the potatoes. I was wondering what happened to make it so there wasn't. Was there an accident?"

Korjan's expression was so sincere and the worry on his face was so real that Kael couldn't help but to hesitate. He just wanted to tell the truth... "I don't know. I was just given a letter yesterday telling me I was needed to work on the fields."

"From whom?"

Did Korjan know? He must have, he was asking too many questions. Kael was eager to end the conversation, so he turned his shoulders slightly towards the exit. Hopefully Korjan would get the message that he had other things to do. "I don't know. The letter was anonymous."

"I can't afford to lose you, Kael. It's really difficult to replace an apprentice, especially in this blasted city. I need your help. Isn't there some other way?"

Kael shook his head.

"Huh, well, you be off then Kael, and good luck." Korjan was good at hiding his emotions, but before he turned around, Kael could see the disappointment in his eyes.

"Thank you." Kael turned at last and exited the tent. He could feel the blacksmith watching him as he left, but he never looked back.

The next person Kael would visit would be Bunda. He had intended to say his farewells to countless others, including his boss at the mill and Helena, but is seemed that he wouldn't have enough time to visit everybody today. But maybe that was for the best. Kael couldn't take lying to his friends. He had done a terrible job lying to Korjan; Laura would surely know what was wrong.

Shaking his head, he decided to think about this later, after he had visited Bunda.

Bunda was chopping meat when Kael arrived at her shop. He walked in and stood in front of the desk for a moment and watched as she brought her cleaver down zealously on a hunk of steak. She was grumbling to herself, a sure sign that she was upset with something. Kael didn't say anything for awhile hoping that she would notice him, but she didn't.

He cleared his throat. "Good morning, Bunda."

The butcher took notice of him and she put down her cleaver. "Kael, how are you my boy? You look pale, what's wrong?"

Running his hand through his hair, Kael braced himself for more lies. "I'm fine, just a tad under the weather's all."

"What are you doing here, shouldn't you be at work?"

He wasn't forthcoming with an answer, so with a concerned look, Bunda spoke again. "You forgot to come back for your birthday present last night."

"Yeah, th—that's why I came back," Kael lied. "It was late when I got back yesterday. I came to get it."

Bunda grabbed the cloth sack from underneath the counter. "I salted some of it, and put honey on the other half. You know how to cook, right?"

Kael managed a dry laugh. "Yes, I know. I have to soak it in water before to get rid of some of the salt first, right?"

Bunda smiled. "That's my boy. Now, what's wrong with you? You can tell me." She winked, a fiendish smile playing on her lips. "Is it girl trouble?"

Kael chuckled. "Girl trouble," he echoed. *Hardly.* "No it's just that..."

Kael looked up at Bunda's awaiting face. One of her eyebrows was raised still in concern. She was such a nice woman, and she had lost too much already. No, he couldn't tell the truth her and he couldn't lie to her either. "Nothing," Kael said at last, "nothing's wrong, I'm just really tired today, that's all."

The butcher stared at Kael for a moment. When she spoke, Kael could tell by her tone that she was unconvinced. "Well then, you better get yourself a good night's sleep tonight, eh?"

Kael nodded, picking up the package of meat. With a wave of his hand and saying nothing more, he left the butcher's shop and re-entered the streets. It was getting busy now. He sighed. For once, he was tired of the hurried woman going about their business; he was tired of the young boys running around while their mothers tried to round them up. One boy had a wood sword in his hand. Kael looked away. He just wanted to be alone.

Kael dropped the package of meat off at his house. Instead of visiting those he would be leaving, Kael decided instead to visit the closest courtyard to him.

There were seven courtyards in Vallenfend. One of them was within walking distance from his house, two more were a reasonable trek, and the others were too far away from him to visit on a busy day. He had once gone to all of them with Laura when he had a few days off, but despite each one's beauty, none of them could compare to his courtyard; in his opinion anyway.

The courtyards were built in the last king's reign, more than fifty years ago, in more peaceful times. It was said that that king had been one of the best Vallenfend had ever seen. The king had been deeply concerned with making his subjects pleased and content. So, on a whim to make the kingdom more beautiful, he had ordered the courtyards to be constructed. Essentially gardens, each one was spectacular in its own way and no two were alike. The king had the courtyards decorated according to different times of the year, with seasonal flowers planted that would light up that section of the city when their time came to bloom. They served as a calendar of sorts. But even when the flowers planted weren't in bloom, other plants, shrubberies and decorations kept the courtyards pleasantly lavished throughout the year.

Kael walked on the courtyard's stone path, looking around at all the flowers that were beginning to bud. It was just about that time when this courtyard's flowers opened up. Birds sang happily on the various trees. Kael quickly lost himself in the serenity, enjoying the gently sloped path. The entire kingdom was slanted, being built on the very foot of the mountain ranges.

This park was decorated with flowers that were mostly red, like tulips and yarrow. Even the copper beech trees bore red leaves this time of the year. Perhaps that was the reason why Kael like this particular courtyard more than the rest, red was his favourite colour.

Kael sat down on the soft green grass. He stared up at the cloudy sky, searching for solutions. How tranquil it was. All his fears and troubles seemed to melt away. He would miss this... He closed his eyes, thinking of all his friends he would be leaving.

When he opened his eyes again, the sky looked different. He squinted and stretched his tired limbs. Wait! What time was it? The clouds parted, giving him a full view of the sky. It was almost noon! He had fallen asleep? No, he didn't have time to fall asleep, how could he have done something so foolish? Now he couldn't see any of his friends even if he wanted to.

But, perhaps that was for the better. Now he didn't have to say goodbye to Laura, something he knew he wouldn't be able to do. Now he had an excuse not to go visit her. *Forgive me,* he thought as he got up off the grass, leaving an imprint of his body.

He rushed out of the courtyard and turned towards the centre of the kingdom.

As he approached the castle, he could hear women's voices growing louder. The king was having another public appearance. Whenever he had these, almost half the kingdom would show up, either to genuinely learn what he was up to, or to throw curses and—

if they were braver—tomatoes at him. The events were always crowded and covered with soldiers. It was said that the men who guarded the king at the time would be sent off to die not a week later. It was a wonder why they protected him at all.

As he had suspected, the large reception area reserved for public displays was packed with women. Some shouted up at the king, others simply stood there, shaking their heads, and some were even crying. Kael peered up over the heads. Bunda liked to attend these things to make sure the king knew how she felt about him...

That's when Kael spotted him. King Morrindale. The king was standing atop the battlements, with two guards on either side of him.

Kael hadn't seen the king in months, perhaps even a year now. And although King Morrindale hadn't changed his look or personality in a long time, his very appearance was very profound indeed. Not because he was an outstanding person, but that so much influence came from one individual. It shocked Kael to know that such a simple man ran a kingdom like Vallenfend. It just wasn't fitting.

The king was wearing a green robe today, with tracings and intricate designs done in gold. Scarlet and royal blue adorned the sleeves and hems of the robe, and although it was a lavished garment, it wasn't striking. Sometimes the king was known to overdo his appearance or wear things that were just plain ostentatious. Gold rings adorned his thick fingers and sparkled as bright as his pebbly eyes as he waved to the crowd. King Morrindale smiled down at the growing throng of people like a child with a new toy. He was an aloof man, and held the flustered appearance and rosy cheeks as one who has consumed too much wine. From what Kael knew, the king wasn't a very smart person, although there was a hint of a deeper, more cunning intelligence behind his eyes.

The roundish man continued to wave as people threw curses up at him. Down below, the guards were trying to silence the crowd and keep them from hurling things at the king. Morrindale seemed to be stalling.

Finally, a door opened just behind the king up on the battlement. The king turned around and beckoned the new figure outside. It was his royal advisor.

Kael never liked the king's advisor. Zeptus was his name. It was name which seemed to have a life of its own and seemed to breathe contempt towards civilians. He was a tall, gaunt figure, draped with elaborate purple cloth befitted with silver seams. His hubris clothing hung from his thin shoulders like drapery in front of a window and overall he carried a vulture-like appearance. Perhaps the strangest and most chilling fact about him was that his eyes were an unnatural purple which neatly matched his clothing. Whenever the rare chance arose when Kael set eyes on the advisor, when he gazed into those sinister, leering purple eyes, he shivered.

Zeptus peered down at everybody in a scornful sneer, as if they were cockroaches underneath his boot. Atop his dark, oily hair he wore a silver diadem that seemed dull contrasted to his rather pale and bony face. When he spoke, it sounded as if he had phlegm in the back of his throat and needed to cough; it was raspy and cold and made Kael's spine tingle.

Kael always wondered why King Morrindale had chosen Zeptus as his advisor, instead of a more appealing subject. Malaricus would have been far better. But, then again, any reasoning the king used was beyond him.

King Morrindale's silly smile widened as he brought Zeptus into full view for the people. A hush ran over the crowd and even the upturned dust seemed to surcease its wild swirling, aroused and frightened by the chilling advisor's presence. All was still.

"Ladies and gentlemen," the king began, breaking the tense semi-silence, but he didn't get far.

"What gentlemen?" somebody yelled out, "they're all dead!"

The king put a finger gently to his lip, as if to bite back a retort. His smile faded somewhat. He tried again. "Ladies and gentlemen, as you probably know, I have issued another drafting."

The crowd erupted into a tumultuous uproar. The guards had drawn their swords now, waving them at the crowd to try and calm them. Several archers appeared on the battlements, notching arrows.

More than once, people had been shot at these displays. Through the flailing arms and screams, Kael managed to push his way through the crowd, wishing to find a better viewpoint and positioning himself closer to the castle gates.

"Silence, silence. I assure you, it is necessary for your own safety," the king continued. Another volley of screaming interjected. "If it weren't for...if we didn't..." King Morrindale faltered, trying to fight the crowd and find the same words at once. He wasn't very good at multi-tasking, let alone talking to crowds to begin with.

Zeptus leaned over and whispered something into the king's ear. Morrindale looked up at the tall figure and nodded, stepping back to let the advisor speak, looking like a frustrated child who hadn't gotten his chance to speak.

"People of Vallenfend," he sneered, "this is the regular mandatory enlistment that happens every year. It is necessary to keep this city safe, I *assure* you."

"How so?" somebody yelled, most people knew why the king enlisted young men, but the same questions seemed to be repeated at every one of these meetings. Perhaps they wanted bother the king and his advisor, or possibly the person asking truly didn't know. The latter was unlikely.

"The dragon that lives to the east, Shatterbreath—thrice accursed be her name—is a savage brute. We are waging war against this monster! Is it not necessary to take drastic action in war?"

"The dragon hasn't attacked us for several years, it is no threat!" That voice sounded like Bunda. "Why must we send our children off to fight it? It is a waste of precious lives."

"Insolence," Zeptus yelled, swinging his arm out to the crowd with a flourish of his robe. "Have you not considered that because our soldiers fight it, that it is kept at bay? Consider this; if we stopped sending our soldiers, what is stopping it from attacking the city? Without us, that beast would be free to destroy everything we fight to defend!"

The crowd was silent for a moment. The general throng seemed to accept this answer, but not willingly. "Why so often? Why can't we just send a few prisoners or thieves every so often, instead of whole battalions of young men at such unusual intervals?"

Zeptus squinted, his lip rising in a challenging sneer. Even from where he was, Kael could see the man's purple eyes narrow. "Strength in numbers. The more men we send, the more likely it will be that we can keep it at bay or even kill it. Think about that, *kill it,* if we send two men, the chances of success are slim. It is only because we have a limited amount of men that we don't send an entire army right now to slay it once and for all."

"I heard you have," one voice lashed out.

Zeptus backed away from the ledge he had been leaning on. "We underestimated its strength at the time. It used tactics that were unfamiliar. But that will not happen again. We have learned its secrets and tricks. Still, it seems as though the dragon has placed us in a stalemate. If we try and stockpile our soldiers and amass a proper army, surely it will attack before then and catch us unaware. Or we can send these smaller battalions every so often and keep it away for longer. Which would you prefer?"

A whisper rushed over the crowd. The women were dissatisfied, but could not think of a good enough question to challenge the advisor. The slightest twinge appeared on his lip, perhaps a faint semblance of a smile. His eyes gleamed. He straightened his back, a sign that he was through with the conversation.

"We do everything we can to keep this kingdom safe. I apologize sincerely if this upsets you, but believe me, there is no alternative. We have tried." He licked his lips, his sarcastic tone utterly detestable. "Thank you for your patience."

With that, he backed away from the ledge, letting the king take the stand once again. King Morrindale clapped his hands and started to rant about something, but Kael lost interest. He leaned against a large structural pillar set in the wall of the castle and resolved to wait until the crowd thinned to enter the castle. In front of him, two women were having a conversation.

"...not sure about that Zeptus character," a brunette woman was saying, "He's too secretive, too dark."

"I know what you mean. He seems to make the same excuse every time, but nobody can beat his logic!" the other woman replied.

"I hope Icecrows will eat them both, that creep Zeptus first, then King *Murderdale*."

Kael interrupted their conversation, pushing himself away from the wall. "You better watch what you're saying," he said. "I may not turn you in, but others could."

The brunette scrutinized him angrily, but her expression softened. "Ah, thank you. We will have this conversation later."

The two women left and joined the rest of them as they filed out of the area in front of the castle. Kael shook his head. Despite the severe penalty for referring the king as Murderdale, people still continued to call him that.

When he had first made the decree banishing the use of that name, King Morrindale thought he had solved the problem. Years passed and King Morrindale heard rumours that people still called him by that name. He figured there was nobody to catch them doing so, so he issued another decree which stated that if the one saying the name was caught by two separate people in the action, those two could turn them in for a sum of money. His two orders had significantly reduced the amount of people saying his nickname, but the title had still stuck.

Kael's thoughts were interrupted as Bunda sprang out of the crowd. "Kael? What are you doing here? I'm seeing you everywhere today!"

He flinched but nevertheless faked a smile. "Hi," he croaked. His mind was still two steps backwards. "I came...to see the king."

"You to, eh?" Bunda turned back to where the king had been moments before. He had retreated inside already. "I hate that man. I hate his advisor. He always has a comeback to everything, it's so aggravating!"

Kael nodded, at a loss at what to say.

"Bah, never mind him, you don't seem to be busy today, join me for lunch."

Frowning, Kael shook his head, his mind racing to come up with an excuse. "Nah, I'm meeting a friend here in a little bit. I'll catch you later though."

Bunda nodded, the same look of anxiety she had worn before on her face. "Okay then..."

She left along with the last remaining people, leaving Kael leaning against the shaded wall. His gut twisted and he could feel his face had gone pale. That's twice he had lied to her, *today!* That's more than he had in his life!

Kael waited a few more minutes for the people to clear out. With everybody nearly gone from the scene, he moved towards the gate. There was a young man guarding it. He had a large scar across his face and kept his eyes towards the ground as Kael approached.

"What do you want?" he growled, ignoring the fact that Kael was his own age. Kael gulped and removed his letter from his pocket. The young man's face stayed stern. He inhaled and exhaled deep and slow. Still avoiding Kael's gaze, he nodded, turned around and unlocked a small door set in the castle's main huge gate.

The small door swung open. Kael stood where he was for a moment, trying to see inside. Whatever lay behind was out of view. This doorway was like a portal to another world, and he did not want to make that journey.

Forlornly, he stepped through the door and into the boundaries of the castle.

Chapter 4

As Kael discovered, the inner workings of the castle walls were much different than he had anticipated. The castle grounds were large and spread out, most of the area covered by simple brown gravel. Kael coughed, trying to breathe through the heavy cloud of upturned dust that three horses were kicking up in the middle. From what Kael could tell, there was a large target field to the right used for archery practise, and to his left was a sparring area.

There weren't many soldiers practising, which surprised Kael. He had been expecting a large number of young men to be hustling to and fro, stiff and erect. All he saw as he stood there, surveying the scene, were four boys walking in a cluster. Their heads were bent low and they seemed weighed down by their loosely-fitting leather armour. One of them dragged a halberd on the ground, which was not a wise way to handle a weapon like that.

Kael began to walk towards a large building to his right. It looked like a barracks or something similar, and since he was unsure what to do, perhaps there would be a good place to start.

Off in the distance, past the horse ring, with another building resting at its feet, was the Royal Castle itself, richly lavished with gleaming white stone. Its eight precipices rose high above the scene, as if to watch over the soldiers below. Two large stone walls jutted out of either side of the castle and wrapped around the field which Kael was standing in, meeting together to form the castle gates. The castle was about as large as the area walled in. Kael could imagine that from overhead the whole area would look like a large figure-eight. There were buildings attached to the twenty-foot walls, mostly positioned closer to the castle, all built in the same pointy style and bone white hue. It was rather unnerving, actually, to be closed in like this. It felt as though he was in a cage.

Kael stopped moving, still unsure what he should do. The poster he had seen earlier had specified when to arrive and where, but not what to do once he was inside, plus he was half an hour early. He relaxed when he saw a man walking towards him. Expecting the man to guide him, Kael took a tentative step towards him. He was about to open his mouth to say something, but the man continued walking at his same eager pace and showed no sign of slowing down. He brushed past Kael without even so much as a glance, making Kael feel rather insignificant. Where was he going so fast that he couldn't help a new recruit?

"You look lost," a stern voice said from behind him. Kael wheeled around to come face an older man, perhaps about thirty years of age. Although he appeared young, the man's moustache and hair glowed almost as white as the clouds above.

Kael stuttered, surprised by his sudden and stealthy appearance. "Y-yes, I was drafted. I thought I'd come early to get myself orientated."

The man cocked his head so that his chin swayed near his collarbone. His eyes listed halfway closed, he seemed impatient with Kael already. His hair wasn't white, Kael realized, just very, very blonde. "Came early, eh? Don't know why you'd do that."

Kael shrugged; he really didn't have an excuse.

"Fine. You can wait in that barrack over there, see it?" He pointed to a medium sized building across the way to the left. "Or you can explore the area. I really don't care."

The man strutted away, leaving Kael no better off than he had been before. He repositioned the backpack on his shoulders. Following the man's advice, he walked over towards the barrack, giving the horse riders in the middle a wide berth. They fought each other using staves. They didn't hit each other hard, but it still looked very dangerous. Would he have to learn to do that?

Also on his way, he passed the sparring area, which was fenced in. Against the wall there was a large shack that reminded Kael of a school building. Along one of the side of the fence, there was a wide rack covered by many dented weapons. Kael marvelled at the variety of weapons. Given that this place was a training centre for soldiers, it was surprising that they would not simply settle for giving out the same basic weapon. It would cut costs for one thing, but would also be more efficient to train all their soldiers at once, instead of teaching them how to handle their preferred weapon individually. Oh well, maybe this was more effective in some way.

Passing only two other soldiers, Kael arrived at the barrack. The condition of this building was appalling. Although it was made of stone, the walls were weatherworn and held cracks; the ceiling was tattered and in need of new shingles and the white colour that it could have once held was gone, replaced by a malignant yellow. When Kael opened the door, it squealed and scratched against the ground, making it tough to open the door.

The inside wasn't any better. The bunks were tightly packed, despite the limited amount of attendants, and none of them held cushioning to sleep on. Kael scrunched his nose in disgust. What was that smell? He walked through the aisle between the bunks, squinting in the semi-darkness to see. Where were the windows? Even through the darkness, he could still see a light coating of mould caking the edges where the walls met the ceiling and floor. He would have to sleep in the middle, to stay as far away as he could from that mess.

Kael jumped as something rustled deeper in the room. What now, were there rats in here too?

"Are you a new recruit?"

Letting out a sigh of relief, Kael replied. "Yeah. How about you?"

A figure rose up off of one of the lower bunks. It propped itself on the edge of the bunk. Kael watched him shake his head slowly. "No," the young man replied, "I've been here for awhile. They don't release you into battle if you're sick or injured. I had the flu, couldn't get out of my bed for a week. I suppose I'm lucky."

Kael threw his pack down on a bunk near the boy and sat down opposite him. "That is lucky."

The boy sniffed. "Not really. You'll soon find out, this place gets you down."

"It's better than death, isn't it?"

The boy took his time to reply, so Kael got a good look at him. He was the same age as Kael, but shorter. His features were thin and dark lines surrounded his eyes. His hair was thin and held a dusty sheen. Overall, he didn't look healthy.

"I suppose it is," he replied at last. Kael had nearly forgotten what he had said at first. "What's your name?"

"Kael Rundown."

"Don Huntson," the boy replied, shaking Kael's hand formally.

They sat there in silence for a bit, Kael was too worried to ask him what the training would be like. Don simply stared at his feet.

"I like you, Kael," Don stated suddenly, "I'm going to do you a favour. Listen up. When they ask you a question, the answer will either be A or B. Don't worry; this is their cruel way of picking which battalion you will belong to. Pick A, believe me, it's the easier one, the trainers aren't as tough."

Kael pondered this for a moment. "Thanks, Don. I take it you're in A?"

With a strange, sly smile, Don answered, "yeah."

Kael didn't like his tone, there was something more to this than he could see. Don was insulting him or it was some sort of inside joke, but Kael vowed to take his advice—what else could he do?

The time came along when the rest of the new recruits rolled in. Kael had left the barracks to find a group of boys standing just inside the front gate. He walked over to them. They were all mostly his age, although there were a few men standing amid them. They all looked frightened however, and a couple were even crying, streaks running down their faces. Kael took his spot in the ranks, between an oily boy and a shorter boy.

It was surprising how many boys were there. Vallenfend had a population of about twenty thousand and about an eighth of that was male. Although most of them weren't in any condition to fight, being either children or old men. The fact that there were perhaps forty-eight young men and a few older men there was impressive. Kael didn't think it would be that easy to find enough to make even a small group of warriors. He felt somewhat relieved that he wouldn't be as alone as he thought.

The blonde man who had told Kael to go to the barracks arrived on the scene. "Shut up," he barked, "all of you. You're in the military now! We don't tolerate cowardice."

At once, the boys were silent, fear towards their fate replaced by immediate fear of the man. This was unlike anything any of these boys were used to, Kael could tell. Most of the young men in the city were treated like gold. Few ever got a real taste of the hard life. Kael had an understanding of both.

"I am Captain Terra, but you scum will refer to me as just Captain. You understand?"

There was a small ripple of tentative response from the crowd.

The Captain uttered a small growl, his face twisting into a sneer. "Do you understand?!" he roared.

"Yes, Captain!" Kael responded, along with the rest of the crowd.

The Captain scrutinized them. He placed his arms behind his back and slowly paced in front on them, chewing his lip. "That's better," he said at last, "but still terrible. You will work on that, won't you?"

"Yes, Captain!"

"Good. Now before you put away your personal effects, I have a skill-testing question. You there!"

He jabbed his finger out at one of the boys in the front row, a pale, skinny little kid. "Me, Captain?"

"Yes, *you*," Captain Terra scoffed, "tell me, quick, A or B?"

The boy hesitated, confused by the random question. Kael smirked, staring forward like the rest of them. So Don hadn't been trying to fool him. This would play to his advantage. *Thank you, Don*, he thought—until the Captain reached the next boy.

"You, C or D?"

Kael flinched, C or D? What? But Don had said A or B! No matter, maybe he was just doing this for one boy. By the time he got to Kael, he would surely be back to asking A or B, right?

"No, rutabaga is not an answer!" the Captain hollered at one kid who had decided to try and crack a joke. The boy winced violently. "I'll ask you again, up or down?"

The Captain, as he went on, said something different each time. "Blue or red? Cat or dog? Today or Tomorrow?" Kael tried to figure out if he had any pattern, but so far, there seemed to be none. He either put you to a left group, or right. Whether or not he was doing so according to the answers he was given was unclear. Kael closed his eyes. He was getting too stressed over a trivial matter such as this.

"Cake, eh? You go over there," he said to the greasy boy beside Kael. He stepped directly in front of Kael. "Quick, heads or tails?"

Kael stuttered, giving no clear answer. His brain suddenly froze. "Uh... A?"

"A?" the Captain whispered softly, leaning in close. Kael didn't dare look up, expecting the Captain's face to be red with total anger. He chanced a glance. There was an expression of amusement spread across the Captain's face. "You really want A?"

"Yes?" Kael said with a shrug.

"A it is." A fiendish smile spread under the Captain's moustache. "Go over there."

Kael went to the left, trying to hide his burning face. The Captain watched him over his shoulder, still smiling dreadfully. He snapped back to the next kid, straightening upright. Under normal circumstances, Kael would have laughed at this mishap and had a good joke about it, but by no means was he entertained. He was frustrated already, and embarrassed.

The Captain finished grouping the boys off. There were more in Kael's group than there was in the other. Captain Terra stood in front of the boys and surveyed them. He nodded in approval. "You boys will go to the barracks to your left," he pointed at Kael's group, motioning over his shoulder, "and you to the right. You have the day off today to get yourselves orientated, but tomorrow will start off with a bang. Failure to have yourself ready on time and at your proper locations results in punishment. By no means are you ever allowed to set foot in the Royal Castle, or be within the white circle that represents royal land. If you do not comply with these rules, again, you will be punished. You have been warned—failure to listen to your superiors and you will be punished accordingly. You got that?"

"Yes, Captain," the boys replied. As Kael glanced sideways at the other group, he noted that all the men—those that appeared older than twenty—were on that side.

"Good, now be off, I don't want to look at your carcasses anymore. Dinner will be in three hours. A bell will sound for you to come. It would be unwise for you to be late." With that, the Captain wheeled around and headed off towards a building near the castle gates which Kael hadn't noticed it before. It must have been the trainer's hut. He watched the Captain enter it with a pang of jealousy; it was much nicer than the barracks he had to sleep in.

Kael didn't go to the barracks with the other boys; instead he resolved to become familiar with the training grounds. If there was a chance the Captain might get cross with somebody for not knowing their way around, he dearly didn't want to be that person. He was going to slither his way through this and draw as little attention to himself as possible.

The sparring pit and the archery ranger were both exact opposite of each other, and also perpendicular to the castle and the gates. Closer to the castle, near the archery range, was a large building that Kael guessed would be the cafeteria. There was a building beside the sparring pit, a medical tent judging by the insignia above the doorway. On the other side of the sparring pit there was a simple narrow building. Curious, Kael headed that way.

The narrow building turned out to be the armoury, and it was much larger than he had predicted. When he entered, Kael was shocked by the depth of the shack. It must have gone under the wall as well, which made sense for if the castle were under siege, archers would need to fetch their bows as fast as possible to guard the walls. Like the smaller display outside, the armoury held a huge variety and amount of weapons. Halberds, glaives, swords, bows, falchions, any weapon he could think of was here.

The weapons weren't amazing concerning their craftsmanship. Everything was shoddy. They were made to fill soldiers' empty hands, nothing else. Quantity sacrificed quality; Kael had learned

49

that the hard way when he had tried to make a sword in a mere day. The weapon was useless and had to be scrapped.

There was a gruff-looking man polishing a blood-stained mace sitting on a bench. Kael didn't notice him until he had almost tripped over his stumpy leg. The man stood up sharply, startling Kael. He shook the mace threateningly close to Kael's face. "What are you doing here?" he rumbled.

Kael caught his breath, his heart pounding. The man had blended into his surroundings. He was covered in greasy old rags, which is also what hung behind him; cloths for cleaning tarnished weapons. "I—I'm sorry, I didn't know I wasn't allowed to be in here."

"You are," the man moaned, sitting back down. He began to wipe the mace again, scrutinizing Kael carefully with one good eye. The man rather stunk and was missing a few teeth. Kael was eager to escape as soon as possible, his interest lost with the armoury. "Just not yet, youngin'. You'll get your chance to come in here later, depending on which side you picked, heh heh."

Kael nodded, and struggling not to heave from the man's overwhelmingly foul presence, extricated himself from the armoury, running several paces until he thought the air would be clean again. When was the last time that guy had a shower? And what was that last bit he had mention about which side Kael had chosen?

Since there wasn't anything else to look at, Kael decided to retire back to his barracks. It would be more entertaining to talk to the youth in there than anything else out here, although he did find the castle rather fascinating. He stopped halfway back to the barracks to marvel at it. The architecture was so much different than anything else in the kingdom. So unique, and so bright! The spires stabbed into the air, each at a different elevation. It was surprising how large and wide it was. Kael had never been so close to it.

There were three barracks on Kael's side, and two on the other. It was odd that they would have so many barracks for such a slim amount attending, but then Kael realized the place had once supported an entire, thriving army. He couldn't even imagine what having over a thousand soldiers marching around in there would be like.

The barrack was thrumming with activity. People were still choosing their bunks, but most were laying bedding down over the hard wood. Kael fetched his own standard-issue bedding after asking somebody where to get it. He shoved his way through until he found where his pack already was. He frowned as he noticed the top was lying wide open. He threw his blanket and pillow on his bunk and leaned over his pack. Somebody had been ruffling through clothing! One of his shirts was lying off to the side, but otherwise everything was accounted for. Had somebody thought he would bring something valuable? Doubtless that's what they were searching for.

Kael scoured the crowd. Don Huntson, the recruit he had met earlier, was nowhere to be seen. That rat, had he been the one who had gone through his stuff? He was the only one who could have, there was no way that any of these boys could have in the time Kael had been gone. Don had tricked him concerning this, what else had he tricked Kael with? It struck Kael to remember what had happened earlier...he had chosen A...was that a bad thing?

No matter, it wasn't important who rummaged through his meagre things, as long as everything was here. In the back of his mind, he felt hurt in a distant way. It was disturbing to know that somebody who had talked directly to him would do such an underhanded deed as soon as he left. It made him feel as though nobody here could be trusted.

The day dragged on sluggishly. The compound wasn't complex, just large due to the horse ring in the middle, so most of the boys had their fill of exploring it within the hour. The rest of the time was spent moping around and getting to know the other boys. Kael was surprised how much they all had in common. A lot of burden was placed on the shoulders of the young men, Kael had just never thought that anybody else could have more work to do than he—after all, he did have three jobs—but he was mistaken. Some boys did four, up to five jobs.

Remus, for example, was a hard-working individual. Throughout the day, Kael tried to get to know him better. His shoulders were massive and his chest barrel-like and was a boy thick with muscle.

Talking to him didn't get anywhere though. There was no time to talk when one was too busy, it was more efficient not to.

Where some boys were quiet like Remus, there were others that never seemed to stop talking. Horan and Joran, twins, talked up a storm. Both of them combined spoke more in an hour than the rest of the boys could in an entire day. All they had to say as well was nonsense, trivial facts that nobody cared about, useless memories. They even ranted on about their dreams. How they had both managed to get into the same group was baffling, and very annoying. If the two were separated, Kael would bet that they would be much quieter.

Otherwise, most of the other boys were alike, and getting to know them individually would be an undertaking of its own. Kael, like the most boys, simply leaned against the sparring fence and stared at the dusty ground in silence, waiting for the day to end. Although he didn't look forward to tomorrow or the day after that, his body ached for action. Idleness was not a flavour he hadn't tasted often, and he didn't like it.

Some of the boys carried on idle conversations and the twins continued to blabber on. He ignored them and stared across the horse pit at the group across the way. They were doing a similar thing, just loitering against their fence. What set them apart from them? He supposed he'd find out soon enough.

A bell sounded off from the dinner hall. The boys hesitated for a moment, and then began to strut towards the building. The other side, naturally, arrived there first by the time Kael's group had reached the middle of the grounds. Feeling uncomfortable for taking so long, Kael set out at a medium jog while the rest of the boys continued their snail pace. He could feel their eyes grinding his back. *Why is he running? Is he trying to make us look bad?* He could feel these questions caress the back of his ears, thrown at him from the other boys. He hoped something simple like this wouldn't set him apart so soon.

Returning to a regular pace once he reached the building, Kael found the other side already seated and eating their meals, which, from what he could see, looked like a simple stew with a slice of bread.

"Good work, soldier." A hand clapped down on Kael's shoulder. He gasped and turned around to face the Captain yet again. How in the world did he do that?

"Hello, Captain. Um, thanks?"

Captain Terra chuckled. "You rushed to get here, I like that. That's how you're supposed to move in the military. You have much promise so far. Continue to please me, and I believe you will do well."

Kael bit back a remark. "Thank you, Captain," he said.

"Now the rest of your group...they could learn something from you." Just then, Kael's troupe walked in. The Captain's iron gaze halted them as they came in the doorway. Some of the boys in the back yelped in surprise, asking the ones in front why they had stopped. They soon got their answer. "What took you so long?"

"Captain?" a boy in the front questioned.

"When we ring the bell or call for you, I expect you to rush to wherever it is that your scrawny hides need to be!" Spittle flied from the Captain's mouth. "Do you understand me?!"

"Yes, Captain!"

He eyeballed a couple of the boys. "Good. You'll go without dinner tonight for your tardiness. Consider this a warning. I have the authority to take away all your meals for two days, so I suggest you listen to me." He placed a hand almost lovingly on Kael's shoulder. "Now follow this boy's—what's your name?—follow Kael's example and you will live to be great soldiers."

Kael could see the contempt in their eyes, but none dared to retort. They nodded instead and turned out the door. Kael watched them leave, feeling guilty. Was this his fault? Maybe they would have gotten away with a warning if he hadn't run...

He ate his dinner culpably, feeling alone. He knew some of the young men in his group somewhat, but he didn't know even a single one of these guys. Dinner was short and unfulfilling.

Kael returned to his barrack, fearing what they would do when they saw his face. But when he opened the door wearily, nothing happened. Most of the boys were already asleep, and the ones that were awake did not even glance at him at all. The twins, of course, were still yapping away like they had been all day.

Sensing that the boys around him didn't want to talk, Kael slipped into bed. He was about to strip down to his undergarments, but the blankets were scratchy, so he decided that sleeping with a tunic on would be better. He wrapped a thin sheet around himself, closed his eyes and willed sleep to come upon him.

What a dreadful day it had been, surely one of his worse. But it didn't help his mood any more to think that things could only get worse. Much, much worse.

Chapter 5

A ringing arose in the distance. It started off small, so Kael ignored it. He turned back to Laura, oh how good it was to see her again! Her presence was so soothing; his troubles seemed to just melt away. He wanted to stay with her forever, what a stupid thing it had been to leave her in the first place, he couldn't even remember why! But that didn't matter now.

She smiled serenely, but her face told Kael that there was something wrong. Kael wanted to ask her what the matter was, to touch her cheek gently and reassure her that everything was right. She opened her mouth to speak.

"Wake up you pestilent scumbags!"

A wave of moaning swept over the barracks, breaking Kael free from his dream and reminding him where he was and what had happened the day previous. He buried his face in the pillow, wishing the dreams had been real and that he could return to them.

"Get up you dogs! I've seen a corpse move more than you—and faster too!"

"Was it, by chance, an undead monster?" one of the twins jested.

Kael looked up to see the Captain staring down icily at the thin, blonde boy. Was it Horan or Joran? It was impossible to tell. The Captain leaned in closer to him, grabbing him by the scruff of his shirt collar, his face so close that bangs of his bright blonde hair nearly touched the boy's forehead. The twin's face smile dropped. "Get up," Captain Terra snarled, his moustache rustling from his breath.

The Captain looked as though he might pick up the boy completely off the ground and throw him across the room. Instead, he gave the scrawny kid a shove and wheeled around to scream at the rest of them. He was in a foul mood today, or worse, maybe he was always like this...

Kael hastily threw himself out of bed. He yawned as he stepped outside. What? The sun wasn't even up yet! Or it could be...it was hard to tell with those walls...

"Today we start the first course of your training. I will be your group's trainer. Over there, they are having the same discussion, but they have a different trainer." He gestured over his shoulder at the other group. A rippling of distress ran through the group. The Captain didn't seem to pick up on it. He was their trainer? Was Don lying, or could the man on the other side be even worse? "First off, before we can do anything, you will receive your uniforms."

The Captain nodded and the large man Kael had bumped into in the armoury can waddling out, pushing a large cart full of blue cloth.

"Thanks, Larr." The Captain picked up a tunic from out of the cart as the one named Larr waltzed away. "Don't be so eager to put these on now," he exclaimed. "These beauties are standard issue. Having all our soldiers look so stunning makes our army look that much more imposing."

Kael could almost hear the comebacks the boys were biting back. He could think of a few himself. *Why did they need to look imposing to a dragon? Surely it wouldn't be intimidated when it was several hundred times their size.* But of course, he didn't utter a word. As he looked sideways, he saw one large redheaded boy almost say something, but he caught himself.

Captain Terra threw the outfit at a boy. "Find one that looks your size and put it on."

"Now?" one of the twins asked.

"Yes, now! You think I mean tomorrow?"

The twin flinched and dropped his trousers, commencing to put on the new blue ones. Kael followed suit, first finding an acceptable tunic and then replacing his regular clothes with the outfit. Unlike the bedding, it was quite nice. The cloth was soft and far more comfortable than the tunic and pants he had just been wearing. He was impressed by the quality of the outfit. It was much different than he had suspected, judging from everything else. He liked the look of the outfits as well.

"Good," Captain Terra stated once the group had all changed. Each boy had an outfit that was his perfect size. Kael's fit tight, but comfortably. Just the way a good tunic is supposed to. "We will begin with our training at once, come."

He preceded the lead them to the building at the back of the sparring pit. It was a classroom of sorts. It brought back old memories back when Kael had attended school. He was one of the only boys that attending the school at the time. School was considered a higher-end luxury and most didn't see the practicality of education. Kael's mother, however, insisted that he go.

He had liked school; it was good to stimulate his brain. Even from the short time he was there, his education gave him many things to ponder, as well as moderate problem-solving skills.

The group entered the building. There were desks filling the room. Kael sat down at a desk near the wall. The Captain stood in front of a big mahogany desk at the front before starting.

"The time we spend in here will be short-lived, so don't get comfortable," he said. "I feel the best way to learn something is by practising it first-hand, but only after reasonable classroom education." He paused, scowling at the red-head for no reason. He cocked his head, birdlike. "If you hadn't figured it out already, we will be learning the delicate yet powerful art of swordplay, or depending on your specific preference, how to use a different weapon."

A few of the boys gasped. "Are you kidding? Don't we get a choice in this?"

The Captain pounded his first on his desk, at once all the young men who had risen out of their seats in outrage sat back down.

"You did get your choice, and you picked this path. Do you honestly think that anybody would willingly choose this side? If you got your choice, our army would be comprised of snivelling, whining archers. Bleh."

Kael didn't quite understand. What was wrong with being a knight? That's what they were going to become wasn't it? In his eyes, knights were courageous and powerful. Shouldn't it be considered an honour to learn how to swordfight?

Shrugging off his confusion, Kael listened diligently as the Captain began to teach them the beginning aspects of swordplay. It was very basic stuff, mostly common sense facts such as not sticking your sword in your own team, and how to wield a sword properly. The pace that they went at was brisk enough, but even so, after several hours, Kael was finding it hard to concentrate. The Captain wrote on a slate board at the front, illustrating the beginning footwork of swordplay. He drew arrows and lines on the board, but not a word. It was clear he was illiterate. It wasn't uncommon.

Kael was very bored by the time the Captain called for lunch. He knew most of the things that the Captain was teaching already.

Lunch, like dinner the night before, wasn't appetizing. The boys quickly marched out of the hut, stretching their aching joints and talking amongst themselves. Kael didn't want to say anything at first, but he thought better of himself and urged his troupe to jog to the cafeteria, lest they suffer the Captain's wrath again.

Despite how the group practically ran to get there, they were all surprise to see that the Captain was already there, leaning against the wall adjacent to the door, munching on a piece of bread with soup slathered on it.

The food wasn't disgusting, but it was horribly similar to the stew they had eaten the night before. Still, he was grateful for whatever sustenance he was given because they had skipped breakfast to receive their uniforms. His belly had begun to ache in the classroom. He was afraid that the Captain would verbally explode at him if his stomach issued a growl.

There was small talk flowing through the boys, so Kael decided to join in. He turned to the boy next to him. What was his name again? "Brudo, what's wrong with being a foot soldier?" he asked.

"What's wrong with it?" the boy scoffed. He had been one of the boys who had yelled out when they had found out that they would be learning. "Think about it, who's gonna die first, the foot soldier, or the archer—who is standing several yards away from the battle?"

It didn't take Kael long to think about it. His heart fell an extra two notches. Soon it would be in his feet. "Oh."

Brudo leaned in closer to Kael. "Do you think there's something wrong with the Captain?" he asked, his eyes flickering around, trying to find Captain Terra. "He seems a little off."

"A little?" Kael exclaimed. "The Captain is more than a little bit off, don't you think?"

Just that moment, Captain Terra yelled at some recruit. Kael didn't recognize the boy, perhaps he was an archer. "Is there something wrong with my face, boy?" The Captain screamed. "You look me in the eyes when I speak to you, show some respect!" He smacked the bowl the young man was carrying, spilling the contents over a couple others and all over the floor.

"He's a lot off," Brudo agreed, stifling a laugh, hunching over his bowl as the Captain, nostrils flaring, turned to face the rest of them. "But why? Was he just born a terrible person?"

"Nah," a short, pale boy interjected from across the table. Portus was his name. He was an intelligent boy from what Kael had deduced so far, but spoke slowly. "My brother was in here two years ago. He said in his letters that there was something wrong with the Captain—he was kicked in the head by a horse when he was younger, something similar to that. He said that was the reason the Captain was still here, they don't send sick soldiers out to fight."

The Captain walked by. They halted their conversation, sharing careful glances to silence each other. But as he strolled past, Kael stole a quick glance. Sure enough, there was a scar near his eye right, just below his temple. Maybe it was true; maybe the Captain had a mental deficiency. It explained a lot.

Lunch was soon over, and it was time to return back to the classroom. Kael gazed up at the sky as they reached the edge of the sparring pit. Perhaps going inside where it was sheltered was a good thing. The sun was beating down on them and it was getting hot already.

The Captain called them to a halt. Without warning, he chucked a large stick at the chest of the redheaded boy, who barely managed to catch it before it hit his meaty face. He grunted. "What was that for?"

Blinking slowly, the Captain smiled. "You've learned a lot today, it's time to put that footwork to rest. My theory is to train a soldier quick and effective, half his time should be spent in the class, and the other half should be putting his knowledge to use. A week from now we will begin specific training for the specific weapons you choose, but for this week, I want everybody comfortable with using their legs properly. Come to think of it, give me back that training sword, you don't need it yet."

With a sour look, the redhead threw the stick back to the Captain, who caught it, blank-faced.

The rest of the day wasn't any more eventful. In fact, it was just about as exciting as the first half. They just practised the footwork they had learnt inside the classroom, prancing around with nothing even in their hands to guide them. The Captain strutted around and gave orders on how to step properly. He threw a fit at a couple boys, that redheaded one especially, but otherwise kept quiet. The Captain's emotions seemed to flare at any given moment. One moment he could be satisfied with what you were doing, but the next he would explode at nothing. Kael's thoughts returned to what Portus had told him. What is true that the Captain had brain damage?

Finally, when the sun had nearly set, the Captain decided that they had enough. By the end of day one, Kael was confident that every single person there had almost mastered basic footwork. He certainly had already. But once they split into individual weapon studies and had the chance to wield a blade, the footwork would be totally different. So, in a sense, everything they were doing would be irrelevant. They should have picked their weapons first.

Dinner was different that night. They actually got a well-rounded meal, with vegetables, a slice of bread and a small hunk of meat. It was better than the stew they had earlier, but not the best meal Kael had ever had, though it was fulfilling and did its job satisfying his belly.

The Captain dismissed them after dinner. By then, the sun had already crept below the confines of the walls, sending a deeper-than-usual twilight over the complex. Kael found himself weary and headed straight to his barrack. The other boys followed suit, some lingering around the complex for a bit, but discovering there was nothing to do.

The barrack was noisy, but at least it wasn't cramped like it could possibly be. It was a large structure that could easily fit three-hundred and Kael would hate to be trapped inside it when it was full.

After changing, Kael sat himself down in the bunk. A sorrowful emotion crawled slowly over him. What had his life been reduced to? This place was truly horrifying, and all this was for what? To fight a large dragon and ultimately be killed? It didn't seem very fulfilling. The chatter in the room subsided, the same sinking feeling coming over the rest of the boys. Except for the twins, they kept chattering away long after Kael fell asleep; perhaps it was their way to try and shy away the sense of impending death.

The next day was just as bleak, a complete repeat of the day before. The third day was also boring, except they finally got to use wooden sticks when they began their physical training. Kael had to admit, Captain Terra was a decent teacher, but his irregular emotional swings and lightening fast temper kept him from being a true master.

"No, no, no!" he hollered at the redheaded boy again. "Haven't you been listening? It's like this, do exactly as I do."

The redheaded boy, Ernik—Kael had learnt his name last night—wasn't good at paying attention it seemed. For that reason, the Captain enjoyed tormenting him. Well, either that or he simply had a bias against him. He followed the Captain's movements as carefully as he could, his beady eyes following the Captain's wrist, but for whatever reason, he just couldn't do it the same.

The Captain twisted his sword, took a sharp step backwards to dodge an imaginary foe, then with a flick of his wrist, shot forward and plunged his stick through the air. Ernik did a terrible job replicating it.

The Captain screamed at Ernik, hitting him across the back with his stick. It didn't look like the strike hurt the boy, but it still shocked Kael. Teachers had struck students in school, but never like that. Kael reminded himself that this wasn't school.

Kael had mastered his footwork the first day, and even with a stick in hand, he still found it child's play. He wanted a real weapon; he wanted to spar with an opponent to sharpen his skills. This was doing nothing for them, stabbing at non-existent enemies. He ached for some sort of challenge.

Even though they were only three days in, Kael longed for some variation in the course. He didn't say anything, of course. He caught a glance over at the archery range. He almost considered himself lucky as he watched them taking aim at their targets. That must be twice as boring, taking shots at the same thing all day long. How terrible.

Supper came as a relief again. The food, like the two days before, was lacking. He was grateful for it, considering how much worse it could be.

The Captain's piercing voice reverberated through their barracks earlier than usual this morning.

"Get up you rotting corpses! Today we start off early!" He seemed in a good mood today, which was hard to believe. He marched them all outside after they had put their usual outfits on.

Kael gasped. The sun wasn't even up yet! Why did he wake them so unbearably early? Remembering how he had thought he archery side was worse the other day, he glanced over. They weren't up yet.

"Keep your eyes over here, soldier," the Captain called out to Kael. He immediately snapped to attention, closing his mouth which had been open in a wide yawn. The Captain stood up on a low box that he had brought near the barracks earlier. "Today begins your physical strengthening. We only have a short time to make you strong, but I promise you, I'll do my best." He smiled sinisterly. "Now give me eight laps around the track, now!"

The Captain was referring to the horse ring in the middle. So far there had been no horses in it. Kael had wondered why they would use up so much room for a race track like that. He now knew that it doubled as a jogging track as well. How swell.

A few sighs could be heard, tired moans that said nothing in specific.

"You don't like it?" the Captain said, leaning forward on his box. He twitched like a bird, a scowl spreading across his face. "Good, give me ten laps then, see how you'll like it now."

An extra loud moan erupted. The Captain smirked and watched them as they started to run.

Kael thought that he was in good health, but he underestimated how long ten laps around that ring really were. He was sweating profusely and the sun was high in the sky by the time he finished. He hadn't been the first, but he was far away from being last as well.

He collapsed in front of the Captain, where most of the other young men had so far. It seemed to please the Captain to see them panting at his feet, so Kael, dodging his eyes, moved somewhere else. He breathed heavily and stared up at the sky as if to plead for it to make this all better.

The Captain let the boys catch their breath and relax while the others were finished up. The last one to finish was a rather plump looking boy with a smattering of freckles across his beat-red face.

As soon as the red-faced boy finished, the Captain clapped his hands loudly together. "Well done," he exclaimed, beaming. "Now drop and give me double fifty. Fifty push ups and fifty sit ups—go!"

Kael flopped to the ground and started. Fifty push ups? That was easy, he usually did fifty push ups every morning anyway. He couldn't help but to check on the boy who had finished last.

"Captain, can I wait a little bit, please, I'm still out of breath," the last boy wheezed.

"No. In fact, do double."

"What? Why?" Some of the other boys stopped what they were doing to watch the argument.

The Captain's face remained calm. "You finished last, consider this a punishment. Do better next time or the same will result. Understand?"

"Yes, Captain."

Kael was outraged by the Captain's insensate behaviour, but what could he do? It wasn't right to give a boy who couldn't help but be

63

slower a punishment like that. The young man was out of breath, he could hardly lift himself off the ground. Kael could see the same anger he was feeling from this injustice in some of the other's faces. Nobody said anything, fearing the Captain would make them do something worse.

Finishing both tasks before everybody else, Kael sat down, waiting for the others to finish. The distinct sense that somebody was standing behind him came to him. He slowly turned around, facing the knee of the Captain's trousers.

"What are you doing?"

Kael hesitated, unsure how to answer. He could hardly see the Captain's face from the sunlight behind. He shielded his eyes. "Resting," he said delicately.

"Resting?" the Captain repeated, tasting the word. "That's unacceptable, soldier. When you are finished with your exercises, you will ask me what your next task will be, do you understand?"

Kael bit his lip. The Captain's logic made no sense. They were allowed to take a break earlier, what made now any different? Controlling his voice, he said, "yes, Captain."

"Good. Now, what are you going to do?"

Kael hesitated again, trying to keep up to the Captain's confusing mind games. He stood up and faced the Captain. "I'm done what you ordered me, Captain, what should I do now?"

The Captain was satisfied, but his tone was less friendly. "Do you see those four lines over there?"

Kael nodded. Sure enough, there were four white lines lying just outside the entrance to the horse ring. They were set several feet apart and perfectly parallel to each other. Each was about twenty feet long. "Yes, Captain."

"You go over there and stand in the middle of the two innermost lines," he explained, coming sickeningly close to Kael. His breath smelled sour, as if he were sick. "When I tell you to, you run to the first line on your left, then to the line on your right, then to the outermost line back on your left, then to the outer right. Repeat until I tell you to stop. Is that clear?"

Kael nodded. It was straightforward enough, just run to each line. How hard was that?

"Get to it then, Soldier. I'll come get you after breakfast."

Kael winced. He was going to miss breakfast. What's more, he was going to have to do this all through breakfast! How was this fair at all? He thought what the Captain had done to that thickly boy was bad, this was far worse! The Captain turned on his heels and stood in the centre of all the boys who were still doing their sit ups.

"Why did you stop, you bedraggled maggots? Get back to work!"

Kael could see it in their eyes. They were sorry for him, but nobody would say a thing, frightened they might have to do the same thing as him. They immediately resumed their sit ups.

Standing where the Captain had pointed to, Kael stared at the man acidly. He had a vague smile on his face and a slight skip in his step. Was he proud of what he had done? Did torturing young recruits give him that much pleasure? What a twisted, degenerate man.

"What are *you* looking at?"

Kael snapped to attention. "Waiting for you to tell me when to start, Captain," he said briskly, trying to control his emotion. Doubtless the Captain could read what he was thinking, but he smiled anyway.

Captain Terra laughed. "That's a good soldier. Now, get to it."

Kael couldn't believe how hungry he was. Hungry and tired. The archery side had eaten their breakfast a lot sooner than his group. In fact, it was getting close to lunch by the time Kael's group exited the building. But he didn't stop. If he paused for a moment, the Captain might throw another tantrum and make him do something worse.

Kael was on the verge of collapse when the Captain finally freed him of his task. Kael hadn't run the entire thing; he had run out of energy after two or three times and had walked most of it. However, all that had taken its toll, and without any food to replenish him either! What a day this would be. Hopefully they wouldn't be doing anymore of that soon.

They proceeded to go inside for their usual lessons. It didn't seem like there would anything else to learn, but of course, there was. The Captain began to teach them about the vital areas of enemies and how to strike them there, but Kael wasn't listening anymore. His heart wasn't into it. After his humiliation, he was neither in the mood or feeling lively enough to pay attention. Everything the Captain said wafted in one ear and out the other.

The nagging thought arose in Kael's mind, however, one which he found impossible to ignore. How would any of this help them in battle against a colossal dragon? Perhaps it was too soon to say whether or not they would indeed learn how to slay a dragon, but Kael had the feeling it was all a waste of time.

After a couple of hours, Kael looked outside a window and noticed the archery side was going in for their lunch break. It didn't look like Kael would be having lunch either. He turned to the boy beside him, Portus. They shared an overzealous expression of boredom, telling each other of their disappointment through one simple funny face.

"You boys, what are you doing?"

Kael flinched, turning to the front where the Captain was standing. How did he catch things like this? "Portus had an eyelash under his eye," Kael lied, "I was showing him where it was."

"By making a face like that?"

"Yes, Captain."

The Captain frowned and narrowed his eyes. He considered the answer for a moment, and then with a twitch continued his lesson. Kael caught his breath. Was he actually satisfied with that answer?

The lesson dragged on as usual. The Captain caught the redheaded boy, Ernik, napping and absolutely exploded at him, but otherwise the lessons were drab and boring. Once again, Kael learned nothing new.

They dismissed for lunch at last. It was brisk and disappointing. Even despite his hunger, Kael found it unfulfilling. Watery, cold soup was outright unappetizing at that point.

After lunch, they continued to do simple workouts like earlier. The whole group had to do the line-run, Kael included (which he found immensely frustrating) and then a lovely activity where they had to dodge stones that the Captain hurled at them to heighten their reflexes. Whenever Ernik's turn came to have the stone thrown at him, Kael could swear that the Captain threw it twice as hard. Why did he hate that boy so much?

When Kael went to bed after supper, he was feeling the most miserable he had in years. He was bruised, fatigued, upset and still hungry. Could this get any worse? He quickly tried to take back that thought, as if it was a bird he had accidentally released. Whenever he thought something like that, things did indeed get worse.

Perhaps this was all an issue of perception. He had a couple of bad experiences, but wasn't the worst off in the group. In fact, he should consider himself lucky. Compared to Ernik, this was like a day off work. The redheaded boy sat in his bunk, staring at the ceiling dismally. He had a dull glint to his eyes. Kael felt sorry for him.

From now on, he would try his best to obey orders and avoid for any reason for the Captain to yell at him for. Who knows, maybe he'd actually enjoy himself; maybe he could learn something important.

After a week, Kael wasn't enjoying himself anymore than he had when he had arrived. He tried to stay positive, but there was nothing to like in this place. Everything they did had to be picture perfect. Everywhere they went they were accompanied by the Captain, and every little move they made had to be carefully observed and corrected.

There was some consolation, however, at the end of week one.

Kael awoke with a start as somebody jumped down from a top bunk. Something was wrong. His heart began to race. It was past their regular roll-call, he could tell just by the sickening feeling in his gut. The other boys knew it as well. Was this some sick trick the Captain was playing? Was he going let them sleep, and then punished them for missing the normal beginning time?

Voices began to rise as the boys started to question each other. Some boys slipped on their uniforms, but stayed rooted to the edge of their bunks. Light shone through the crack under the door at the far end of the barrack. It was far into the day already, later than the Captain allowed. Kael edged to the end of his bunk, slipping his feet into his boots, ready to stand at attention if the Captain burst in.

A general decision was made, one which was suggested by words, but finalized by the boy's inaction. Ernik sat back down into his bed, pulled the covers back on himself and said with a loud voice, "well, if he's going to wait outside for us to come out, we're already in trouble. I'm going to catch some more sleep."

About half the boys agreed and settled back into bed. Kael, however, was already wide awake, his senses stimulated by that short spurt of fear. If he was going to be punished, he would rather it be now as opposed to later, when the sun baked the ground hot. Better to do it in less heat.

He girded himself, and then headed straight outside. Brudo followed him. Instead of finding Captain Terra outside his door, Kael was surprised to find the archery trainer. The gray-haired man smiled at Kael, his beard ruffling. He was a kindly, medium-set man. By any means, Kael liked him a lot more than the Captain so far.

"Good morning," he said, addressing Kael. "You're Captain is...sick right now, I will be conducting your training today."

Kael and Brudo exchanged glances. "Alright," Kael replied. "What's wrong with him?"

The archer shifted his weight. "Let me put it this way, undoubtedly you've heard rumours about the Captain, yes?" He tapped his right eye, near his temple. "Well, most of them are probably true then—within reason of course."

Kael nodded. Portus, who had come out of the barracks a few moments ago stopped just outside the door. He was surprised that the archer was there, but didn't seem affected by the information the man had just told them. In fact, he wore a smug look of triumph on his face.

"So, what are we doing then?" Kael asked.

The archer turned around to check on his group before answering the question. "Your friends may sleep as long as they want, but today the ones that are awake will learn how to ride the horses if they wish."

Kale was already wide awake, so he decided to follow Sergeant Mahone's advice. He headed towards where the horses were kept.

The horse stall, Kael discovered, was built inside the wall, just like part of the armoury. The reason was so that people on the outside could send horses, hay and oats through the gate on the other side, which was heavily padlocked. The stables were built into the bottom of a large cylindrical pillar that acted as the elbow of the wall. There was another staircase in the building as they entered. It wound upwards and out of sight so Kael guessed that it would be a pathway to the battlements. Kael imagined that such a small, enclosed area like that would bear a terrible stench. But to his surprise, he was wrong. The stables weren't the cleanest thing he had ever seen, but he was impressed even so. And the stench wasn't as bad as he expected.

Kael strolled through the stables, feeling hay crunch under his feet. He was trying to decide which horse he would choose to train with, but it occurred to him that he knew next to nothing about horses. He eventually picked a dark brown horse, on no thesis whatsoever besides his liking to the colour of its coat.

It was kind of wonderful, moving at such a slow pace. When the Captain was around, they were always rushing to get somewhere or do something with ridiculous speed, all while being as precise and perfect as they could. It was a nice change.

The archers were also there, but Kael's group was allowed to choose their horses first. They would take turns with the animals, first Kael's small group, and then the archers themselves. This was also a pleasant thing, before the archers had beaten them to everything. Well, dinner at least, but to Kael, that *was* everything.

Kael returned outside, leading his horse by its reigns. It was strange to him, ordering a strong animal that was twice the size of him around so easily. It seemed unnatural in a way. It was somewhat disconcerting as well.

The archer, whose name was Sergeant Mahone, taught Kael the basics of horse riding and it wasn't until long before Kael was

69

tentatively seated on the animal's back, leading it right and left. He wasn't a professional yet, far from, but the new experience was thrilling and he enjoyed every moment of it. For once, this place was fun for a brief moment, and he was learning something for the first time.

He was sad when his turn was over.

However, the day was still young, and Kael had his several more chances to practice his horse riding. He was getting good at it as well. He ate breakfast quickly, eager to get back outside. How strange the day was.

Eventually, the rest of Kael's group woke up and joined them as well. They all went to the middle of the ring to take their turns riding the horses. The line became long and soon Kael became tired of waiting. He had his fill and there would always be another time. Wouldn't there?

Kael decided to take advantage of his time and just relax. He found a nice, shady section of the dusty yard and settled down, leaning up against the wall and folding his arms over his stomach. To have time to think again, that was something he had missed dearly. But as he sat there, trying to think of better times, the inevitable thought of the friends he had left behind floated into his mind. Laura, Faerd, Bunda, Korjan, Malaricus—each took their turn plaguing his mind as he sat with his eyes closed. Oh how he missed each and every one of them so much. It hurt him even more to remember how he had left them with nothing more than a lie. A pang of guilt stabbed his heart as he remembered how he hadn't even said goodbye in any form to Laura. He hadn't visited her nor did he touch her smooth face before he left. He had never gotten the chance to tell her how he really felt about her...

Somebody shook him awake. He stared at Portus, who hovered above him with a goofy smile across his pale face. "Lunchtime!" he said happily. Portus enjoyed talking to Kael at lunch; it was something the boy looked forward to in the day. Kael like to talk back to him as well, it passed the time by and made him think of something besides raging infernos and shining scales.

"Thank you," Kael said painfully, rising off the ground and stretching his sore muscles. "You go; I'll meet you in a bit." Portus ran off towards the dinner hall.

Kael stood for a moment longer. He took a deep breath. No matter how good of a day it was in here, it was nothing compared to those spent outside, with his friends. The deep, dark remembrance of why he was here suddenly struck him again. He was going to die.

Chapter 6

Apparently, the Captain was feeling better the next day. Which meant that the rest of them were going to feel worse.

"Wake up, scum!" The Captain's familiar voice struck Kael hard. It seemed as though somebody was ringing a really high pitched bell right beside his head. "I have something you all need to see." A sadistic grin met Kael as he opened his eyes. The man was standing right beside him. Why was he smiling like a criminal who had just gotten away with murder?

Aroused by the insane look in his eyes, Kael quickly got dressed. The Captain, without yelling at anybody else, exited the building, slamming the door shut behind him. He may have been sick the previous day, but today he was back to his normal self, perhaps a little bit giddier. Although giddy was too pleasant of a word to describe him.

With a huge yawn, Kael followed the general throng outside. Eyes still closed, he bumped into the boy in front of him. Why had he stopped? Kael squinted in the early light, and then moved around the figure in front of him. One of the twins who had been standing in front of him had stopped. Confused, Kael looked into the twin's eyes, then followed his gaze. Mid-yawn, he completely froze.

In the middle of the horse ring, tied up onto a large wooden pole, was something Kael would remember for the rest of his life. Still wearing their leather armour were two lifeless young men, both hanging by ropes attached to the top of the pole. They were covered in gore and dirt and there was a ring of blood splotched on the ground underneath them. Their mouths hung agape and they stayed chillingly still and pale. Nobody said a word, not even the twins. A morose gloom rapidly descended over the complex. The sky bubbled and churned overhead, stirring the fright and overall shock that hung over everybody.

Except one person.

"I can tell, you're wondering about them," the Captain said loudly so that both factions could hear. He had snuck up behind Kael's group once again, startling a few of them. The archers had joined as well at the front of the horse ring by then, all their mouths hanging open or covered by shaking hands. "Bad things happen when you try to run away. It's a long way from here to any other city and these mountains surrounding are filled with perils." The Captain paused ever so slightly, as if to inhale the sullen mood. A smirk was slowly spreading across his face. "We found these two in the south-eastern part of the mountain range. It looks as though both were attacked by wolves or fell off a cliff. Like I said, trying to escape your mandatory enlistment is high treason against the crown and highly unadvisable. Anybody who tries to run away may sooner or later end up like these two—as...*unfortunate* as that would be."

Kael's eyes never felt so wide. He had never seen a dead body before. Sure, he had seen many corpses, but those were all of animals. These were *human!* With a shudder, he realized that he recognized them. No, it couldn't be! They were the boys he had seen at Bunda's butchery. *The very same boys!* He had talked to them! This was too real, it couldn't be happening. Kael grabbed his hair with both hands. He didn't want to end up like them, either in the belly of a dragon or mauled by wolves. He didn't want to die!

Wheeling around, Kael bolted to the latrine, but it was far away and there was no way he was going to make it. He keeled over and heaved. Despite how sick it made him feel, he couldn't help but to look back at the young corpses hanging from that pole as he wiped bile from his mouth.

"This is what happens to runaways." Kael didn't have to turn around to know whose voice that was. He refused to get up. "You better learn to hold that stomach. Humph, some soldier you will make."

Kael furrowed his brow. He stood up, swaying. Kael was taller than the Captain, but if the shorter man was bothered by this, he didn't show it. He met Kael's angry eyes and squinted. "Maybe I don't want to be a warrior," Kael shouted, throwing his arms up into the air. "Maybe I don't want to be a knight." Kael knew it was a

73

terrible idea to yell at the Captain, but he didn't care anymore. His nerves had run raw.

The Captain smirked. "Then you can join those two."

Kael winced as if he had been struck. The message was quite clear. He shirked from the Captain's gaze, hunching his shoulders. Kael didn't say anything.

"Very well." The Captain returned to the rest of Kael's group, which had either begun to disperse or were still staring dumbfounded several metres away from the bodies. "Let's go, you maggots, unless you are content with sitting there all day. I have another surprise for you."

Kael was quite through with the Captain's surprises for the day, but he couldn't help but to feel curious. He was about to follow the man but he hesitated for an unsure moment. Was the Captain going to show them something even more or equally gruesome? There was no better action, so Kael followed his group as the archers followed their own leader. He joined in the throng and together they followed the Captain like a group of chicks to a hen to the far side of the complex.

It suddenly struck Kael. He scoured over the crowd as best he could. Remus, Horan, Joran, Portus, Brudo, Ernik and everybody else. All of them were there, even the boys Kael recognized from before, the ones who were doing their second term. Every single person—except for Don Huntson. As soon as Kael had left his barrack after meeting the boy, he had never seen him since, the conniving snake. But that was of little concern now, he supposed.

They congregated just outside the sparring pits, where Larr, the official weapon master, had detached all the weapons from their racks. During practise, Kael had regularly glanced over to these weapons, wondering when they would get the chance to use them. His heart skipped a beat. Would today be the day?

The Captain cocked his head, delaying his announcement that Kael could tell he was about to make. He waited until they all itched with anticipation. Small shuffles echoed here and there as the boys shifted their weight. Everyone was eager to get to use a real weapon. Remus had a large smile on his face. He never smiled.

Finally the Captain broke the excited silence. "Congratulations. You've done well at your training thus far. Well, most of you." His voice bit out as he scowled at Ernik. "It is my decision that you are ready to start the next level of your training."

A few mild cheers erupted.

The Captain smiled, his teeth gleaming under his bright blonde moustache. "Well then," he chuckled. "I didn't know you'd be so excited to get your armour!"

The crowd went silent.

Their armour was disappointing. Kael had been suspecting grand shining plate mail or chainmail at least, something worthy of a true knight. Instead, they were given a set of leather armour. After the first person received their armour, Kael wanted to kick himself for thinking so foolishly. He had *seen* other soldiers wearing leather amour before. Two of them were in his group right now! Why had he been expecting something better?

There were seven separate pieces of armour. The breastplate consisted of four pieces of large leather studded together by large metal rivets. There were two shoulder pieces that wrapped around and connected together about his neck and over his shoulders and down to his elbows like large scales. Also, there were two vambraces that would protect his forearms and wrists. Lastly, he had greaves that were studded with bits of metal similarly to the other parts. Kael couldn't help but to think the set of leather armour wouldn't be very protective in. When they were to be facing a dragon, what help would this be? Metal would have been much more preferable. Nobody complained, however. A little protection was better than none.

The armour fit perfectly over his tunic. It was relatively light and flexible, but sturdy. It wasn't that bad in reality, but Kael would have loved to see how impressive he would have looked in a full suit of armour while holding a powerful weapon. In his mind, that's what a knight should look like.

After all the armour was given to the boys accordingly, the Captain didn't stall to begin their training at once. They skipped the classroom study and instead went for a two-lap jog. By the time breakfast rolled around, Kael was already spent for the day. Although the armour was light, having just that extra amount of weight took its toll.

The rest of the day, before and after lunch, was spent sparring with wooden swords. It was slightly more difficult with that armour on, but as usual, Kael excelled at it. He found the Captain watching him often, with a scrutinizing look on his face. Maybe Kael was too skilled for his own good, it had set him apart from the beginning, and even as the others improved, they were still leagues away from his level. It drew attention to him, so Kael tried to ease up.

All throughout the day, Kael's gaze kept returning to the two boys hanging on the pole. Would he share their fate?

Two days passed where the boys trained in their armour. Kael was already awake and dressed in his armour by the time the Captain rolled in, screaming as usual. There was something different about him. Before Kael could get a good look at him, he had already strolled out the door. With a sigh, Kael followed him.

When he went outside, Kael saw what was different. For one, the Captain was wearing armour today, a mixture between chainmail and leather armour plating. For another, he was wearing a medium-sized sword on his hip, shielded by a worn, black leather sheath. Judging by the hilt of the blade, it wasn't intricate, but of a better design and quality than the weapons Kael had seen over a week ago in the armoury. Just having the blade at his hip made the Captain seem a lot more imposing. Many of the boys snapped to attention at once, even quicker than before. The thought flittered through their minds that he just might be wild enough to use it on one of them.

This morning, all the Captain had to do was point to get the boys out of the barracks and lined up in front of him. They filed outside with a silent air of anticipation. Something important was about to happen, they could tell. Kael flicked his eyes towards the middle of the horse ring. The bodies were long gone, but the image of the both of them hanging there was burned in his memory.

Captain Terra stood in front of the group once they had all congregated together. He took a deep breath. Kael groaned under his breath. He was going to give them another lecture.

"You've mastered your footwork for any basic weapon, and applied that knowledge while wearing armour. Now, for the next two weeks, I will train you how to use specific weapons that are right for your particular style." An excited whisper ran through the crowd. This is what many of them had been waiting for, weapons at last! "Now, I know two weeks isn't nearly long enough, but I will do my best to teach you as well as I can. Although you won't be perfect warriors, you will have the basic knowledge and skill to survive—if you use both in harmonious synchronization." He spread his arms, his tone making him sound as if he was wise and poetic. A few boys snickered, including Ernik, but the Captain continued, ignoring them. In fact, it seemed as though he was enjoying himself this morning.

They marched over towards the armoury. The building was just big enough for about six boys to go into. Kael was near the middle of the group, so he relaxed and joined into a silly conversation Brudo and Ernik were having until it was his turn to enter. The Captain stood at the mouth of the armoury, arms crossed.

Kael saw some young men exiting, holding a variety of weapons. Brudo and Ernik entered. A moment later, it was Kael's turn. At once, Kael noticed how much darker inside and cooler it was. The change in temperature was nice, considering how hot it was outside. Kael scanned the racks of weapons. A potent stench wafted into his nostrils, and he could tell that Larr, the weapons master, was standing just behind him. Kael turned sideways, surprised by how short and stunningly smelly the gruff man was. He was harbouring a thick, wiry moustache under his short, bulbous nose.

"What weapon do you think I should use?" Kael asked. He already he had his weapon picked out in the back of his mind. His other two friends who had entered with him walked farther into the armoury, awing at all the weapons.

Larr looked him up and down with his semi-hidden, dark eyes. "Halberd," he said.

Kael couldn't help but raise his eyebrows. "Halberd?"

"Yes, halberd. See this? This is a halberd." Larr pulled a weapon off the shelf, a large spear-like pole with a small axe head attached to the top. Kael scrunched his face in disdain. That was hardly a knight's weapon.

"I was thinking of something different."

Larr pounded the bottom of the halberd on the ground. "No, this is a proper weapon for someone like you."

"How?"

"Who's the weapon master?"

Kael hesitated and turned his head, scouring over the other weapons, hiding his doubtful expression. Something caught his eye. "Oh, how about this?" He hopped over to a short sword lying flat on a shelf. Perfect!

Larr scratched his chin. He seemed reluctant to let Kael have his way. He shrugged and said, "Fine, you take that instead, see what I care. When you're lying on the ground, dying because you chose the wrong weapon, you're going to regret not listening to me."

Mortified, but still unconvinced, Kael picked up the short sword. What a comfortable weapon! It was as though this sword was built for him. He tested it, holding it balanced on his palm. He knew a lot about swords. This one was a fine specimen. Well balanced, straight as an arrow, a little dull but otherwise a good weapon indeed.

"Oh, also," Kael grabbed Larr's shoulder as the weapons master turned around, "do you have a shield by any chance? A buckler or something similar?"

Larr frowned, obviously irked by Kael's persistence. "Shield? We don't carry shields that often. We train our soldiers to be offensive, not hide behind their shields like snivelling..." Larr stopped himself. "Uh, never mind. We might have a few rolling around. Take a look in the back."

Doing as he was told, it wasn't long until Kael found a suitable rectangular shield buried under a stack of spears. He slipped it over his left arm, bouncing it up and down with his new sword in his other hand. Shaking his head, he put it back and reached for the next. Yes, this one would do. This shield wasn't any more intricate than his sword, simply a thick, black hunk of circular wood with metal reinforcement studs and lacings on its front side, but it could very well save his life.

Satisfied with his findings, Kael moved to leave. Ernik's girth blocked his way, so he waited until the redhead finished choosing his weapon.

Larr was unsure what to do with Ernik. He would take a weapon off a shelf, hand it to the redheaded boy, stare him top from bottom, cocking his head, and then quickly take the weapon out of his hands. He did this several times until another boys waiting for Larr's help became impatient and chirped at them to hurry up. With a frown and a shrug, the weapons master reached under a lowermost shelf and retrieved a thick wooden club. Testing it in his own grip first, Larr surrendered the hunk of studded wood over to Ernik. The club suited him all too well. Rolling his eyes, Larr ushered them out and called for the next group of boys to come in.

There were about ten boys who had already received their weapons waiting outside. No more than three had the same type of weapon. Kael saw a one-sided axe, a mace, a large battle-hammer, and a couple of spears. Brudo was holding a curved blade with a reluctant, rather confused look on his face. Remus, however, was very please, for in one hand was a broadsword, the tip resting in the dirt.

"I've had some experience with this type of sword before," he was saying smugly, "my father taught me how to use one before I was drafted."

Brudo walked over to Kael. "What am I supposed to do with this thing?" he exclaimed, "I mean, at least Remus got something he could work with, but I'd rather have something fiercer. I don't even know what this is!"

"It's a scimitar," Kael said, biting back a snide remark. "Anyway, it's better than what Ernik got."

"Why, what did Ernik...?"

Ernik stopped swinging the club around for a moment. "What? No, I like this thing! Finally, something I can use!"

"That's because that thing requires no brains, finesse or skill to use," Brudo said, "simply swing it around and hope you hit something. Actually, you're right, it's perfect for you!"

Once they had all received their according weapons, they met back together at the sparring area. There Kael got a better look at everything that the group was using. It seemed to him that every weapon didn't seem appropriate for each boy. Portus, short and scrawny, had been given a broad axe. The poor boy could barely lift it. And a larger, stronger boy had been given a shorter, weaker weapon. If Kael didn't know better, Larr had given them the exact opposite of what would have been good for them. Was this place *trying* to be as inefficient as possible? But he could be wrong. After all, it was the man's profession to hand out weapons. He had much more experience than Kael did.

Kael had to dodge through the crowd as the boys swung around their weapons experimentally, getting a feel for them. He ducked as a spear shaft nearly struck him in the head. He pulled his own sword out of its sheath (he had picked one up before he had left), and gave it a thrust. Yes, this was a comfortable weapon.

The Captain appeared out of nowhere again and began instructing them. He told them that the footwork for each weapon was basically the same. Kael didn't quite believe him though. From his experience, each weapon had its own style that made it unique. However, in the short time that they had, he could understand why the Captain would suffice in teaching them the basics. Still...

After breakfast, Captain Terra split them into two groups. Half of the group would go back inside and learn how to use their weapons to begin with, while the others holding swords or already knew how to fight would spar with each other outside. This time, they were allowed to choose which side they preferred, so Kael decided to stay outside. From the ones outside, Kael recognized the twins and Remus, otherwise the rest of them were relatively unfamiliar to him.

The three boys that were doing their second term were all outside. They had already knew what to do, so two of them began to spar immediately, clashing their sword and axe together, while one other watched absently. He seemed hesitant to go with anybody else, and none of the others were making any effort to pair up, so Kael walked over to the lone boy and offered to spar with him.

They stood opposite of each other, swords at the ready. The other boy brandished a standard military sword. Kael readied his shield and tightened his grip on his sword. They had done some one-on-one sparring with wooden staves before, but those practises were dull and lacking, often moving at a snail's pace to compensate the slower ones. But this, this was the real thing, with sharp blades that could cut through flesh. Kael's heart began to beat furiously and adrenaline began to flow through his body. His skin itched in anticipation. The other boy wore a confident smile across his face. Doubtless, he was expecting to win. Kael would give him a little surprise.

Kael's sparring partner made the first move. He rushed over and swung his sword overhead. Kael blocked it with his shield, the blade glancing off and hitting the dirt. Kael then swung his other arm at a sideways angle, but the other boy stopped the attack with the flat of his blade. Continuing with his attack, Kael retracted his sword, paused for the slightest second to read his enemy's defence, and then lunged at his chest. He was much faster, so he stopped half an inch away from his opponent's exposed chest when he saw that he wasn't going to be able to stop the attack. The other boy froze. He smiled, impressed by Kael's speed.

"I won't let that happen again," he bragged.

"We'll see," Kael said.

This time, they locked blades a few times and Kael blocked many of his enemy's attacks, grateful that he had chosen to use a shield. This battle was far longer, more intense and physically demanding. The other boy's sword was much larger and took more effort to stop than Kael's would have. But he was faster and it took the other boy as much effort to bring his sword around to block Kael's attacks as it did for Kael to block any of his. The boy's style was generic and repetitive, which was the way they were taught. Kael's fighting style, however was very different than his opponent's, and that was beginning to wear the young man down as well. Kael had more fluidity and grace and followed through better than anybody else in

81

his group could. In all those years as a blacksmith's apprentice, he did far more than work with the weapons, he also practiced with them as well. Korjan had been a very good warrior in his day and had taught Kael everything he knew. That's why he excelled in his training, Kael already knew everything. In fact, he probably could have taught the Captain a thing or two.

Eventually, sheer fatigue won over and Kael took advantage of his foe's weariness. He ducked under the opposing blade—a risky move considering he wasn't wearing a helmet—batted the sword away with his shield and brought his sword to a stop on the other boy's chest.

"I win," he declared.

The other boy, exhausted, took Kael's hand. "You fought well, better than I thought. Well done. My name's Bruce Nendara."

"Kael Rundown."

A cheer erupted from around them. Kael hadn't realized, but a crowd had grown. He had been too engulfed in his battle to realize it. The Captain was standing there as well, looking impressed. Kael blushed. So much for not drawing attention to himself.

The rest of the day was spent sparring. Captain Terra decided that Kael was so advanced that he didn't need any classroom training, so he spent the whole day outside. After all was said and done, he must have fought every boy his in group. He even fought against Bruce again, and although he lost due to his great fatigue, it was still a lot of fun.

For the second time so far, Kael was enjoying himself. There were times when he was content, like when he was talking with his new friends or thinking fondly of the ones he left, but never a day like this, when all seemed to be right. It was fun to use a weapon, and fun to engage in competition.

He went to bed that night wearing a smile. He gave his sword one last check to see that it was alright where it leaned next to his bed, and then popped into his sheets. He loved that sword already. It felt like a part of him. He felt strong and brave, just like a real knight.

But once again, that deep dark thought crawled up through the back of his mind. He tried to shove it away, but it took over once again. *What was this all worth? What was the point? He was going to die.*

In two weeks time, he was going to die.

Kael's smile faded. Two weeks wasn't long enough.

Chapter 7

Those two weeks went by fast. Far, far too fast. As much as he wanted to be done his training and be done with Captain Terra, two weeks was a short time to live.

But even in that short time, he had improved. Gone was his mediocre training he had received under the Captain's tutorship and gone with the more advanced training Korjan had given him. He was easily one of the best fighters here, save for Remus. Remus was unstoppable wielding that broadsword. Unlike Bruce, Remus didn't slow down, nor did he tire. And because he was strong, he could swing that blade like it was a twig.

Most of his friends showed significant improvement as well. Ernik loved the dull club he was given and could hammer his opponent with it. Often he never knew when to quit and would give his sparring partner a large bruise on his leg or arm. Kael didn't like sparring with him.

Brudo had eventually warmed up to his scimitar, but his initial dislike for the weapon set him back on his training so he wasn't as skilled as he should have been. Portus had the most difficulty out of all of Kael's friends. The poor boy was so small! He had to drag his broadaxe everywhere he went because it was too heavy for him. But the physical training they did every second day was working on them all and Portus had managed to get somewhat skilled with his axe. Kael didn't like to fight him either.

Even though Ernik was improving, Captain Terra enjoyed tormenting him. Ernik had developed apathy towards it and sometimes countered the Captain's snide remarks with less-than-bright flouts of his own, which usually earned him three laps around the jogging track. The twins had joined in Ernik's torture as well, making them even less likable. None of the boys enjoyed being near them for too long.

During their two weeks, they had another day off to train with the horses. The Captain's absence was a well-deserved gift for everybody except the twins, who were pushed around and bullied the whole day. When he was around, the twins clung to the Captain and nobody could get near them without him knowing. However, without Captain Terra to guard them, they were defenceless to whoever felt they deserved revenge.

Kael didn't partake in that though, he preferred to spend the day doing something more productive than beating up a couple of skinny wimps. Like last time they had day free of the Captain, Kael spent his time riding horses. Once he had his fill of that, he found a nice warm spot along the fence of the sparring area and settled down there. His friends soon joined him, disturbing his homesick thoughts. He liked his friends, no doubt, but he enjoyed his privacy just as much.

"I heard the Captain had a seizure today," Portus announced, sitting down beside Kael. He was always first to report if something was wrong with the Captain.

"Where'd you hear that from?" Kael asked sceptically.

"Sergeant Mahone told me," Portus said, looking hurt.

"Really? Wow." Kael watched the horses in the middle for a moment. Two boys were swinging lances at each other. He cringed as one of the lances nearly struck on of them in the face. "I didn't know he got the shakes."

"Makes sense though," Ernik grumbled, "it can happen to people who get hit in the head. It takes quite a blow."

"How'd you know that?" Brudo asked quizzically.

Ernik shrugged. "My cousin had the shakes. I know all about how it works. He was born with it though, kept him out of the army." He went strangely quiet, so no one ventured further.

Kael got thinking about Ernik's statement though. He had seen a person on the street get the shakes once. They had started to convulse and froth at the mouth. Nobody helped the man either. Kael had learned later that there wasn't anything that could be done. It was better to let him be than intervene, and wait until his shaking was over.

That brought up a question though. If the Captain was one who got the shakes, why was he there? Only important people to the

85

economy or those who are sick or wounded were exempt from the drafting. The Captain was clearly not well. Why was he allowed to train recruits if he had such a condition? Kael recalled the scar on the side of his head. He must have gotten the shakes from that injury. Perhaps his injured had occurred after he had become a teacher. Or maybe there was something more Kael was missing. He shook his head. There were more to the situation than he could see. He would have to think about it later.

"Ernik, you oaf!" The Captain was better the next day. His face was pale and his eyes were red and blotchy, but apparently he was well enough to resume their training. Unfortunately for them, his mood was just as sour as his appearance. And with only three days until graduation and then departure, he was in a flurry to get as much training done as possible. He had them working like farm animals, doing both physical exercises and great amount of sparring. He even joined in, duelling several of the boys to see at what level they were at.

Right then, he was beating Ernik to a pulp. "Don't expose yourself like that!" he yelled at the boy. Ernik was doing his best, he really was. However hard he tried though, a club was simply no match against a sword, especially against the one who trained him to begin with.

Ernik attempted to strike Captain Terra with the club, but the Captain easily sidestepped and smacked him on his left leg with the flat of his blade. Many boys in the crowd flinched or grimaced every time this happened, whereas the twins laughed and pointed.

Captain Terra didn't ease up there. He knocked Ernik's club away slapped him hard on his side with the flat of his blade, then took total advantage of Ernik's howl of pain, swung his left hand and struck Ernik right in the middle of his face.

Ernik screamed, clutching his nose which had begun to bleed profusely. The Captain backed off, the tendons in his neck flaring. He inhaled heavily and grinned like a predator that was playing with its prey. "Come on! Put up a fight!"

Growling, Ernik threw a volley of attacks at the Captain, who blocked them with ease and then parried with his own slaps. Ernik fell to the ground, too tired and beaten to fight anymore. "Get up," the Captain said. "Get up! If you don't fight me, you won't eat for the rest of our time here! Get up!"

"Stop!" Kael screamed. He had enough, he couldn't stand this anymore. This was far too cruel. The Captain wasn't teaching Ernik anything by beating him like this. "Stop!"

The Captain twisted his head and sneered at Kael. "What did you say to me soldier? You want me to *stop?*" He walked over to where Kael stood along the fence. The two boys on either side of him shuffled away. Kael was conscious that his whole group was watching. He wished it could somebody else who had said something.

He gulped, trying to hide his anxiousness. "I said stop. This is unreasonable. You're hurting Ernik and being unfair."

"Unfair?!" The Captain's voice grew loud and shrill. Across the way, out of the corner of his eye, Kael could see the archers stop their practise and turn to see what was wrong. "I've been here for fifteen years, waiting for my chance to exact my revenge on that hell-lizard! I've been trapped! Don't you dare tell me what's unfair!"

Kael blinked, wiping the spit off his face. The Captain was unnervingly close to him, his eyes wide and his lip twitching. "What do you mean?" he asked.

"I've always wanted to go fight that dragon, like my father before me," the Captain said. "I would do anything to die like my father, in the face of danger, fighting courageously to defend my city. That's all I long for, an honourable death that would make my ancestors proud! But after my *accident*, they decided I wasn't fit to go fight. So what did I do to try and help this war? I decided to train future soldiers so that they could exact my revenge for me. All I want is to die honourably, but I'm stuck here instead. Tell me, stupid boy, how is that *fair?*"

Kael understood. As hard as it was to comprehend why someone would want to die on purpose, he understood why the Captain would want to follow in his father's footsteps. He didn't say anything.

The Captain only became more infuriated by Kael's lack of response. "Fine, you want me to stop? Fight me then. Let *him* go off and let you and I duel."

Kael furrowed his brow, his throat constricting. "What? What will this prove?"

The Captain laughed boomingly. He was becoming ludicrous. "I'll just continue beating him then, and you can stand and watch. Which do you prefer?"

Ernik pleaded at Kael with his eyes to help him. Blood was flowing out of his nose and mouth and one of his eyes was swollen and bruised. He clung to the fence to support his weakened knees. Kael had to help him. "Okay, okay. I'll fight you."

The Captain laughed again. "Compassion, a true warrior has no place for it. It will be your downfall, mark my words. If I win, however, you and your troupe will go two days and nights without breakfast, lunch or dinner."

The crowd erupted with complaints, screams and roars. Kael tried to block their swearing, cursing and yelling from his mind. "Alright, but if I win, you will leave Ernik alone for the rest of his life. And we will get the rest of today off."

Captain Terra's smile intensified. He wiped some sweat from his brow, ruffling his hair in a way that made him appear crazed. It was then Kael realized how much he hated that man. "Good." His voice was low and ominous. "I like a challenge."

Chapter 8

Kael hopped inside the sparring pit as Ernik stumbled out. His heart beat more furiously than he thought it could. It felt as though it was about to burst out of his chest. In the back of his mind, a voice was screaming at him, asking him what he was doing. His whole body felt uneasy and sore, a stomach ache added to his silent torment as well. He took a deep breath as he stood opposite of Captain Terra. He pulled his sword out of its sheath, removed his shield from his back and placed it on his left arm with some difficulty. His hands were shaking.

His focussed on the wild man just a few metres away from him. He seemed so much farther away. Everything else melted away into darkness as he focussed as hard as he could on that man. All he could see was the Captain and his blonde, nearly white hair. All he could hear was his own heartbeat. All he could smell was the soft, sandy ground beneath him. His skin itched from the heat of his own body and suddenly his light armour felt too heavy and restrictive. He cleared his throat, almost choking on his own spit.

The Captain, contrarily, was very calm where he stood. He hardly moved at all and wasted little movement as he brandished his sword just out in front of him. His eyes focussed on something distant. Kael hesitated, had something happened to him, or was this some trick or part of his style? He would wait for Captain Terra to make the first move.

A small rustle of wind managed to make it over the walls of the compound. It swept over the ground, picking up a dusty smell along with it. The grit from the wind was flung into Kael's eyes. He didn't notice. He continued to stare with iron concentration at the Captain. The crowd around them murmured but was otherwise silent. Being a defensive person, Kael was reluctant to make the first strike, but the Captain was making no move whatsoever.

One quick stride, that's all Kael dared to make. The Captain's eyes flittered towards him, but he still remained still. This was killing him, why wasn't the Captain doing anything? *He's just bothering me,* Kael thought grimly, *just toying with me and making me skittish as a bird.*

Kael struck. He dashed forward and made a move to swing his sword a couple feet away from the Captain. The other man finally moved and swung his sword to block, but Kael had already stopped. He waited for the Captain' sword to travel past and then moved in to attack. They locked blades.

The Captain snarled as the two sharp pieces of metal clinked together. A loud *ping* echoed across the compound. Again, the sharp sound broke the otherwise still silence. Kael thrust out his other arm, successfully blocking an attack with his shield. Thank goodness for his shield! His arm shuddered from the trauma, but a little shock in his limbs was better than a hole in his chest.

They broke off, both panting. The Captain glowered at him, his lip trembling in anger. Before Kael was ready, the Captain lunged forward and stabbed at him with his sword. The tip of the blade came so close that it brushed against Kael's leather breastplate. His breath stole away from him. The Captain was being far too overzealous. He was making this as more than a simple duel. He wanted to hurt Kael. Batting the sword to the side, Kael made a swipe of his own, but he only slashed air.

The Captain, nostrils flaring, doubled over to dodge Kael's attack, and then thrust his foot out, kicking Kael in his stomach. Winded, Kael took a few steps backwards. He struggled to catch a breath and fight at the same time. He hopped backwards to try and put some distance between him and the Captain.

Kael placed his hands on his knees, leaning over the ground to try and make the cramp in his gut go away. Keeping an eye on the Captain, he muttered a curse. The man was glaring at him through his sweat-drenched hair, his moustache flaring as he inhaled. Kael was getting frightened and discouraged by the Captain's ferocity. But he had to do this, if he didn't he would get beaten up afterwards by the other members of his group for disallowing them food. But more than that, he needed to prove a point to the Captain, and deep down, to himself.

Kael, when he felt ready, brandished his sword and shield, his lips pursing in concentration. Once again, he made the first move. Less tentative than before, Kael rushed forward, faked a stab and instead sideswiped his blade at the Captain. Surprising them both, Kael's attack actually worked. The Captain made a move to block his first attack, leaving himself exposed. Bemusement struck Kael. He hesitated for a slight second, his sword hovering just under his opponent's arm. But the Captain recovered, batted the sword away and elbowed Kael in his chest.

"You are unsure of yourself," the Captain said, his tone scornful. "Next time, you won't get an opportunity like that to strike. You have to react and act with speed; never double think what you are doing when there is no time to think to begin with."

Frowning, Kael pretended like he wasn't listening, but he drank in every word. Next time, he wouldn't pause. How foolish that had been, he should have brought his sword up to the Captain's neck to end this, or even struck him in the side with the flat of his blade. Frustration burned inside him.

Aggravated that he had let Kael make such a move, the Captain threw a hard volley of attacks at Kael, one of which he barely managed to dodge. Kael's arms were getting sore from this battle, his shield arm especially beaten from having a sword clash against it so many times. With every slash, cut and lunge that either he or the Captain made, he was getting more and more eager to end this.

The Captain was relentless. Kael couldn't keep blocking his attacks. He was running out of energy. He suddenly realized that the only way he was going to be able to stop this flurry was to make his own offensive move.

Time seemed to slow as Kael's welled up frustrations surfaced. With his anger came a hidden strength he didn't know he had. It was as if somebody had opened a source of energy within him that had been locked. With renewed vigour, Kael scanned the Captain's moves in distorted time. Everything seemed so clear; every detail seemed to jump out at him. Slash, cut, slash, and lunge. That's it! He had a pattern!

Kael let the Captain follow through his routine one more time. Furrowing his brow, Kael ducked under the Captain's lunge, his opponent's blade coming mere centimetres from the top of his head. He shifted his weight forward, falling to his knees for a moment, letting his sword fall behind his body. In one fluid moment, he brought his coiled body explosively upwards. In a flash, he slammed his shield into the Captain's face and chest. A groan emanated from the other side of Kael's shield as it struck soft flesh.

Captain's Terra's sword fell from his grip, clanging to the ground, useless. Kael withdrew his shield without pausing in the least, spun around and kicked the Captain straight in the chest, felling him like an oak tree. In a glorious moment, Kael watched in slow motion as the Captain careened towards the ground, his face scrunched and arms flailing. In that small amount of time—which seemed to last an eternity—Kael felt like a true warrior.

Captain Terra landed on his back and Kael stepped forward, aiming his sword downwards. As he lay still, gazing up at him with blood oozing from his nose, Kael put one boot on the Captain's chest, pointing the tip of his sword close to his throat.

"I win."

The crowd remained silent for an eternity. The Captain's eyes were full of so many emotions, each one glinting in his eyes in turn as he stared at Kael in terror. Disbelief, anger, humiliation and even a flash of admiration. But his face remained still, locked in an expression of shock. Kael raised his chin, enjoying the Captain lying at his feet.

The crowd began to cheer, their voices raising and filling the inside of the castle walls with their joyous shouts. Kael turned to face them, noticing with a tinge of embarrassment that the archery side had joined in to watch as well. Sergeant Mahone was wearing a lugubrious expression, one which sent shivers down Kael's spine. His arms were crossed and there was a frown creasing his lips.

There was the sound of a large door being opened from towards the castle. The crowd turned to face a new figure that was strutting confidently across the training ground. They all went silent in a flash, as if suddenly standing inside a church. Even in the dirt of the compound, the figure was still wearing a lavished purple robe. He walked with a fierce gait towards the sparring area, bringing along a sour disposition. Kael's heart caught in his throat. *Zeptus?*

The Captain gasped as he saw who was coming towards him when the crowd separated silently to let the stolid man through. Kael's gaze lingered on Zeptus's eerie purple eyes as the man stopped a few feet away from away. He quickly looked away as Zeptus shot him a pernicious look. The King's Advisor transferred his sharp gaze from Kael to Captain Terra, who cringed as if he was being burnt.

"L—Lord Zeptus! What brings you here?" the Captain spluttered. For some reason, he couldn't get up from where he was, even though he seemed to be trying.

Zeptus sneered. "I came to see what all the recruits were gathered for. I came to see what our swords master was doing, duelling a recruit as if life was on the line." He leaned forward as he spoke, belittling Captain Terra even more. So fierce was his conviction that Kael even started to pity the Captain. "I wouldn't have been bothered by this waste of time, but seeing our most highly-regarded knight defeated by a thin, stringy *boy* has made it abundantly clear to me that perhaps you are not as fit for this job as I would have previously thought. I am disappointed indeed."

The Captain's eyes went wide and he put an arm out in front of him as if that would help shield him from Zeptus's controlled fury. Kael's wanted dearly to clear his throat—the advisor's voice sounded so coarse!—but he restrained from doing so, lest he bring Zeptus's wrath away from the Captain and onto him instead.

"Come with me, Captain Terra. We have much to discuss." With a flourish of his robe, Zeptus wheeled around and proceeded to stride back towards the castle. The Captain, now very white in the face, hesitated. Catching Sergeant Mahone's sad gaze, he reached out in a gesture for the archer to help him up to his feet. The Sergeant shook his head and instead ushered his pupils back to their side.

The Captain's face twitched and his eyes went unfocussed. Nevertheless, he managed to bring himself to his feet, which was quite the production. Kael couldn't understand. What was so frightening about having an audience with Zeptus? Sure, his appearance and overall presence was intimidating, but what else was there to fear? Obviously, the Captain and Sergeant Mahone knew something more about the shifty advisor.

Kael's group watched as the Captain slowly followed Zeptus. He didn't even look back.

Captain Terra came back far sooner than anybody had been expecting. When he did, only a few hours later, he had a skip in his stride and a smile in his eyes. As soon as he appeared out of nowhere from behind Kael and his small group of friends, he could already see that the Captain's disposition had greatly improved. For once, he saw the Captain truly happy.

The Captain acted as though nothing had ever happened between Kael and him. He did give Kael an angry look once, but otherwise he remained pleasant. Kael watched closely to see what the Captain would do around Ernik, but to his relief, the Captain didn't sway even close to the boy.

Throughout the day, the Captain grew sour once again. It was almost a relief, however. Kael had been unnerved by his cheery mood. It was unnatural seeing that man happy.

Even with the Captain's disposition back to normal, nothing upset Kael now. He went to bed that night with a feeling of fulfilment. He had defeated a weathered swordsman. That was no little accomplishment. Duelling Bruce Nendara or any of the others was a simple thing. But defeating the *Captain?* Kael fell asleep that night wearing a smile. His friends would be proud.

The new day brought a strange feeling with it. An omen, it seemed. Two days left. Two days left to live. How unreal that seemed! Kael's heart leapt in his chest as he thought about it. It was as if the dust he inhaled everyday was some sort of drug that quickened his pulse. There was no way to escape the dust, so his pulse stayed wild all throughout the day. It didn't let him forget what waited at the end of their training.

The Captain didn't wake them that morning, nor did he even glance when they waited around for their orders. He seemed to have given up on them entirely, content to spar with an unseen enemy instead.

With no instructions, Kael began to meander around the compound, feeling quite lost. Anxiety itched underneath his skin. He wished that their training would continue under the Captain's supervision. Without any tangible instructions, there was nothing to keep his mind from wandering. And invariably, it always wandered to the same thing—Laura and all the friends he had left behind.

He couldn't take it, so he began to practise in the sparring area as well, giving the Captain a wide berth. Every time he looked at the man, he felt awkward at the stare he gave back to Kael. It was an angry look, but not entirely scornful. There was a silent thanks somewhere in those eyes.

Two days past. Time was up.

Kael had done the same thing for two days. He simply trained, to get his body and mind as prepared as he could. He had kept busy, as to keep the ominous feeling and reminiscent thoughts away. But now, as he lay in bed, he couldn't bring himself to move.

There was an eerie silence to the barracks. It was dead quiet this morning. Usually the sleepier boys in the bunch would be snoring or the early-risers would be having soft conversations with each other. This morning, every single boy was lying in their cot, just staring. Like Kael, they had hardly slept the whole night.

The Captain eventually came. He snuck up to the front door quietly, choosing to startle the boys instead of clomping up to the barracks in his usual manner. He flung the door open and screamed at them. Several of the boys, nearly all of them, yelled in surprise, flinching violently and flailing their arms.

The Captain's laugh boomed through the barracks. He laughed so hard and so long, Kael was beginning to wonder if the Captain would pass out from lack of oxygen. Captain Terra stopped abruptly and wiped a tear from his eye. Voice stern, he said, "Alright, time to go, boys. Come meet me outside and line up."

It didn't take long and soon they were all lined up. He looked at each of them in turn, squinting from the early morning light. He stopped when he reached Kael, his brow furrowing in thought. He pointed to his right. "You, over there."

Kael obeyed wordlessly, conscious of the group's gaze that followed. The Captain watched him for a moment, then wheeled back to face the rest of them. He stopped at Remus and repeated what he had said to Kael. Remus stood beside Kael. They exchanged a nod.

The Captain did the same to several others, including Portus, Brudo, Ernik and one of the twins to stand by Kael. By the time he finished, there was about eleven of them, about half of what their group had started out with. Suddenly, Kael's new group felt small.

Captain Terra stood between the two groups for a moment, chewing his lip. With a twitch he said, "As you know, today is departure. Today, you leave to fight in the war. Today, you will confront the dragon and help save this city. You are fine boys, which is why I have placed you on this side." He was addressing his group, Kael realized. "You have all excelled at your studies or have become acceptable warriors in the terms of your training." He gave Kael a nod. "That is why I have decided that this group," he paused; Kael's heart began to beat faster, "this group will be the first to depart."

The Captain remained oddly patient as curses and swears volleyed at him from Kael's new group as they erupted in outrage. The Captain turned his back on them completely and instead talked to the other group. "You boys will continue your training for another month, at which time you too will be sent off as well." He turned back to Kael's group, and the uproar escaladed. "What are you swearing at me for, you maggots? You have to get ready, we leave after lunch." They became silent.

Kael was easily packed by lunchtime. There wasn't much to pack. Throughout the morning, he and the members of his group grumbled and growled amongst themselves, angry towards the Captain and the king. Brudo was so outraged, he even cursed the dragon. Some boys remained silent and pale. Eventually, their addictive silence won over and Kael had stopped talking. Most of the boys stopped talking. Kael scanned their morose faces, feeling depressed.

Those last hours dragged by at a crawl. It was agonizing. Lunch was quickly and solemnly eaten, then, after which Kael's group congregated in the middle of the camp, coupled with an equal amount of white-face archers that had been chosen from the other side. Kael didn't pay any attention to the archers, or anybody else around him for that matter. All he cared about was himself at this point. He had no interest in talking with any of them or getting to know them like he normally would. What was the point?

Ernik was talking rudely about the Captain. He was swearing vigorously and flailing his meaty arms to corroborate what he was saying, making offensive gestures all the while. "...If the Captain had any pride at all, *he* would go fight the dragon instead of us, the—" he stopped when the boys he was talking to looked over his shoulders. Eyes wide, he turned around to face the Captain.

Kael was about to intervene. The look the Captain's face was utterly sour. Kael caught his breath and eased off when the Captain spoke. "In case any of you were wondering, I *am* going to go fight the dragon," he said calmly, "I will be leading you."

Kael understood why the Captain had been in such a good mood earlier. He had finally gotten his wish when he had talked with Zeptus. He was going to die, like his father before him.

Once they had prepared themselves, they departed. They went the most direct route east through the city to get to the mountains, which was fine with Kael. As long as they went this direction, there would be no chance of seeing Laura. For if he did see her, he knew that he would run to her and never let go. If he did that, he would be killed for insurrection and cowardice. The image of the two boys he had met in Bunda's shop flashed in his mind.

The people of Vallenfend gave the boys sad looks as they marched past. The procession reminded Kael of a funeral. In a harsh way, it *was* a funeral march. Nobody spoke, nobody moved. The women simply stood there, watching them with swollen eyes, holding their children. Everything was silent except for the occasional sniffle and the dull shuffling of the soldiers' feet as they marched on through their former home.   This was the most depressing walk Kael had ever been on.

They exited through the city's outer gate, which was secured by a small group of female guards. With a nod, one of the guards opened the gate and issued the group through.

Right away, the land began to slop upwards on a slight degree. With the city behind them for good and the mountains looming overhead, Kael had to turn his head downwards as if to be fiddling with his armour. In reality, he was hiding the tears that were forming in his eyes.

Chapter 9

Their group was twenty-four strong. Well, not necessarily twenty-four *strong*. They all looked rather young and weak—and frightened. As soon as they left the safety of Vallenfend's immediate area and entered the wilder, untamed confines of the forest, the boys' rose more and more with each passing minute. Every step they took, the trees were thickening, becoming more densely packed, wider and taller. Wild shrubs, bushes and plants sprouted up everywhere around them, making Kael appreciate the worn path they were travelling on, as narrow as it was. Even still, it was rather hard to walk properly with his leather amour, shield, sword and heavy backpack full of supplies. He could only imagine what it was like for boys like Portus, who were hefting large broad axes or large battle-hammers. The Captain was wearing a real set of armour, including chainmail and an iron breastplate, but he had distributed his pack items among the others. Kael wouldn't feel sorry for him if he became tired.

The Captain had set an unruly pace. He clopped along eager as a mountain goat, one hand resting on the hilt of his sword. He worn a blissful expression under his moustache and there was a twinkle in his eyes as he gazed up at the blue sky overhead—well, he had the last time Kael had checked anyway. They were travelling in a single file due to the narrowness of the path. Evidently, it was the same path every group took to get to the dragon's cave. It was a good thing it was here, the underbrush was getting thick and Kael doubted some of the others would have been able to keep without it.

When one of the boys—an archer—asked why they weren't taking the horses up the mountain. "After all," he said, "we did train with them."

The Captain shrugged. "Why waste perfectly good horses?"

His answer was simple and straightforward. It summed up everything Kael had learned during his stay in the training grounds.

They were insignificant. Their lives were worth less than horses'. The archer's face paled.

Although Kael's heart beat in his throat the entire time, he found that looking at the surroundings kept his mind off grim fate waiting for them at the top of the mountain. There were beautiful bushes and wildflowers that grew around here, some of which he had never seen before, (he had never really strayed too close to the mountains), and he was reminded of Laura. She loved wildflowers.

There were animals too. Squirrels chattered in the trees above, angry at these intruders that tread through their forest. They squeaked to one another and at the boys, and Kael could swear that he saw one drop a nut on one of the boy's heads. Aside from the squirrels, birds sang endlessly to each other. There was an entire orchestra up there, composing a wordless symphony just for them, the boys who marched up their mountain to fight its deadly inhabitant.

Kael sighed.

"Hey, you." Kael turned around to face an archer behind him. "Yeah, hi!"

Kael returned his wave with confusion. "Do I know you?"

The archer chuckled. "No, but you do now! My name's Vert Bowman. What's yours?"

Kael smiled feebly, the boy's infectious cheerfulness catching him off-guard. "Kael, Kael Rundown." He looked the boy over. He had flat, black hair and a decent amount of stubble across his chin. He was thick and stocky and held an air of laid-back confidence. He held in one hand a weapon that looked like a spear with a sword attached to the end. It kind of reminded Kael of the halberd Larr had tried to give him. He used the weapon like a walking stick, striking the ground with the blunt end.

"It's a pleasure to meet you Kael," Vert said cheerily, placing a hand on Kael's shoulder. Kael nodded in return and turned back around, preferring to stay to his own thoughts, but apparently Vert did not get the message.

"They gave you a short sword, eh?" Vert piped up from behind. Kael rolled his eyes before turning back around. Instantly, he wished he hadn't as Vert strolled up behind him instead of staying where he was. Now the path was even more crowded. "That doesn't seem very effective for slaying a dragon."

Kael furrowed his brow. "Does that thing fare any better you think?"

Vert chuckled. "No, not really, but at least I can prod at it from a distance. With your weapon, you have to practically stand underneath it to hack at its kneecaps." Kael laughed. Despite how grim the conversation really was, Vert's tone was jocular and teasing.

"Oh yeah?" Kael scoffed.

Vert shrugged. "Yeah. In this battle I figure that having distance between me and a fire breathing monster would be a good idea. Plus I have my bow."

Kael eyed Vert's weapon for a moment. "If you're an archer, why do you have that thing then?"

Vert kept up the pace, but answered Kael's question. "I have had lots of training with this glaive. They had originally placed me on your side, but I was already a master with this blade. As soon as I found out we were to be footsloggers, I demanded to be switched. Figured I might as well learn *something*. I was only on your side for maybe a day or two."

Side by side, Kael and Vert walked together throughout the day. Vert had a strange humour to him Kael found catching. He was nonetheless a smart boy and seemed to know a lot about the military and various tactics. He reviewed with Kael many historical battles that had been won with clever battle plans and tricks of sorts. It was interesting and passed the time quickly. However, the other boys near them were getting somewhat annoyed by Vert's boisterousness and vigour.

The group stopped for the night at last and Kael had a chance to see how much ground they had covered. He hadn't been paying that much attention to his surroundings because he had been talking with Vert. It surprised him how much the land had changed. There were more rocks protruding out of the ground than before, and the trees were thinning ever so slightly. The underbrush had significantly reduced, leaving more room to tread than before. Vallenfend lay far below, semi-hidden by the sloped forest canopy. How much different it looked to him than what it felt like when he had been inside it. It was *that* big?

The Captain stood where he was, watching the boys as they began to build a fire. It was painful for Kael to watch at first as some of the novices tried to start it with just sticks alone, so he took over for them, taking a flint stone out of his pack and striking it against his sword. Soon they had a roaring fire which they all settled down around.

Many of the boys were moaning or complaining, rubbing their feet or inspecting blisters. It was apparent who had brought hiking-worthy boots and who had not. Although Kael's were old, they were perfectly worn in, so his feet weren't sore whatsoever. It was a good thing he hadn't had enough time to get new boots.

Kael heard Joran moaning somewhere. The poor boy had been sobbing the entire day, whining that he had never been separated from his twin for so long. Kael felt sorry for him. He couldn't even imagine what it would be like to lose a brother that was so close to him. He had never had any siblings.

Vert unrolled his pack near Kael, gazing up at the sky. The sun had shot down swiftly tonight, sending the forest into an eerie blackness that Kael had never experience before. Things seemed to be creeping everywhere out here. Twigs snapped somewhere out in the distance, making Kael imagine that great beasts with huge teeth and claws were watching them right now, waiting for one of them to take a step out of the safety of the light from the glowing fire. His eyes were wide open in fright, constantly scanning his surroundings for any movement.

"You know what I think?" Vert exclaimed suddenly. His sharp whisper made Kael jolt. He shook himself mentally for being such a coward.

"Huh? What?" Kael asked. "What do you think about what?"

Vert chuckled at Kael's poorly worded sentence, but continued. "What I think about all this. I mean, why we are going to fight this dragon in the first place. It seems pretty unreasonable for us to go and fight a dragon that seems to never attack the city to begin with."

"Oh," Kael said. He waited for Vert to continue. The boy stared right back at him expectantly. "What do you think about this?" he asked with a sigh.

Vert took a deep breath, checking to see who was listening. Portus had joined them, but otherwise nobody else was listening. Portus stared at Vert lazily. He wasn't very enthused by Kael's new friend either. "Gold. Think about it, what are dragons known for? Gold! Dragons *love* gold! They stash it in giant heaps in their caves and sleep on it at night. Everybody knows that." Kael nodded, it was true that fact was well known, but Shatterbreath had never been known to have a stash in its cave, so he pointed this out. "True, but it's never been proven for sure if the dragon does or does not have a collection of treasure. After all, everybody who has been sent to its lair has died in the process."

"Okay then, so what if it does have a huge stash of treasure, how does that affect us?" asked Portus sceptically.

"King Morrindale has been known to be extremely greedy. A huge treasure like that must be more than tempting for him." Vert shoved a spoonful of stew into his mouth, letting Kael brood over his words as he munched. Kael stared at the embers of the fire, which began to look strikingly similar to gold coins.

He cocked his head, realizing what Vert was getting at. "Are you saying that King Morrindale is sending us to try and kill the dragon to try and capture its treasure for him?"

Vert shook his head. "I love Vallenfend deeply, don't get me wrong, but Morrindale doesn't strike me as a person who could hide his intentions so well like that. No, I think that Zeptus is the true mastermind behind this. He probably goaded the king to do this so that he could get his own share. You know? A fifty-fifty kind of deal."

"Even still," Kael said, "you'd think that the king or Zeptus would give up after thirty-five years of failure."

Vert shrugged, finishing his last spoonful of stew. "They say greed knows no bounds."

That one sentence alone struck Kael as hard as a sword to his chest. His understanding was shattered. He had always assumed that

103

there was some hidden reason behind the kingdom's loss of men, but he would have never imagined it would be for gold alone. Could the leaders of Vallenfend really be that corrupt? Any trust or belief he had in the king or his advisor disintegrated right then. Kael's patriotism that he felt towards his home was tainted, as if mud was just stirred into clear water.

"That's enough," the Captain declared suddenly. Had he been eavesdropping? "We still have a day and a half left to travel. You better get to sleep promptly so we can resume our hike right away tomorrow."

Kael did what he was told, but he couldn't shake the disturbing thought that Vert had just introduced to him. The very concept was appalling and went against every moral code that he had. He tried to shake the feeling off, but he couldn't. It stayed in the back of his mind for the rest of the night keeping him up long after his friends had fallen asleep. *How could somebody be so corrupt?*

The Captain stopped their march at last. The ground had become steeper and steeper and pretty soon they were zigzagging up the inclining hill. They still had a long way to go though.

The threat of predators also stayed in the back of Kael's mind throughout the day. Wasn't it fabled that there were ferocious bears in this forest? And mountain lions and other terrible creatures? What was keeping them from being attacked? Kael cursed himself for his own foolishness. Their large number was certainly a deterrent, and even if they were attacked, each one of them was holding a razor sharp blade.

"Break for lunch," the Captain yelled. "Archers, go hunting to see if you can find us anything to eat after I make sure everyone is accounted for." The Captain began counting their ranks. He seemed annoyed that they had ignored the line he had established, but he didn't say anything about it. "Wait a moment. There is one missing. We are supposed to have twenty-two soldiers."

A few mutters ran through the crowd. Kael was wondering who could be missing. Out of his immediate friends, it looked as though everybody was there. The Captain recounted several times and even the majority of the boys began to count their numbers as well. Every count turned out the same. Twenty-two.

One boy perked up. "Oh, I think I might know who's missing!"

"Do tell," the Captain said sharply.

"A while back, maybe two hours ago, the boy behind me was huffing and puffing," the boy explained, pale-faced. "He was lagging behind and told me that he was going to take a quick break and then catch up to us later. I didn't think anything of it, so I let him."

The Captain's face twitched ever so slightly. Kael could tell that he was fighting back the immense urge to explode at the boy. "And what position are you in the ranks?"

"Wh—what?"

"Where were you in the line?" he hissed, "were you at the front or the back? Is it that difficult of a question?!"

The boy cringed. Being an archer, he wasn't used to the Captain's harshness. "Uh, we were at the back, me being second to last and him...last."

The Captain swore. "You fool," he said despondently, "you might as well have killed him. There's no time to search for him. We're moving on at once."

"Wait," Kael cried. "Shouldn't we wait for him? He could still catch up!"

The Captain scowled. "We can't afford to *wait*. We'll let the bears deal with him now. Let's go!"

The boys were terrified; Kael could see it on their faces and feel it inside his chest. They were going to leave a boy behind? Just like that? He shared scared, wide-eyed glances with the young men around him. From now on, he would stick even closer together with his comrades.

The Captain, however, was not dismayed. "There's one less to the attack," he said callously. He didn't say it under his breath either. Kael's heart sank even lower.

The boys didn't stop long for lunch. As soon as they were finished eating, they were on the move again. Even Vert stayed quiet as the reverence towards the boy they had lost settled over them.

Without Vert to distract him, Kael had a chance to survey his surroundings. The mountain was starting to jut upwards sharper than ever now, making the path craggy, steep and narrow. They had to resume their ordinary line and hug close to the wall now as the path became more treacherous and cliffs began to form underneath to their immediate left.

But if Kael managed to ignore the steep, nearly vertical drop and the jagged rocks below, the scenery was quite startling in beauty. Here and there, waterfalls of varying height sprouted out of the mountainside, spilling out and over the awaiting expanse. They splashed down below into small pools that foamed and sputtered, thirsty for more and more water. The pools were beautiful and inviting. Kael wished dearly that he could leap into one of them to escape the hot mugginess that engulfed him.

They passed directly underneath a large waterfall, which stole Kael's breath away as he looked up to behold the huge amount of water flowing just overhead. How amazing this all was! Amazing, and dangerous. At least four times, he lost his footing and nearly tripped from the slippery film that had enveloped the path from the constant mist the waterfall produced, something that could spell death most certainly if he fell over the edge.

Past the waterfalls, the craggy wall to their right rounded and became more welcoming as the slope became less harsh. The ground grew drier and rocky again, as opposed to that fine mossy film they had just been walking on. However, the cliff to their left became even steeper and the bottom of it stretched farther out. Kael had never imagined that the mountain just beside his city looked anything like this! It was unbelievable, he had thought it was the same all over, smooth and covered by the same plants and scenery.

Yelling caught his attention and Kael turned around. His heart jumped forward like a racehorse as he saw what the din was about.

Hanging just on the edge of the cliff was one of the archers, a rather plump boy who was hanging on to a clump of grass for dear life. He kicked his legs frantically, trying to find a foothold, but none came to his rescue. Ernik had his hand outstretched, but the boy was just out of his reach. Ernik was lying on his stomach, trying to save the boy, hollering at him incoherently. Nobody else was making a move to help.

Cursing, Kael pushed Vert to the side and rushed over to where the young archer hung. Picking up Ernik's club which the redheaded boy had thrown to the side, Kael yelled at Ernik to grab the club. Ernik seized the club and swung himself back over the edge, reaching the wooden weapon out to the boy. Kael held onto Ernik's feet, letting him inch out even farther over the edge.

The archer reached out with one hand, but he was still too far. His grip faltered. Kael's heart beat even faster, so fast that it hurt every time it resonated through his ears. Once again, time itself seemed to slow down as Kael watched in absolute horror. The boy's grip failed completely and he succumbed to gravity.

Kael gasped deeply and brought himself and Ernik away from the ledge, not wishing to watch the young man fall to his death. The boy's scream echoed over the mountain, sending chills up his spine. There was no way he would survive that fall.

The Captain finally rushed over. He paused to see what the boys were up to, noticed that Ernik was straddled over the edge and peered over. His face went grim. "That's two down already," he muttered, so quietly that Kael, who was standing right next to him, was the only one who heard. "March! There is no reason to linger any longer, we must get going."

One by one, the boys began to follow the Captain's lead once again. Kael and Ernik stayed where they were, frozen. After a few minutes, Vert urged them on and coaxed Ernik to his feet. They resumed their trek.

"Who was that boy?" Kael managed to ask some while later, breaking the thick silence that had befallen them.

"An archer I had become friends with," Ernik said, staring at the ground. "I couldn't stop it, he just...he just slipped and fell off without any warning. There was nothing I could do." Kael tried to reassure him, but Ernik was becoming frenzied. "I swear that I will avenge his death. I will kill that dragon, so help me!"

A few boys up ahead snickered. Ernik glowered at them from under his still-bruised eyebrow. "You don't believe me?"

107

Brudo laughed, elbowing the boy next to him. "No offense, Ernik, but look what you're using as a weapon. You're hardly a threat to a dragon, let alone any trained warrior."

Ernik moved closer and waved his fist threateningly in Brudo's face. "I don't need a weapon at all to beat the tar out of you!"

A sword quickly interrupted their conversation, passing deftly between the two, stopping in the direct centre. It turned so that the sharp edges were pointing towards either boy's chest. The look that the Captain gave them could only be described as malicious. Kael could easily tell that he was tired of having to babysit kids like these. "You two stop this at once. Do you forget who the real enemy is?" he said. His voice echoed over the mountain as if carried away in a crow's talons. "Do you forget why those two boys had to die? Remember why we are doing this! Remember what we will fight for!"

"And what is that?" Brudo scoffed.

"Vallenfend. We fight for our city, for our people and for our king."

Brudo snorted. "How can you be so blind? The king's an oaf and our city is dying with all its men. To fight for such a cause is purely idiotic. If we were given the choice..."

With that, the Captain lunged forward, giving Brudo a great shove over the edge of the cliff. But before he fell to his demise as the unlucky archer had only moments earlier, Captain Terra seized Brudo's leather breastplate and held him in that position, with his feet still on the ground and body leaning over a sure death. "You talk big words," the Captain hissed, swinging his sword through the air, "but you are yellow on the inside." He spat over the edge. "Take back what you just said."

Brudo, swallowing his fear, shook his head. "No, I'm not going to deny what I believe."

The Captain shook him fiercely, loosening a strap that kept his breastplate together. Brudo gave a yelp of surprise. "These straps won't hold forever, son, you take back what you said or so help me, I will let you join that other boy in the afterlife."

Chest heaving, Brudo hiccupped, wordless. He began to tremble. He was gasping, as if searching for the correct answer. Another strap broke and half of his breastplate swung open, nearly flinging him over the edge. "Fine, fine! I take back what I said! You were right!"

With a satisfied growl like a dog who had just wrestled a bone away from another dog, the Captain yanked Brudo back onto the safety of the path. Brudo sprawled to the ground, panting from the sudden terror. The Captain wheeled around and proceeded to hike up the path.

"Deranged imbecile," Brudo spat from where he was still lying down. He must have thought he had said it quiet enough. The Captain heard it all the same.

Howling in anger, the Captain charged towards Brudo, raising a hand high above his head, as if he was going to strike Brudo, or worse, grab him and throw him off the edge for real. But instead, and before Kael or anybody else could react, he thrust his fist down, grasped the handle of Brudo's scimitar, wrenched it out of its sheath and hurled it as far as he could over the cliff and down the mountain.

Brudo watched helplessly as the blade fall down and out of sight. The Captain, spittle flying from his mouth, drew close to where Brudo still lay on the ground. "Let's see how tough you are without a weapon when it comes time to fight, eh?" He looked at the rest of them. "Let's get going!"

Nobody helped Brudo back up onto his feet as they continued.

A thick, gloomy mood befell the company. Kael could almost feel the hatred towards the Captain permeating the air around him. The archers had soon realized how terrible and senseless their leader was. And now, everybody glared at that man with animosity thick in their eyes.

The Captain, however, was doing his best to remain calm and unconcerned. Kael could see through it. He was stressed. He twitched his head in a certain way that only spelled danger for them and his lip trembled ever so slightly, as if he was restraining from screaming at them.

The day was finally spent as the stars came out to perform their nightly ritual, sluggishly dancing in circles around the sky, their twinkling reminding Kael of laughter. He wished he could be a star. How simple it would be! Wait for the sun to come out, then the night was their playground. Instead he was stuck down below.

The archers had found and killed a deer, which came as some consolation for the terrible day they had just been put through. After sprinkling some of his personal seasoning from a can of spices he had brought, Kael gratefully devoured the meat, elated that he could consume some real food for the first time since he could remember. It was absolutely delicious! Its warmth seemed to flow through his entire body as he swallowed it, helping to dissipate the sense of sorrow that had overcome him.

They had picked comfortable position to sleep tonight, a wide glade in the forest that was set into the side of the mountain almost like a crater. It was well protected, with a cliff wall to their left and with thick trees barricading all but two exits. Kael finally let himself wind down, breathing in the smooth, sweet smells of the forest at night. He was far calmer than the night before. It was particularly cool this night, and indeed, even in the later hours of the day it had been chilly. Probably due to the limited light they received this close to the cave, where the mountain's girth stole away most of the light, setting many parts of its backside in almost permanent twilight.

Kael welcomed the cold. It made his senses come alive and his skin tingle in refreshment. Plus it made him appreciate this warm meal even more.

The boys sat around the campfire for a long time. They swapped stories from when they were younger and hadn't felt the sting of the military yet. Things were so much simpler back then. Kael said his share of stories, which he thought were somewhat bland compared to some of the others adventures, but it was felt good to hear his own voice. It reassured him he was still alive. And with death surrounding them, that was important to him.

Remus began to tell a story, and although it was rather exciting, he as a person was not and soon his monotonous voice lulled Kael into a deep sleep, one which bore no dreams.

Kael awoke in a frenzy. He beat his fists at an unseen enemy and gasped. He blinked a few times, realizing that reality was once again upon him. He rubbed his eyes and licked his lips, trying to shake the lingering sleep that held on tight. This morning felt different than the mornings before. There was some sort of greater importance that seemed to be riding on the wind. Kael struggled to listen as a breeze rustled the trees surrounding, but soon gave up, realizing how silly the prospect was.

He already knew there was something important about this day. He didn't need the forest to tell him. Today was the day he would die. He gulped, fearing what this last, final day would hold. He decided to find something to ease his mind. Ernik was already awake and rambling about something. Kael moved closer so he could hear what he was saying.

"...Doesn't stand a chance against me!" Ernik was saying. Kael could already deduce that the redheaded boy was talking about how he was going to slay the dragon again. He had become so sure about himself, confident to a fault.

Kael rolled his eyes and instead began fold his bedroll back up. Soon it was strapped back on his pack. Little by little, the other boys followed suit. Everybody was moving slower today, obviously unexcited that today was their last. At least Vert, as always, was wearing a broad, silly grin. Did anything get that boy down? "Good morning Kael!"

Kael rubbed the sleep from his eyes, slightly angered that Vert was acting as though nothing was out of the ordinary and that this whole thing was nothing more than a camping trip. "Good morning?" Kael repeated in a doubtful tone. "What's good about it?"

Vert huffed. "You're breathing and alive—"

"For now."

"You're breathing and alive," Vert continued, ignoring Kael's interruption, "you should consider that a blessing for one. The air is clear and it's not very hot out. That makes for good travelling!"

"Very good." Vert gave him a sorrowful frown. "Uh, sorry."

Vert took a deep breath. "Don't worry about it," he said with a shrug. "Well, better pack up your stuff, there's no point in delaying the inevitable."

Kael took his advice, and not a moment after he had finished, the Captain suddenly popped up in the middle of the glade, his voice rising over the trees. He threw an impressive volley of curses at them, which set them all moving.

The surrounds changed dramatically as they marched onward. The trees thinned out, whether due to the altitude they were at, or the lack of sunlight on that side of the mountain. Kael shivered. There was no sunlight at all this early in the morning because the sun rose on the opposite side of the mountains. As such, frost delicately sprinkled the ground everywhere, like a light layer of frosted sugar on a rich cake Kael had once seen. It was beautiful. And chilling.

And for the first time, he noticed a large, dark crevice set up high in the side of the mountain. It was shrouded in darkness, and from the oblique angle it was at, it looked as though very little light could escape into there, if any. Kael shivered again. They had to go in that?

The crevice in the side of the mountain grew bigger as they crawled their way towards it. As they did, the mood of the boys descendent lower and lower into depression, opposite of their ascent up the slope. The mountain rose up into a rough point, still high above them, but the cave was set in the bottom of the cliff that spiked to the top.

So thick became the tense silence that even Vert held his peace, staring at the ground with a pained frown fixed across his usually cheerful face. He may have hid it well, but even Vert feared death.

In less than half a day's journey—far quicker than the Captain had stated before they left—they had already arrived at the very edge of the cave.

Night seemed to re-emerge as they slipped into the mouth of the cave, and Kael felt as though he was rudely plunged into another world.

Chapter 10

A tingle ran under Kael's skin. The cave. He was *in* the cave. All the terrible rumours he had heard about it... He remembered swapping horror stories with other children when he was younger. It had been exhilarating to talk about it, as if they were breaking an unspoken rule. It had felt like death was rolling on his tongue when the very mention of it struck his lips. And now, he was in one of those tales.

Ancient stalagmites and stalactites rimmed the mouth and throat of the cave and it felt like he was walking into the maw of some great beast. The walls were cragged and sharp, irregular bends and crystalline shapes protruding at obtuse angles in no specified pattern.

A dull listlessness clung to the inside of the cave. Coupled with the rumble of a deep, blackened expanse, it made the cave feel colder than it actually was.

A harsh, unnatural light splayed into the cave, the remnants of sunlight that the overlaying mountain had been unable to steal. The leftover light bathed the cave in a strange ethereal blue, like the twilight before night when all the colours cease to differentiate.

A thick blanket of mephitic stench issued out of the belly of the cavern, like a large dog yawning. The heavy scent bore the remnants of old, fetid meat. The drifting, unpleasant aroma also held the hot, sticky smell of flame and singed metal, which stung one's nostrils.

The years of battle were present from decades of wear and tear in the floor. The ground was pounded flat from soldiers as they trekked deep into the cave to battle the monster within and indeed, centuries of a large beast roaming in the cave had left the rock ground unnaturally smooth.

A deep, throaty growl surfaced out of the inscrutable depths, sounding as if the mountain itself forbade the presence of the unwanted, terrified intruders. A monotonous wind rushed through, the reoccurring whoosh of calm, heavy breathing.

113

Grasping the reality of the situation, Kael's heart began to thrum wildly in his chest. He could feel it in his hands and feet as it pounded. A cold sweat broke out under his feeble armour. The hairs on the nape of his neck stood on end and his breath stole away from him. *This was real.*

Kael's breath came shallow and quick. He tried his best to stifle his fear, but it wouldn't obey. It was like a caged animal that wanted to escape with every fibre of its being and he was struggling to keep the door closed.

They kept to the sides of the cave, groping their hands against the craggy walls in a vain attempt to find their way in the near-darkness. Kael could hear one of the boys whimpering from in front of him somewhere, he could only assume it was the twin. It was hard to tell, however, the odd acoustics in here warped and bent any noise. The Captain quickly chastised the boy, and judging from the dull *thud* that resonated, Kael guessed he had done so with his fist.

They were all bunched up now, with the melee fighters up at the front and the archers at the back. The Captain had reviewed with them earlier how their tactics would work; it had been one of the conversations Vert had entertained Kael with earlier. The boy couldn't stress enough how ineffective this strategy could be.

It was painfully dark. Kael could hardly see his hand in front of him. If he hadn't been holding on to Portus's armour, he may have lost his group entirely.

One thing kept on his mind; *where was the dragon?!*

Kael exhaled, his breath coming out choppy. In his mind, he had pictured the dragon erupting out of the depths of its cave, wreathed by a halo of fire. He imagined immense heat, a roar, human screams and then blackness for himself. So far, there was none of that. He scowled. Wasn't that what the dragon was known for? Its ferocity? So far it seemed as though it was either intimidated by visitors or wasn't home.

The cave gradually lightened as they continued onwards. Kael was awed to see that there were luminescent stones set into the roof of the cavern, or what appeared to be stones anyway. The ceiling was very tall and it was hard to see them. For all he knew, it could have been glowing fungi or some sort of cave-dwelling creature. Either way, he was grateful for the light, as scant as it was.

A fog enveloped them, but it was strangely thick and swirling, more like smoke than anything. The Captain drew his sword as a hollow sound echoed through the cave and a soft whisper of humid wind ran over them. Was that a breath? With it, more fog oozed out of nowhere. As quietly as he could, Kael drew his sword as well, fixing his shield to his arm. Suddenly, he felt underequipped for this. His shield seemed so weak, so useless! His leather armour now seemed more useless than it ever had before.

Ernik made a strange noise from where he stood, perhaps six feet away from Kael. Ernik pointed straight forward, wiggling like an excited puppy that had just spotted a strange and interesting animal. "There it is!" he whispered far too loud. "I see it!"

Kael squinted, trying to see through the intense blue miasma. He could see it too! Just ahead, hovering seven feet off the ground was a tapered shape. It seemed to stare at them calmly through the fog, sizing up their expeditionary force, deciding whether they were worth the trouble. Kael's throat constricted. The dragon! Hmm, it was smaller than he had expected...

His confidence rose when he beheld how small it truly was. From what he had heard, this dragon was much larger. He began to feel bold, as a man does when they have drunk wine. They could do this.

Ernik jolted forward, his armour clunking as he did so. A few boys struggled to restrain him back. The triangular shape in the distance twitched at the noise, startled by the sudden movement. It didn't strike Kael as an especially intelligent beast.

"Let me at it!" Ernik was thrashing, trying to free himself from the two boys who held him back. "Let me tear its throat out with my bare hands! Let me avenge my friend!"

Their cover was blown now, thanks to Ernik. Assuming they had it to begin with. The two boys that were holding him back shot a look over their shoulders at the Captain questioningly. The Captain, giving a sly smile, nodded his head and flicked his hand. The boys, still unsure, let Ernik go and crouched down, ready for whatever happened.

Unrestrained, Ernik ran towards the dragon with his club held high above his head, screaming as wild as a barbarian. Kael and the rest of the foot soldiers watched him while archers notched their arrows to give Ernik some cover. All them except for Vert, who had joined Kael's ranks as the archers moved back to put some distance between the two groups. It seemed as he would prefer to fight close-range. He glanced away from Ernik and gave Kael a nod.

Kael made his way over to the Captain. He gave him a shove. "What are you doing? Why did you let him go?"

The Captain blinked. "Excuse me?"

"You're going to just let him get killed! I know you hate him, but this is insane!"

His grin intensifying, Captain Terra twitched. "When you disgraced me that day, you told me to leave that boy alone for the rest of his life. I am a man of my word. But soon, I won't be able to uphold my promise any longer."

Kael's face twisted in horror.

Just that moment, Ernik reached the dragon. With one final roar, he swung his club at the shape. It retreated, far quicker than any of them would have expected. In fact, it withdrew so quickly and in an unnatural way that Ernik froze right where he was, bemused. His club rested at his side.

A strong wind pushed all the fog away and out towards the mouth of the cave. The shape which Ernik had mistaken for the dragon's head was in view now. A growing expression of mortification ravaged Ernik's features as he followed the shape towards its body. The tapered shape was triangular and led up to a thick, sinewy tendril which wound its way to the base of a large pelvis and hips. The shape hadn't been the dragon's head. *It was its tail.*

The dragon itself was clinging to the side of the wall, straddled against the stone, appearing like an enormous squirrel climbing a tree, except it held none of the cute charm a squirrel does. One hind leg remained on the ground to steady itself and its wings were spread out and pressed closely to the wall, otherwise it clung firmly to the craggy wall. Its storm-blue colouration was nearly perfectly matched to the dull blue of the cave and its scale-armoured hide and spines were rough and hard like the backdrop it rested against. It matched its surroundings so perfectly, they had missed it completely. *They had walked* past *it*.

And it was big—its head alone was the size of a horse. Neck flexing, it lifted its great head away from the surface of the wall, glaring at Ernik with large, feral green eyes, its jaws slightly open, showing a row of fearsome ivory daggers. Kael gasped and heard somebody else yelp.

Ernik, gaping up at the tapered, sharp muzzle above him, took a deep breath, thrust his arms out to the side and screamed. His high-pitched, solid note resonated through the cave and even the dragon flinched from the intensity of it.

With a roar that shook the very ground beneath them, the dragon extricated itself from the wall. Its other three feet slammed heavily into the ground, sending a ripple through Kael's legs, causing him stumble. The dragon, tail thrashing, lifted one great limb off of the ground, where it hung above Ernik for a grisly moment.

Kael turned his head away as the paw came down. There was a thunderous *thud* and Kael knew at once that Ernik was no more.

At this point, the archers let their arrows fly. Kael witnessed in altered time as the dragon inhaled, lips curling. Its magnificent, armoured chest widening as it drew in air. A moment later, like the break after the calm before a storm, the dragon let a venomous jet of molten fire escape from its jaws. The searing-hot fire exploded on impact with the condensed group of archers, as fast as the arrows they had shot at it. The heat was so intense that Kael felt it from where he stood, several yards away. Kael looked away, feeling the heat against his eyes. A rancid smell of burnt meat quickly filled the cavern. Kael barely managed to hold his stomach.

The dragon took one more breath, pausing for a moment before it released it, glaring down at the remaining soldiers as if to decide who it would aim at next. Vert answered its question by notching his bow which he had retrieved from his back. He let an arrow fly at its chest, perhaps hoping to take advantage of its exposed underbelly. The arrow rebounded off its scales harmlessly.

The dragon's eyes narrowed to slits and it released its pent-up flame at the group of soldiers, who had since diverged unlike the archers.

Most of the soldiers, including Kael, had the common sense to dive out of the way of the incoming danger. Some, unfortunately, did not.

Kael lied sprawled on the ground, coughing up ash and wiping his brow. He had hit his head when he had dove. He licked blood off of his upper lip, aware that his nose was bleeding. The world swooned around him, making him deeply confused. He was aware of a great danger and the imminent need to continue moving.

His ears rang, as if a loud firework had just burst off near his head and there was a strange chemical smell clinging to his nostrils, again, as if a firework had just detonated. Placing one hand on the ground to help support him as he stood back up, he cast his head from side to side, trying to recall what was happening.

He heard a shriek and glanced further to the side. A figure ran past, flailing his arms and engulfed in flame, screaming in pain and terror. A moment later, slumped to the ground, still as a statue.

A strong arm grasped him, yanking him completely to his feet. "Kael Rundown, *run!*" Vert launched past him, his glaive in hand. He must have discarded his bow somewhere, realizing how useless the weapon was.

Kael quickly and all too rudely remembered where he was and what was happening. He jumped forwards to dodge a large paw that took a swipe at a boy who had been running past him and ducked as a body flew past him, slammed by the dragon's tail. He changed direction sharply, so fast that he nearly tripped, one hand caressing the ground as he did, and tried to get to cover.

It was difficult to navigate through the room. The occasional burst of flame did little to help Kael as he scrambled through the cave, looking for shelter. Not before long, he was able to hide behind a thick pillar where two separate stalagmites and stalactites had merged together. He placed his hands on his knees, heaving and cringing from the pain that flashed across his chest. This was all so real!

Kael stood back up straight, noticing that Vert was hiding behind a similar structure adjacent to his. They shared frightened glances for a moment, Vert's face blackened by soot. Cautiously, Vert peered around his pillar and Kael did the same. The scene was chaotic. The dragon was slashing at what was left of the survivors, sitting up on its haunches. What resistance was left was faring relatively—and surprisingly—well. Led by the Captain, they were doing a fine job dodging the dragon's slashes and bites. However, once and a while, it would succeed and catch one of them around their legs or right in the chest, killing them almost instantaneously.

Vert exchanged one last final glance at Kael. His brow was furrowed in a serious frown, an expression that scared Kael. Motioning for him to follow, Vert burst out from his hiding place. Kael tentatively followed behind, brandishing his sword with white knuckles.

Vert swooped around the dragon while its back was turned, dodging its flailing tail. Kael had some trouble, but managed to stay just behind him. Fearlessly, Vert raised his weapon high above his head before Kael could say or do anything to stop him. Spinning it around his body expertly, he brought the weapon down on the dragon's rear right leg.

The dragon roared mightily in pain as a large gash opened on its lower leg. The wound poured blood on the ground, spilling over his boots and making Kael feel sick.

Before Vert could make another slash, the dragon had already turned its great head to see what petty creature had dared to harm it, ignoring the Captain and the rest of the survivors. Kael took notice and bolted. There was no way! No way would he stay! He needed to find cover!

Kael glanced behind as the dragon kicked its hind leg out, sharply hitting Vert right in the chest. The boy was sent flying from the kick and careened into the wall. He fell to the ground, where he remained motionless. Kael's fear caught in his throat and he nearly choked on it.

119

Kael hid behind another pillar and listened as the last of his group struggled to stay alive. They were losing, but that wasn't stopping them from continuing to fight.

"Kael!" Kael turned to see Brudo standing idly off to the side, watching the fight with concerned eyes, but unable to do anything without a weapon. "Kael, why aren't you fighting?"

Struggling to speak, Kael answered. "I can't, Brudo, I can't!" he wailed.

Brudo nodded, still sitting in a low crouch. "Lend me your weapon; I think I see an opening! Quick, hurry!"

Kael nodded in agreement. He tossed his blade towards Brudo, aiming is so that the blade would land at his feet. Just before his sword reached him, however, as Brudo was turning to get up, a gigantic blue tail swung out of nowhere, hitting him from the side and sending him out of sight into the other part of the cave. Even from where Kael was standing, he could hear the *crack* as the boy's neck broke when he was struck.

Kael screamed as the same tail swung back and collided with the pillar he was hiding behind. Large boulders fell all around him and he lunged forward into a somersault as one landed just where he had been. Time shifted again as he dodged two more boulders.

Catching a glimpse of the fight, Kael noticed that the dragon had its back turned to him, preoccupied with the few survivors that were left. Even as he watched, Remus made a mighty attack and plunged his weapon into the paw of the beast.

It roared, lifted its injured paw up and removed the broadsword from its paw as if it were nothing more than a splinter. Remus stood there, bewildered and weaponless. A moment later, the Captain dove out of the way as the dragon brought its great maw down on Remus. Picking him up completely off the ground, it flicked its neck and hurled Remus out towards the entrance of the cave. He flew at such speed that Kael wouldn't have been surprised if he flew out the cave and over the mountainside from the force of the throw.

Kael stopped watching. Pumping his arms and legs, he aimed to put as much distance between him and the dragon as he could. He wasn't cut out for this and he didn't have a weapon anymore. Those were his excuses anyway.

He found a nook at the far side of the cave wall that was well hidden and cowered behind it, placing his hands over his head to try and drown out the screams, roars and tearing sounds as the dragon finished off the last of his troupe. A month of training, all the hell they had been put through, all to end here, like this. Just like that, they were all dead. *All dead.* Kael sobbed silently. There was one last quake through the floor and a booming noise, perhaps a roar. He couldn't tell, his ears were plugged from fear.

And then, everything was still.

Chapter 11

Was that it? Was it all over? Kael forced himself to be calm. He closed his eyes and focussed on his ragged breath. He held the air in his lungs for a moment and slowly, quietly, let it all out, feeling his limbs relax and his heart slow down.

Kael remained still and tried to determine what the dragon was doing. He heard a shuffling that he guessed was its tail. There was a ruffling and the sound of metal sliding against stone. It sounded as though it was walking. The immense noise shifted around the pillar Kael was hiding behind. It was definitely moving deeper into its cave. The noise stopped at the end of the cave and the ground shuddered as the dragon slumped down.

Kael waited as the dragon paused for what seemed an eternity, and then began licking its wounds. Kael could imagine the dragon's soft, sand-papery tongue sliding over its wounds as he listened to it. The dragon licked itself for half an hour before it was finished. Hardly daring to breath, Kael waited another half an hour before looked around his pillar.

The dragon was lying down, curled into a loose ball with its muzzle resting peacefully on its huge paws. Its eyes were closed and its features relaxed. Kael pushed away all thoughts of how docile it looked and remembered the fresh, painful memory of the battle that had just occurred.

He stayed where he was, clutching to the side of the pillar, and stared at the dragon for any signs that it was asleep. It inhaled deeply, a throaty rumble resonating from within its chest. The noise was similar to a snore, so Kael assumed that it was in a deep sleep.

He raised his foot and looked at the resting beast before he took a small step. It didn't stir. A fragment of confidence sliced through Kael and he sprinted to the safety of a stalagmite. He pressed himself as flat as he could against the side of the stalagmite, which reminded him sickeningly of a large canine. He didn't look around, to check whether the dragon was as still as ever, but there was no noise, so he assumed as much.

Kael made a dash to another obstacle, this time a large, smooth boulder set partway into the wall of the cavern. He skirted around the large rock and peered around the corner again.

His stomach twisted. Where was the dragon? *It had been there a moment ago!*

"And where do you think you're going, Tiny?" Kael nearly choked on his own spit and he flinched violently. He hardly dared to look up, but he couldn't help it. Her voice was as powerful and intense as a storm. It was also very demanding.

A large, fierce green eye stared down at him in amusement, the pupil dilated from the semi-darkness. Kael's knees shook and he slumped to the ground.

It detached itself from the wall it had been hiding against, similar to how it had when it had ambushed Kael's party. Kael realized that he had hidden against its knee without realizing it. It blended in so perfectly in this cave!

"What do we have here?" it mused in a strong, surprisingly deep female voice. Kael grimaced, shocked that it could talk and less surprised that it was female. He had supposed it was male all this time. "A survivor? That is rare, that is rare indeed. Hardly a sight I've even seen in all these years. How did I miss you, hatchling?"

Kael's mouth was wide open, but no noise came out.

He could see the dragon's features better now. She was large, that was the most obvious and striking thing about her. A thick neck supported her bulky head, which was perhaps the most impressive part of her body. Large jaws filled with pointed teeth rested in front of a ball of muscle that worked her jaws and above that, her overlaying brow, which cast a shadow over her emerald eyes. A beautiful, yet simple crest adorned the back of her head and jaws, with two large horns sprouting from behind each eye, just behind her temple, like the centrepiece for a banquet. Kael noted that one of her horns was shorter than the other, broken off halfway, splintered and jagged.

123

Her massive chest expanded as she inhaled and a warm rush of air washed over him, smelling of fresh blood. Overall, she held an almost smothering muskiness which seemed to come at Kael in waves. She smelled of earth and rain as well the essence of everything feral and untameable. Her body so close to Kael was threatening.

The dragon had a crooked grin across her muzzle and the end of her tail flicked. Standing up straight, she paced around Kael, sending vibrations through the ground and up Kael's spine from her weight alone. And although it seemed as though she spent her days within this dark and dank cave, her physique was no less lacking. Her hind limbs were massive and rippled as she moved them, covered in strong, sinewy muscle. Her front legs were not as impressive as her back, but nonetheless powerful, equipped with longer, scaled fingers, each one bearing a massive, razor-sharp claw. Large, leathery wings covered her back with sturdy muscle used for supporting flight surrounding the area around her shoulder. She flexed those wings while she scrutinized Kael carefully, running those emerald eyes over his body several times over. Kael felt as though she were the Grim Reaper sizing up his next victim.

"You do not seem like the type that would run away from a fight." She prodded him gently with her snout, making Kael cringe again. "You've got some muscle on you. Judging the way you carry yourself, you could be a formidable swordsman. But the question still remains, how did I miss you?"

Kael kept silent, a spasm making him shudder.

"Answer me!" the dragon said with a growl.

Closing his eyes for a moment, Kael summed up enough courage to answer. "I—I was hiding."

The dragon's smile returned. "Hiding?"

"Yes."

"How cute," she scoffed. "And what were you hiding from, besides me? Why do you fear death?"

It took Kael some time to answer. His fright caught his breath, but more than that, he couldn't come up with a feasible answer. "I—I don't know. I guess I fear the unknown."

The dragon brought her head back up, away from Kael's level. She studied him closely over her muzzle, her leathery wings flexing. "The unknown?"

"I suppose I fear what I haven't accomplished, what I'll never accomplish. So many things I should have done, so many things I *could* have done. A life unfulfilled is hardly a life worth dying for."

The dragon made a purring noise, satisfied with his answer. She kneaded the ground for a moment, contemplating something to herself, creating large scratch marks in the floor. Kael stared at her claws, feeling the blood rush from his face. This was it, the end.

Crouching lower, as if she was about to pounce, the dragon brought her head back to Kael's level. "You speak as if your fate is already determined, Tiny, as if I have already predestined to kill you."

Kael perked up. "Wh—what are you saying?"

The dragon scrutinized him with one eye. Amusement was thick in her voice when she spoke. "I'm saying I'm not done with you quite yet. You still have heartbeats left to use, young warrior of the colour yellow. You still have tasks to accomplish. I have need for you still."

Kael blinked in surprise. "You—you're sparing me?"

"Yes."

Was she telling the truth, was this some sort of dragon trick? Was she really going to let him live, or devour him later? "How do I know you're telling the truth?" He made his tone as delicate as possible.

The dragon cocked her head. "It seems to me, Tiny, that you have no choice in the matter, unless you'd rather join your comrades." Kael shook his head vigorously, but the dragon continued. "I give you my word that will not kill you until I have decided your usefulness has run its course or if I decide that you are not ready to meet death."

Kael was no further persuaded by the dragon's oath. But he really did have no choice in the matter. What choice was there? It seemed pretty obvious to choose life over death. "Fine, I accept."

"Very good," the dragon declared. "It would have been a shame if you had disagreed. You're just so darn cute, I would have had a rough time digesting you in regret." She chuckled.

Kael didn't find it funny.

"What is your name, Tiny?" she asked suddenly.

Kael hesitated. What would the ramifications be for telling a dragon his name? "Kael, Kael Rundown."

"Rundown... That name sounds familiar." The dragon furrowed her heavy brow. "No matter. I am Shatterbreath, and from this time forth, you, Kael Rundown, will serve me. You will obey my every whim and command, or else suffer the consequence of ingestion. You will faithfully do everything I order, no matter how dangerous, trivial or obscure."

"In other words, are you saying that I'm your slave?"

Slowly and dropping all mirthfulness, Shatterbreath nodded her head. "Aye. In simpler terms, that is exactly what I mean."

On the inside, Kael was furious. He was nobody's slave! He served only himself and those he trusted. But of course, he said nothing. "As much as I do not wish to, I agree to these terms," he said, gritting his teeth.

"Very good," she repeated. "Formalities aside, we should get down to business then."

Nodding his head, Kael followed her. Shatterbreath, using her fiery breath, lit a fire at the very back of the cave. Coupled with the strange glowing rocks, her cave became less daunting. Somewhat mollified by the warm light, Kael relaxed.

Shatterbreath nodded for him to sit down. Kael stared at the ground. It was covered in a rich layer of fresh blood. He remembered the battle that had happened over an hour ago. Gulping, Kael shook his head. He would rather stand.

The dragon sat down, her rear end crashing to the floor and the rest of her body following like a wave. Kael just barely managed to stay standing as the shudder throttled him. The dragon's size still amazed him.

"Now then," she said once she was comfortable, "tell me what you know about the king of your city."

Kael was quick to answer her. "He is somewhat of an oaf, hardly worthy to lead Vallenfend, in my opinion. I think many others would freely agree with me."

"Hmm, and what of the war they wage? The war against me? What do you fight for exactly?"

"I don't really know. We were told that you are a threat to the kingdom, and that if we didn't fight you, it would give you an opportunity to attack us first."

Shatterbreath frowned, placing one paw over the other. She snorted, a flicker of flame escaping her nostrils as her tail danced. "That is a lie. I mean no harm to your city, not anymore. All I want is to be left alone."

Kael scrutinized her. It dawned on him how old Shatterbreath appeared, like an aged sorceress who had seen her fair years go by. As he watched her stare at the ground, he believed her.

She turned her muzzle, facing one large eye towards him. Her eyes weren't especially big in comparison to her head or body, but still, each one was as large as Kael's face. She didn't blink often, but when she did it was slow and meticulous, as if such small actions were of a greater, more significant importance.

"Then," Kael ventured, "if you're no threat to us, why are our men still sent to fight you?"

"Well," Shatterbreath said, breaking free of the trance she had momentarily been captured in. "Either your king or one of his close associates has a personal vendetta against me, or more likely, there is something more to this than it would appear."

"How so?"

"Well, a little more than two months ago, I followed a dark figure towards the coastline. He seemed suspicious, and kept glancing around, as if he didn't want to be seen, like a deer who doesn't want to be captured and eaten. Eventually, he reached the shoreline, where he proceeded to light a fire. His signal was returned by a boat out on the water and a small vessel armed with three people went out to meet them." She paused. "They talked about something, which I couldn't hear. The figure who had arrived on the boat handed something over to the other man, who inspected it. If I'm not

127

mistaken, the object was a diamond as big as a small rabbit. After which they both proceeded to return to wherever they came from."

"A diamond?"

"Yes. It was a transaction of some kind."

Kael tried to recall anything that might be important. "What did the first man look like? The one you were following?"

Shatterbreath inhaled deeply, something in the cave wall catching her attention. "He was dressed in black, so I couldn't see his features that well. But one thing that I saw and distinctly recall was his eyes. Purple like a wyvern's egg they were. Like little amethysts they peered at me, cold and devoid of compassion. Even for a dragon, they were chilling to behold." Shatterbreath's exhalation ruffled Kael's hair, hot and smelling of ash.

He shivered, despite how warm he was. "Zeptus," he muttered.

"What?"

"The man you saw, he was undoubtedly the king's advisor, Zeptus. Everybody knows he has purple eyes; it's just one of his more unsettling features."

"Interesting," Shatterbreath said. "There is obviously more to this that either of us thought. Go back to your city and find out anything you can pertaining to this plot."

Kael shook his head, uncertain whether he heard her clearly. "Excuse me? Just...go back?"

"Yes, you are free to go. But you will return in one week's time," she warned, coming in close, "or else I will personally find you and hunt you down, wherever you are."

Kael retorted. "You just expect me to waltz back into Vallenfend as if nothing happened? I've been gone for a month from everybody I know! I am supposed to be dead!"

Shatterbreath cocked her head in a strange dragon way, the equivalence to a shrug. Kael was annoyed by her nonchalant manner. "Lie. Oh, and work on hiding your emotion, young Kael. You are as readable as a scroll. It is a good thing I have very good patience, because I can tell you've wanted to say a lot of rude things to me throughout our lovely conversation. You are far too easy to decipher. Work on that."

Kael forced his expression to go blank. At least he tried to. "Alright then," he sighed, "when do you want me to depart?"

Shatterbreath yawned, showing her wide array of pointed teeth. She began to lick her wound that Vert had given her, ignoring Kael, making his frustration escalate. "Oh, you're still here?" she remarked at last, "I thought you left five minutes ago."

Kael bit his lip. "What about my sword?"

Shatterbreath stopped her grooming for a moment. She frowned angrily at him. "It's always something else. Go check that nook over there, that's where I keep the metal skin of all the soldiers I defeat. There will most certainly be something over there that will appease your complaining."

Kael did as he was told. He pinched his nose shut when he neared the great pile of armour hidden within a recess at the back of Shatterbreath's cave. Now he knew why a wave of stench had met him when he first entered the cave. It wasn't the dragon. True to her word, Shatterbreath did keep all of the armour from her foes, but she had failed to mention that the armour also contain the *corpses* of them as well. There must have been a thousand skeletons back there!

"Ugh!" Kael exclaimed, nearly vomiting.

"Oh, sorry," Shatterbreath replied from around the corner. "I may have lied, that's not *all* the soldiers I've defeated; those bodies are maybe only ten, twenty years old. Your guess is as good as mine. If I would have kept the bodies from the original *army* they sent at me, surely this cave would be filled with their pestilent bodies." Kael would expect her to gloat about this, but her tone was sorrowful.

They seemed to have been organized at one time. The older skeletons, which were browned and splintered, were laid out to the right, as if she had deliberately placed each on in an according spot. But the fresher skeletons, the ones more intact or with small pieces of flesh still attached to the bones, were more and more scattered. It seemed to be the fresher the skeletons were the less Shatterbreath had cared about their organization. The piles to the left were simply heaped together, looking as though she had just shoved them all there and continued on her way without a second thought. It saddened

Kael to see the display of death. It sunk his spirits in a way he had never experienced before. There, lying unceremoniously on the stone floor, were the men of Vallenfend.

Shaking his head, Kael took a step closer to the spread-out piles, trying his best to ignore the hideous stench they emitted. Without touching any of them, Kael inspected the rancid piles first to see if he could spot a suitable sword before he went in there. One in particular caught his eye and *very* carefully, he weaved his way through the mess and untied the scabbard from a skeleton. Thanking the corpse silently, Kael made his way back out of the pile of bodies.

Awed by the blade's beauty as he unsheathed it, Kael spent the next several minutes inspecting its beautiful surface.

It was flawless. The blade widened ever-so slightly and gracefully at the tip, adding to its overall prowess. A symbolic lion stretched along the metal's surface, intricately crafted and detailed, so that a real animal seemed to inhabit the surface of the blade. The words *Noble, Strong* and *Proud* encircled the guards, written in an elegant manner. The three simple words seemed to describe the blade perfectly. The hilt was formed in the shape of a snarling lion's head.

Compared to his *borrowed* sword, Kael's round shield was a hunk of rubbish. He would have to fish around for a new one later, although he doubted he could find a shield as marvellous as his new sword. Obviously whoever owned this weapon before him was a knight of the highest order. Kael felt honoured to hold the blade, but felt it a disgrace for a coward like him to steal such a grand weapon. But no matter how badly he felt, he couldn't bring himself to give up such a weapon now.

Looking back one last time, Kael left the cave, stepping around his fallen comrades with solemnly.

It surprised him to find that it was still daylight outside, how dark it had been only moments earlier! Armed with a new sword and a new fate, Kael started towards him home, which seemed so small from where he was, standing high up on this mountain. Never again would he look up at this cave in the same way.

Kael swallowed. *What would he tell his friends?*

Chapter 12

As Kael trekked down the mountain, the reality of his situation set in. He had just survived the impossible. But at what price? For the first time, he had a chance to think about the friends he had just lost. It had cost them all of their lives for just his. That wasn't a fair trade, not in the least. He was a coward; he had only bought life because the dragon had pity on him, because of the way he had cowered. What kind of a man was he?

His grief became so great that he had to stop and lean against a tree. There, in the horrible solitude of the forest, Kael cried like he hadn't cried since he was but a baby. He cried for those lost, he cried for the lies he had told and the lies he had yet to tell. Most of all, he wailed for what fate had to burdened upon his shoulders.

Composing himself, Kael set out again, heading at a sturdy pace. He had not forgotten what had happened on the way here. This forest was dangerous. He would need to stay on the lookout.

Eventually, fear wrapped its clawed tendrils around him and Kael was once again engulfed in it. He flinched at every snap in the brush and every crunch that his own feet made on the ground. When night arrived, his paranoia only grew worse.

Stopping for only a brief moment, Kael quickly decided that the forest would be more active at night. It would be wise to continue on his way so he wouldn't wake up in the middle of the night with a cougar gnawing at his legs.

As the night stole away his vision, leaving him barely able to see the ground beneath him, Kael relaxed. The night was strangely tranquil in the forest, and he had the distinct feeling that there was nothing out there that wanted to harm him. He loosened up on his pace, realizing for the first time how truly tired he was. He ached, he was thirsty and his head throbbed with every step he took.

At long last, he couldn't fight sleep any longer. In a haze, he set up his bedroll and settled down, falling into a troubled sleep.

A roar. There was a flare of fire, like the crack of lightening. Within the periodic flashes or brilliant orange, he saw the faces of his friends, stained in blood. One by one, each one of them met their according doom. A slash here, flames engulfing them there. They all died.

Kael jolted awake at once. He was perspiring, and a chill ran up his spine, feeling like a spider crawling on his flesh. He swallowed, feeling his stomach rammed in his throat. They were all dead. It seemed cruelly ironic that he now served the one who had killed his friends. Was he a traitor?

The mountain side was still bathed in darkness, but Kael could tell it was morning by the rays of sunlight spilling out onto the farmland of Vallenfend. He suddenly remembered. Before he had left, he lied to Korjan that he was going to be working out on one of the farms. Maybe his lie would still work... Perhaps the others would believe him, as well as the blacksmith himself. He hated to bring himself to more lying, but what other choice was there? They would surely consider him a traitor and hang him for his insubordination. He had to lie.

Eyes set in grim concentration, Kael continued his trek down the mountain, ignoring the beautiful scenery that had infatuated him earlier. After a while, he stopped at the base of a waterfall to clean himself. He took off his armour, put his sword, shield and backpack to the side and scrubbed himself down in the frigid pools, which gave him a temporary boost of energy. His clothes quickly dried as he continued.

Now this was something he hadn't been expecting. He was alive. *He had survived.* A month ago, he had considered his life over. He had been a dead man. But now, now he had a second chance. He would get to see his best friends again, although he would have preferred to not have to lie to them. Few got a chance to cheat death like this. He should consider himself lucky.

But yet...

Kael didn't stop to rest that night. He wanted to get home so badly. A small thought in the back of his mind pressed against anxiousness, forcing him onwards even after he reached the point of exhaustion. *Maybe this was a dream, all of it.* Maybe all he had to do was lie in his bed at home and wake up and realize that it was all just a nightmare. The whole month, it could have all just been a horrendous, painfully realistic nightmare.

That's what he was hoping for, but the logical side of his brain told him otherwise.

Without incident, Kael finally reached the borders of Vallenfend. And in the middle of the day as well. He had made good time, nearly halving the time it took him and the rest of his group to get up there to begin with.

He strolled up to the gates, putting on the most innocent and pathetic look he could muster, remembering the dragon's words to shield his emotions.

The female guard standing near the gate eyed him. "Who are you?" she demanded, holding her spear tighter in her grip.

Kael hadn't foreseen this. He put his palms out defensively. "I live here, it's alright."

The guard furrowed her brow at him, unconvinced. "Oh yeah, who's the king?"

"Morrindale."

"His advisor?"

"Lord Zeptus."

"How about his scholar?"

Kael rolled his eyes and huffed. "Malaricus. Malaricus the Wise, if you want to be specific. Also, there are seven courtyards, each pertaining to a different time of year. Need to know anything else?"

The guard raised an eyebrow. "Okay, I believe you, but tell me what you're doing way out here then."

Kael hesitated. "Well," he began, scouring his mind. The only thing that he could think of was his farmer lie. "I was returning from a trip out from the fields, right. This other guy and I were having an argument. It got really fierce so we decided to split up, in case we decided to throw fists at each other. He went in the nearest entrance to the south, but I got stuck having to go all the way around finding another way in."

The guard cocked her hip, reminding Kael of the look Laura would give him if she knew he wasn't telling the truth. "That's plausible enough. Who were you arguing with? You mentioned he was a guy. What was his name? Chances are I know him."

"Chances are..." repeated Kael sluggishly, his tired brain processing what was happening. "Uh, no, I meant that I was travelling with a girl. Sorry, I didn't sleep well last night. I'm a little slow today. My nerves are shot from that argument too; boy did she get me angry." Kael feigned his anger, hoping he wasn't overdoing it.

The guard yawned. "Alright then, I'll let you in, one moment." She knocked against the large wooden door to the stone gate. Vallenfend had firm stone walls bordering it. It had been built solely for defence. There came a muffled query in which the guard replied to. "Open the door," the guard said.

The door swung open, revealing another bored-looking woman, younger and prettier than the lady Kael had just been talking to. "Well then," she said, her voice going softer as she caught hold of Kael. He gave a sheepish smile. "Come in."

Kael's spirit jumped. Home!

At once, all the family sights, sounds and smells greeted him. How he had missed them so. He had planned on taking the most direct route home so he could sleep the day away, but Kael couldn't help but stroll through the market where delicious, heart-warming smells hugged him, making him feel happy from head to toe. The cheerful sounds of the market filled him with a nostalgic, familiar feeling that he didn't want to leave behind.

After the market, the city wasn't as stimulating on the senses, but Kael enjoyed every waking moment of being home. In fact, he was surprised that with the amount of people that noticed him, still garbed in his armour and reeking of soot and blood, that none of them said anything, or that his friends hadn't found him yet. That was for the best though; he didn't want to see them quite yet, not until he had more energy.

Somehow, he managed to grope his way to his meagre little house. He fished around for his key but realized he didn't have it.

He stared at the handle for a numb moment, unsure what to do. Eventually, in his weary stupor, he remembered that he also hadn't locked it either. Slowly, he pushed open the door and stood there in the doorframe.

He smiled. Just how he had left it.

Not willing to fend off sleep any longer, Kael threw off his armour, let his newly acquired sword fall to the ground with a clang and took off his shield, nudging all three under his bed. Comforted, he wrapped himself in a tight layer of blankets as he lay down on his bed.

Despite how tired he was, it took him a long time to fall asleep. He feared what the dreams would hold, recalling his nightmare on the mountain. He lay there with his eyes wide open, listening to the city as it blissfully went about its regular business. After perhaps an hour, he fell asleep at last.

His dreams weren't any better than when he had caught some sleep up on the mountain. They were chaotic and filled with turmoil, danger and death, quite like the experience he had just gone through. He found no comfort in sleep. His whole world was turning upside-down.

Kael was dimly aware of something...something familiar. It pounded at the side of his dreaming state, making the terrifying images shudder and fade. Reeling between two worlds, Kael struggled to grab onto either. There came another pound, and he left sleep entirely. Reality came flooding back and at once and for a blissful moment, Kael forgot what had made him so tired in the first place. Then he remembered.

Kael opened his eyes, blinking away his disorientation. His vision slowly returned through his heavy eyes and focussed. A warm smile met him. At once, he realized who it was and despite himself, smiled back.

"Kael, you're back!" Laura's sweet voice welcomed him. For a split second, Kael thought that he heard Shatterbreath's voice emanating from her lips. He shuddered. "We've missed you so much!"

Kael, wiping his brow with his sleeve, leaned up in his bed, noticing that Faerd was standing in the room a few feet away. Although he didn't say anything, he too wore a look of relief. Kael tried to speak, but his voice cracked on the first word. Swallowing, he tried again. "Yeah, sorry I didn't come to you first. I am really, really tired."

Laura shook her head. "Don't worry about it, I'll let you sleep. I just wanted to see your face again! How long has it been since I last saw you?"

Faerd cleared his voice. "A month, give or take a *week*."

Leaning in, Laura whispered in Kael's ear. "Don't mind him; he's just sore that you didn't tell us where you were going."

Kael blushed. "Oh, that's right. I—I'm sorry, I had to go so quickly there was no time for goodbyes."

Faerd sniffed. "But you had time to see Korjan, eh? And then Bunda told us that she talked to you in front of the castle, when the king was holding a public display. 'No time to see us,' he says."

Kael repositioned himself in his bed, hurt by Faerd's biting attitude. He wanted to tell them what happened, but that could comprise his mission. If anybody heard about this, he could very easily be killed for treason. He was, after all, assisting the enemy the kingdom had declared war on. Choosing his words and tone carefully, Kael scrambled to think of an excuse.

"Well, the real reason I didn't see you," he began. Come to think of it, he wasn't lying at this point. His throat relaxed and he found the words flowed easier than before, although his emotions were still astir. "...is because I couldn't bring myself to. I hate to leave you guys, and I hate sorrowful, long goodbyes. I was hoping to skip all that and apologize later." Okay, maybe he stretched the truth on that last part.

Laura was smiling sadly. She could relate. She hated long and sorrowful goodbyes as well. Faerd however, crossed his arms and turned to the door. He didn't say anything, but threw Kael an acid look before marching out of the room. Laura watched him go and waited a few moments before she spoke.

"You had us all worried, Kael."

Ashamed, Kael looked out the window, pretending to spot something interesting. All there was outside was that neighbourhood cat, but he preferred to look at that than Laura's disappointed eyes.

"I—I heard rumours that you had been drafted," Laura said, her voice trembling. "After a few days when you didn't show up...I started to believe them. I didn't want to, but the very thought of you...gone forever. It was torture!"

Kael's heart was being torn, but he still didn't say anything. He turned his attention away from the window. "I'm sorry," he said. As if that would justify what he had done. It was a good thing she didn't know what really had happened. He imagine how she would have felt if he had told her that he was drafted and suddenly, he didn't regret not telling her was leaving. He wouldn't have been able to let her go, and he would have been dead that very moment.

Laura paused for a moment and wiped a tear from her eye. "You're safe now, that's all that matters. Rest, I know how tired you are. I can see it in your eyes. Come over to my place tonight, and we'll have dinner, our little family, all together again. You can tell us exactly where you were." Kael smiled, he would like that.

Assured that he was safe, Laura took her leave. Kael watched her go. Once she had left, he let his head, which seemed to weigh as much as his sword, fall back onto his pillow. He quickly fell asleep again.

He only had five days left until he had to return to the dragon, Shatterbreath. He shrugged, five days was enough, wasn't it? He had spent one travelling down the mountain, then another catching up on sleep.

The first place he would go to today would be the Royal Athenaeum to see Malaricus. His heart leapt at the very prospect of seeing the old scribe again, but it was the most obvious place to start his search for Shatterbreath. More importantly, however, he would be able to clear his drafting issue up with Malaricus. It dawned on Kael that Malaricus had promised to get Kael out of the training grounds. But Kael had stayed there the whole term. He had even been sent off to fight! Oh, they were going to have a serious talk.

Kael hadn't realized how much he had missed since he had been gone. Although he had made a decision to visit Malaricus first, he took the long way to get there. Kael's favourite courtyard was in full bloom and there was a general hustle about the city as the crops just started to come in. Everybody had to get ready for fall.

The Royal Athenaeum rolled into view. Kael walked up to the front of the building, emotions stirring in his chest. He espied the same poster he had seen as he left over a month ago, still pinned to a nearby column. Burning inside with rage, he seized the poster with trembling fingers and tore it up violently, scattering little pieces all over the doorstep to the Athenaeum. Flustered from his sudden fit of anger, Kael slipped inside.

He climbed the stairs up to Malaricus's study, feeling tense. This hallway was too stuffy, too tight. For whatever reason, he felt as though the walls were constricting around him and his overflowing emotions. He wanted to be outside.

Pounding on Malaricus's worn door, Kael placed a hand on his chest, trying to calm his heart. He kicked at a scuff in the floor, trying anything to rid himself of this accursed anger.

Malaricus opened the door at long last. The scholar stared at him through his spectacles for a solid minute, neither of them saying a word. At last, his glasses slipped from his nose and he thrashed out, trying to catch them. Kael caught them gently on the toe of his boot and frowned. Ever since that first battle with the Captain, his reflexes were amazingly sharp. Time seemed to slow whenever he was in battle or even in an instance like this.

Malaricus grinned as Kael gave him back his glasses. "Kael, my boy! You—you're back! Oh glory, this is excellent news indeed!" The scholar bode him inside. "We have a lot to discuss about! But firstly, I am happy to see that my request to Zeptus went through. They let you out at last! I doubted that man would listen but—"

"Wait," Kael interjected, "you made a request to the king's advisor to let me go?"

Malaricus cocked his head in a young, spry way. He seemed rejuvenated by Kael's return, as if he had been broken and then fixed. "Um, yes. It took a whole month it seems, but he finally listened to my reasoning and let you go. I was beginning to worry; I thought they had sent you away to go fight!"

Kael feigned a laugh, trying to match Malaricus's jovial tone. "It was you then! I couldn't figure out why they just let me go all of a sudden, I was so confused!"

Smiling like a thief who was exceptionally clever, Malaricus tapped his nose. "Ha, that's alright, no thanks are in order. I assume you were just coming up here to say just that, but don't worry about it, my boy. You go and visit your friends now."

Kael shifted his weight. "No." Malaricus raised his brows. "Well, I mean I've already seen them today. I was here to ask you something else."

Shrugging, Malaricus situated himself down on his favourite chair. "My knowledge is your knowledge."

Kael licked his lips. This was good. Malaricus's knowledge was vast, and if he didn't know, his books surely would. "What do you know about the war against the dragon? Besides all the basic answers they feed us."

Malaricus scratched at his beard, leaning back. "Well, for starters, King Morrindale, under the advice of Lord Zeptus, declared war on the dragon nearly thirty-five years ago."

"Zeptus had advised him?" That wasn't surprising. Vert's theory sounded like it had some truth to it, but there had been no gold in Shatterbreath's cave, he had seen so himself. What other motivations did that man have? Kael cleared his throat. "Why?"

"I don't recall. It was so many years ago, there's only so much I can remember. Although I do remember him being young, Basal, he was only seventeen or so. About your age, yes?"

"Basal? That's the king's first name?" Kael shook his head. "But why? Why did he declare war? Was the dragon attacking?"

Malaricus scratched at his beard again. It was his way of thinking. "Whatever the reason, I remember it being really trivial, otherwise it would have stayed locked in my memory. Believe me, if the dragon did attack, such carnage would be hard to forget."

"Hmm." Kael sat down as well on a fluffy armchair adjacent, placing his elbows on his knees. "What else do you know?"

"To be honest, Kael, nothing. The king and Lord Zeptus are touchy on the subject; they do not discuss it with me freely. If you want to know more, you'll have to figure it out on your own."

Kael sighed. That's the end of that road. It looked as though he wasn't going to learn anything else on that subject. That wasn't all that bad though, at least he would get to spend the next few days with his friends. Kael stood up to leave as Malaricus lit his pipe, but stopped himself, sitting back down.

"Oh," he said, picking his words carefully. "Is there anything you can tell me about...dragons?" He cursed himself for that pause.

Malaricus hesitated, stroking his long, snowy beard with a wrinkled hand. "You want to know more about dragons, eh? And why would that be, young Kael?"

Kael shrugged, trying to force the blood from flowing into his cheeks. He hated it when he blushed, and it would only give away what he was hiding. "I figure that I should learn more about them, seeing as I was nearly sent away to get eaten by one."

Nodding, Malaricus considered him for a moment. He chewed on his pipe. He seemed to be peering into Kael's soul. "Are you alright, Kael?"

Kael didn't say anything for a long time. He furrowed his brow, trying to keep his composure, and trying to keep his face blank. His lip twitched. "I'm just fine." His voice quavered, but he coughed afterwards, hoping Malaricus would dismiss it for a sore throat.

The scholar studied him behind his shiny spectacles. "What would you like to know, my boy?"

"Anything," Kael said. He was trying to keep the edge out of his voice as he spoke. He didn't think it was working. "Well, anything that could be useful."

"Hmm." Malaricus stood up and walked over to a bookcase. He paused, running a finger alone the perfectly aligned spines until he found what he was looking for. He pulled a thick brown book of the shelf and blew the layer of dust off of it and out the window. He wheezed from the floating particles and handed the book to Kael. "This is a very informative book if you want to learn every little detail about dragons, their mating behaviours, anatomy, preferences and habitats...all that nitty-gritty detailed stuff that doesn't really matter. If you want to know anything relevant, it's good that you've come to me, my boy, I was once an expert on dragons. I hope I remember everything."

Kael took the book out of his hand, surprised by how heavy it was. Grunting from the effort of holding it, Kael decided it would be best to just leave it on the table and get it later. He placed it down with a *whumph*.

"So, where to begin...?" Malaricus said. He took a deep breath. "Such a vague topic. Well, first off, dragons are ancient creatures. Older than the human race, in fact. Consequently, they are also very wise and philosophic at times, although they can become savage and unruly in an instant if something aggravates or threatens them. They are very driven by their emotions, you see. Oh, they also, they have the uncanny ability to use magic."

"Magic?" Kael interrupted, "I've never seen any magic before, isn't it just a folktale?"

Malaricus waved the end of his pipe at him. "Not at all. In fact, magic is very real, just...*uncontrolled.* Magic is everywhere, but to my knowledge, humans have not yet found a way to harness its power. Dragons, on the other hand, have magic coursing through their veins." He ran his fingers down his wrist to emphasize. "For so long have they controlled magic that they have completely forgotten how they managed to conquer it to begin with. Every dragon is born with an instinctual rule over magic. Most of the time, however, their use of it is purely accidental."

Nodding, Kael scratched his chin. This was all very interesting, if not a little hard to digest. *Magic,* the very thought of it was very foreign to him. This was perhaps something he would need to experience firsthand to believe.

Malaricus sensed his scepticism. "Take, for example, a dragon's ability to breathe fire," the scholar said, scrutinizing Kael over his spectacles. "Everybody knows that all dragons know how to breathe a jet of flame, or in rare cases, different forms of energy. It is only through magic that they can achieve this incredible feat without burning themselves."

"That makes sense I suppose."

Malaricus could tell that Kael still held some doubt, so he moved on to the next subject. "Dragons pair off when they are old enough to mate. They usually stay paired until their offspring are old enough to fend for themselves, but in some cases, it has been recorded that some stay coupled for life. Whether they do this through love is unknown."

Kael stroked the armrest on his chair. "Love? Can dragons love?"

Malaricus shrugged, blowing a smoke ring towards an open window at the other end of the library. Kael shuddered as he watched the smoke. Malaricus seemed unaware of Kael's discomfort. "It is unsure," he said, admiring his smoke rings, "whether dragons have the emotional capacity to love."

Responding quickly, Kael said, "It seems like they could have that feeling."

Malaricus raised an eyebrow at him. "Oh? And what do you base that on?"

Kael blinked, letting his body go limp in the chair. He averted his eyes. "I don't know. It just seems like they're smart, smart enough to feel love anyway."

"They might know how to love, but either way, dragons are usually solitary creatures, content to hide away alone in their dens for most of their lives."

Kael nodded. That was about all he wanted to know. He thanked his old friend, hefted the thick book in one arm and exited the library. That had gone well, surprisingly well. Malaricus was now as fooled as the rest of his friends. Which wasn't terribly comforting, considering how poorly-pieced together his lies were. Still, Kael's tower of deceit was staying together.

Now he would go see Bunda.

Within twenty minutes, Kael had arrived at her house, taking the same busy route as always. It lifted his soul to see all the people going about their business. It made him feel at home to walk with the flow of the crowds. Being around regular people again reminded him he was alive.

Kael strolled up to Bunda's shop, pausing with his hand on the door handle. He took a deep breath and then flung the door open. As he was expecting, Bunda was ecstatic to see him. She hugged him so tight he thought his head would pop right off of his shoulders.

"Kael, where have you been? I missed you so much! I feared the worst! I heard you—"

Interrupting, Kael gently removed himself from her grip, wearing a wide grin. "Bunda, Bunda, I'm all right! Look," he said, waving a hand over his torso, "I'm all right, all in one piece, I'm fine."

Flustered, she wouldn't hear of it and continued to rant on about how worried she had been. Suddenly, she stopped, her face going blank for a moment as it processed what she was going to say next. "Where did you go?"

Kael laughed, this time for real. His laugh ended short as he realized what was coming next. "I was working out in the fields," he lied, "they were short of workers and only needed me for a month or so."

"Why in the world would you want to work out in the fields?" she demanded. Her eyes as wide as saucers and her hands were resting on her hips in a comical way.

Kael laughed again, shrugging his shoulders. No matter how bad he felt, Bunda never failed to make him happy again. "I thought they would be paying me better. I thought it was going to be a learning experience as well. I was wrong."

"Oh? Why were you wrong, what happened?"

Kael blushed and looked at his boot, kicking at a bump in the floor. He glanced back up at Bunda. "Nothing really, to be honest, it was very boring."

Bunda smirked. "That's too bad. At least you're back now, and here to stay I presume."

Kael desperately wanted to corroborate her query, but that would be just another lie. He would just settle for a lighter lie. Was there such thing? "Uh, no. I'm actually going back there in a bit, about four days or so."

Bunda frowned. "That's too bad," she said, her expression blank. "How long will you be gone?"

143

Shrugging, Kael finally told the truth. "I have no idea. A week, a month, who knows? However long they need me."

Bunda, more relieved than anything else, placed a hand on Kael's shoulder, as if she was still in doubt that he had come back. "As long as you will return, I bid you good luck."

Yeah, Kael thought to himself, *he was going to need all the luck in the world.* "Thank you," he said.

The last person on Kael's list to visit today would be Korjan. He was reluctant to visit the blacksmith, recalling how awkward and forced their last conversation was. Would he actually swallow the lies Kael was going to feed him? He didn't seem to buy them last time. Unsure, he set off towards the blacksmith's tent. Hopefully, Kael's reappearance would make Korjan believe his previous lies and any further he would have to tell. This was all terribly difficult. It tore Kael on the inside to have to do this over and over. It wasn't right, *it wasn't him.*

The familiar smell of hot metal reached Kael's lungs as he neared the blacksmith tent. Everything at this place seemed to remind him about the dragon in some way as he entered. The smelting oven roared and blazed, bringing up a terrible image in Kael's mind of a great, toothy maw belching fire. The bellows Korjan was holding heaved, strikingly similar a dragon taking a breath. Even the worn, black-stained wooden pillars that kept the tent upright seemed to remind Kael of the legs of Shatterbreath, each one ridged and rough. He shuddered.

Korjan put his bellows down, wiping his sweaty brow with a gloved hand. He was actually wearing a shirt today, although it was as wet as his forehead. "Kael? I'm surprised—I mean, you're back. This is good news. When did you arrive?"

Kael frowned. So Korjan hadn't believed him. That didn't surprise him. "I got back yesterday."

Korjan was at a loss for words. "I didn't think that you were..."

Kael cut him off. "That's alright," he assured him, leaning up against a table. He inspected all the swords that were being worked on or otherwise displayed to the public. He smiled inwardly; none of them were even close to the magnificence of his new weapon. "I left in a hurry; I couldn't explain the situation to you properly."

"Or the others I suppose."

Kael sighed; upset how he had left so many loose ends when he had first left. "No, not the others, either. The farmers needed my help right away."

"Hmm. Well," Korjan said, at a loss for words. Kael studied him closely. "I heard another story from somebody. A rumour, I suppose."

"What was it?"

Korjan shifted his weight, picking up a dagger and inspecting its edge. "I heard from somebody on the street, maybe one of your friends, that you had been drafted."

Kael's heart skipped a beat and his breath came up shallow. Jaw working, he shook his head. "That's a lie. Who did you hear that from?"

Korjan put his hands out defensively. "Calm down. A girl told me, but I can't remember what she looked like. I didn't believe her at first, it seemed outrageous. But when you didn't show up after a couple weeks, I started to believe her. After all, you didn't say how long you were going to be gone."

"Huh. Oh well, I've had a rumour go around about me before, it's nothing I can't handle."

Korjan nodded, eager to get back to work. "It's been rough since you've been gone, Kael. With nobody to help me, I've had to do all the work myself! So, are you ready to start again?"

"No," Kael replied, "I have to go back in a little less than a week." He would have liked to return to his job as blacksmith's apprentice, anything would be better than having to return to that stinking cave.

"That's a shame. Well, when this troublesome business out in the fields is over with, you will return right?"

Kael nodded. "Of course."

"Alright then, I'll see you around."

Satisfied that he had tied up all his loose ends, Kael decided to loiter around until it was time to visit Laura. Enjoying every moment, Kael meandered through the streets of Vallenfend peacefully. Such a glorious city it was! Making his way through the varying crowds, Kael wandered to places he hadn't visited in years, such as the church that occupied a large section of the south-western part of the city.

Saint Briggon's Monastery, named after one of Vallenfend's forefathers, was massive, far bigger than Kael remembered. It had been so long since he had set eyes on it that he spent at least fifteen minutes staring at it in awe from across the street. It towered over the buildings surrounding it, easily one of the biggest structures in the city, although still dwarfed by the castle. Daunting in stature, it was also incredibly intricate, with carvings of angels and demons fighting eternal wars upon its surface. Its precipices tapered to sharp points, as if they were silently praying to the heavens. Large stained-glass windows adorned the front of the building, portraying two deceased kings from centuries ago. One was the king who had ordered the monastery to be built, and the other was Saint Briggon.

Priestesses made their way across the church grounds, their clothes pearly white and gleaming in the afternoon sunlight. Children tugged at the hems of the priestesses' dresses as they followed the women. Orphans. Saint Briggon's Monastery served two purposes. It was a place of god and a place for orphans. Kael watched as one of the priestesses picked up a little girl, holding the crying child in her arms. Kael gritted his teeth and looked back up towards the towering precipices. Seeing that child reminded Kael of who he was. An orphan. Just like them.

Once he had his fill of marvelling at the holy church, Kael set on his way to the Stockwin household. He figured by the time he reached Laura's house, it would be time to eat. But as Kael smelled the alluring scents wafting out of the houses and shops as he strolled on, he quickened his pace.

When he arrived, Mrs. Stockwin ushered him in, a comforted expression on her face. Kael could only imagine how worried she must have been during his absence.

The dinner Mrs. Stockwin had made was glorious. The warm foot comforted Kael and he ate until his belly threatened to burst. It had been far too long since he had last eaten a real meal. He had almost forgotten what good food and company was like.

It was wonderful to talk to Laura and her mother once again. Life felt normal once again. The stories they told were full of life and good times, which lifted Kael's spirits to a level he hadn't experienced in weeks. Once, Kael and Laura caught each other's eyes in the middle of a fit of laughter. At that moment, as time stood completely still, the world was the most tranquil Kael had ever experienced. They gazed into each other's eyes until Mrs. Stockwin broke their trance. Awkwardly, Kael took a piggish bite out of a hunk of bread while Laura pretended to fix her hair.

The only thing that would have made the dinner perfect would have been for Faerd to be there. It seemed as though he was still upset with Kael.

Laura suddenly gestured at Kael. "Where did you get that tunic anyway?" Laura asked. Mrs. Stockwin also looked expectantly at Kael for an answer.

Blushing, Kael struggled to come up with a reply. He opened his mouth to say something, but closed it, having thought of a better lie. "I was thinking a while ago that I needed some new clothing, but rather than buying shoddy clothes like I usually do, I decided to spend a little bit more money to get something nicer."

Mrs. Stockwin clicked her tongue. "Aw, Kael, why would you do that? You don't have the kind of money to be doing that."

Kael shrugged, keeping his voice steady. "I thought as a way to celebrate a month's worth of working out in the fields, I would treat myself. I had a bit of extra money to spend anyway."

Laura chuckled. "Yeah, there goes all the work you did out there!"

Kael smiled. "Hey, I made more than that!" Kael was in an even better mood than before. Not only had they accepted his lie, but he had hidden his disappointment that Mrs. Stockwin had sparked. Usually when her mother said something like that, Laura would chastise her for saying something rude about Kael. This time, she hadn't even noticed that he was upset. He was getting better at hiding his thoughts.

147

Dinner came to a close and Kael reluctantly left. Mrs. Stockwin had to get up early the next morning and she couldn't afford to stay up late.

Kael couldn't shake his elated mood that he had gained from spending time with the Stockwins again. Everything seemed perfect right now, just the way it was supposed to be. Even when he thought about returning to the dragon empty handed, he stayed as happy as he was. Nothing could get him down now.

And though he had to return to Shatterbreath in less than a week, he was fine with that. The sun was shining, the grass was green, and he had seen his friends one last time. Right now, that's all that mattered to him. With or without any helpful information, Kael was perfectly content.

Chapter 13

Shatterbreath was used to waiting, oh yes, it was something she had experienced all too well over the years. But this time... This time was different.

She huffed, a jet of flame licking around her nostrils, upset by her own anxiousness. She was eagerly awaiting the boy's return. *What was with her?* Her tail flicked angrily across the ground, bumping into a corpse on the floor.

Waiting was something she should have patience for; after all, she was a dragon. This type of waiting though, it was different. What she had done before could be better described as...*doing nothing.* Perhaps waiting was a different experience now.

She growled. She hated waiting.

An even louder growl escaped her jaws a moment later as she continued to brood and fester. Why did she even care? What was the life of a puny human worth to her anyway? She had killed hordes upon hordes of them; they were bugs under her colossal—

Curse that one boy! She licked her leg angrily as another spasm of pain erupted from where that bold young man had cut her. What kind of weapon had he used anyway? It had been new to her. She shouldn't have underestimated him. She was getting lazy. May he live a thousand years without sleep in the great sky above.

Where was she? Oh yes, she had been thinking about Kael. Why was she so concerned? Not just about his success, either. For whatever reason, she didn't care if he attained crucial information. Just as long as he was *safe.*

She dug one of her claws into the cave floor, creating a large new crack in it. *Why did she care?* There was something different about that boy though...something that the rest didn't have. For one thing, he had a certain *innocence* about him. And there was the clever answer he had given her, about why he had to live. Even for a dragon, she had been impressed, and also greatly amused. Hardly anything she would have expected from a little bag of grease that he was—what all humans were.

She flicked a bone out of her teeth in disgust, remnants of the fight that happened a few days ago. Humans. Disgusting. She would prefer to eat a rock. Battles did occasionally require her to devour a human or two. She did that reluctantly, hating every chew.

Shatterbreath shook her head. It had been so long since her mind had been aroused, she hadn't realized how off-track it could get.

Despite her conflicted mind and confusing emotions, Shatterbreath was ecstatic. She hadn't had this kind of adventure in ages. Trapping a boy, *working together with him,* trying to figure out a dastardly plot. This was almost too much excitement, she wasn't used to it! She sighed; she would have it no other way. It was good to jumpstart her old heart now and again.

When she had first seen that boy cowering pathetically in the corner something more than just pity persuaded her to spare his feeble life. She peered down at the lowly humans as though they were insignificant little creatures. But that boy, *that boy*, there was something more about him, deep courage, a greater...*importance* that he didn't know about. When she had mused down at him, there was a strange feeling, a dull listless in her chest that seemed to speak gently in her ear. It had told her that there was something different about Kael. She had felt this feeling before, only a long, long time ago.

She closed her eyes and bowed her head, remembering the pains of the past and where this familiar feeling had first been experienced by her. Such a long time ago...

Shatterbreath stood up. She shook her head, feeling the spines on her back shake as well. She flexed her wings. That's all this was, boredom. She had just been in here too long, that's all. Maybe it was time to relocate, find a better place to live.

Blast the humans. She was there first, why should she leave?

In three graceful bounds she made it to the edge of her cave, careful not to scratch her back on the ceiling which seemed to get slightly lower after every decade. Examining her kingdom, her land, her *world,* she decided to spend more thought on the boy Kael later.

Right now, she would hunt.

Letting out a shattering roar that startled nearly all the birds on her stretch of mountain for a mile, Shatterbreath took to wing, letting the wind guide her. She didn't care if her prey heard her warning call. They could run all they wanted; they could even dig into the earth as far as they wanted. They would hide or fight for all she cared. She was a dragon, and when a dragon hunts, no prey can escape.

Content as a sated wolf, she angled her wings and banked off in the direction of her favourite hunting grounds. Casting her long neck back to get one last glance of the kingdom, she silently bade the young warrior, Kael Rundown, good luck.

Chapter 14

His week was up, but Kael didn't mind. His friends all believed he was leaving on another 'business' trip and he had spent four whole days with them, catching up on everything he had missed in his month of absence.

Eventually, Faerd warmed up to him once again, which was quite a relief. Kael's days wouldn't have been the same without him. Faerd still was somewhat sore that Kael did indeed have to leave, but he tried to hide it. Kael could tell all the same.

There was a small pang of regret for not trying to find any information for Shatterbreath, but Kael didn't care that much. If she wanted to find out anything concerning the king or his advisor, she should have given him better instructions, or at least a way to get the information she sought. He had to admit, that did seem highly unlikely.

The whole thing was unlikely! How was he, a blacksmith's apprentice, a coward, supposed to attain any knowledge on a subject like that? Surely the only way to do so was to do something either incredibly clever or equally brave. Kael didn't think he would be able to sum up enough nerve for the latter and doubted he could outwit Zeptus or any of the king's close attendants, or even get near the castle for that matter.

So, without learning anything useful and feeling very reluctant to return, Kael decided that today would be the day he would leave. After saying his goodbyes, Kael headed back to his house. Strapping his leather armour back on, as well as his sword to his hip and shield over his backpack, Kael checked to see if anybody he knew was watching and headed out and away from the area where all his friends lived.

It was a hard choice for him to make, but Kael decided that he didn't want to travel back up the mountain for a second time unassisted. He didn't want to go back at all, Shatterbreath's warning echoed through his mind. If he didn't willingly come back, she would hunt him down. Kael doubted Shatterbreath made idle threats. Kael sat down on a bench that was situated across from leather merchant's hut, watching the people and ox-drawn carts of this section of the city go by. It sure was odd how varying each area of Vallenfend was. There was a stone road underneath his feet, but years of heavy animals tracking in the mud from outside of the city and all but covered the stone up. The smells of working animals as well as the tanning vats nearby permeated the air around him. He cleared his throat, feeling the musky air fill his lungs. This particular subdivision was where they kept animals.

Kael stood up and walked towards Vallenfend's outer wall, trying to act as casual as he could. He couldn't stick right to the wall because there was large chicken coup, but he was as far away from the general throng of people as he could get.

His plan, regrettably, was to steal a horse so it could take him up the mountain in safety. How he was going to manage to thieve such a large beast was beyond him. The actual stables were located just outside the city walls, enclosed within a smaller wall of their own. This location was chosen to keep the smell and feces of the animals outside, but also served to keep the horses out of enemies' hands in case a neighbouring kingdom attacked them, in which case, the invading army would most likely come from the east, pass through the mountains and sweep in from north. Vallenfend was fundamentally designed for war; it was ironic how their army was lacking.

Kael stood outside a hut near the stables. The owner of the horses lived in that hut. If you wanted to buy or rent a horse, you would have to speak to him first. Kael had no intentions of speaking to him, however, so he quickly moved past.

It hadn't been hard to get out of the gates; the guards here were lenient and would let almost anybody through without a second glance. Some gates were designated for the flow of workers or livestock.

Spotting the stables, Kael pretended to keep walking in a straight path, keeping an eye on the stables where he could see the horses.

What he also saw were at least four stable-hands tending to the animals, feeding them, grooming them and making sure nobody tried to steal one.

Now, how to deal with them...

There was a small girl playing among some chickens not far away. Kael changed his direction and walked towards her, double-checking to see if he could spot her parents anywhere. From what he could tell, she was alone. Aware of the crunching his worn boots made, the little girl noticed Kael and stopped her frolicking. She crossed her arms as he approached, sticking out her lips in a pout.

"Daddy told me never to talk to strangers," she interrupted as Kael tried to speak.

"My name is...Don, Don Huntson," Kael lied, kneeling down in front of the girl, keeping his composure calm and friendly. "What's yours?"

The little girl considered him for a moment. "Morey."

Kael smiled warmly. "There, now we're not strangers, are we?" There was something wrong about this conversation, but still he persisted. "Do you want to do me a huge favour? I can pay you."

Morey's eyes lit up. "Really? You would pay me?"

Kael nodded, keeping his smile. "Yes, I've got a few gold coins in my pocket I'd be happy to share, but first you have to do something for me."

Morey looked frightened for a moment. "I'm not going anywhere with you, Mr. Don!"

Kael shook his head. "No, we're not going anywhere. Listen, I just want you to go over there, see, by the stables? All I want you to do is try and climb the wall to the stables. Do you think you can do that for me?"

"Sure!"

Kael deposited all the coins he had brought with him into her tiny, awaiting hand. "Oh, wait," he said, placing a hand on her shoulder before she tried to run off. "One other thing, do you have any friends nearby? They can help as well if they want."

Morey nodded vigorously. Kael was charmed by her energetic personality. "Perfect! You go get them quickly and then do as I told you, okay?"

She nodded and then skipped away.

Kael, acting quickly, stood back up and loped further down the animal-worn path. Ducking out of sight from the stable-hands, he hid behind a large boulder situated close to the stables. He poked his head out, checking to see if anybody had seen him. There was nobody there besides the stable-hands, who were all female. This close to the kingdom, there weren't really any farms. Most of the livestock or crop farms were further away. There wouldn't be chance of many people spotting what he was doing.

Kael watched patiently as two of the workers placed a saddle on a dark brown horse with a black mane. He guessed they must have been taking it out for practice. That would be the one he would steal.

After several minutes, Kael spotted what he had been waiting for. Morey, with a squad of small children in tow, was sneaking up from around the back to attempt what Kael had told her. There must have been at least ten kids. Where had she gotten all of them in such a short time? Kael had a new encouragement to be swift. If he could escape with the horse fast enough, then he wouldn't have to pay any of the other children. Surely some of them would be expecting the same bribe.

As the children began to try and climb over the wall, Kael pulled a cloth out of his backpack. He tied it around his head, leaving a horizontal gap for his eyes. One of the stable-hands caught notice of the raucous children as a young boy flung a rock at them with his slingshot. She rushed over to them, where Morey had actually succeeded in climbing over the wall. Kael was surprised by how wild the children were, but relieved. The more distracting the stable-hands were, the better.

Once all four of the women looking after the horses rushed over to stop the rampaging children, Kael made his move. He ran over to the saddled horse as fast as he could, his armour and sword clanking together as he did. He made it all the way across the field to the front of the stable before one of the stable-hands noticed.

"Hey, you!"

By the time she had yelled at him, Kael had already swung himself up onto the horse, which nickered in fright. He seized the reigns and gained control over the horse. Three of the four stable-hands had given up on the children and were now running towards Kael, but he unsheathed his glorious sword and waved it threateningly at them.

"You stay where you are unless you want me to cut your face clean off!" He didn't mean it, but his tone was serious enough that they stopped dead in their tracks.

The horse Kael was on beat its hooves impatiently, sensing the tension that had just risen. Kael, eyes wide from excitement, spurred the horse forward. It bolted, nearly bucking Kael right and sprinted at full speed away from the stables.

"Darn," one of the stable-hands said to another. "We nearly had that horse trained."

The woman beside her laughed. "Yeah, but who cares if he steals that one, it's always been trouble. Good riddance I say. He's doing us a favour!"

The lead stable-hand, frowned. "Still, thievery is punishable, and I don't think our boss will be too happy that one of his horses is gone, even if it was *that* one."

Another stable-hand walked up, holding a struggling little girl. "I think this one was the leader," she said, grunting to hold back the child's flailing arms.

The lead stable-hand bent down, her lips set in a serious frown. "Did he tell you to do that?" she asked in a disappointed voice.

"Yes, he gave me money too!"

The lead stable-hand gave a playful smile. "He gave you money? Oh, that's not a good thing."

The girl's face scrunched up and she looked like she was about to cry. "It isn't?" she asked over a trembling lip.

"Not at all, but I'll tell you a secret." She leaned in closer and so did the girl. "If you tell us his name, I promise you that I can let you go, and nobody will ever know you were involved."

The little girl's face lit up. "Really?"

The lead stable-hand nodded, smirking.

"His name was Don Huntson."

The lead stable-hand nodded to another. "Okay, you may go, just don't tell anybody about what happened here, alright?" The little girl nodded and skipped away happily. The lead stable-hand stood up straight. "Go tell the authorities."

Kael yelped as his horse jumped clear off a rock ledge down onto a grassy plain. It was wild! He was having the hardest time just holding onto the reigns and even when he did try and change its direction, it wouldn't obey. It was still running as fast as it could in the wrong direction. Annoyed by the horse's disobedience, Kael yanked the reigns as hard as he could to one side, digging his boot into its side.

The horse screeched in protest, but Kael won over and it pitched right and back towards the kingdom. Satisfied, Kael let it continue to run at its maximum speed. It could burn all the energy it wanted, just as long as he was going where he wanted to go.

The horse's energy finally ran dry when they were near the south-eastern section of the wall around Vallenfend. The horse heaved and foamed from the mouth, exhausted by its quick adventure, and slowed down to a peaceful gait.

Even though Kael was worried that people would spot him, going at this easy pace gave him a chance to survey the land. It was beautiful. Green grass spread for several kilometres, most of it changing into the sandy-brown of the wheat fields far off in the distance. Off to the east, the great mountains loomed overhead, painted a dazzling conflagration of blue and olive as the last rays of the sun poured over its face. Kael sighed. He loved Vallenfend.

The workers from the fields began to pour back into the city from the south, but by the time they did, Kael was far enough away that nobody would pay attention to him.

As he reached the foot of the mountain, memories of last time he had climbed its slopes began to flitter through Kael's mind as he rode on the back of his stolen horse. This was all so familiar. An hour

157

later he realized he was even walking on the same path his troupe had taken before.

Having to do no work himself besides hanging on, Kael started to get drowsy, being rocked back and forth with every step the horse took. He even closed his eyes for a moment and slipped into sleep. He jolted back awake as he almost slid off.

He checked the sky, which had become dotted with stars. The moon was nothing more than a sliver tonight. His horse was slowing down, so Kael decided it was time to rest for the night.

Quickly setting up camp, Kael decided to forgo a fire he and instead tied his horse to a tree off in the near distance and then settle down to sleep. He was frightened as he had been on the way down, but for some reason, this time was different. He felt stronger tonight, more confident than he had before. Perhaps it was his horse's presence that comforted him, or maybe it was a stronger feeling of purpose that he hadn't felt before.

Whatever the reason, Kael fell asleep with a grin on his lips.

In the morning, Kael resumed his journey, feeling bored on the horse's back. He didn't even have to lead the animal. It followed the path without Kael's assistance. If it was any consolation, he was making excellent time, much faster than going on foot and not having to wait for anybody else now that he was alone.

His thoughts were interrupted and the image of Laura in his mind disappeared. *What was that noise?* He stopped the horse, gazing into the bushes worryingly. A twig snapped somewhere. He supposed it wasn't anything significant, probably just a squirrel.

Another twig snapped, louder than before, followed by a rustle of leaves. Whatever was out there had to be larger than some squirrel to make such a sound. His horse swivelled its ears, proving that Kael was not just imagining anything. He tried to follow where the horse's ears were pointing, but it seemed just as unsure as he was.

Tension hung heavy in the air. A sweat broke out on the back of his neck and Kael's stomach lurched. There was something out there. He could feel it watching him. He inhaled deeply, trying to catch his breath. He instead breathed in a bunch of pollen. Kael sneezed.

A tawny shape erupted out of the bushes. As the form flew towards him, Kael slipped off of his horse as it reared in surprise. The cougar just barely missed his chest with its outstretched claws as he fell off to the side.

Kael shook the bewilderment out of his system and scrambled to his feet, pulling out his sword and swiftly strapping his shield to his arm. Just in time, too, because right as he finished, the cougar attacked again.

Thick feline claws struck his wooden shield, sending a jolt up his arm. It didn't stop there and pounced right at Kael, who still had his shield out in front of him. He rocked backwards, onto his back, with the cougar pressing down on top of him, crouching on his shield and snarling furiously.

Kael's one arm was pressed down across his chest, making the edges of his shield dig into his neck and stomach. He gasped for air. The situation slowed down and Kael witnessed in horror as the cougar lifted a paw to strike him in the face. As fast as he could, he moved his free arm to put his sword in the way of the claws.

There was a terrible screech as the claws met the metal surface, slowing the cougar's attack, but not stopping it entirely. He screamed as sharp claws torn his cheek. As fiercely as he could, Kael managed to lift the end of his shield that was lying on his stomach up, which also brought the huge cat close to his head. He wedged his knee into the gap he created below his shield as the cougar made another attempt to slash at him, widening the distance even more. Kael let go of the handle in his shield and kicked it away as hard as he could with both feet, and with it, the cougar as well.

The cougar flew off of him and landed on all fours. Kael's shield disappeared into the tangle of the trees. He scrambled once again to his feet, holding his sword out in front of him defensively.

The cougar's muzzle wrinkled and it hissed at him, baring its shiny teeth. A moment later it pounced at him again. But this time, he was ready. The cougar neared him, seemingly floating through the air as time travelled as slow as a snail. His eyes narrowed in concentration. Now!

He brought his sword around his body with, and then with two hands, lifted it high over his head. When he brought it down, the blade struck squarely between the cougar's neck and right shoulder, sinking in at least a foot into its flesh.

The cougar let out a pained snarl. It fell to the ground in a heap and began to convulse and whimper as Kael removed his sword. For a moment, Kael was convinced to simply leave the animal to suffer, but compassion moved him and he plunged his blade into its chest. A pool of blood surrounded the area, painting the path maroon red.

Gingerly, Kael touched his cheek. It smarted, but it was not nearly as serious as it could have been. At least it hadn't reached bone.

Moaning in pain, Kael reached into his bag and fetched the same clothe he had used to disguise himself earlier. He pressed it hard against his wound, trying to stop the bleeding. He peered around, looking for his shield and his horse. Neither was in sight.

Gritting his teeth, he searched through the bushes closest to him where he thought his shield had gone. He found it pretty quick— snapped into two separate pieces. He moaned loudly as he picked up one jagged half, the wood groaning right back at him as the one fibre keeping the two halves together severed. Now he needed to get a new shield! He swallowed his anger and residual fear. He would get a new one at Shatterbreath's cave. If he had found a sword this nice, surely there would be a shield of equal quality.

Leaving the shield in the bushes, he started to follow his horse's hoof prints. Large clods were taken out of the ground as the horse had fled, leaving deep gouges in the ground. Feeling impatient and even warier than ever, Kael followed the tracks up the path, his eyes darting all around in case another, more dangerous animal was watching him.

Kael was surprised by how calm he had reacted during the whole ordeal, and indeed, even at that moment. Two weeks earlier, he would have been traumatized. *I guess having met the largest, scariest predator out there, everything else seems small and weak in comparison,* he thought, *now I have to return to that great beast.*

Kael could hear his horse before he saw it. It was braying and thrashing wildly because its reigns had gotten caught on a thick limb of a branch. Walking slowly up to it, Kael put his hands out, speaking to it in a calm, reassuring voice. The horse eyeballed him, and then quite surprisingly, it landed back on all fours, mollified.

Patiently, Kael untied the horse from the branch, patted its great neck and hopped into the saddle. Shaken still by the cougar, Kael spurred the horse forward, exhaling slowly. What a wild adventure this was turning into.

Kael pulled some salted cooked meat out of his pack after a while and began to absently munch it. The morsel of food wasn't the most appetizing thing he had ever eaten, but it would have to serve as lunch for today. He stopped to let his horse nibble on some grass.

The bushes looked the same as always, the trees swayed with their usual lethargic dance as a meagre wind clawed its way through them, but Kael was still awed by the beauty of this forest as he had been when he first entered. There was always something to look at! It struck him how much he liked this place, despite the dangers it held.

The trees thinned as they had before, and a deep fog enveloped Kael and his horse. There was no more wildlife as the ground became craggy and thick bushes turned into stubbly moss. Impressed by its swift speed, Kael dismounted his horse and packed up all his things which he had strewn over its back. He patted his faithful friend's hide one last time and then slapped it in the rump, sending it back down the mountain. He had become quite attached to that horse in the last day and a half, he was sad to see it go. However, he doubted it would be able to tolerate Shatterbreath's overwhelming presence.

The cave, unfortunately, beckoned overhead, just up this last, gravelly hill. Expression set in grim detest, Kael worked his way up the mountain, pausing just before the gaping opening to gaze into the blue expanse. Sighing, Kael entered the cave, trying his best to ignore the heinous stench and instinctual push to go the other direction and escape.

Shatterbreath was waiting for him.

Chapter 15

Shatterbreath was lying at the back of her cave, surrounded by her glowing stones. Her scales shimmered like tiny pools of water after rain. She reminded Kael so much of a thunderstorm, it was startling. She had been curled up against the wall but Kael came in, she lifted off of the ground and sat on her haunches. He was surprised at first because he hadn't seen her until she had begun to move. For his own sake, he would have to memorize this cave so she couldn't hide from him like that anymore.

"Tiny, you're back," she said, tone neutral. "And late as well, I was just about to come get you."

Kael gave an awkward bow. "My apologies," he griped. He considered, for a moment, whether to address her by name or by title. He doubted she would like to be patronized and he wasn't comfortable enough to call her by name. He continued. "I thought I had an extra day."

She dismissed it with a shake of her muzzle and a smoky snort.

Tentative, Kael Threw his pack to the ground and sat down on the cold, hard floor, just in front of Shatterbreath, who was watching him with one large eye. She cocked her head, swinging it closer to his face. She squinted at him.

"Why, Tiny, what happened to your face? What sort of trouble could a measly little morsel like yourself get into in just a week?" she asked, a touch of concern lacing her strong voice.

Struggling to even breath through the waft of her heavy breath, he waved his hand in dismissal. "I was attacked by a cougar on the way up here, don't worry about it."

Shatterbreath huffed, a sound that resembled more of a growl. "I am not *worried* about you. I simply thought that in your pressing investigations to find useful information, you had gotten hurt somehow, perhaps by an angry guard who had seen you."

Kael blushed as he took in all the dragon had just said. Terror wrapped its fingers around his throat and he couldn't speak, couldn't give her an excuse.

Shaking her large head, Shatterbreath rose on her hind legs and placed her two front legs up against her cave wall. With a terrible grinding noise, she clawed the side of the wall, digging her talons into rock. Large chunks fell out of the ceiling, which she pushed flat to the side of the cavern with her tail. Whether she was doing this to sharpen her claws, or to intimidate Kael further, he would never know.

Kael grimaced as the large chunks of stone hit the ground, sending a shiver through the floor.

"So," she said, landing back on all her legs, "I take it you didn't discover anything new?"

Kael shook his head, feeling very uncomfortable. Would she kill him because of his failure? "A month wouldn't be enough time to discover anything by simply snooping around. I couldn't even find out why they started this war on you in the first place."

Shatterbreath rolled her eyes, her expression grave. At least, Kael thought it was grave. It was harder to read her emotions. It seemed she expressed herself more in body language than facial expressions. "You failed me, Tiny," she said slowly.

She took a threatening step towards him, and Kael scrambled to his feet. "Wait," he cried, taking a few steps back, "I—I can still help, really!"

"How?" the dragon mused. "Even if I did let you have a month, you said yourself it wouldn't be enough. What makes you think a second attempt will prove anything?"

Kael scoured his mind, searching for some solution. An idea came to mind. "The castle," he said, snapping his fingers. "If we're going to find anything, surely it would be in the castle. Perhaps in Zeptus's study, or in the king's chambers. But getting there," he thought aloud, "would be nearly impossible."

Shatterbreath's tail swished on the floor as she pondered the concept. "The castle, eh? That's not as impossible as it would seem.

I've flown over that hubris building before. It doesn't look heavily guarded. If you were stealthier, you could easily infiltrate it."

As glad as he was to still be breathing, a new dread was forming in his gut. Infiltrate the castle? If he was caught the penalty would be death. But he didn't share this thought with Shatterbreath, as the dragon had made it abundantly clear that she didn't care much for his life. "But I'm not stealthy," he insisted. "They'll catch me right away."

"What a *shame* that would be. Fear not. I am a master at stealth," she said, putting her head to the side in a proud pose. "And although you are...clumsier than I, I will still teach you the ways to be *sneaky.*"

Shatterbreath brought her head close to Kael. There was a smile in her eyes and her tail danced playfully off to the side. He looked into her large green eye, to her tail and back again. He felt the blood drain from his face. She was serious. He was going to have to spend *more* time with her. Kael could feel the stress building in his chest.

"Where is your shield," she said suddenly, backing away. "I thought there was something different about you today."

Kael blinked, confused by Shatterbreath's strange observation. He would never know how this dragon's thoughts worked. Tentative as ever, he said, "It broke when I was fighting the cougar."

Shatterbreath stared down at him for a passive moment, as if she had just heard what he had done, even though this was his second time telling her. "Oh yes," she said, "well done, Tiny, you are braver than either of us expected."

Deciding this was indeed a compliment, Kael nodded. "Thank you." Despite the flattering remark, Kael remained wary as ever. He wasn't going to let her sudden good mood get the best of him. He hadn't been with her long, but he already knew how fast her emotions could change. One wrong word, one wrong body movement, and she could interpret it as something different. He would be dead before he even knew how he had offended her.

"Get yourself a new shield then, you're going to need it," Shatterbreath said, turning her great body around. She flexed her wings, yawned and then slowly rested herself on the ground. "While you're doing that, I can figure out where to start your training."

Kael walked over to the nook at the side of the cavern. The same overpowering stench met him as he reached the fetid pile of corpses. With a pang of disgust, Kael realized all the fresh new bodies that Shatterbreath had created were all piled atop as well. He met Brudo's pale, lifeless gaze for a heartbeat, then quickly looked away, his courage failing him. Eyes held closed, Kael stood there for a moment, trying not to remember the horrors that lived in his dreams.

That day Shatterbreath killed them all was etched in his memory. Every time he heard Shatterbreath begin to speak, images of his friends dying flashed across his vision and he could still remember the screams, the roars...

"What are you doing over there?" Shatterbreath called out to him from behind the corner. He shivered.

Summing up some bravery, Kael replied. "Nothing. Just...give me a moment."

Kael heard a mumble in response and then Shatterbreath was silent. He stared at another body for a split second, then stepped onto the pile, giving the fresh bodies a wide berth. He began to scrounge around for a shield, keeping his hands hovering above all the equipment that was fitted around loose bones.

After a while, he found a shield that would suite his purposes. It was a kite shield made of metal. He gingerly plucked it off of the body that was still holding it and held it at arm's length, wiping away the dust on its surface. It wasn't that scuffed and the insignia inscribed, a rearing wolf, was still shining and as impressive as it would have been when it was first made. Although it was metal, it was surprising light for its size, just slightly heavier than Kael's old shield. Yes, this would do nicely. It was sturdier than his last, and would last far longer.

Kael fitted it to his arm and then headed back towards where Shatterbreath lay. She inspected him patiently as he adjusted the shield's position on his wrist. He was unfamiliar with its new weight, but it wouldn't take long to get used to it.

"That's a rather unfitting pair," Shatterbreath observed. "A lion for courage and a wolf for cunning."

Kael glanced at her. "Pardon?"

Shatterbreath made a low rumbling noise. "The lion and the wolf are two totally separate predators. Your armour and weapon should match under normal circumstances."

Kael furrowed his brow. "How do you know so much?" he asked, ever careful to keep his tone respectful.

She gave a playful shrug, rolling onto her back, keeping her head pointed at Kael. "I've been around a long time, Tiny. You don't go so many years without knowing a little about the world."

Kael was about to say something when she cut him off. "Now, because of my knowledge in such areas, I can teach you both how to fight and how to be as silent as a butterfly."

"I know how to fight."

Shatterbreath rose up on her feet in one smooth motion. She always moved smoothly, as if her muscles were made of silk. The end of every movement would end sharply, a flick of her tail, a snap of her wrists as she placed her paws on the floor. It made her actions more pronounced and noble. She was truly unlike any animal Kael had ever known.

Shatterbreath let out a strange growl, amused. "Not that well I presume. Sure, you know *how* to fight. But how well? And against what foes? A true knight can fight multiple enemies at once, both defending and striking at the same time. Especially when holding a shield, as you prefer." Kael's interest was roused by the mention of a knight. How alluring the prospect was to him.

She brought one green eye down to his level, blinking in her slow, methodical manner. "Tell me, how many enemies have you ever successfully battled at once." His silence proved her point. "Good, now, which should I teach you first?"

Kael he stared up at one of the glowing stones in the ceiling, pondering her words. "You can really teach me how to fight?"

Shatterbreath grinned from cheek to cheek. "Yes, hatchling. Although it will be somewhat...different than regular training methods, I can teach you the ways of the knight."

"Alright," Kael agreed, "where do we start?"

Shatterbreath yawned. "First you have to go get some real armour. That weedy set of leather won't be much use. Go fetch some better armour."

Taken aback, Kael looked himself over. She was right, his armour was worthless. "From where?"

The great blue dragon rolled her eyes. "From where else? Go over to that pile of metal skin and find something that fits."

Kael groaned, but otherwise obeyed. The stink met him as he rounded the corner. He stood there for a spell, refusing to take another step. How had he gotten into this mess?

"Get a set that has some room in it," Shatterbreath called to him, "in case you decide to grow."

As quickly as he could, Kael seized a rotten, blackened body and pulled it free of the other bones. He choked on the stench, but nevertheless dragged it back to Shatterbreath, letting it slump in front of the dragon's paws.

Shatterbreath snatched the body up in her jaws, sensing Kael's reluctance. Grabbing its legs with her teeth and holding tight it with one paw, Shatterbreath proceeded to yank the body out. With a loud, sickening *crack,* she wrenched the body out of the breastplate and let the metal fall to the ground. Then, being more careful, she pried the greaves and bracers off of the body. Finally, she threw the corpse itself aside.

"Now that that's settled, let us begin," she stated, cocking her head.

Kael stared at the five pieces of armour resting on the ground. He scrunched his face and wordlessly glanced up at Shatterbreath. She frowned at him, her eyes dark underneath her heavy brow.

"Fine," she declared, "you don't have to wear it right now. There's a lake on the top of my mountain. Later, go there and clean your armour. For now, I suppose we'll have to make do without."

Kael nodded. Shatterbreath slumped to the ground, lying on her side. She stared at him for a long time. Kael squirmed under her gaze. What was she playing at? Several minutes passed by where she didn't say a thing. The cave was silent save for the periodic of Shatterbreath's inhalations.

"I've decided," she said at long last. "Time is of the essence. I will teach you both at the same time. That way you can apply each study to each other as we go along."

Kael bit back his anger. She spent the last fifteen minutes thinking about just that? Kael hoped her thinking process wasn't always this slow. "That's fine. Just as long as we get going soon."

"No," Shatterbreath said quickly.

Kael twitched and waved his hand in frustration. "What? Why not?"

"Watch your tone, human!" Shatterbreath barked. Kael cringed. "I am tired right now. We'll wait until tomorrow to start. Is that alright with you?" Her tone was sweet, but her face still said otherwise.

Kael nodded, pursing his lips.

"Good," she said, complacent. "I thought so. Wake me in the morning."

With that, the great blue dragon rolled over onto her other side, making Kael stare angrily at her back. It wasn't even that late out! The sun was still creeping along the edges of the cave near the entrance. But there was no use arguing with a dragon, especially with this one...

With nothing to do, Kael stared at the walls for a while longer. He was curious about those glowing rocks. He hugged his knees, a sudden chill running through his spine as he spotted a bloodstain.

"Shatterbreath," he whispered. Nothing. He inhaled slowly, worried that he might wake the dragon and consequently make her angry. Was she even asleep or just ignoring him?

"Yes, Tiny?" the delayed reply came at last from the other side of her body. She lifted her head lazily, looking over her shoulder at him through a half-closed eye. Her voice and gaze were gentle. Right then, Kael's fear towards her melted away.

"Why do those stones glow?" Kael asked, pointing at one in the ceiling.

169

Without looking up, Shatterbreath yawned again, showing her pink tongue and glistening teeth. "Honestly, I have no idea how those rocks work. They're not from here, that's all I know. I took them from another cave."

Kael nodded, still gawking at the glowing stones. How mesmerizing they were. He hadn't really paid attention to them earlier. They flickered, as if in each one was a little roaring fire. They were beautiful, and shed a surprising amount of light into the depths of the cave.

"Where did you get them?"

Shatterbreath rested her head on her side. "I can't really remember. Some other deep cave. They're really nice, but I have to breathe fire on them every so often to keep them bright. Small price to pay, I suppose..."

There was something else hidden in Shatterbreath's voice. A deeper secrecy that was laced with pain. Kael could sense it. He didn't venture any farther as Shatterbreath turned her head away once again. She gave him a look that told him their conversation was over.

It felt strange to him, to have a full conversation with Shatterbreath. Mostly, it was just her giving orders or making comments and him more or less agreeing.

Bored, Kael stood up when he heard Shatterbreath's heavy inhalation. It would seem that she had fallen asleep already. He kicked a small rock on the cave floor, sending it skidding across the ground. It bounced off a small crook in the ground, flying several feet before landing. Catching up to it once more, he kicked it again, and again. Pretty soon, he found himself back at the mouth of the cave, staring into the thick fog that enveloped the mountain's peak.

Sighing, Kael picked up the rock, sizing it up in his palm. His shield was beginning to feel heavy, so he took it off his arm and swung it over his back in a more comfortable position. This view was disappointing, he wanted to see Vallenfend! The city was so small from up here, but so wonderful to behold, like a tiny, precious jewel. Upset, Kael hurled the rock off the mountainside. It careened downwards and out of sight.

Dropping all caution towards waking Shatterbreath, Kael took a deep breath, threw his head back and yelled as loud as he could, letting all his pent-up emotions escape at last. His furious howl echoed over the mountain.

Shatterbreath, from where she lay at the back of the cave, lifted her head off of the ground. Slowly, she turned to face Kael. He was unaware of her gaze. She cocked her head, curious to his behaviour. She licked her lips and swished her tail, an inner turmoil boiling. As the boy turned back around, she placed her head back carefully onto the ground, resuming her sleep.

Chapter 16

Shatterbreath laughed as Kael fell to the ground. She hadn't laughed in so long that the deep, thrumming sound resonating from deep within her chest startled her at first.

She was teaching him, as she had promised, how to fight and sneak. Right now she was teaching him how to defend against multiple enemies at once. It wasn't easy of course, to teach Kael everything that she knew. She had done her best to explain and now they were putting that information to practise.

Kael was scrambling in front of her, trying his very best to dodge all of the attacks she volleyed at him. She lashed out with both front paws, her tail, occasionally her mouth and even a back paw once. One zealous attack on her behalf had knocked him clean to the ground. He, other the other hand, didn't find it as funny.

"What are you laughing at?" he griped, scrambling back to his feet, a bead of sweat falling from his brow.

Shatterbreath stifled her chuckle, realizing Kael wasn't as amused as she was. She wasn't particularly impressed with his sharp complaint, but she would forgive him this one time. She nodded her head apologetically. "Sorry, Tiny. You fell in such a humorous way."

He muttered something rather impolite, but Shatterbreath overlooked it once again. After he had stolen a moment to catch his breath, they continued.

Shatterbreath would strike in rather predictable moments, trying to make him learn how to read an enemy's strategy. In return, he would lash out with his sword or block with his shield. When his blade did make contact, it hardly ever cut through her first layer of tough skin. But when he did strike a little too hard, a tad bit too deep for comfort, she would let him know.

Shatterbreath wouldn't admit it out loud to Tiny, but her stamina was incredibly low. Sure, she kept fit when she hunted, but when she started to train with Kael, she realized how out of shape she really was. The first day they practised, she could hardly keep up with the boy, let alone go on for a whole day. They stopped several hours before she would have liked to, her muscles sore and her body exhausted. But every day, she could feel her dexterity improving, her stamina returning to its youthful extent. Silently, she was grateful to the boy. He had awoken her from a lethargic, repetitive lifestyle she wouldn't have been able to shake. In a strange, distant way, he had *saved* her.

But being a proud dragon, she didn't say anything to him. She simply admired his eagerness with one beaming eye as he practiced day in and day out, occasionally applauding him.

She would have to do something nice for him later...

Teaching the boy how to sneak was a whole different story. Fighting was easy. All she had to do was swing her paws at him, but teaching that tiny bag of clumsiness how to sneak was out of her league. She tried to recall, had anything like this ever occurred in dragon history—a dragon, training a human? The very thought seemed humorous.

Basically, their sessions focussed on stealth would just be Kael trying to creep closer to her without making too much noise. She would give him the occasional advice, but that's all she could do to help.

Shatterbreath hunted for her small companion, bringing him all the fattest deer to feast on. She liked to watch how he insisted to cook it first, the small hunk of meat that she left over for him once she had her full. He patted a small tin can over it, sending a cloud of spices wafting through her cave. The substance tickled her nose and had an interesting, delicious smell to it. But after it made her sneeze, she decided quickly that she didn't like *spice* and had taken the can from him, hiding it, perhaps to give back later if she decided.

173

She liked to toy with him, but sometimes he became frustrated with her restless attitude and would give her a small shove in whichever leg was closest to her. It was playful, reminding Shatterbreath of a feeling she hadn't experienced in a while.

Sometimes, when Kael was fighting, she would see something else in him... As he batted at her paw, she imagined tiny claws instead of fingers... Soft, unused wings instead of blue tunic... A small figure with its rear end wiggling, ready to pounce mischievously...

On the fifth day the illusion was so strong, Shatterbreath had to tear herself away. She turned around abruptly and bowed her head, closing her eyes as she did. She curled up into a ball and hid her wings around her head, refusing to let Kael see the pain spread across her muzzle. The boy was getting better at reading her emotions while she was getting worse at deciphering his.

She listened carefully as Kael stood where he was for a moment. He walked over to her and tentatively placed his warm hand on the membrane of her wing. She flinched at the touch.

"Shatterbreath, what's wrong?" he said, concerned.

Taking a deep breath, she blinked a tear out of her eye. "Nothing, Tiny," she struggled to find the right words, struggled to control her voice. "A fit of fatigue has struck my old body. We will conclude for the day."

Shatterbreath remained silent. She heard the boy turn around and walk to the mouth of her cave and then out. He liked to explore the top of the mountain as of late, as if the answers he sought for would lie conveniently on top. She let him go, trusting he would return.

Kael recognized Shatterbreath's behaviour, it was similar to Korjan's, in a feral, animal way. She was hiding something.

The mountain top was the same it had been every day that week. Foggy and cold. Yet, he felt comfort on top. There was no cover for animals to hide and there was a cool touch to the air, a gentle kiss on his skin that the mist lovingly placed as he strolled along. He took a deep breath, feeling the crisp moisture in his lungs. He had been afraid of this mountain before. Now he rather enjoyed it.

He sat down on a rock, gazing up at the sky. The sun was trying its best to poke through the mist today. He took an extra-deep breath, still not used to the elevation. The lack of air was quite noticeable.

The tranquil moment became even more beautiful as the sun finally succeeded in its battle against the fog. A crack opened in the clouds, which let Kael catch a full view Vallenfend and the surrounding area. The city was bathed in glorious light, making Kael's homesickness return. Shatterbreath was getting more and more bearable each day, but nothing could replace the feeling of home, where everybody loved and respected him.

There was a certain respect that Shatterbreath had for him; there was no doubt about that. Malaricus's words were still stuck in his head though. *They're solitary creatures,* Kael said to himself as a fond image of Shatterbreath flashed through his mind. *She's only using you to figure out this plot. She doesn't actually* like *you.*

Kael pushed all thoughts aside. He didn't want to think about that now. He didn't want to think about his training. He didn't want to think about anything. All he wanted to do was enjoy the moment.

When he had his fill, he headed back inside. He paused at the mouth of the cave. He could hear Shatterbreath stirring inside. Crouching lower and tucking in his shirt to reduce noise as the dragon had told him, he moved silently along the edge of the cave, slipping in between the cover of the stalagmites. He froze as Shatterbreath repositioned herself where she was sitting. She was licking her right hind leg where Vert had slashed her. That wound really bothered her, although she tried to keep it a secret. She must not have known he was there because she feverously nursing it, which she wouldn't do in front of him. Kael had deduced that hated to show weak emotion around him.

Holding on to the edge of his shield to keep it as silent as possible, Kael dashed to another pillar, making barely a sound. The dragon looked up; her tongue stuck halfway out her mouth in a comical way, but decided the small amount of noise was nothing.

There were two more pillars between him and Shatterbreath, if he was silent enough, he could give her a good surprise. Holding his breath, he made his way painstakingly to the next pillar as silently as he could. He was impressed by his own skill, and to think, he had only been learning for five days now. Shatterbreath hadn't a clue what was going on.

He peeked around the corner. *Oh no, not this again.* The great dragon was gone. From the short time he hadn't been paying attention to her, she had disappeared, just like a whiff of smoke. Just like before.

But he knew better this time.

Keeping his back pressed against the stone, Kael worked his way around the stalagmite, surveying the area carefully. He didn't want her sneaking up on him again, or worse, to end up hiding against her leg like he had before.

Deciding it would be the best option, Kael walked right out in the open where she had been sitting. Keeping himself low, he darted his eyes around the cavern, trying to catch a glimpse of her claws or wings. She blended into this cave all too well.

A force gave him a big shove from behind. He sprawled to the ground and spun around onto his back. There was nothing there. His heart beginning to race from this silly game, Kael stayed where he was on the ground. He was focussing as hard as he could in the area where the shove had come from, but there was nothing there. Every crag seemed like a claw or cheekbone.

He yelped as something snatched his leg. It tugged on him, sending him sliding three feet across the floor. He gawked over his chest. It was the tip of Shatterbreath's tail. The tail unravelled itself from his ankle and then lashed out towards his torso. Before he could do anything, it wrapped itself around his body and hefted him completely off the ground.

Kael struggled to get free, but realized that would be a bad idea, so he let Shatterbreath lift him all the way to the ceiling and in front of her grinning muzzle. She had been clinging to the ceiling, upside-down, watching him. She turned him over so that her muzzle appeared upright in his view.

"You're getting better," she said, "a couple more days and I think you'll be ready to set off."

Kael nodded, holding on tightly to the rough tail, his face burning from the sudden rush of blood. He was struggling to hold his lunch down at this very awkward angle. "Can," he stuttered, "can you let me down now—nicely?"

Shatterbreath chuckled and released her grip. Kael screamed as he pitched towards the ground. Shatterbreath let go of the ceiling and caught him easily with her paw before she landed. She placed him gently on the ground, but the sudden excitement had made Kael dizzy and he collapsed.

"Come on, Tiny, we have work to do!" she exclaimed, her nostrils flaring in amusement.

Kael scowled at her.

Two days later Shatterbreath decided Kael's training was complete for now. Kael was ready to set off to find information. Which meant he was going to trespass into the castle. His stomach churned at the prospect. He couldn't help but to think that Shatterbreath's training had been...inadequate. Still, he was going to try and hope for the best. He had no other choice.

Kael picked up the armour he had cleaned. He was about to fit it over his head, but Shatterbreath stopped him.

"You better not put that on yet," she said.

Kael squinted at her, holding the rather heavy armour over his head. "Why not? Why'd you clean it in the first place then?"

"It's going to impede your stealth," she explained, her tail dancing across the floor. "You better leave it behind and save it for a time where you'll actually need its protection."

Kael put the armour back on the floor. "Well then," he said with a grunt. "I should get going"

"Wait," she said, "I have a better idea."

"What's that?"

"I can get you down the mountain much faster. And safer too. Would you like that?"

Kael sensed something more in her tone. "What's the catch?"

"Come on, Tiny, hop on my back."

Kael flinched. "Absolutely not!" he said, taking a step back. "I'm not riding you down the mountain. Uh-uh, nope. Never."

Shatterbreath took a step forward. Excitement twinkled in her eyes. There was a wild look on her features and her tail swished even more than usual.

"Why not? You should consider it an honour. A human being giving the privilege to ride a dragon hasn't been granted for centuries."

Kael shook his head, his stomach twisting. "No, heights scared me, and so does the very thought of flying. I'd rather walk and get attacked by a cougar again." He turned away and set a brisk walk towards the mouth of the cave, hoping she let him be.

Shatterbreath wouldn't take no for an answer. She leapt forward and Kael burst in a run as she bore down on him. In one smooth motion, she scooped him up. With him dangling by his tunic, she bounded to the mouth of her cave, Kael's screams going unheeded. Just before the entrance, she swung her head around, throwing Kael onto the crook of her massive shoulders.

Kael landed on his back, but quickly rocked himself forwards, careful to not impale himself on the sharp ivory spikes ridging her back, each one as large as his forearm. He clutched onto the spine in front of him as Shatterbreath prepared to jump. She landed on the very edge and flared her wings. Time slowed down. Kael felt every muscle in Shatterbreath's body flex and tense in preparation for flight. She raised her head proudly, aiming for the skies.

And then the next moment, she took off.

Pushing off hard with her powerful hind legs, Shatterbreath was airborne. Kael was buffeted by the sudden force of pitching forward so quickly and he was just barely able to hang onto the spine in front of him. Air rushed past his face, stinging his cheeks and making tears form in his eyes. The wind screamed in his ears, as if it was angry at him.

Kael was dimly aware of Shatterbreath's huge wings beating on either side of him. With every *whoosh* they made came another pummel of wind. Head down, Kael hugged the spine as hard as he could, trying to outlast this flight. How long was this going to take? How far were they?

Cautiously, Kael opened one eye just a crack, trying to catch a glimpse of anything down below. To his alarm, all he saw was blueness surrounding them. His stomach lurched. They were still *rising*.

"Ah, Shatterbreath, what are you doing?!" he screamed. "Send us down, not up!"

Kael could sense her elation before he could hear it in her voice. "Aha! Enjoy the moment, Tiny! Stop cringing like a frightened rabbit and throw your arms out! Breathe the fresh, crisp air out here! Feel the wind flow through your hair! Oh, this is bliss!"

She was so ecstatic that Kael had to try what she suggested. Reluctantly, he poked his head out a bit and sat up a little straighter. He squinted in the cool breeze and tried to forget his fear. He wasn't in danger; there was no reason to be scared.

He managed to work up some courage to loosen up. His grip relaxed—slightly, and he raised himself up even higher. Now that he was calmer, he noticed how wonderful the wind felt against his skin. Shatterbreath was right, this felt good.

He closed his eyes, feeling the exhilaration of this new adventure taking hold of him. He shuffled forward off of her shoulders and placed his legs more comfortably around Shatterbreath's thick neck, surprised how similar it was to sitting on the back of a horse.

"You better watch out," Shatterbreath warned over the din, "your legs will chaff pretty badly. Just kneel, or even stand up, if you're so brave. Don't worry about falling off, I have you, Tiny."

Kael did as she said. Shakily, he released his grasp on her neck with his legs, instead clutching on with his arms. She arched her neck, making his grip easier to maintain.

She beat her wings, sending them far above the land below. They had left the mist of the mountain a long time ago, so Vallenfend was clearly in view below. From where they were, higher than even the mountain range, the city was puny. Kael put a thumb up and the entire circle of the city fit behind it.

Kael laughed, his voice swiftly drowned out by the wind. Feeling happier than he had in a long time, Kael lifted himself into a crouch and wobbled for a second. Grinning from ear to ear, he stood completely up off of Shatterbreath's back.

She slowed down for a moment and consequently, the wind calmed down. Kael thrust his arms out. He was standing on top of a dragon, higher than the very mountains. Kael suddenly realized how lucky he was. How many people would ever get the chance to do this?

Suddenly, Shatterbreath pointed her great muzzle downwards and together they pitched. Kael stumbled backwards, but to the side as Shatterbreath rolled slightly to one side. He snatched onto her spine again, sprawled on her back.

His vision began to shake as Shatterbreath pointed her entire body into a nose dive. She tucked in her wings close to her side and they plunged into freefall.

An enormous whistle started up in Kael's ear. His heart began to race faster and faster as the ground grew larger underneath them. His fingers began to ache from holding on so tight. He could see the field of wheat below, just past Shatterbreath's horns. They were getting closer and closer. Pretty soon he could see people dotting the fields.

Excitement quickly turned to fear.

"Shatterbreath!" Kael screamed, pounding on her back. "Shatterbreath, pull up!"

The dragon wasn't listening. They came so close to the ground, Kael could see the frightened expression on one of the worker's face. As fast as she had pitched, Shatterbreath pulled out of her dive.

She beat her wings forward fiercely, roaring as she shuddered to a stop, several yards above the ground. Kael slammed into her back. Cupping the air with her wings, she rose back up to a more comfortable position.

Both Kael and Shatterbreath were breathing heavily as she caught a lazy thermal. Shatterbreath craned her neck to see how Kael was doing. His knuckles were white from holding on, and he still held a look of terror across his face. Dazed, he returned her gaze for a shocked moment as everything that had just happened sunk in.

All of a sudden, he burst out in laughter. Shatterbreath chuckled as well.

"Th—that was close!" Kael said through joyous tears.

Shatterbreath nodded. "My wings are so sore now, you have no idea!"

Kael laughed some more. "Well, next time you're going to do that, warn me, alright?"

Shatterbreath cocked her head and raised a brow. "No promises."

Kael patted her back affectionately. "That was fun, better than I thought it would be anyway. You really scared me on that dive."

Shatterbreath bobbed her head meekly. "I've gone higher. I'd show you some more tricks, but my wings are *really* tired. I need a break. Besides, I don't want you getting sick right now."

Although he was disappointed their flight was over when they landed, he was also very glad to have solid ground underneath his feet once again. Shatterbreath looked around to make nobody was watching before talking to Kael.

"Now, walk that way before heading into the city. They won't suspect you of anything. I just hope those people I nearly landed on didn't see you."

"Does it matter?" Kael said with a shrug. "They won't recognize me. Even if they do, I doubt they would do anything about it."

"Don't be so hasty to jump to conclusions," warned Shatterbreath, "if people find out you've been helping me, you'll find they'll be less loving towards you. As much as they hate your king, as you claim, they will probably hate me even more."

Kael nodded, taking her advice to heart. "Alright, how long do I have then?"

"Before I pick you up?" Shatterbreath scratched at her neck for a moment with a hind leg before continuing. "I'll fly here every day at different times. Just wait here and I'll come. Good luck, and stay safe."

"Understood. I'll see you in a couple days I suppose."

Shatterbreath nodded in agreement, turned and crouched to pounce into the air, but stopped. "Oh, and Kael."

"Yes?"

She glanced at the ground, embarrassed. "Could you bring me some medical supplies? My leg hurts badly."

Kael frowned. "Of course."

"One last thing." Shatterbreath hesitated.

"What, what is it?"

"I've been thinking that you need a little something extra to help you."

Confused, Kael asked, "like what?"

Shatterbreath took a deep breath. She licked her lips before speaking. "How about my vision?"

Kael blinked. "Your what?"

"My vision, of course. My sight. I want to lend it to you, Kael."

Kael shook his head, waving a hand through the air. "You're serious?"

"Oh yes. It is a little known fact that dragons can share certain abilities that we have, our vision being one of them."

Kael's heart began to beat faster. "R—really?"

Shatterbreath nodded. "I haven't done this before though. I hope it works. Stay still."

The dragon leaned in closer. She paused, her great muzzle hovering inches away from Kael's forehead. He could feel her hot breath as she exhaled, ruffling his hair. A chill ran through his spine as he looked into her wide, knowing eyes.

With a cock of her head, she moved in even closer and ever-so-gently touched Kael's forehead with her snout, closing her eyes as she did. Her body relaxed and a moment later a surge of energy flowed through Kael's body. He closed his eyes as well.

"Whoa," Kael muttered, exhilarated by the strange experience.

"Open your eyes, Tiny," he heard Shatterbreath say. "Look around."

A whole new world presented itself as Kael lifted his eyelids. He gasped. Never had the world appeared so beautiful! The colours of the field were so rich, so alive! The grass, the soil, it was all so crisp, so clear! Kael gazed around in amazement. Nothing seemed to be out of view. He could see miles in all directions without his vision becoming blurred and witness the smallest details that had remained unnoticed before.

The corners of Shatterbreath's lips curled into a playful grin. She blinked several times, rearing back as if something were tickling her nose. Her eyes where brown for a moment, just like Kael's, but slowly reverted back to their usual green. Her lips curled in distaste.

"You humans have such terrible vision, how do you cope with it?"

Kael laughed, interested by how intricate her features were now. "I've never known anything else."

"Well then, I'm glad you like my vision. Don't get to comfortable though, I'll be seeing you in a few days."

With that, she leapt into the air and beat her wings, sending a wave of air washing over him. He shielded his eyes for a moment as she flew into the sunlight. She roared as she flew off into the distance, back up the mountain. Her roar sounded exactly like the sharp clap of thunder when it's directly overhead.

Kael girded his pack tighter around his shoulders, thankful it hadn't fallen off during their flight. He had completely forgotten it was on his back the whole time! Face set in determination, Kael started off in the direction Shatterbreath had advised, still awed by how interesting and detailed everything was now. Even the simplest beetle was amazing to watch for a moment. Kael had to force himself to keep his head straight forwards because he kept getting distracted. He set his eyes on Vallenfend, which loomed far off in the distance.

This time, however, he wasn't so eager to head back home. He had to go trespass into the castle without being detected, which alone was a seemingly impossible feat. To make things worse, he didn't even know where to start. How would he get close enough to the castle to—?

An idea struck him.

A sly smile crept onto Kael's face. He knew just how.

Chapter 17

Kael leaned against a tree, leaning around the corner as to get a better view of the south-eastern gate. He was still plenty far away from the gate, but with Shatterbreath's telescopic vision, he could spy in the guards with ease, whereas there was little chance they could see him.

It was the same gate he used to pass through when he had worked out in the fields. He watched some workers enter. He wished he could just do the same, but his blue tunic, shield and sword would surely catch attention. The last thing he needed was attention. The guards, seeing a lone soldier, would be suspicious. Doubtless, they would apprehend him for questioning.

Kael furrowed his brow, pondering. A familiar creaking sound interrupted his thoughts. He swung around the tree, and cupped a hand over his eyes. He smiled as he spotted an ox-drawn cart filled with pallets of plums.

"Helena," Kael called out. He ran towards her, waving her hands.

Helena blinked in the bright light and squinted. She was wearing her hair in her usual messy manner. "Kael?" she said. She stopped her cart. "Kael! Now there's a face I haven't seen for a long time! How are you my boy?"

Kael grinned as he approached her cart. "I'm just fine."

"Just fine indeed..." She placed her hands on her hips. "Where have you been? You've had us all worried sick!" Helena paused to throw him a plum. "Heard talk you were out in the fields, heard talk you were in trouble with the guards. I even heard a rumour you had been drafted!"

Kael scoffed. "Do I look like I've been drafted? I was out in the fields. In fact, I'm just coming home right now for a brief visit."

Helena eyed him top to bottom. She pointed at the sword scabbard at his hip. "Working in the fields, eh? Well, judging by that, I'd say you *were* drafted." She interrupted him as he tried to reply. "And if you weren't, where'd you get that thing then?"

Kael winced. He refused to look down at his sword. "I, uh..." He scrambled to think of a lie. "I mentioned to my boss that I used to be Korjan's apprentice." Helena blushed at the mention of Korjan's name. "Knowing how excellent Korjan is at his work, my boss figured I'd have the same appreciation for craftsmanship." Kael paused to carefully place the plum back in Helena's cart. "It so happened that my boss thought I was a very hard worker. He was so impressed, he offered me his sword as extra pay."

Helena frowned. "And you accepted? Oh, Kael."

"I couldn't take no for an answer. He *insisted.* He didn't need it anyway, said if I didn't want his sword, I could trade it in for some coins instead."

"Well, that was awfully kind!" Helena put a hand to her chest, as if aghast that somebody would display such generosity. "But you still shouldn't have accepted. That looks like quite the sword!"

"Hmm, well... Speaking of generosity," Kael said, shifting his gaze, "can I ask of a favour?"

Helena gave him a look. "What?"

Kael pointed to the gates off in the distance. "See that guard over there?"

Helena stared at the gates. "No. Oh wait, yes, the one to the right?"

Kael hesitated. He had forgotten that the gate was too far away for Helena's vision. "Sure. I was wondering if maybe I could— could hide in your cart."

"What? Why?"

Kael kicked at a rock in the dust. Helena's ox shifted its weight. It seemed uncomfortable for pausing so long. "Faerd said something rude to that guard—something I'd rather not repeat. You know him. I was there at the time and even though I had nothing to do with it, that guard *hates* me. I doubt she'd let me in. I would just go to another gate if I wasn't so tired. It's been a long day." He dropped his shoulders slightly to corroborate what he was saying.

Helena considered him for a moment, her mouth partway open. "Sure," she said with a shrug. "Put yourself in between some crates and throw that blanket over you. I'll let you know when we're inside."

Kael let a grin spread across his face. "Thank you!"

He hopped on and shoved a few crates aside, placing himself in the middle of the cart. With some effort, he managed to conceal himself underneath a blanket in a way that he hoped didn't look suspicious.

With a snap of the reigns, the cart creaked forward. Kael set his jaw as the cart rumbled on the road. It wasn't the most comfortable ride, but it was an effective way to dodge the guards at the gate. Within ten minutes, they passed through the gate undaunted. The sounds of Vallenfend accompanied the groaning of the cart.

Kael's legs were starting to tingle when Helena pulled the blanket off of him. With a gasp, he sat upright.

"Comfortable?" Helena asked.

Kael shook his head and scrambled off of her cart. "Not one bit! Thanks, Helena."

The woman folder her arms with a sly smile. "Oh the trouble you kids get into."

You can't even imagine, Kael thought. "Yeah, can I ask another favour?"

Helena sighed and rolled her eyes. "What now?"

"Can we keep this our little secret? Laura doesn't know about our squabble with that guard. I don't want her to worry about it. She doesn't need any more reasons to worry about me."

Biting her lip, Helena nodded. "Of course."

Kael turned to leave. "I'll see you later, alright?"

Helena chuckled. "Of course. Have a good day, Kael."

He nodded and without further hesitation, set off towards his house. He hadn't realized how late it had become—or how tired he was. For what he was about to do, he wanted a full night's rest before he set off. He would need it.

Going to the long way home took more time, but Kael figured it was worth it. He weaved through the back alleys and took a few detours. He didn't want to chance seeing one of his friends. He had told them he'd be gone for a long time, if he returned to them in less than a week, they'd suspect something. He could only hope Helena was going to speak of their encounter to anybody.

Kael's house seemed to be waiting for him. He threw open the door and took a deep breath, expecting a warm, nostalgic feeling to wash over him. To his surprise and disappointment, he felt nothing. He studied his humble house. It was drab and unexciting, almost as if it was missing something.

Promptly, Kael undressed and slipped into his bed. He felt uncomfortable. It was as if his house was no longer *home*. It was just another building.

He fell asleep with a frown.

After Kael woke up, he left his house at once. He jogged towards the castle until he was only a few blocks away. He stopped and took a breath, leaning around a corner to catch a glimpse of the gates. It was the same young man guarding the gate as before, with the long scar on his face. Kael walked leisurely towards him. As before, the guard kept his head pointing at the ground as Kael approached. He seemed bored.

Without looking up, the young man spoke loudly to Kael. "What do you want?"

Wearing a confident smirk, Kael answered him. "I'd like in, please."

The young man finally looked Kael in the face. "What?" he said far louder than necessary. He scrutinized Kael for a moment, twisting his halberd in his grip absently. "You're familiar, do I know you?"

Kael sniffed, pushing the guard's pointing finger away from his chest. He raised one eyebrow as if the he thought the boy was crazy. "You should, I was recruited more than a month ago. If you were wondering, I *wasn't* part of the group that already left. If I was, why would I return?"

"Oh, alright," the boy said sarcastically. "How'd you get out then?"

"I took Sergeant Mahone's key, went to the back gate and got out. I wanted to have some *fun* before I leave." Kael winked at him.

The boy hunched over again, contemplating what Kael was telling him. "Why didn't you get in through the back?"

Kael's temporary personality faltered for a second. Luckily, the young man was still looking down. "They put different locks on the back doors," Kael lied, "I couldn't get back in through that way. So, I came here."

The guard considered him for a moment. With a sneer, he opened the doors.

Once again, Kael found himself inside the dusty confines of the castle's walls. He sighed morosely, remembering all the torment he had been put through before.

Dropping his fake overconfidence, Kael strolled over to where the archers were practising. He inhaled deeply, the reminiscent smell of the sandy grounds meeting him. He faltered as he came closer to Sergeant Mahone, who was standing near the archery range, surveying his students. Surely the archer would recognize him. What would he do then?

"Ahem."

The archer turned around. His white brows furrowed as he looked Kael top to bottom. "Yes?"

Surprised by the Sergeant's reaction, Kael hesitated. He quickly found his voice again. "Oh, uh, I—I'm a new recruit," he stammered.

Sergeant Mahone's white moustache twitched. "What? You're a little late, aren't you?"

Kael bowed his head sheepishly. "Yeah, um, I tried to hide away when they enlisted me. But I eventually came to my wits and well," Kael shrugged, "here I am."

The Sergeant inspected him for a moment longer. He squinted at him closely. Kael tried to keep his composure and stop the blood from flowing to his face.

"Do I know you?" Sergeant Mahone asked slowly, "you look familiar."

"I guess I have one of those faces."

He scanned Kael's face for a moment longer before he was interrupted by a familiar voice off to the side.

"I know why you recognize him." Larr, the smelly weapons master, waddled over to where the Sergeant was still staring at Kael, "this bugger owes me money. Isn't that right?"

Kael was about to retort, but Larr gave him a slight nod, raising one eyebrow. Kael closed his mouth, thought for a heartbeat and then spoke again.

"Ah, you got me," he gasped, as if he was disappointed. "I was hoping you'd forget."

The Sergeant turned confusedly from Kael to Larr, then back again. "You two know each other?"

Larr laughed, putting his arm around Kael's shoulders. Kael tried his best not to gag, disturbed by both the man's stench and his more noticeably disgusting features that Kael's new vision displayed for him. "Of course we know each other! Why, old friend, you know him too! Remember, before the recruitment, we went out for a drink? I played this bugger in a game of cards and won! I've been waiting for my money ever since."

He winked at Kael and then beamed at the Sergeant. "Isn't this lucky that he can finally pay me back?" There was a touch of warning in his voice, a tone Kael regarded with distaste.

The Captain scratched his chin thoughtfully. "Hmm, I suppose you're right. Well, you know how I am with faces." Larr nodded. Sergeant Mahone clapped his hands together. "Well then, it looks like you might already know a thing or two about swordplay," the Sergeant said, nodded towards Kael's sword. "Figure you might as well learn some archery."

Kael frowned and placed his hand on his hip as Larr let go of his shoulders. He had forgotten about his sword. He quickly looked back up and smiled. "Yeah, m'dad taught me how to use it. It's our ancestor's sword and I'm the only son in the family. He thought I should carry the blade into battle, considering our family name will die out after me." He put some sadness into his voice, trying to convince the Sergeant.

"That is a nice blade indeed." Sergeant Mahone sounded bored. He turned away. "Go join the rest of the archers; I'm going to go check on the foot soldiers on the other side."

With that, Sergeant Mahone briskly set off to the other side.

Kael sighed. That was a close one. It was a good thing Larr had come to save him. But there was the issue that Larr had recognized him. He turned to the smelly man and opened his mouth to speak. Larr interrupted him.

"Hey, don't worry about anything. I do recognize you, you were here before. I distinctly remember you going off to go fight."

"Why didn't you tell Sergeant Mahone that?"

Larr grinned like a sly coyote. "I figure the only reason a man would return to this place is to find something. Something, say, of value? I don't care how you managed to escape from the dragon, supposing you did climb up that mountain, and I don't care why you're back here—just as long as I'm rewarded for my silence."

Kael could feel his anger spike, but he remained calm. "So you're blackmailing me?"

Larr put his hands out defensively. "I meant what I said earlier to Sergeant Mahone. You owe me money. And please, don't get angry, I'm just a man of business."

"How can I be so sure you won't speak out?"

Larr raised his eyebrows. "Like I said, you can do anything you like, I don't care whatsoever. As long as I get something out of it."

Kael rubbed temple, tired from all this. Could Larr be trusted? It seemed as though Kael's only option was to trust the weapons master at the moment. "I can't pay you right now."

Larr frowned. "I suppose I have no choice but to tell Sergeant Mahone the real reason why he recognized you."

"No, wait," Kael said quickly, grabbing Larr's shoulder as he tried to turn away. "Listen, I—I'm going into the castle sometime...soon. I don't intend to steal anything, but rather find out anything useful for an...associate of mine. However, if I *do* find anything worth taking..."

Showing his yellow teeth, Larr smiled. "It's a deal then. I'll keep my trap shut, and I'll even find you a safe way into the castle if you bring me back something shiny."

Larr thrust out his hand. Kael hesitated. He was making an odious deal with a greedy man he hardly knew. If he accepted the offer, he would be hitting an all-time personal low. Dealing with crooks. How further away from his morals would he be forced to go?

Pursing his lips, Kael took Larr's hand in his own.

To his surprise, there was more to archery than Kael had thought. On his initial attempts, he was hardly able to get the arrow across the field, let alone stuck onto the target. On top of that, as if they were trying to prove something to the new boy, the rest of the young men were striking close to the middle each time. Whenever Kael shot an arrow, the two boys on either side would then let one loose, making Kael feel even worse.

Perhaps it was the fact Kael was new, or maybe it was his habit of inspecting his gleaming sword whenever anybody did approach, but the archers left him alone. He didn't mind though. He wanted to be let alone.

Kael spent all his time on the archery side of the grounds. However, both the foot soldiers and the archers would mingle for dinner. Kael did his best to stay unseen by the foot soldiers, getting his meal and leaving the building as fast as he could. On one occasion, he had stumbled directly into the other twin who had been left behind. Luckily, the boy kept his head down as Kael apologized, so the twin—Kael believe he was Horan—didn't notice who it was that he ran into.

During his lunch on the third day of being an archer, Kael met Larr in the armoury where they proceeded to organize their plan. Larr unfolded a large map out on a tabletop. Kael inspected the map closely. It was a layout of the castle with all its levels and rooms. Kael could even spot smaller, winding lines that represented tunnels underneath the building itself.

"Alright, as you should know by now, this is a map of the castle," Larr said. "Here's the entrance here, at the front," he pointed to a little rectangle on the far side of the map. "And here's the back entrance, the one that you can see if you poke your head out the door."

Kael placed his finger on the small rectangle, recognizing the outline of the castle's walls. "We're going in through there?"

Larr shook his head. "No, that's too obvious and well guarded. I've decided to find you a more discreet way in."

Furrowing his brow, Kael scanned the map. "What other way in is there, besides through the outer walls, which I'm sure are also guarded."

Larr paused for a moment, his finger hovering above the map. He squinted for a moment under the feeble light radiating in through a small window and then placed his middle finger down on the map. Where he pointed to, Kael could see nothing, even with his superb vision.

"I don't see anything," he remarked.

Larr grinned. "Exactly. A while back, I stumbled upon this entrance while I was cleaning the grounds. It was hidden under a wooden trapdoor, which, under centuries of weather, had become rotten and broken. I fixed the entrance up and hid it again, in case I needed a quick way in. It seems my discovery will have some use."

Kael's lip twitch. He didn't like Larr's greedy, detestable personality. The weapons master wasn't a person Kael enjoyed spending time with. Nevertheless, he was impressed by Larr's intuition. "That's perfect," he said.

Larr chuckled throatily. "Thank you. I just hope you are a very subtle person, otherwise you'll get caught for sure."

It was Kael's turn to smile mischievously. "I have some experience. Don't you worry."

"It is settled then. I'll get you in and let you gallivant around all you want in there, and you steal something of value for me. If all goes well, nobody will suspect a thing."

Kael shifted his weight, listening for anybody that might be coming near. "I have your word on this?"

Larr placed his hand over his heart. "You have my word."

"Good."

Kael stared at the map for a while longer, aware that lunch was almost over. He ran his palms over the many lines in the parchment. There were so many paths, so many hallways! It would be near impossible to navigate his way through there! How would he be able to find anything? He didn't say a word to Larr, but he could sense the man's gaze lingering on him.

Trying to break the tenseness, Kael asked, "how come Sergeant Mahone didn't know who I was? He recognized me, sure, but he didn't actually realize who I was. When I duelled the Captain, he was there watching. Surely he would remember me for that?"

Larr sighed. "We're an irregular lot, all of us who work here. The Captain had his...obvious issues and the Sergeant has a knack of forgetting every face that he sees."

"What do you mean?"

Larr rested his elbows on the table. "Sergeant Mahone is the type of person who hates having to say goodbye to people. Not just friends or family, but everybody he meets."

"That doesn't makes sense, why did—"

"Let me finish," Larr snapped with a scowl. Kael leaned back. "To compensate for all the loss around him, Sergeant Mahone built himself a kind of barrier in his mind. He forgets a face almost instantly. No matter how special or skilled a youth may be, he will not remember them. He's built a complete shield from all the recruits. He is as nice and pleasant as could be, but there's really no point getting to know him unless you're somebody who spends a lot of time with him."

Kael frowned. "Really? That's kind of..."

"Sad?"

"Yes."

Larr twiddled his thumbs over the map. "That's how things work in this blasted city. Zeptus works that way. If you haven't guessed, this operation we've got here isn't entirely effective."

Kael shook his head. "I've noticed all right."

Standing up off of his stool, Larr began to fold the map back up. "I'll meet you there tonight."

Kael tore his eyes away from a huge broadaxe handing on the wall. "Tonight? Okay, that's fine. Can I have that map to help me through the halls of the castle?"

Larr shook his head. "I had to go to some extreme lengths to get this, they don't just hand out secret castle plans left and right. You can find your own map or just find your own way."

Larr exited the building with Kael. When they were outside, he pointed to a section of thick bushes across the way. "There it is," he whispered with a slight nod. "I'll see you tonight."

Larr turned back inside. Kael looked to and fro to see if anybody was watching, then started back towards the archery range.

It wasn't the easiest thing to sneak out of the barracks, but Kael managed. As he slipped out of his bed, one boy did inquire to where he was going, but he lied to the boy, telling him he was going to relieve himself. The young man believed him and without any other interruptions, Kael was outside.

As he strolled over towards where Larr had said the secret entrance was, he gazed up at the castle, wondering why everything was so bright. He quickened his pace, worried that the cause might be somebody carrying a torch nearby. He calmed down as he realized it was just his new vision he wasn't used to. To his astonishment, he discovered he could see in the dark. This could play to his advantage; he wouldn't have to light any torches inside if he happened to stumble into a dark room.

Kael silently rushed over to where Larr had directed him to go when they had met during the lunch break. There was a large patch of bushes nestled in between the archery barracks and the entrance to the castle. The trapdoor was hidden somewhere in the tangle of bushes.

Larr was already there when Kael arrived. He flinched when Kael snuck up behind him.

"What in the—? Oh, it's just you. Don't do that to me, boy!"

"Sorry. Are we safe? Is there anybody around?"

Pulling a thicket of brambles aside, Larr shook his head. "Who would be out here at this time?"

Thieves and liars, Kael thought grimly. He peaked into the tangle of thorns. He couldn't see the trapdoor, and judging by how thick the brambles were, it was several metres into the thicket.

Pursing his lips and trying not to complain, Kael pushed partway into the bush. He glanced back at Larr, who raised his thumb. "Good luck, boy," he said, gently pushing the branch he was holding back into place.

Biting back the pain from the scratches and scrapes that the nettles gave him, Kael wormed his way through. An even thicker darkness surrounded him as the brambles nearly cut out all the light from the moon above. Kael's eyes soon adjusted and the dark didn't bother him at all. Now, if only Kael could borrow Shatterbreath's scales right now. Even as he thought about the colossal dragon, Kael didn't know if he should curse Shatterbreath for making him do this, or bless her for saving his life. He would think about it later.

The brambles were getting thicker and their thorns seemed to get longer and sharper. Tears welled in Kael's eyes as he felt their stinging points dig into his flesh all over his exposed body. He covered the still-raw scab on his face from where the cougar had slashed him as he felt a thorn slice it back open.

Blood dribbled down his cut and towards his mouth. He wiped it away, feeling anxious. This was getting unbearable! He was just about to turn back when he spotted something with Shatterbreath's keen vision. Something brown...

He shuffled closer and the brambles widened out to reveal a small gap just big enough for Kael to fit into without brushing against the brambles. In the middle of the gap was the trapdoor Larr had spoken of. Thankful for the small shelter, Kael paused before he opened the door. Suddenly, the reality of the situation gripped him. What if this was all a trap? What if Larr reported directly to Zeptus? What if there were twenty soldiers awaiting him in the tunnel beyond?

Prying open the handle to the one of the two doors, Kael looked inside. It was pitch black. Going down into the darkness would be better than going back through the brambles. The doors fit perfectly in the gap, both standing upright. Kael slithered down into the black expanse, head first. He gently closed the trapdoor behind him, submitting himself to an uncomfortable darkness. Even with Shatterbreath's vision, he couldn't see a thing.

Hands outstretched, Kael made his way through the cavern like a blind man, stumbling every once and a while as his feet struck hidden obstacles. There was a faint dripping sound somewhere that sent echoes through the cavern, but otherwise all was still. The familiar stench of wet earth made Kael curl his nostrils. Kael's breaths came up short. The air was thick and moist. After only half a minute, Kael felt panic setting in.

After stepping in a dank puddle, Kael finally caught a glimpse of light. Surprised by a sudden incline, Kael made his way towards the crack in the ceiling. He pressed up against the ceiling, running his fingertips along it. There was a hard object, a thick tile it seemed, just overhead. Light poured through two edges and Kael caught the faintest aroma of cooking food.

Bracing himself against the earthy, sloped ground as best as he could, Kael pushed against the tile. It lifted open a crack and Kael peered through. Torches lined the walls of a large, square room and a fireplace still smouldered in the centre. A huge cauldron hung over it. There were multiple shelves holding various types of food and counters still bearing the stains of last night's meal. He was in the kitchen.

Kael waited for a moment to see if the cooks were still there. This early in the morning, he doubted anybody would still be awake.

He shoved the slab of marble to the side. Pausing one last time, Kael hefted himself up and placed himself on the edge of the tunnel's entrance. He tore his dirt-caked boots from his feet and left them inside the passageway. He had loved those boots, but his muddy prints would give him away. It was time for a new pair of boots anyway.

Thinking for a moment, Kael pulled out his sword and, using a hand to stabilize his precision carefully, scratched the edge of the tile. Now he wouldn't have trouble finding out which one it was. The scratch was faint as well, so hopefully nobody else would think twice of it.

He was in the corner of the room, at the very back where large crates lay orderly against the wall. Luckily, one of the heavy boxes hadn't been laid over top of the secret entrance; otherwise he wouldn't have been able to get in.

Tip-toeing silently in his socks, Kael made his way to the front of the massive kitchen. He marvelled at the magnitude of it. He could imagine it in the daytime, thrumming with activity, people carrying around sweet smelling spices to put in the king's stew, freshly-slain poultry cooking over one of the fires of the many hearths. He could still smell the delicious aroma of whatever had been cooking in the cauldron.

Kael had to stop once he started to drool. There were other things at hand besides fantasizing about eating. In any case, he would never get the luxury of a meal prepared this way.

He pressed himself up against the door, took a deep breath and gently pushed it open. The hall was dimly lit by the moonlight flooding through one window on the opposite side, but otherwise the lavished halls were dark, the torches burnt down to stubs by this time at night. Kael welcomed the dark. It no longer bothered him.

He slipped into the hall, closing the door behind him, and taking a crouching stance, he began to work his way through the castle halls. His first objective would be to try and find where the guards in the castle kept their equipment. He needed new boots and another tunic.

Kael heard a noise, a faint shuffle from around the corner. Thinking fast, he squeezed in behind a suit of armour that was placed in a small niche at the side of the hallway. Holding his breath and staring at the picture across the way, Kael patiently waited for the person to pass by. Whether he was a guard, a cook or the King himself Kael didn't see, he was busy staring at the painting. Shatterbreath had told him that some people could sense when somebody was watching them, especially at shorter distances. If Kael didn't look at them as they passed by, there would be less chance they would notice him.

After the person had passed, Kael waited a few moments before extricating himself from his hiding spot. He peered back at the individual who had just passed. She was a cook, most likely heading towards the kitchen. If he had waited any longer, he could have been caught by her.

Saying a silent prayer to whatever gods rest above, Kael stole on.

He wove through the hallways, quieter than a mouse. This castle was immense! He couldn't believe how many times the hallway he would be following would branch off to yet another wing of the castle. Why the king would need such a grand castle was beyond him. He found the stairs, at least two separate sets, but he bypassed them, suspecting if there were living quarters for the guards, they would logically be located on the ground floor.

His foresight payed off and Kael found the guard's quarters. He crept up to the door, but paused, unable to think of how to get in without being noticed. He let his head droop in thought. Smiling, Kael bent down to what he had discovered, taking hold of the boots somebody had left outside the door. He snuck away to a more secluded part of the castle to put them on and quickly did so. To his surprise and extreme relief, they were a perfect fit. As for the tunic, he'd have to make do with the one he had.

Originally, he had been worried that the guards in the castle would have different-style tunics than the soldiers outside, but his anxiety had been for naught. At least two guards had already strolled, yawning, with boredom in their eyes. Still, Kael kept up his guard, staying as quiet as he could and keeping one palm on the pommel of his sword in case the occasion called for it.

It took Kael some time, but he found the one of the staircases he had seen before. He gazed up the spiralling escalade of stairs. He frowned. Unless he intended to climb up the outside walls of the castle, this was the only way up.

Gulping, Kael began to ascend the stairs, hoping dearly that there wouldn't be anybody going down them at the time. He must have been halfway when there came a shuffling from above. His breath caught in his throat. His body screamed for him to run back down, but it was too late. There was no way he could turn around without making some noise and consequently alerting the person of his presence.

His face contorted for a moment as he contemplated what to do. Straightening his spine and acting as bored as he could, he began to climb the stairs.

A woman garbed in a white robe, a cook, caught his eye as she passed. She smiled faintly and nodded a simply greeting to Kael. Returning the gesture, Kael sighed, feeling his body relax. Only a cook... Once she had past, he clutched the handrail for support. Only a cook! What else had he been suspecting?

Kael reached the next level. This section was less guarded than the ground level, so he guessed there wasn't anything of significance on this floor. He took the opportunity to catch his breath and let his heart calm down. Without incident, he made his way to the other end of the castle and climbed up a different set of stairs to the next floor.

Kael dashed out of the stairs and around a corner, pressing himself up against the wall. He heard a yelp come from the hallway that branched off to the right. He closed his eyes and smacked his head lightly against the wall. Somebody had seen him. He cursed himself for being so hasty.

Using the same, bored look as before, Kael walked around from the corner, giving whoever had yelled at him a full view. A guard holding a torch approached him.

"What's the hustle, soldier?" the man barked, he looked Kael head to toe, "why are you all jittery like that?"

Kael stared down at the man for a moment, lost for words. This guard was wearing a hauberk and a mail coif on his head. There was a patch on his right shoulder, signifying he had a higher level of authority. Kael groaned under his breath. The man bent in closer, furrowing his brow.

"What a moment, who are you? You're not in my ranks!"

In a flurry of movement, Kael drew his sword and held it up to the man's neck. He nodded for the man to walk towards a doorway just to their left. "Check if it's empty."

The man gave him a nasty scowl. Kael ignored it. "Do it," he demanded, pressing the tip of his blade harder into his neck. Any more pressure and the blade would break skin.

Lips pursed, the man turned around and opened the door. He stuck his head inside, and then pulled himself out. "It's empty," he stated, void of emotion.

"In, go in."

199

The man did as Kael ordered. The room seemed nothing more than a small study, a reading room for royalty. Still holding his sword to the guard's throat, Kael pulled his shield from his back and carefully strapped it to his left arm.

The man opened his mouth to say something rude, but Kael thrust his shield at him and bashed him in the side of his head. The guard fell limp to the ground.

Propping a chair up against the door handle in case somebody might chance to enter, Kael seized the guard under his armpits. Grunting, he sidled his way over to the corner of the room. Then he placed the guard in between a large bookshelf and an equally large couch. He took a few pillows and a blanket and draped them over the guard. It was a poor disguise, but it would suffice until morning—hopefully. Kael had a strange thought as he brushed against the massive couch. *How hard had it been to get all this stuff up here, anyway?*

Kael removed the chair holding the door shut and casually exited the study. Seeing nobody was near, he resumed his low crouch, trying to gain as much stealth as possible. A sense of urgency struck Kael. He was working against the clock now. It was only a matter of time until the guard he had knocked out woke up or somebody discovered him.

He moved down the hallway, checking each door fleetingly. It dawned on him that he didn't even realize exactly it was that he was looking for. It also struck him how much he could have missed already. All these doors, any of them could hold the vital piece they needed to finish this puzzle.

A beam of light protruded through a small window, casting a ghostly tendril through the hall that seemed to be reaching for the floor on the other side. Kael crept up to it and gazed out through the glass. Half of the city was in his sight, illuminated by torches that lined the streets. He paused there for a moment, appreciating the orange glow, but turned his attention closer. He opened the window and poked his head through, gazing upwards.

He was on the upper floor—that much was certain. There was a narrow stretch of wall above him which he guess must have tapered out to a point because he couldn't see any further. Off to the left, the wall bent at a corner and he couldn't see beyond that way either. To his right, however, the tallest spire lunged up at the heavens high above the rest of the castle. Kael couldn't explain why, but there was significance to that tower. It seemed to him if there was anything important, it would be in there.

Trying to get his bearing before he set off, Kael pulled himself back into the hall. Keeping his sword and shield at the ready, he made his way over to the spire. He stopped, however, as he came across a richly adorned set of doors. There were purple cloths draped on either side and the doors themselves were carved describing ravens, wolves and other nightly creatures. Kael placed a finger over a particular carving, feeling the smooth wood under his touch. A small, neat *Z* was traced in the middle of both handles to the door. Kael caught his breath. *Zeptus's study.*

Kael knocked on the rosewood door and placed his head close to it, breathing in its rich aroma. He could hear nothing on the other side. Kael didn't know if he should have been worried or relieved. Zeptus was the most powerful and most hated man in the city. "Then why," he whispered to himself, "are there no guards?"

Shaking his head, Kael took a deep breath and held it. Before he could second-guess himself, he grabbed the handle to the study and twisted it. He flung the door open, cast a quick glance to check there was indeed nobody inside and then closed the door behind him.

Kael gasped as he beheld Zeptus's room. Large, sturdy pillars of the same craftsmanship as the door held up the ceiling. Candlesticks of highly polished brass lay here and there, gleaming like gold as the white light from the moon flooded through a large, open window. Bookshelves that closely resembled the ones from the Athenaeum lined one wall, fitted perfectly together to leave no gaps. Off in the corner was another door that Kael guessed led to Zeptus's bedchamber and another which he guessed was the bathroom.

Small purple flowers that Kael didn't recognize sat in small vases, filling the room with their tart scent. It was no longer unsure whether or not purple was Zeptus's favourite colour, this room made that certain. But that wasn't going to help him.

He strode over to the great, mahogany desk, stepping around a large sofa. A gust of wind swept over Zeptus's desk as he sat down on the chair. Almost disturbing a chessboard that was on the table, Kael placed his palm down on a stack paper and was about to start rummaging through them when he noticed a large blue silk bag. It was the finest silk Kael had ever seen. He frowned and grabbed the bag, surprised at how heavy the contents where. He unfurled the top and reached inside. His hand felt something smooth and cold. He gasped and pulled it out. It was the diamond Shatterbreath had been talking about. This confirmed it, Shatterbreath had been right!

But this wasn't information enough. Kael already knew about the diamond. He shoved it back inside and placed it down on the desk. He needed more.

Turning his attention back to the pile of papers, Kael began to haphazardly search through them. He picked them up, one by one, scanned them to see if anything caught his eye, and then placed them in a different pile. Finally, something caught his attention. It was a folded piece of parchment as smooth as glass and as white as snow. There was an insignia of a hound with the letters *B* and *H* inscribed underneath. Kael unfolded the paper, his heart racing, and read the first paragraph.

Basal Morrindale, King of Vallenfend, sorry this payment is less than last time. We would have given you more but something arose. I'm sure you'll understand if we pay double at our next visit...

Kael jumped as he heard footsteps approaching. He quickly threw all the papers back onto the desk.

A million thoughts seemed to dash through his mind as the knob on the door slowly turned. Time stood still for a grim moment as he imagined the consequences for what he was doing. Should he hide? Should he attack whoever entered? Should he run past them?

Indecision and fear kept him rooted to the spot as Zeptus entered his study. The man caught eye of Kael and a wicked sneer spread across his face. He straightened his back and strutted over to Kael, standing a mere foot away.

"What are you doing in my study, *soldier?*" he barked.

The way he said 'soldier' so coldly gave Kael an idea. "I'm sorry sir, just—just doing my rounds, sir!"

Zeptus raised his brow. "Is that so? Don't you know this place is off limit? This whole tower is off limit!"

Kael shook in his boots, adding more fright than he was experiencing. He couldn't explain why, but he almost told Zeptus the truth about why he *really* was there. "I'm sorry, sir. I didn't know this place was off limits," he said foolishly, "me comrades down below, they haven't quite taught me the routes yet. I didn't know, I swear.

Zeptus eyed him top to bottom. "You're new, I take it?"

Kael nodded furiously, pretending to be as ignorant as he was sounding. "Of course, sir."

With a wave of his hand and a slight flourish of his robe, Zeptus dismissed him. "Be gone with you then, and consider yourself lucky I don't punish you for your impudence."

Kael bowed. "My thanks, sir," he grovelled. He made his way to the exit. "You're most kind, sir. I won't come here again."

Zeptus scowled at him angrily, his nostrils flaring. "See that you don't."

Kael nodded one last time, avoiding the advisor's violet eyes and slipped out of Zeptus's study. Once outside, Kael shut the double doors and leaned up against them. That was far too close. He couldn't believe he had just gotten away with that.

Kael made it half way through the hallway before Zeptus burst out of his study. "Guards!" he shouted, sending unpleasant echoes through the cramped hallway. "Intruder!"

Before Zeptus had even screamed the second word, Kael had sprinted forward. He dashed through the halls, giving up all hope for stealth. Right now, all he wanted was to get away.

A rustle came from behind and Kael chanced a look. He yelped in surprise. There were two darkly-clad figures already in pursuit. By the style of their clothing and the bulk of their bodies, they weren't regular guards.

He ducked as one lunged forwards with surprising speed, a blade sprouting from the depths of his clothes like a stinger. The blade sunk into the stone beside Kael's head, chillingly close.

With a sound that resembled a growl, Kael slashed his sword at the figure. The blade sliced through the black cloth of the figure's outfit and Kael felt it sink into flesh. The figure groaned and slumped to the ground. Kael stared at his sword in shock for a moment before another figure took the first one's place.

Holding out his shield in a defensive stance, Kael braced himself for an attack. The figure scowled at him through the folds of his cloak, just his blue eyes visible. Kael faltered, recognizing that stare.

"K—Korjan?"

The eyes twitched in confusion under the cloak for a moment before the figure attacked. Kael blocked the blade that twisted out of the figure's sleeve and followed through with a kick to the man's chest.

Rather than trying to avoid it, which Kael suspected the man could with ease, the figure let Kael's kick hit him and he sprawled to the ground. Kael dashed in the other direction.

Right now, nothing mattered more than to find the stairs. But for the life of him, Kael could not find them in this labyrinthine level. He ran through hallways, turning at random branches in some vain hope that he would eventually find the way. The thought of those dark, sickly blades and the shadowy figures kept him from thinking straight.

Kael flew around a corner. There was a guard midway through the hallway, guarding a door with a heavy metal padlock. He wore a dark blue tunic and his body was thicker than the guards down below. Judging by the depth of his chest, Kael expected he was wearing a hauberk. Kael raised his shield and despite the armour barrelled through the man like he was an unlocked fence.

The man's face scrunched as he smashed against the thick door he was guarding. The force of Kael's tackle was so strong, the door cracked across the middle and the top hinge was wrenched from the wall. Kael would have then continued forward, but he skidded to a halt as his superior vision espied something irregular through the crack in the door. Something shiny.

Double-checking to see if the man he had just clobbered was indeed knocked out, Kael turned towards the tall, heavy door. Whatever had caught his eye was through there. Kael pulled against the door, but the padlock kept it shut. He twitched as he heard a noise somewhere. Kael set the tip of his sword in the lock's bar, adjusted his grip and braced his sword against the door's handle. With a fierce shove, the lock broke free, skidding down the hallway. Kael flung himself into the room.

His jaw dropped as he entered. He thought Zeptus's study was grand, this display made the advisor's room look as humble as Kael's little house.

The room was filled with treasure. Crates were stacked halfway to the ceiling, with smaller chests scattered about the room. Here and there, the tops of crates were open and the lids to the chests folded back, showing diamonds, rubies, pearls and a great abundance of gold. There was so much treasure! Kael wouldn't have believed such a wealth was possible if he hadn't seen it with his own eyes. He walked in between the stacks, where gaps in the crates displayed the telltale glimmer of gold and silver.

Now it was clear why King Morrindale didn't charge high tax prices. What need did he have for the citizen's petty gold when he had all this? But this discovery, rather than clearing up anything, set a new question in Kael's mind. *Where had all this come from?*

There was a pile of gold set at the back of the room where it appeared as if several of the crates had fallen over and smashed open. The pile glittered at him, seeming to be alive and breathing. Kael moved towards it, dumbstruck. With just an armful of the treasure, he could be richer than a nobleman! He would never have to work again. He could help pay for all the Stockwin's needs and ensure all of his friends' safety and comfort. With that gold, he could...

Kael shook himself, remembering that he was still in danger. He pulled a sack out of the nearest pile, sending a sprinkle of gold coins cascading down the hill of treasure. He craned his head, worried that somebody would hear. He peered into the sack, which was filled with precious stones. There was extra room left over, so he stuffed a gold idol of a cat into the bag as well.

Kael heard some noises. A soft whisper, the creak of a broken door. He skirted around the pile of treasure and settled down at the base of it, crouching low and placing a hand on the floor, careful not to disturbed the coins scattered by his feet. As he did, the door burst open, wrenching from its hinges and clanging to the ground. A moment later, several men clad in black entered. They peered around the room, their hands outstretched and ready to seize their weapons.

Sword at the ready, Kael took a slow breath through his mouth, watching the black-clad soldiers. He was impressed by their stealth as they meticulously made their way through the room. They moved with the grace and efficiency of prowling wolves, wasting no energy with quick, useless movements as they scoured the room.

A soldier bumped into one of the crates, spilling some gold coins onto the floor. Kael cocked his head, interested. Kael had forgotten that with Shatterbreath's vision, he could see in the dark, and they could not. This could work to his advantage.

A flicker of light came from the other end of the room and a soldier wearing blue walked in with a torch. He had an anxious look on his face as the soldiers in black turned to give him orders. Obviously, the men clad in black were not part of the regular guard force. The man with the torched took a few steps and lit another torch that was resting on a pedestal. The room was soon filled with the soft glow of two burning torches.

As the one holding the flame made his way around the room, lighting more torches, his comrades stood where they were, throwing their heads to and fro, hoping to catch any glimpse of their intruder. Kael crouched lower; there was no he was getting out without a fight.

The man with the torch neared closer, Kael held his breath. The man stopped just a few feet away from where Kael hid and paused to light another torch. Getting up slowly, Kael's free hand brushed against the gold coins lying on the floor, making a slight noise. It was enough. The man turned his head and looked right at Kael.

With a cry, Kael cut the torch in half with a diagonal backslash. Startled, he dropped the handled and both halves of the torch fell to the ground. Before either landed, Kael followed through with his attack and struck the figure in the side of his head with his closed fist. The man fell to the ground in a heap.

The others were instantly alerted.

Kael just barely managed to block an attack that was directed at his chest and parried another with his sword. Three of the figures began to all attack him at once. As he managed to hold his own against them, Kael was suddenly grateful for Shatterbreath's training. He hadn't thought it had done much for him, but now he could see. These men were much better trained than the soldiers down below and Kael struggled to stay alive.

He blocked one attack and, getting desperate from weariness, plunged his sword through the man's foot. He had wanted to refrain as much as possible from harming anybody, but he had no other choice. The man fell back with a cry, clutching his bleeding foot.

Enraged by his comrade's injury, another man lunged out zealously. Kael was preoccupied with another blade, so he didn't see the sword until it was inches away from him. It was too late to block the attack with his shield, so with a yelp, he tried to sidestep it.

A cold sting rushed into Kael's body where the blade struck his flesh. He winced as he noticed blood on the figure's sword as he pulled it free from his tunic. Shocked at the sight of his own blood, Kael pushed himself harder.

Not a moment later, another blade bit into his left shoulder. Time slowed down as pain shot through his upper back. He twisted around and wrenched the blade free and kicked the man who had stabbed him. The black-clad man stumbled back a step and Kael took advantage. He slashed the man across his chest with one stroke and turned his attention towards the last soldier standing.

With a wild cry Kael lunged forward. His attacker backed off, startled by Kael's sudden ferocity and tried to block. Instead of striking at him, Kael sprinted past him. The man spun on his heel, ready to engage in pursuit. But Kael had stopped running.

A loud and painful *crack* resonated through the room as Kael struck him in the side of his head with the flat of his blade. He slumped to the ground, unconscious.

Kael dashed out the door and into the limited safety of the hallways.

When Kael reached the staircase, he threw himself down it, nearly tripping as he did. He barrelled into a guard wearing a blue tunic, sending him sprawling down the stairs. Kael literally ran over the young man as he worked his way down the stairs, eager to leave this place as soon as possible. The scenario rushed through his mind as he ran down the stairs three at a time. He would sprint back to the secret entrance and if he couldn't reach there, he would simply barge through either the front entrance or the back and then high-tail it back to the field where Shatterbreath would hopefully be waiting.

Huh, safety at a dragon's cave. Kael shook his head. Now was not the time for idle thoughts.

The last step caught him by surprise. His ankle buckled and Kael lost his balance. At an uncomfortable speed, Kael fell head over heels. As his shoulder hit the ground and his body went limp, the world around him slowed to a crawl. He became unnervingly aware of the situation as his shoulder cracked on the stone underneath. His face scrunched up from the pain and from the frustration of being unable to stop what was happening. His gaze spun upwards and he saw, as clear as day, a gleaming sword slicing above him, right where his neck should have been if he had not fallen.

Time returned to its normal pace with a jolt. Kael rolled at least once more before coming to a complete stop. Although his body screamed at him to stay still, although his shoulder ached and his head throbbed, Kael forced himself into action. He somersaulted forwards onto his feet and swept his leg in a wide arch, tripping the dark soldier who had tried to decapitate him not a moment earlier.

Kael was off again.

He found himself running through a hallway, clutching his shoulder haphazardly with his shield arm. He could feel blood and sweat drenching his shirt, but he did he best to ignore it, instead glaring down the hallway, ready to act if anything arose.

Shatterbreath's vision caught a flicker motion from the other end of the hall and before the guard could round the corner, Kael tackled a door to his right and slammed it behind him. There was a lock in the door, so he quickly turned the little piece of metal, pressing his ear up to the door and held his breath. Footsteps echoed through from the other side, starting quiet and working up loud. The footsteps went quiet again as whoever was on the other side kept going down the hall.

Kael caught his breath and turned away from the door. His mouth dropped open. This wasn't good. At once, he knew whose room he was in.

Elaborate furniture filled the room, from the massive four-poster bed, to a gigantic mirror hanging on the wall, with a fat oak dresser resting underneath. There were flowers in vases spread at random in the room, which was painted a mahogany red. There was no doubt. This could only be the princess's room.

Kael had heard stories about her, Janus Morrindale. Somebody had told him that the king neglected his daughter. Instead of spending time with her, he chose instead to let servants attend to her every whim, so she always got what she wanted. King Morrindale was also overly-protective. He never permitted to let his daughter leave the castle and because of this, Janus had little social experience—especially around men.

The room held a strange smell to it. Probably due to the many bottles of perfume on top of her dresser. Whether the smell or the fact that Kael couldn't tolerate spoiled children, he didn't want to spend any more time in the princess's room that was needed.

Kael sheathed his sword and turned back to the door. The guard he had bypassed would have been gone by then. Just in case, he pressed his ear up against the door. Wincing, he drew away. He had heard voices. From the high pitch and indignant tone, Kael guessed Janus herself was coming back to her room. She wasn't alone.

Kael put some distance between him and the door. He scanned the flowery room warily, searching for a means of escape. The window! He rushed over and flung it open. A lofty vertical drop met him. Kael spun away from it and put his hands to his head at a loss. He espied something beside him. In the corner of the room, there was a screen used for changing. It was partly folded up and leaning close to the wall, a long blue dress folded over it.

Shaking his head, Kael pulled himself behind the screen and opened it up. His disguise was horrible; he was completely exposed from one angle. Janus would surely notice him. He closed his eyes, saying a silent prayer. There was nothing he could do now.

The door opened up.

"Janus, stop all this. You've stayed up too late already." Kael let out a hopeless sigh. *Not King Morrindale!* This night was getting worse by the minute.

"No, daddy, tell me what the excitement is about!" Kael cringed at Janus's voice. It was so shrill! "There's something going on. You're not fooling me!"

Kael leaned forward. There was a slight gap where the screen was bent. He could just see King Morrindale through it. The king was standing in the middle of the room, holding his daughter's shoulders. She wasn't facing Kael, so he couldn't see her face.

"Janus," the king said, his voice warm. "Don't you worry about a thing. There's nothing going on. I just want you in bed. You know I don't like you roaming around the castle at night." King Morrindale waved a finger at her. "Especially when you're pestering the guards. They have better things to do."

Kael listened intently. Perhaps he had been wrong about King Morrindale and his daughter. The look in the king's eyes didn't seem like neglect. Although it appeared as though Janus's issue with men was quite real.

There came a knock at the door. Kael repositioned himself so he could see. A tall, gaunt figure entered. All Kael needed to see was the purple of the man's cloak to know it was Zeptus. Kael leaned away from the screen, biting his lip.

"Basal, the perpetrator has not been apprehended yet," Zeptus said. Kael ignored the urge to clear his throat. "I advise you retire to your quarters immediately."

"Thank you, Zeptus," King Morrindale said, "for assuring my daughter she was correct about an intruder."

There was a moment of silence and then a shuffle. Janus was moving towards her bed. Kael held his breath. If she looked his way...

Janus sat down at the foot of her bed in one smooth motion. Kael now had a few view of her features. Her hair was cut short, straight and was a similar colour to fresh corn. She held a particular beauty that few seemed to find appealing, but by no means was she an ugly girl. Her face was longish and her eyes where positioned in such a way that her face vaguely reminded Kael of a donkey's. She stared forward intently as a new man entered. He stocky and garbed in the same black clothing as the other soldiers Kael had avoided. He didn't say a word.

King Morrindale spoke. "Why has the intruder not been caught?" Kael peered through the screen. King Morrindale glanced back at his daughter and then walked towards the door.

Zeptus muttered something, but Kael couldn't hear.

"What are you doing to find him?" King Morrindale asked, stopping a foot away from his advisor. If he was trying to speak soft enough that he daughter couldn't hear him, he wasn't doing a very good job. "I don't want some vagabond running amuck in my castle."

Zeptus nodded. "We're doing the best we can, Basal. He seems to have...*disappeared.*"

The king cocked his head. "You're really upset about this intruder, Zeptus. Do you have something personal against him, or are you still bothered that I beat you at chess?"

Kael cringed. The king played Zeptus at chess, *and won?*

A harsh sneer spread across Zeptus's gaunt face. "Hardly. The intruder rummaged through my personal documents. I think it's in *your* best interest that he is caught and interrogated. He may have attained vital information."

Morrindale waved his hand. "Don't worry, we'll catch him alright."

"You'd better hope so." Zeptus nodded at the man in black standing beside him. "Jobra, double your efforts."

The thick man gave a short bow. Kael couldn't see all of his face, but his eyes were dull, listless, as if he was incredibly bored with the scenario. King Morrindale stopped the man before he turned to leave. "You're the leader, right?" he said. "Get a guard positioned outside my daughter's room immediately, I don't want any..."

Movement caught Kael's attention from the corner of his eye. He completely forgot about the conversation. Janus had spotted him. She gawked at him, eyes wide, body rigid. Kael put a finger to his lips. Her expression softened and she seemed to size him up. Then, with a flick of her neck, she faced forward once again, acting as if nothing was out of the ordinary. A sly smile played at the corner of her lips. She folded her arms over her lap. Kael let out his breath. Whatever the reason, she wasn't going to say anything.

Janus twitched. She stared at something at the floor. Kael followed her gaze. His heart sank. There was a spot of blood staining the carpet. Kael put a hand to his chest where he had been cut. There was blood on his hand when he removed it. He could feel blood oozing down his back as well, where his shoulder had been slashed. He was bleeding all over!

With a flourish, Janus stood up. "Enough of this," she cried, taking a step forward so that she hid the blood spot underneath her nightgown. "Get out of my room, all of you! I need my beauty rest."

Zeptus's expression was less-than-pleasant, but the king nodded gently. "Of course, my dear. We will leave. Have a good night."

"Thank you, daddy," Janus said. Promptly, King Morrindale, Zeptus and Jobra, the man in black, exited. Now, it was just Kael and Janus.

Kael waited a moment before coming out from behind the dressing screen. "Thank you, uh, Princess," he said with an awkward bow. "Thank you for not screaming."

Janus laughed, sounding more like an irritated bird than a mirthful young woman. White teeth glimmered in between her pink lips. Although Janus was roughly Kael's age, she seemed very childish. Kael would have expected that a princess would be more mature. She kicked at a scuff in her carpet and bit her lip.

"You're welcome," she said, beaming. Janus walked over to her dresser and scoured over her many bottles of perfume. She picked up a silver comb and began running it through her hair. She continued to stare at Kael, amazement twinkling in her eyes.

"I, uh..." Kael coughed, feeling quite awkward. Janus didn't say anything—just staring. Kael remembered his wounds and clutched his stomach. "Ah, I'm bleeding all over, I'm so sorry! I should...be on my way. Is there any way I can repay you?"

Janus stopped combing her hair and instead played at a seam in her nightgown. "You could give me a kiss."

Kael grimaced. "Excuse me?"

Janus blushed. "Just a small kiss. A peck on the cheek, that's all I want. No harm in a kiss..."

"W—why didn't you alert the guards when you saw me?" Kael asked, trying desperately to avoid the payment she had just suggested.

Janus took a step towards him. "Well, I thought you were handsome. I don't meet many handsome men. I've never been kissed by a handsome man."

Kael tried his best not to gag. There was no avoiding this situation. The least he could do for Janus was give her an innocent little kiss. The very thought revolted him. Still, he leaned in close. She closed her eyes. Kael pressed his lips against her awaiting cheek. Her pale skin was cold against his chapped lips and he withdrew quickly.

Janus giggled.

Kael, not wanting to draw out the moment any longer, made a swift movement to the window. "Well then, I—I'd best be off."

Janus gave him a longing look. "Of course."

Kael leaned out the window again. The drop was just as high as it was before. He noticed this time that the castle's wall was just underneath Janus's bedroom window. If he had a rope, he could climb down onto it and escape. Torches burned along the wall's length. There were a few guards, but Kael was positive he could make his way past them.

Now, about the rope...

Kael noticed a pile of large sheets resting nearby. He scooped them up. "Can I borrow these?" he asked Janus.

"Anything you want," she said, fluttering her long eyelashes at him.

Kael quickly tied one end of a sheet to Janus's bedpost and threw another over his shoulder. Checking to see if it would hold his weight, Kael inched his way over and out of the window, holding on for dear life to his improvised escape rope. He paused.

"Princess, I have one last question," he said over the windowsill.

"Yes, handsome?"

Kael hesitated, disturbed by what she had just said and the tone in which she had said it. "Your father mentioned he had beat Zeptus in a game of chess. Do you know if that's true?"

Janus smiled. Kael marvelled at the whiteness of her teeth. "No, silly. Daddy hates it when people patronize him. Zeptus is no fool; he would not let my father win on purpose. He's beating Zeptus fair and square. But there are the times he loses..." Her voice trailed off.

Kael pondered her words. *Fair and square.* Surely Zeptus was a mastermind. The fact the king could beat him in a challenging game of chess was disturbing indeed.

His grip faltered, bringing Kael's thoughts away from chess. He tightened his fists around the soft cloth. "Thanks again, Princess," Kael said, lowering himself.

"Farewell," Janus's voice followed him down the improvised rope, "handsome."

Kael shuddered. He was sure glad that was over.

He grappled his way down the blanket until he thought he was low enough to land safely. Letting go of the sheet, Kael bent his knees carefully as he landed, making hardly a noise at all.

Just then, he noticed a guard stationed on top of the wall. The man was looking out over the training grounds, leading against the edge. Kael snuck up behind the man and smacked him with the pommel of his sword, letting the body slump at his feet.

Kael tied the other sheet around his shoulders to a torch set in the side of the battlement, and repeated the process he had just done. He was only halfway down the sheet when he heard a loud snap from above. His rope suddenly went limp and he careened to the ground. He landed heavily on his back, his rope falling beside him, the other end still tied to the broken end of a torch. He wheezed and rested let his head go limp against the ground.

The weariness that had been kept at bay by his adrenaline suddenly engulfed him and Kael succumbed to unconsciousness, the rope still caught in his clutches.

Chapter 18

Kael awoke with a sharp pain across his face. He yelped in surprise, his body as tense as steel. He groped for his sword, but realized it wasn't there. A strong arm grasped his shoulder and forced him back down onto the bed.

"Ah, you're awake!" Larr said in a gruff voice. "It's about time. Sorry I had to slap you to get you to wake up. You were sleeping like the dead!"

Kael rubbed his face with a scowl, doing his best to ignore Larr's heavy stench. A stab of pain made his arm go limp. He gingerly lifted up his tunic partway to see his left shoulder. It was all bandaged up, the gauze painted maroon.

"You got in quite a bit of trouble there, boy. I thought you said you was going to be sneaky about it, eh?"

"Well, desperate times call for desperate measures." Kael patted his waist. The sack that held his treasure was gone. "Did you like what I picked out for you?"

Larr beamed. He sat down on a chair with a large cloth in his hand. He seemed to be rubbing something underneath the fabric. Kael looked around as the man spoke. They were in a small room, darkened by curtains and smelling as bad as its owner. It was a simple room, with nothing more than the chair Larr was sitting in and the bed Kael was lying on.

"Very much so, thank you dearly."

"No problem." Kael winced in pain as sat up in the bed. His body ached all over and there was a burning sensation across his chest where he had been slashed. It too was bandaged up.

"So," Larr ventured, bringing whatever was inside the cloth closer to his face. "Did you find what you were looking for?"

Kael shrugged, bringing another sting across his shoulder. "I suppose. I have to relay what I've...recovered to my accomplice."

Larr frowned. "And who would that be?"

With a glare, Kael was quick to answer him. "None of your business."

Larr chuckled. "Of course." He paused to admire whatever was in his hands. "This thing you picked up for me, it's like nothing I've seen before." Kael realized the object he was polishing was the cat idol he had stolen from the treasure room.

"How so?"

"The craftsmanship, the detail, just everything about it is foreign to me." Larr paused, letting a fold of cloth droop, giving Kael a better view of the little golden cat. Indeed, it glimmered like no metal Kael had ever seen. "I don't consider myself a master as this sort of thing, but I've spent enough time around gold to know this is beyond anything Vallenfend goldsmiths could make."

"So it's foreign?"

"Foreign?" Larr scoffed, "this thing might not even belong to our continent! The skill, the precision, it's baffling! You picked me up something very nice indeed." He scratched his stubbly chin. "Where'd you say you got this then?"

Kael shot him a glance. "I didn't." He stood up and gathered his things, including his sword at the side of the bed. "Thanks for mending me and for your help. I have lots to think about and I should take my leave."

"I would imagine so. The castle is buzzing with activity like a wasp's nest, they don't want to admit it to the public yet, but they are furious that you escaped. I heard you had a run-in with the king's daughter, and that she alone is the reason for your escape."

Kael nodded. It hadn't taken them long to figure out that Janus had helped him escape. "In truth, that is what happened."

Larr smiled, the gap in his teeth profound. "That's impressive. You're lucky I'm not interested in the reward they're going to put up for your head soon then."

Kael's heart skipped a beat. He wheeled around, his shield in hand. "What?"

Larr leaned back on his chair, inspecting his treasure. A glint of light flashed across his face for a moment. "Well, you gallivanted through the castle, ran away from the king's daughter. Naturally

217

they're going to want to bring you into justice. Plus, I understand that running away from a dragon has a nasty consequence indeed."

Kael swallowed. There was no room for delay now. He would have to leave the city at once without any stops along the way to see his friends. Strapping his shield to his back and sheathing his sword, Kael gave a brief bow to Larr and opened the door.

"Take care," the man called to him as he left. He chuckled deep and throaty, his voice echoing in Kael's mind. Kael shivered.

Larr's room, or house, or whatever he lived in, was at the very back of the armoury, so deep in the wall of the castle that Kael was surprised in didn't cut all the way through. As he made his way through the armoury, he was shocked to learn that it was dark out. *How long had he been out for?* An hour or a day? *Oh well,* Kael thought with a shrug. It didn't matter how long he had been out for, just how fast he could get out of Vallenfend.

Kael stuck his head out of the armoury. He had been checking to see if he could borrow some better armour from Larr, but all he could find was the shoddy leather armour. He had seen a chainmail hauberk, but it had been too small for him. Perhaps he could scrounge some in Shatterbreath's cave, as distasteful as that would be.

Under the cover of night, Kael stole through the castle's inner grounds, making it to the gate in a matter of seconds. He stopped as he noticed a large padlock on the gate.

At first, he thought of simply cutting the lock off, but he decided otherwise. The noise would draw too much attention and that would only dent his sword.

Kael went back to the armoury.

Larr was still inside. He wasn't polishing his new treasure, but meandering near the back, as if to protect it from any shifty people. He scrutinized Kael with his good eye. "What are you doing back here? Shouldn't you be gone by now?"

Kael ignored his sudden curtness. "I need some rope, do you have any? Oh, and a bow and a quiver full of arrows would be nice."

Larr huffed. "I wouldn't usually give you either but I am *most* pleased with what you gave me. Here, one moment." Kael waited patiently as Larr fetched what Kael had asked for from various places in the armoury. "There you go, youngin'. Now, go for real this time."

Without saying goodbye, Kael walked out the armoury and to the stables. The doors, to his relief, weren't locked. Spotting the staircase that climbed up the atrium of the large pillar, Kael checked to see if there was anybody near. There wasn't, so he ascended the stairs.

Once he was on top of the wall, this time on the other side, Kael quickly checked for onlookers, whether civilian down below or guards on top. He tied one end to a torch, this time checking to see if it would hold and then swiftly repelled down the face of the wall. Checking one last time to see if the coast was clear, Kael left his rope dangling there and disappeared into the streets of Vallenfend.

He had only run into a minimal amount of people, none of which recognized him. Kael felt far more conscientious now that he was a wanted man. He stuck to the back alleys, weaving in between houses and avoiding any major streets.

Kael passed close to the Royal Athenaeum. He stopped. Perhaps Malaricus had more to say. Plus he felt bad for lying to the scholar. Slipping out of the alleyways, Kael climbed his way up the spiralling stairs to the top of the library and knocked on the scholar's door.

There came no reply, so Kael knocked harder. Eventually, a voice brusquely and a second later the door swung open. Malaricus stopped his cursing and he gazed at Kael through his wise glasses. His mouth hung open for a moment but he shook himself of his stupor and ushered him in.

"Kael, my boy, what brings you in so late?" he asked, sitting down in a chair. Kael was surprised how thin the man looked in his night robe; he had hardly ever seen him without his other clothes on.

Kael sat down in his usual chair. He didn't reply for some time, struggling to find the right words. *How to start this...* "Malaricus, I—I'm going to be honest with you."

"How so?"

Kael chewed his lip for a moment. "You didn't save me from the dragon. I went."

Sagging deeper in his chair, Malaricus's disposition whitened. "Oh, is that so? H—how did you survive? You didn't... Oh, Kael, that rumour going around about an intruder in the castle...is—is that you?"

Nodding, Kael laced his fingers together. He sighed. *Oh, how quickly rumours spread in Vallenfend.* "Malaricus, before you call me a traitor or a thief or a trespasser, let me explain. Shatterbreath, the dragon, isn't as bad as we all thought! She's incredibly kind and sweet and caring. Zeptus has it all wrong."

Malaricus sighed. "I trust you, Kael, more than Zeptus, that's for certain. But what proof do you have? And why on earth would you intrude into the castle! What ludicrousness is this?"

"Shatterbreath told me that she saw Zeptus making a deal of some kind with a stranger on the beach. She said he was anxious and kept peering around. A boat with three people riding it came in from the water. One of them talked with Zeptus and gave him a large diamond. It was a transaction of some king. Shatterbreath thinks that there's more to the war we wage against her than we all know. She thinks that Zeptus has persuaded the king into something...we just don't know what. We don't know who these strangers are either."

Malaricus searched his desk for a moment, looking for his pipe. He didn't find it. "Did you find any concrete evidence in the castle?"

Kael smiled. *Malaricus believed him.* "Yes, I found the diamond in Zeptus's study. Shatterbreath's story was true. I also found something else, although I would prefer to discuss this with her. There is definitely something going on in the castle, Malaricus. I was attacked by guards in black who were far better trained than any other soldier I've met in this city."

"An elite group of soldiers? Kael, you must guard yourself closely, even outside the city. I've heard rumours on my visits to the castle. These men are not to be trifled with, understand?"

Kael nodded. "Before I go, Malaricus, is there anything else you can help me with? Do you know anything else that will help?"

"No, but I'd like to say one thing." Malaricus took his glasses off. He gazed into Kael's eyes with compassion. "I'm so sorry this has fallen on you Kael. I thought I could keep you from going, but my old, foolish heart was wrong. I believed the story you told me even though I had my doubts. I wanted it to be true with every fibre of my being. But alas, a great responsibility has been put on your shoulders. I am so sorry."

"You speak as if I'm fighting against a legion on my own. Malaricus, I'm trying to see what Zeptus or the king has planned." Kael's expression was grim and defiant. "I'm just trying to set things right."

Malaricus's sad eyes seemed so hollow, so cold. His sullen expression intensified. "Whatever it is, this plan of Zeptus's has been in motion for over thirty years, Kael. I doubt whatever this is about, it's not going to be so trivial."

A chill ran up Kael's spine. He gazed into space for a moment. Suddenly, he felt very small and scared. Snapping back to reality, he shook Malaricus's hand and turned to leave. A thought struck him as he reached the door.

"Malaricus, do you have any medical supplies?" he asked.

"Of course, Kael. Give me a moment." Malaricus disappeared behind a door to the side and came back a moment later with a thick bag. "Here you go."

Malaricus placed the bag on a desk. Kael frowned. "Oh, I don't have any money to pay you with." He reached into his pocket subconsciously. He was startled to find he *did* have money. When he withdrew his hand, there were several gold coins resting in his palm. He had forgotten he had filled his pockets with treasure when he had been in the castle. He had only assumed that Larr had taken away this gold as well.

Malaricus eyed the gold coins. He seemed tempted to take the money for a moment, but he waved his hand in dismissal. "No, Kael, you probably need it more than I do at this point. You keep it."

Kael could tell he wasn't going to take no for an answer, so, saying goodbye one more time, he picked up the bag and walked out of Malaricus's study. As he did, he glanced back once more to make sure the scholar wasn't looking, then left six gold coins on a tabletop. The dark streets of Vallenfend welcomed him as he stepped outside.

221

For the first time, the true vastness of his situation grasped him. Kael he hadn't realized how big of a mission he had really been on in the castle. Maybe this was more than the sake of Shatterbreath's comfort; maybe this was for all of Vallenfend. He began to feel burdened, as if the weight of his city and everybody inside it was bearing down on his shoulders.

Before Kael knew it, he had reached the southern wall. The gate far away to his right, but he didn't have any interest in going through. Instead, he tied one end of the rope he had left to an arrow. He scoured the tops of the wall. With Shatterbreath's vision, he could see a guard patrolling near where the gate was, but otherwise, all was clear. Taking aim, he drew the bow tight. With a *twang*, the arrow soared up towards the top of the wall. It bounced off and clattered to the ground. Kael wound it back up, making sure no one was watching and tried again.

Success! After a few more tries, his arrow finally stuck to something. Kael tested the rope, making sure it was secure, then proceeded up the face of the wall. It wasn't easy, but at last, he clambered over the wall's inside guardrail. He untied his rope from around the arrow, which had stuck itself into one of the many parapets that lined the top of the wall. Then, he tied the rope around the parapet itself, again, making sure it would support his weight first.

It was far easier going down a rope than up, and in no time at all, Kael was out in the fields, far away from the city. The sun glowed on the horizon, shooting tendrils of light into the sky.

The troublesome thoughts returned as Kael found a large rock to wait on. Every situation, scenario or possible explanation for the king's hoard of treasure flittered through his mind, but no solid solutions came to mind. Not quite yet.

He sat down on a rock, contemplating as he waited for Shatterbreath. The skies overhead rumbled and churned, threatening to snuff out the early-morning light. Thunder boomed somewhere in the distance. Was it thunder or Shatterbreath? Definitely thunder this time.

Zeptus meeting on the beach with a stranger, a stockpile of gold from somewhere foreign, perhaps overseas. *Were* there countries overseas? He had always assumed the continent he lived on was the only in this world. He couldn't understand any of it. *How did this all tie in with Shatterbreath?*

A sudden gust of wind caught his attention, and altogether, a huge ice-blue shape raced into view. Kael yelped and fell backwards off his rock.

Shatterbreath turned her great muzzle down at him, scrutinizing him carefully with one green eye. "Oh, Tiny," she remarked, shaking her long neck, "where did you come from?"

Kael scrambled to his feet, flustered. "I've been here for an hour! How did you not notice? You nearly landed on top of me!"

The dragon rumbled. Kael knew she was holding back a chuckled. He frowned. "I'm sorry. Your vision is so terrible! It's not very good for flying either... Never mind that now, did you find anything useful?"

"Yes, but I'd rather speak about it in your cave, where it's safer."

Shatterbreath cocked her head, digging her claws into the soil. "Safer? What troubles have you run into now, Tiny?" She leaned in close and sniffed his shoulder, concern evident in her voice. "And why do you favour your shoulder like that?"

"I'll tell you later. Let's just get back."

"Climb aboard." Kael pulled himself up onto Shatterbreath's foreleg and she lifted him up onto her back, where he sat down in the crook of her shoulders. "Uh, Tiny," she asked once he was comfortable.

Kael sighed and leaned back onto his pack. "Yes?"

"Did you bring me...what I asked for?"

Smiling as he closed his eyes, Kael nodded. "Of course. I have some medical supplies. I'll fix you up back at your cave."

With that, Shatterbreath let loose a mighty roar as was her custom. She unfurled her great, leathery wings and with one mighty flap, they were airborne. Where it had taken two days to climb up her mountain before, they made it to her cave in less than five minutes.

223

Alighting near her cave, Shatterbreath let Kael down. He hesitated at the mouth of her den. He didn't mind the cave anymore, and he now enjoyed Shatterbreath's company, but the stench, the stench was unbearable.

Holding his breath, Kael entered the cave, following Shatterbreath as she loped into the darkness. His footsteps reverberated off the walls as usual as he walked onwards. Eventually, the size of the cave won over and he was forced to take a deep breath. He was pleasantly surprised, however, by a new aroma that greeted him. He breathed in deeper, enjoying the new scent which reminded him of the crisp mountain waterfalls.

Shatterbreath greeted him cheerily in the main chamber, the tip of her tail dancing. She seemed to wear a smile over her muzzle. "Do you notice anything different, Tiny?"

Kael nodded, gazing around the dimly-lit cavern. The walls no longer had such prominent bloodstains littering the craggy surfaces and the ground was no mostly clear of debris, except for a large pile of metal and armour off to the side.

"I cleaned up the cave," the dragon said, beaming and puffing out her chest.

Kael's eyes were wide in surprise. "That's rather uncharacteristic of you, don't you think?" His tone was rather jocular, but no less cautious.

Shatterbreath lowered her large head near his. "Well, you were complaining so much, I thought it was time to clean this place up. A dragon of my obvious sophistication can treat herself with a nice, clean cave once and awhile. Besides, I was getting sick of your whining."

Kael, despite how wary he was, was impressed. "This must have taken you a long time! What all did you do?"

Shatterbreath beamed even more. "I flew up to the lake and fetched some water to clean the floors and walls, I emptied these metal carapaces of their rotting bodies—I thought you might need some more armour or some other trinkets just in case. Lastly, I stripped some branches off of a few pine trees and pounded them with my feet."

Kael inhaled deeply. Indeed, the cave now bore a strong, almost overwhelming aroma of pine. He noticed a pile of mush which must have been the poultice she had mentioned not a moment ago.

"That smell is quite unbearable, I have to admit," Shatterbreath remarked, wrinkling her nostrils and curling her lips in distaste, "but I thought it would please you. Don't worry; I'll remove that mess in a couple of days. Hopefully by then the stench you were complaining about will be gone."

"I'm flattered, Shatterbreath," Kael said, "but why would you do this for me?"

Shatterbreath lit a fire at the back of her cave. She paced around it and then around him, pointing her thick blue muzzle towards him the entire time. She wore a soft smile across her face. "I just thought you are having tough time with all this. Uncovering the truth, hiding terrible secrets that you cannot even tell your best friends...this is all too much for a hatchling like you to bear. I thought you could use all the comfort you could take." With a heave and an earth-shaking thud, she rested her body on the ground, lying on her side like a content cat.

Kael's brow furrowed. This was beginning to upset him. A former enemy of his, one which was fabled to be savage beyond reason, was doing something as nice as this, *just for him.* It baffled him. An act of kindness like this had never been given to him without expecting anything in return. It made him realize, right then and there, that he could trust Shatterbreath, absolutely. She didn't care if he brought back what he had requested, she didn't even care if he had attained any information on his trip, otherwise she would have waited until *afterwards* to do this. And moreover, he knew that everybody had been wrong about her, Zeptus and the king especially.

Kael made a resolution to himself. He would find out as much as he could in concern with Shatterbreath's past, and why such a gentle creature had such a fearsome reputation. Also, he made a commitment that no matter how trialling or dangerous, he would assist the dragon in whatever way possible to free her of this miserable situation.

Shatterbreath watched him for a moment as he pondered. She made a whimpering noise which broke Kael of his concentration, standing up so that her injured leg was closest to him.

Wordlessly, Kael opened up the bag Malaricus had given him. Inside was a large stash of gauze and cloth, a needle, several spools of thread and a few vials of alcohol among other cleansing agents. He took a cloth and soaked it in the alcohol and moved towards Shatterbreath's injured leg. The cloth hovered a foot away from her wound. *Maybe this was a bad idea.* Kael had seen some extreme reactions when alcohol had been placed over their wounds. But they were just people. *What would a dragon do?*

"Shatterbreath, this is going to sting. A lot. Are you ready?"

The dragon raised a brow challengingly as she watched Kael. She was trying to hide her anxiety but was doing a terrible job. "Tiny, I'm a dragon. It is in our nature to tolerate—"

Kael slapped the cloth over her wound.

The muscles in her massive leg seized underneath his hands and she dug her claws into the ground all the way to their bases. She roared loudly in pain, sending terrible echoes through the cave. Her tail thrashed and she wiggled furiously, but stayed where she was.

Letting his face relax as Shatterbreath's howl subsided, Kael repositioned the cloth on her leg. The dragon growled fiercely at him.

"You could have told me you were going to do that!" For the first time, Shatterbreath showed genuine anger towards him.

Kael removed the cloth for a moment. He struggled to keep his face straight, aware that her snarling muzzle was only inches away from his head and her teeth fully exposed. He placed the cloth back on, making Shatterbreath's body wince. "What were you saying a moment ago? It's in your nature to tolerate what?"

Shatterbreath hissed, baring her fearsome teeth. "That's not funny."

Kael couldn't help himself from laughing. "Oh come on! It's just a little sting! I'm sure you've had worse!"

Ignoring the dragon's angry whimpering, he removed the cloth once he felt the alcohol had done its job. He inspected the wound carefully. The gash was about four feet long and perhaps two inches deep. The tendons in Shatterbreath's legs showed fully, swollen and of a sickening hue. The edges of the cut were covered in caked blood and saliva, although some of it had just washed off onto Kael's cloth. The wound itself was oozing plasma. The scales surrounding were split and cracking, peeling outwards on themselves. Instead of being the sullen blue as the rest of her body, the area around the wound had become a less-appealing mixture of yellow and teal.

Kael struggled not to retch as he beheld it. He quickly put the cloth back over, just for a moment longer.

"Why didn't you see me about this earlier? Shatterbreath, this is terrible!"

Shatterbreath huffed, sending a volley of warm, ashy air into his face. "I didn't know if I could trust you."

Kael fetched a gauze pad from his bag. He patted the wound carefully. Shatterbreath squirmed. "You didn't want to admit it to me more like."

She grimaced. "Ah, stop poking it so hard!" She tried to withdraw her leg, but Kael stopped her by placing pressure on the gauze.

"No, this needs to be attended to. Stop complaining like a frightened little lizard and tough it out."

Sitting back down, Shatterbreath pouted. Now it was Kael's turn to be amused by her behaviour. "Little?" she scoffed, "look who's talking. You're not even as big as my paw."

She lifted her foreleg to corroborate. Kael laughed.

Throwing the gauze absently to the ground, Kael paused for a moment, considering what he could do for a gash this big. He had mended pretty large cuts before, but this, this was immense. If any wound this big was inflicted on a man, they'd be dead almost instantly.

Grabbing a long sheet of bandage, Kael told Shatterbreath to stand up. He made the loose end of the bandage catch on one of her scales and then worked it around her leg. He thought that she would perhaps feel awkward as he went underneath her great body and between her legs, but to his mild surprise, she didn't seem to mind. He felt more uneasy than she did.

Her lungs filled with air, just to the side of his head. A low rumble emanated from her chest and she shifted her legs carefully. What a strange experience, standing completely underneath a powerful creature. It was unnerving, but all the same, he felt a sense of security. He ran the bandage around her leg a few times, then pinned it tight.

Shatterbreath scrutinized his work from afar. Her lips curled and she shook her neck. Once he was finished, she flexed her leg carefully and lifted it off the ground. The bandage covered the lower part of her leg, so it didn't get in the way of her movement at all.

"And this is supposed to help me?" she asked apprehensively.

"Yes, well, sort of. It'll keep dust out of it and keep the scab from breaking as it heals. Just—no, don't bite it—just leave it there for a while. I'll check on the bandage once and a while to see if the wound is clean." She seemed unconvinced, so Kael continued, "I should have stitched it up, but it's just too big, you'll just have to suffer as it heals, I suppose. I'm surprised it wasn't infected. If you left it any longer, it probably would have been. This will act as an extra measure against disease."

Shatterbreath raised her brow. The spines on her back bristled. "Fine, Tiny, I believe you. Thank you very much for healing me."

Kael scratched the back of his head. "I didn't *heal* you, but that will help. Consider this payment for cleaning the cave."

She nodded and leaned in closer. "Oh and by the way, I think you forgot something."

"What?"

Kael experienced the same energy as before as Shatterbreath touched him with the tip of her muzzle, only it was leaving him this time. His vision twisted for a moment and all the colours of the cave melded together. Once all stopped, Kael was disappointed to find his old vision had returned. Everything was dull and fuzzy in comparison to the sight he had enjoyed only moments before.

He frowned as the dragon smiled. "There we go, that's more like it. Maybe I can catch some prey now."

Once Shatterbreath had returned with food, Kael attempted to relay everything he had learned in the castle.

Shatterbreath listened while she gorged, occasionally stopping her bloody feast to remark on some amazing thing Kael did.

Once his story and her meal were complete, the azure dragon remained silent as before. A shadow fell across her face as considered everything they had learned.

"Treasure, a secret deal with somebody unknown..." Shatterbreath murmured.

"I've already considered all these things. Nothing feasibly comes to mind."

The tip of Shatterbreath's tail danced. "Well, let's consider it for a moment. We know the king—or Zeptus—is doing a deal with somebody, potentially from overseas. They gave him the treasure, that much can be assumed."

Kael interrupted her there with a thought of his own. "It dawned on me earlier why the king doesn't charged high taxes. He's a greedy man, there's no doubt about that, but it always confused me why he didn't charge huge taxes on everything. What point is there...?"

"...If he already has so much treasure?" Shatterbreath tapped her black claws on the floor. "So if he's getting paid for this war he wages against me, what's in it for the other side?"

Kael threw his arms up into the air. "That's where I get lost."

"There's another thing that vexes me," Shatterbreath said. "This Zeptus character... Tell me more about him."

"I think he's the mastermind behind all this," said Kael, "the king is childish and stupid; he couldn't pull something off like this." Kael hesitated as he remembered how the king had gloated about beating Zeptus in a game of chess. He shook his head, pushing the thought aside. *What would a simple game of chess affect?* "No, I think this is all Zeptus's work. Plus, in the castle, he seemed persistent to have me killed. He whispered something to the king about me potentially figuring out something..."

"This Zeptus of the Purple Eyes sounds like a threat. Be warned Kael, if he proves any more troublesome, you will have no choice but to eliminate him."

Kael gulped. He had hurt one of the guards in the castle, one who was trying to kill him. Could he murder somebody purposefully, without them attacking him? That was something beyond him. "I—I don't think I can do that."

Tendrils of flame escaped Shatterbreath's nostrils. "Tiny, you must accept that lives will have to be taken. You must not hesitate to take another's life when yours is in peril. Promise me that you will do whatever it takes to keep yourself safe during battle."

Kael hesitated. Shatterbreath looked down at him with concern and earnest. Reluctantly, he agreed. "Okay, I promise. Although I don't like it, I suppose I'll have to learn how to...how to kill."

Satisfied, the dragon flexed her wings and rolled onto her back. "It's not an easy thing to get used to at first, killing. Trust me though, with time, you'll get used to it."

Kael wasn't sure he wanted to, but he didn't say anything.

They sat in silence for a few more minutes, Shatterbreath lying on her back, stretching and Kael sitting on the floor, pondering.

Shatterbreath twitched and rolled back over. "Enough, I need to stretch my wings. Go up on the mountain where you enjoy wandering and return in a few minutes. I grow tired of keeping my mind and body in this cave while such secrecy is happening! I think better in the air anyway."

Before Kael could ask if he could come, she bounded to the entrance and leapt into the air, kicking up small rocks and sending them careening over the edge.

Kael waited for a moment and with a sigh, he got up onto his feet and headed out onto the top of the mountain, where the dull listless and choking mist awaited.

Shatterbreath was proud of her little human, he had done well. She had been greatly impressed by his story, especially when he described how he fought three soldiers at once. Her training had worked after all.

Snap! Her jaws clamped down on a foolish crow that was flying to high. She flapped her wings and twisted into a barrel roll. Pulling out of that and into a lazy back flip, thoughts passed through her mind like water over a rock in a stream. There was so much to process, but so little time to do it all! There was the boy to think proudly of, the secret plan to try and unravel, plus memories that she preferred not to visit to be avoided.

But the memories were particularly strong today.

That boy, Kael, the tiny one, there was something about him...something she had once known before. Something her whole race had tried to lock out of their memory. Something the world had forgotten. Suddenly, she remembered where she had experienced the feeling in her heart she received every time Kael was near.

Shatterbreath smiled. Now she understood, it all made sense! Why she had been drawn to the tiny one to begin with, why he was strangely brave and why time seemed to slow for him, which he had described to her earlier. Why hadn't she realized this before? It was so obvious now.

With her personal discovery came a tidal wave of locked away memories of when she was very young. The meadows far below shifted as the images wafted into her vision. Instead of grass flowing in the wind, she saw metal plating. Instead of the occasional critter hopping to and fro, she saw snarling, vicious dogs trained to kill.

Their marching, how loud, prominent, powerful it was. In unison they marched under the blazing red sky—red as the blood of their enemies that they slew. Bodies were piled up in great stacks in their wake. The smell of death, decay and lust for power clung to the wind, reluctant to ever let go. So strong was it that she could hardly breathe as she flew alongside her father.

She stayed by his side...there was protection with him. She had to follow him; otherwise they would find her and kill her. The only safety was with him, in the air.

He growled, telling her to keep closer. She obeyed, watching the blackened army below. They were blackened from soot, blackened from their corrupted, tarnished souls. How could they slay so many?

An arrow flew past, narrowly missing her head. Her father turned his great maw downwards and roared. But still, the arrows kept coming. Big ones whistled past, as thick as a tree and just as gnarled. Panic struck her. Why did they want to kill them? They weren't harming anybody, they were just bystanders!

"Fly, fly above me, my daughter!" her father called out. She obeyed him, staring at his back with concern.

The whistling continued, and the shouts from below escalated. How demonic their voices sounded, as if they were calling out to them from the depths of hell. A crack of lightening split the sky in front of them. The bolt was maroon and twisted sickeningly, branching off to strike multiple areas on the battle far below.

She watched, over her father's shoulder, watched in horror as the black expanse of soldiers bore down on the large city before them. Like a hideous wave of beetles, they descended on the town. It was set ablaze, the peaks of the towering castle spewing flame high into the air.

Screams of terror escaped the confines of the town, piercing into her very soul. Her heart beat faster and her scales crawled. This was all so terrible, so horrendous!

Another crack of red lightening. But this one was different. She could see the bolt as it branched to strike people. They fell dead where they were. That was no regular lightening...

Her father roared. It was a pitch and magnitude that frightened her. She had heard this roar only once before, when his brother had been slain before their eyes. It was pain.

He craned his head backwards and his wings faltered. He turned his wise, all-knowing gaze towards her as she flew above him. Still

232

the whistles continued, still the screams echoed through her mind, still war raged beneath them, but all she heard was his voice.

"My daughter," he said slowly, his tone full of love and of pain. She loved his strong, comforting voice, but now she found no comfort. All she felt was fear. He winced again, but kept his great green eyes on her. "Do not mourn for me. And stay strong, my sweet, all will be well again...I promise."

With that, her father, one of ten Dragon Elders...died. His eyes closed and his muscles relaxed. She could sense the life drain out of him. His limp, defeated body fell freely towards the turmoil below, activating a whole new tumult of victory below.

Tears well up in her eyes as she watched her father slipped away from her. Her protection, her safety—was gone. No, this couldn't be...he was going to be there for her forever. Now he was...he was...

Lightening struck in the distance.

She roared as loudly as her young body allowed. Her voice sounded so sullen, so broken... She let loose the inner storm that burned within, letting her voice carry her sorrows far across the land.

A terrible pain erupted in her side.

Shatterbreath opened her eyes. She was breathing heavily and there were tears in her eyes. She closed her half-open mouth and blinked several times to wash away the memory. Gently, she placed a paw on the wound on her side, just below her ribs. Her scales were haggard there and soft flesh presided. She still remembered the pain that scar bore. She caught a thermal and floated on it for a moment, brooding. *Kael...*

She set quickly back towards her cave, surprised at first by how far she had wandered. She submerged into the fog that surrounded her mountain and squinted, looking for Kael's small shape over the dull surroundings. She found him.

He yelped and fell over as she landed just in front of him. Normally, she would have found this funny, but her heart was racing too fast.

"Kael," she exclaimed over his silly complaints, "I think I know what the king has planned."

Kael's face lit up. "What, what do you think?"

Shatterbreath paused, the red sky flashing through her mind. "Think about it, your city is basically defenceless without your soldiers and without your men. What is it susceptible to?"

Kael gasped. "Invasion."

"Exactly," her mind was going faster than she could speak. "I've had some...experience with this before. I'm thinking that there must be an empire we don't know about. What do empires do?"

Kael shrugged. "Rule over their dominion?"

"They expand, Kael. They expand..."

Kael put his hand to his chin thoughtfully. "I haven't heard of any empires on this continent, have you?"

Shatterbreath shook her head. "No, there hasn't been an empire on this continent for...for a very long time. Believe me, if there was, I would know. But you said it yourself that the treasure you stole was foreign, perhaps from overseas."

"Then the empire, assuming it is that, is from another continent."

"And they're bribing your king to kill off all his men." Shatterbreath slammed her tail into the ground, crumbling a rock underneath it. "It's all so obvious. They've been sending their men after me all this time to prepare the empire for invasion! Without a proper army, it will be simple to overtake the city."

"Why?" Kael asked, urgency on his face, "why Vallenfend? Why must we suffer?"

Shatterbreath thought for a moment. "Because of Vallenfend's location. If you think about it, your city could be very easy to defend. It is on high ground, backed up against a mountain. If you had a proper army and defences, your city could be nearly impossible to take by force. I'm guessing your city would be the first on a series of conquering. Once they set up base camp in Vallenfend, it would be far easy to ravage the rest of the land."

Fear stuck to Kael's voice. "W—when do you think they'll attack, this empire or army? I mean, it's been thirty or so years, why haven't they attacked by now? We've been in this state for two decades!"

Shatterbreath rolled her shoulders in the equivalence of a shrug. "I don't know. Maybe they had to amass a big enough army first. I image it would take a lot of men to tame a whole new continent. Whatever their reason, I sense we are nearing the end of this rope, Kael. Time is of the essence."

Kael nodded. "What can we do now to stop them?"

Shatterbreath gazed into the fog. "Not much. Perhaps you can go into town and try to convince your people that Zeptus is playing you all on the king's behalf. That seems like our only option at the moment. I'll think of something more if that doesn't work."

The boy was reluctant. "Okay, but I'll need some armour before I go. I doubt the people will take to me kindly. I may have gotten in a bit of trouble..."

"That's alright. Hop on my back and we'll get you some good armour back at my cave."

Kael nimbly climbed onto her back and they lifted off. Shatterbreath tilted her wings and flew into her cave.

Chapter 19

Kael was happy. At last he had a true set of armour! He had scrounged around the pile of armour until he had found a gleaming, polished set.

There were many pieces to the armour to the set, including a flexible cuirass, greaves, vambraces, pauldrons and even a set of gauntlets as well as a hauberk to wear underneath. Kael was impressed by the suit of armour. It was almost entirely intact and of a superior quality. The surfaces of the metal were smooth and shined an iridescent blue and overall, the armour held an ethereal beauty to it, as if it had belonged to a saint at some time. When he first put the set on, he smiled at the strong feeling that arose. Now he was a true knight.

He walked a few paces with his new armour, which clanked together, but not as loudly as he would have thought. It wasn't as heavy as he was expecting either. It was still somewhat burdening and hard to manoeuvre, but Kael was confident he would quickly adjust. He tightened a strap on his arm and looked up at Shatterbreath.

"This is a great set of armour! It is completely undamaged! Hmm, where's the helmet?"

"It came off with the owner's head, if I recall."

The blood drained from Kael's face. He regretted asking in the first place. Her comment brought a question to mind. He was wary to ask, fearing what the answer would be, but he couldn't stop himself.

Fitting his sword to his waist, he squinted up at Shatterbreath. He waited until the dragon had finished breathing fire on her glowing rocks. The cave was lit up with renewed light.

She stretched out lazily as Kael struggled to find his voice. "What's wrong, Tiny?" she asked through a yawn, making her words garbled and almost incoherent.

Kael took a moment to realize what she had said. "Oh, nothing." He picked at a chip in his shield morosely.

Shatterbreath reached out and gently straightened a pauldron with her teeth. "You are getting harder to read, Kael, but I can still tell when you're feeling down. You can tell me anything. Now, what is amiss?"

He continued to pick at the scratch in his shield, avoiding her gaze and staring into the usual fire she kept ablaze for him. "It's...it's just that I've never really knew my father. He left when I was young."

"What for?"

"You."

"Oh." If dragons could blush, Kael imagined Shatterbreath would be doing so at that moment. "In that case, I am truly sorry for your loss, Kael. Believe me, if I would have known..."

"I have come at terms with my father's death long ago," he said sharply, "but it vexes me that I can't remember what he was like...his face, his personality. I was so young." He kept his voice steady somehow, although he was burning up on the inside. "All I know is what my mother told me. She said I looked just like him. He was tall with dark hair—my mother was always saying how handsome he was... He had a fierce gaze, as if he was always calculating a situation, figuring out how things worked. She said he was brave and smart and always strived to do what's right. Did you...? I suppose you wouldn't even know if you met him."

Shatterbreath lowered her head. She moved closer to Kael, ever so slightly. "I remember almost every human I've slain, Kael. Their faces are locked deep within my subconscious. Let me think for a moment." She licked her lips, her green eyes squinting, just barely visible underneath her jutting cheekbones. "Ah, yes, I remember now," her voice went passive. "I remember your father perfectly. Few humans catch my attention, Kael, but your father impressed me.

"He stuck closely to his comrades and was a faithful warrior, but like all those fathers before him, I could tell he was reluctant to fight against me. He didn't want to die; I could see it in his eyes. He didn't want to be there with the rest of them, he wanted to be at home with his family. His bravery astounded me. He stood firm, he stood strong. He would fight and he would die to save his family and his people. I was sad to have to kill him."

Shatterbreath stopped. "I'm sorry, does this upset you?"

Kael wiped his eyes. "No, please, continue."

The dragon wrapped a comforting tail around him. "He was one of the few I ever talked to before I killed him. He was so unique from the others, so much more emotional and passionate. I see a lot of him in you, Tiny. You mother was right, you look just like him...

"I remember, I asked him why he fought against me, why he would not rather be at home, looking after a wife and child. He told me he would much prefer to be doing just that, but said that it was his duty to keep his city safe from the monster they see me as. He told me that he had to fight to keep his little boy safe...safe from me. He told me he had to keep his boy safe..."

To Kael's surprise, a single, great tear welled up in Shatterbreath's eye. "It is cruel irony to see that he did not get his wish. For here you are, Kael, with me. He—he did not get his final wish... Oh, I have disgraced your father's honour!"

Kael placed his hand on Shatterbreath's tail. He was moved by his father's story, but even more moved by the sorrow the dragon felt. She was truly sorry for what she had done, truly remorseful that his father had not gotten his final wish.

"Shatterbreath, you spared my life," he told her, "and you've chosen me over all people to aid you. For that, and the friendship you've displayed to me, I am honoured."

They gazed into each other's for a fond moment. Kael suddenly felt a closeness so strong between them, something more powerful than any friendship he had ever experienced. They were united in this great cause against a common foe, but yet, there was more than that...

Kael was the first to look away. He wanted to learn more about Shatterbreath's past, but he felt shy for some reason. Instead, he asked a simple question.

"Why are your eyes green?"

Shatterbreath gave a short laugh. "What? That is a strange question to ask!"

Kael laughed as well. "I read this book the other day that stated that a dragon's eyes are usually the same colour as its body. Were you just born that way?"

"Well, no. Believe it or not, I used to be green."

"Really?"

"Yes." Shatterbreath's playful mood quickly subsided. "But years of solitude within this cave has caused me to look this way. I'm sure whatever book you read didn't explain that dragon's may change colour depending on what sort of environment they live in or what they're feeling. For example, a dragon that lives in the arctic is white. Or a dragon that may live in the jungle will be a green, maybe brown hue. I've lived in this cave for so long and have felt the same way for so many centuries that..."

Her voice trailed off and she stared off into the distance. There she was, hinting at the same dark incident in her past. Something had emotionally crippled Shatterbreath when she was younger. Kael seriously doubted that habitat alone could bring this radical colour change upon her or even the constant attacks from Vallenfend.

He didn't ask any more questions. He had asked too many already. She was grieving enough as it was. He would try later. No matter how long it would take, Kael would learn about the dragon's hidden past and do everything in his power to set her troubled mind at ease.

"Enough of this," she declared, rising to her feet. Her features were serious and hardened. "Let's get to the skies at once."

It was a strange experience wearing the thick, blue-tinted armour, but an even stranger experience wearing it while sitting on Shatterbreath's back. Because his legs were protected now, he needn't fear about chaffing them against her scales, so he let his legs fall against the sides of her neck. Kael wiggled the caps he had placed on Shatterbreath's spines in front and behind him. They were the broken ends of sword sheaths which he had placed to ensure he wouldn't get impaled if he was rocked too hard. Neither one moved.

Once he was comfortable, Kael gave Shatterbreath the okay.

Without further delay, she bolted forward, surprising Kael with her speed. As she always did, she launched fiercely off of the mountain's side. He could sense her glum mood melt away as she beat her wings and soared through the air. She let out an elated cry, far different than any roar he had ever heard.

After a few minutes, she turned her great head around. Kael could just barely see the green of her eye. "Do you trust me Kael?"

"Yes," Kael said warily.

She laughed in glee. "Hold on then. Here we go!"

Angling her wings, they dipped towards the earth and for a moment, Kael though she was going to do another death-defying nosedive. She pulled out of it and quickly tilted one wing so that her body began to spin.

Kael gasped in surprise and time once again shifted slower. He clutched onto the spike in front of him and squeezed Shatterbreath's neck with all his might to hold on. The world flipped upside-down and when he looked up; she saw the colours of Vallenfend. An overwhelming sense of vertigo gripped him for a moment, but Shatterbreath continued in her roll and soon they were right-side up again. Time returned its normal pace.

She didn't stop there.

She beat her wings, sending them straight upwards. She craned her neck up and once again, they went upside-down. There she stayed for a moment until she pulled into a backwards nosedive.

They picked up speed as they fell and Shatterbreath banked sharp right, and then left, doing gigantic semi-circles in the air. Kael clung on for his life. His heart was beating furiously, but bit by bit, his fear withered away. His frightened, crooked frown slowly changing into a smile.

As Shatterbreath tilted into her turns and twisted he thrust out his arms, as he had before. He gave an elated yell.

Shatterbreath glanced back, a wild look on her muzzle. "This is where the fun begins," she called back.

Beating her wings furiously, she gained a copious amount of speed. The wind whipped in Kael's face and stung his eyes, forcing him to squint. Shatterbreath did a backwards loop-the-loop while in a barrel roll at the same time. The trick was fast and sharp. It took Kael a few seconds to even realize what happened.

For the next hour, Shatterbreath twisted, dove and weaved through the air expertly with Kael clinging to her back. As before, it took a while for Kael to work up his bravery, but once he did, he enjoyed the experience.

Kael was beginning to feel sick from all the tricks, but he was having so much fun, he didn't want to quit. He threw his arms out into the air once again, just as Shatterbreath pulled into a sharp front flip.

The trick caught him off guard and he was hurled off her back. He floated through the air for a moment, propelled upwards by the force in which he had been thrown off by. He watched Shatterbreath in shock as she dipped downwards, far off to the side.

Then, he began to fall.

His body went limp as he careened towards the ground. He tumbled head over heels, all sense of direction lost. The colours of the sky and the ground mixed into one.

He could feel himself fading away into unconsciousness from the extreme forces at work on his body, but he struggled to stay awake. His eyes flittered, trying to stay open. As they did, he was dimly aware of a big, dark blue shape descending on him.

A minute later, he snapped awake on Shatterbreath's back. She was hovering on a thermal, her head set low. Kael watched the rippling of the membrane of her wing for a moment. He shook his head, groaning from a terrible ache at the base of his neck.

Shatterbreath looked back at him. "So," she said, "how was that?"

Kael groaned again. "Great, until I fell off."

Shatterbreath rumbled, sending vibrations through Kael. "Whose fault is that?"

Kael watched her shoulders flexing. "I guess it's its mine."

"There we go."

Without warning, Shatterbreath pulled into a barrel roll, forcing Kael to scramble over her body. He made it to her chest before he slid off and started to plummet again. His fall stopped short as she

241

caught him in her huge paws. He waited for a moment to see what she would do next, but she simply pointed her body down towards the field she had dropped him off at last time, so he settled down against the side of her paw.

Shatterbreath landed with her hind legs first. Staying upright for a moment, still beating her wings to keep herself aloft, she gently placed Kael on the ground. Once he had backed away from her, she fell to all fours with a sigh and a shudder.

"Well, good luck," she stated.

Kael twitched in surprise. "That's it?"

"Fine," she huffed playfully. Her tone quickly became serious. "Don't trust anyone, Tiny. If you are indeed a wanted man, you're going to have to stay even more diligent. I doubt anybody on the streets will try to confront you, especially considering what you're wearing around your body and at your hip. But the guards may feel a tad bit braver. Try to hide all emotion and thought from everybody, you are getting good at that, but try just a bit harder. And lastly, if you *do* get captured, don't struggle. They kill the ones who struggle. If you do get captured, I'll save you somehow."

"Thanks, Shatterbreath." He turned to leave.

The dragon stopped him with her tail. "Kael, don't expect much success. I doubt they'll take kindly to you considering—considering you're helping me. And that Zeptus...there's more to him than you know."

"What do you mean?"

"I'll tell you later. Just stay safe, okay? I'll meet you back here, as before."

Kael was confused by the dragon's comment about Zeptus, but he couldn't inquire about it because Shatterbreath took wing and was off.

Vallenfend. No longer did the city that waited off in the distance seem so heart-warming. No, now that his city was filled with danger, Kael was frightened to return.

The gate he had entered when he first returned wasn't very far away. The same girl as before was guarding it too. She let him in without a fuss, which Kael was grateful for. As soon as he was free to roam around the city, his guard was up and his senses were strained. He doubted he'd be attacked in broad daylight by the guards in black, but there was always the chance.

Although the dragon had instructed him to not trust anybody, there was somebody he had to see first. Something he had to set straight. Face set in grim resolution, Kael picked the shortest path to get to Laura's house.

He stopped at the foot of her door. Taking a quick look around to see if anybody was watching, he knocked firmly on the door. Nobody stirred from inside. Kael sighed morosely. Where were they? Were they in trouble? Kael forced himself to take a calm break. It *was* the middle of the day. They were probably out doing regular things.

He knocked again, louder this time. He was relieved when he heard footsteps from within. Mrs. Stockwin opened the door. She gasped at the sight of Kael, worry set deep in her premature wrinkles.

"Oh, heavens above, where have you been Kael?" she said, grasping his wrist and pulling him inside.

"I'll tell you in a second. Firstly, where's Laura?"

"I'm here." Laura walked around the corner. Kael's throat tightened. *He knew that look.* She wasn't happy.

Kael took a step towards her, his armour clanking. She backed off, putting a hand out defensively. Mrs. Stockwin had a sad smile across her face and Kael wondered at it. She knew something was about to happen between them, something bad.

"Where have you been?" Laura gasped, her soft voice biting into Kael.

"What?"

She bit her lip. "Nolka saw you in town just the other day. I thought you were supposed to be working out in the fields."

Nolka? Kael struggled to remember that name. Nolka was one of Laura's friends. "I—I..."

"Kael, I thought I knew you, but you lied to me. You didn't go to the farms, did you?" Her face was turning a flustered red. "I used to be able to read you, Kael. But now when I look at you, dressed in *that*, all I see is a closed book."

243

She looked Kael top to bottom. "Where have you been and where did you get all that? How did you get that cut on your cheek?"

Glancing over at Mrs. Stockwin, Kael licked his lips and rubbed his wrist where a loose piece of metal was chaffing him underneath his gauntlet. "Actually, Laura, that's why I'm here, I have some confessions to make, some wrongs to right. Where's Faerd? He deserves to know what I've been doing as well."

"He's working right now, but I'll go fetch him. I'm sure he can take the day off for this." Laura strolled calmly past Kael, not even giving him a second glance. Kael's heart felt like it was being torn in two.

Once Laura had left, he turned around slowly, letting his shoulders go limp under the heavy armour. Mrs. Stockwin stared at him with an inscrutable expression.

"You told us you wouldn't ever leave, Kael," she said reproachfully. "You told her that you would never go. You've had us worried sick. I thought I lost another one of my boys, that's what it felt like at least. You better have a good explanation and a better reason for doing this to us."

It took Kael a while to answer, his jaw working. "Believe me," he said, "it's a good reason."

Laura was back faster than he had expected, with Faerd's scarred face in tow. As soon as he saw Kael, his brow furrowed and his lip twisted. He clenched his fists and charged up to him. He tried to throw a punch at his face, but time slowed for Kael and he stopped the blow with his forearm.

"It's good to see you too, Faerd," Kael said.

Faerd growled, but when Laura touched his shoulder, he calmed down. They moved into the living room and sat down around the kitchen table. Whenever they met together, Mrs. Stockwin would fix them up something nice, but this time she simply leaned up against a wall, her arms crossed over her bosom. Kael could sense their eyes burning into his head, but he refused to look up, instead tracing a line in the table with his index finger.

"I'm sorry I lied to you all," he said, taking his time. *So far, this was not going well.* "I would have told you, but I couldn't jeopardise my mission. You've got to understand, I haven't told anybody about this. It's quite a relief actually."

"Go on," Faerd hissed. "Just tell us, then I can decide if your worthy of my forgiveness."

Kael tapped his metal boot on the ground. "About—my word, how long *has* it been? About two months or so ago there was a drafting, you remember, right?"

"How can we forget?" Laura stated blandly, "that's when all this began."

Kael nodded. "Precisely. Despite Malaricus's promise to me, I was drafted into the military."

All expressions softened. Kael continued when nobody said anything. "And I actually *went* into the military as well. There I stayed for a month, learning how to fight with a sword, although I already knew more than those buffoons..."

Kael told them everything that had happened to him during his terrible stay inside the castles walls. He told them of the Captain's insanity and his cruel nature. He told them of how the Captain bullied Ernik around and how Kael had beaten him at a duel. And, with a heavy heart, he told them of how Shatterbreath killed his entire troupe. The memory seemed all too fresh.

By the time he was done, everyone's hostile mood was gone. Instead, they exhibited worry and anguish for his trials.

"How," Faerd said, eyes wide, "how did you get out alive?"

"Yes, Kael, continue," Mrs. Stockwin said. Laura remained silent.

"Ah, now there's the hardest part of the story to tell. The dragon, Shatterbreath...I still don't know exactly why, but she spared me." He left out the part where she called him cute for cowering in the corner. "She gave me the choice to be her assistant in her quest to discover why the king has been sending soldiers after her all these years."

"Why would the dragon spare you? You of all people?" Laura asked.

245

Kael shrugged. "Like I said, I don't know exactly why yet. I think she sees something more in me."

"So that's where you've been," Faerd said, raising an eyebrow, "helping the dragon?"

"Yes. She told me to return home and see if I could discover anything, that's when I saw you last. And when Nolka saw me, I was on my way to the castle. I rejoined in the army and met up with...a friend who showed me a secret way inside."

"The castle?" Faerd whistled. "*That was you?* There were rumours of a break-in, but I never imagined it would be *you!* What was it like in that place? It gleams like ivory on the outside; I can only imagine what lies on the inside."

Kael laughed. "It is not a place you want to visit. While I was in there, I discovered something remarkable, something that helps explain why the king is doing all this. Although I got in a bit of trouble while I was in there."

"Trouble?" Faerd exclaimed.

"Something remarkable?" Laura chimed in a second later.

"Well, let's just say I ran into a few too many guards. To answer your question, Laura, treasure. I found a whole room stacked to the brim with gold. It was only later that Shatterbreath and I figured out what they're planning."

"What's that?" asked Mrs. Stockwin from where she stood. "What has forced me to lose my boys? What could drive the king to kill his own people? Tell me, Kael."

"Invasion," he replied ominously. "With our city nearly defenceless, an invading army—or empire as we speculate—would be free to walk right in and take over without much of a struggle. Shatterbreath saw Zeptus striking a deal of some kind with a person out at sea. We think the invading army is from another continent and that they're paying Zeptus and the king richly for their *troubles.*"

"Zeptus?" Mrs. Stockwin said. "I always hated that man. It only seems fitting he's behind all this, playing the king like a puppet."

"But Kael," Laura said, placing a hand on his vambrace. "Are you sure about all this? I mean, do you really trust that *dragon,* of all things to trust? It sounds farfetched if you ask me."

"Laura," Kael placed his hand on hers, wishing he wasn't wearing gauntlets so he could touch her soft skin. "I trust Shatterbreath with my life. Plus, I found a huge diamond that proved her story correct."

"But—but..."

"Well, I believe you!" Faerd declared suddenly.

"What?" Laura and Kael exclaimed in unison.

Faerd laced his hands together. "I always thought that creep Zeptus had something to do with all this. And I always thought those two had hatched up some evil plan. You're theory sounds all too fitting. Kael, I'm sorry for getting angry at you, you were only doing what was necessary to keep yourself safe, I understand."

"Thank you, Faerd."

"You two are insane! This is all crazy, it doesn't make sense," Laura cried. "Nobody can be so greedy and shallow to sacrifice their own people for riches! It's inhuman; it's preposterous, even for Zeptus or King Morrindale! Mother, help me out."

Mrs. Stockwin stared at the floor thoughtfully. "You don't know that man like I do, Laura. What Kael says is...feasible. King Murderdale is known for his greed and Zeptus," she shivered, *"Zeptus..."*

Laura threw her hands up in the air. "This is ludicrous! Okay, fine, let's play it your way, Kael. Let's say that Zeptus is indeed telling the king to go through with this deal. How are you, Kael Rundown—who has only had military training as of late—going to stop them? How are you going to stop an entire invasion?"

Kael bit his lip, at a loss. "I was going to try and tell the people of what their king is doing, but now that you've said that, I think Shatterbreath and I have come up with a new plan. We can't stop an invasion, you're right. Not our city alone," he gasped, his eyes going wide, "but maybe we can get some help!"

"And," Laura asked, her voice growing weary, "just who are you going to get help from? Who would help us? We've been out of speaking terms with almost every other kingdom on this continent."

Kael leaned back in his chair. "I don't know, but it's worth a shot. Laura, don't you have any hope?"

247

Laura shied away as Kael tried to touch her hand. "I think you and that *dragon* are wrong. There's no invasion coming, so why bother running around, risking your own neck? Kael, just come home, forget all this. I miss the old you." Her eyes became watery. "I miss the old you," she repeated.

Expression firm, Kael rose to his feet. "I don't like what's becoming of me either, but I'm doing all that's necessary to save my city."

Faerd also stood up. "Then as will I, Kael," he exclaimed. "I will join you in this task. Anything you need, don't hesitate to ask. I will help you in any way possible."

Laura looked up at them for a moment, sadness etched across her body. She didn't say anything.

Kael clasped Faerd's shoulder. "Thank you, Faerd. Right now, I'd rather you stay put. I have armour and a sword to protect me if things get messy, but you don't. I couldn't live with myself if any of you got hurt because of me."

Laura made a sound, but Kael couldn't tell if she said anything.

"Alright then," Kael said with a frown. "I suppose I should go."

Mrs. Stockwin pushed off of the wall. "Good luck, Kael." She shook his hand as he made a move to leave.

"Yes," Faerd said, also taking his hand in turn. "Good luck."

Kael stopped beside Laura. She avoided looking at him. He waited patiently until at last, she too, stood. They gaze intensely into each other's eyes for a moment. At last, she threw her arms around him and whispered in his ear. "I wish you didn't have to do this, but stay safe, okay?"

Kael smiled and hugged her tighter. "I'll try, just for you."

The moment passed and they released each other. Kael nodded at them and then left the loving house of the Stockwins. He felt somewhat relieved knowing that Faerd and Mrs. Stockwin trusted and believed in him, although there was a knot in his stomach knowing that Laura did not.

Kael strolled through the streets, receiving strange looks from the women passing by. Unlike his previous visit, he wasn't taking any back routes or making a conscious effort not to be seen. Yes, he stuck out like a sandbar, but he didn't care, he was beyond image now. If anything, he kind of enjoyed the feeling of power that accompanied his armour, sword and shield. There was something...satisfying to the fear in the people's eyes he past. Then again, to blend in with the crowd, to *belong*, that was something he missed dearly.

"Kael Rundown?" an ebullient voice cried out. Kael flinched. He was relieved it was just Bunda who had called his name. She hustled over to him, squeezing through a group of women. "By the heavens above, child, where have *you* been?"

Kael continued walking and she joined him. "It's a long story," he said, "I'll tell you later sometime. Just keep your voice down, please?"

Bunda put a hand to her breast, exasperated. Nobody had ever told her to quiet down, not without her exploding at them afterwards. "What? Boy, you've got some cheek to disappear for so long and then return only to tell me to shut up."

Wincing, Kael tried to calm her down. "I didn't say that," he said calmly, slowing his pace.

Bunda clenched her jaw and halted. "It doesn't matter, you might as well have."

Kael gave a fleeting smile to the small group of bystanders that had already collected. He pulled Bunda into an alley with much protesting. "Listen, Bunda, I'm sorry to be curt, but quiet down! I'm sorry I haven't visited you in a while, okay? I'll make it up to you later. Right now, I need everybody to stay quiet concerning me. Let's just say I've gotten into a bit of trouble."

Bunda frowned, placing her hands on her hips. "Trouble? What kind of trouble? How could you get in trouble? We didn't raise you like this!"

Kael struggled to hold back a growl. "Please, that doesn't matter now. All that does is that you stay quiet; otherwise I could be in *deeper* trouble. Dungeon deep."

With a pout, Bunda nodded. "Fine, I'll stay quiet, but I deserve an explanation first."

Kael sighed. "I don't have time for that now. If you follow me, you'll find out soon enough." She still seemed unconvinced. "Listen, it's got to do with the king."

Bunda's expression quickly softened. Now she seemed intrigued. "Oh? What is it? Tell me! It better be something that will prove how sinister that dreadful king is!"

"It is."

Bunda grinned like a cat.

Checking to and fro, Kael exited the alleyway with Bunda following. He hadn't wanted anybody to come with him, but after that last bit of information he had hinted to her, it was unlikely she would settle to wait at home. Kael could only wonder who was looking after her shop.

Growing more wary with every passing minute, Kael took some minor backstreets to get to the castle. His casual manner had long melted away. Now, he preferred to stay out of sight. Something caught his eye and he stopped. Across the street from the alleyway he was hiding behind, was a young lady with a basket full of parchment. She took one of the parchments and nailed it to a signpost on the corner of a banked street. Whistling an unknown tune, she wandered away.

Kael stole across the street and ripped the poster off of the pole. He stared at it dismally, his throat tightening. Bunda peered over his shoulder and chirped.

It was a picture of him.

Underneath the black and white sketch was written:

Wanted!
Kael Rundown,
For trespassing into His Majesty's Royal Castle,
And fraternizing with hostile individuals.
Reward: 500 Gold Coins dead,
1000 Alive.
Return to Zeptus for reward.

Kael's heart sank. If people didn't know him before, they would now. *How,* he wondered, *did they get my name? I didn't tell a soul, not even Larr.* But then again, he supposed, he had been in the army, his name was on their roster.

"Trouble?" Bunda whispered, "I think that's an understatement."

"I have a new idea, Bunda," Kael said, tearing the parchment into shreds. "Could you follow her and take down all those posters as she puts them up? That would be a great help."

"I want to know what this is all about. You told me that you discovered something dreadful about the king and hinted that you would tell me later."

Kael shook his head. "This is much more important. I won't get to tell anybody anything if somebody sees these posters and then catches me."

Bunda sighed. "You're right."

"Good," Kael said, relieved. This would give him some extra time. "Once you're done, go over to the Stockwins' place. They'll tell you everything; just tell them I sent you."

"I'll see you later, then." Bunda ran off in the direction the poster girl had run, looking flustered from all this activity.

"I sure hope so," he thought aloud. He slipped into the alleyways again, but changed his initial course. He had to talk to Malaricus first.

Shatterbreath watched Kael from the skies, glad that she had her supreme vision once again. The boy, Tiny, was bustling around the city. He had entered a small, meagre building and there he had stayed for a good half an hour or so.

So far, this was all terribly boring.

Circling from above, watching Kael do all the work, she couldn't help but to feel somewhat ashamed—and perhaps a tad jealous. This is all she could do to help at the moment, simply watch. Her body ached for some action, or at least to help in some way.

She laughed where she was, way up high. As if an old dragon like herself needed anymore action. Action was for the young. But that boy...he made her feel young at heart. His presence alone made shiver with energy. She had recovered her youthful stamina once again thanks to him. What was she doing, calling herself old? *She wasn't* that *old*. Not compared to the *truly* old ones. At least she could walk without shaking, and she still had all her teeth.

Tiny was holding something in his hands, a piece of parchment perhaps. He stayed deathly still for a long time, still clutching the paper. A screech caught Shatterbreath's attention and for a few seconds, she chased an eagle around in a circle until she finally caught it.

Spitting out feathers, Shatterbreath peered back down below. Why did she always eat those darn birds? The same thing always happened. She'd be coughing up feathers for a week.

Now, where was the boy? She scanned the crowds below, her precise vision effortlessly gliding over every face that wasn't the one she sought. *There!* She growled. He was going on another detour? He sure was taking his time. This was making her irritable and cranky. She would have to tease him for something later, just to bother him.

The building he entered was grand and had multiple spires. From its stained glass windows, Shatterbreath would have guessed it to be a church. Churches, however, usually had gargoyles perched atop their crevices and besides, there was already a huge church nearby. No, this building must be the library. Pretty good one too, judging by its size.

Shatterbreath surprised herself with how much she knew about humans. She reflected this for a moment. *You don't live this long on this planet without learning a little something,* she reminded herself.

Tiny Kael exited the library at last. Shatterbreath's adrenaline kicked up as she noticed a man robed in red standing behind him. He man took a drag on his pipe and clasped Kael's shoulders. Shatterbreath growled.

They exchanged a few more words and the man in red disappeared back into his library. She watched patiently as Kael made his way towards the big figure-eight in the middle of the city. There, in front of the gates to the inner yard, he stopped. Shatterbreath began to gradually spiral lower, preparing in case the situation got dangerous

Somebody pointed upwards, catching Kael's attention. He craned his neck to see what the matter was. He cursed silently. Shatterbreath was circling above the city, getting lower and lower by the second. This was not good, she would arouse suspicion. As discreetly as he could, he tried to wave her off. She caught his message and ascended higher, peaking off at a more discreet height.

There were many people waiting outside the castle, which was perfect. The king must have been planning on a public appearance, most likely to warn people of the intruder that had snuck into his castle. Little did he know the very same fugitive would be presenting himself right then and there. It occurred to Kael that making an appearance like this would almost certainly land him in prison, which brought up the encouragement for him to do his best convincing the people. If enough people believed him, they would keep him safe from the authorities. It was a whim, but it was the only thing he could think of.

There was a large barrel set against the castle wall, so Kael squeezed his way through the crowd and then dragged it to the very front of the mob, just in front of the castle gates. A few people were already watching him curiously as he hauled the barrel, and pretty soon nearly half the crowd had their attention on him. He could sense that they expected him to say something.

He stood up on the barrel, shaking for a moment, but gained his balance. His fingers trembled and he could feel the moisture building in his armour. He thrust out his arms and took a deep breath.

"People of Vallenfend!" he called out, his voice orotund. Formulating what he was going to say, he waited for their disporting conversations to cease. "I know why your men go off to fight against the dragon. I know why countless brave souls have died because of your king."

A susurrus ran through the crowd. "Yeah, I know why as well. To keep our kingdom safe, why else?" a tall lady called out.

Somebody snorted nearby. "Are you kidding, you actually believe that? You must not be a mother then." An older woman turned to Kael. "Speak, young man, but choose your words carefully, you are touching on a delicate subject."

Working up courage, Kael began. "People, your king is working in secret. He has organized a clandestine deal with a nation from far away across the seas."

"What?" somebody yelled. "What is this folly?"

"I know it sounds crazy, but you have to believe me. Zeptus and King Morrindale have made an agreement to weaken Vallenfend's defences. They have been doing so by sending your brothers and children to go fight Sh—to go fight the dragon."

"Why," somebody called out, their voice pernicious, "would he do this? What gain is there for either side? What could possibly lure anybody to do such a thing?"

"Riches, gold, silver, treasure." Kael shook his head sadly. "That is what they seek."

"And the other side you speak of? What is in this for them?"

Pausing for effect, Kael gave the person the answer. "Quite simply, our kingdom."

Another ripple of surprise ran through the crowd. Their voices began to rise and soon arguments were breaking out among them. It seemed half the crowd believed him, or wanted to, while the other half did not.

"Think about it!" Kael yelled, crouching lower on his barrel for emphasis, "how easy would it be to invade Vallenfend? With no army, no fighting force, it would be a simple task to sack this glorious city. When was the last time the king issued a large taxation? He doesn't need our money, he has his own hoard!"

The crowd grew silent as a familiar, raspy voice broke the deliberations. "How would you know this, boy, even if it were true?"

Kael's gaze shot to the battlements, where Zeptus had appeared, hunched over the railing. He cleared his throat and spoke again. "You make hasty accusations full of deceit and untruth."

Everybody in the crowd craned their necks up to the top of the wall. The king was standing behind just behind Zeptus, his face redder than usual. He fiddled with his hands uneasily.

"I have my sources," Kael replied to him. The city was suddenly so quiet. The crowd didn't even utter a word. The babies the mothers were carrying went silent and even the dogs in the background stopped their barking. A whisper of wind blew through.

Kael and Zeptus glared at each other for a moment until King Morrindale took the stand. Zeptus backed away. "People, people!" he said, sounding surly. "What is this all about then? Who is disturbing the peace of my kingdom?"

The women standing closest to Kael took a few steps away; leaving Kael exposed standing on top of his barrel. Two archers standing on either side of the king and his advisor notched arrows to their bowstrings.

"You? You are but just a lad!" The king squinted and cupped his hand over his eyes to block out the sun. "No matter. Why is it you bother my people and rile up this contention? What message do you have to bring?"

"I know what you're up to, King Morrindale!" Kael yelled, disregarding the consequences for directly accusing the king of a crime. "I know why you've been sending our men to die for these thirty years."

King Morrindale smiled and laughed, his head rolling around on his thick neck. He definitely had too much to drink. "Of course you do, silly boy. Everybody knows! Why do you think I have these regular public appearances? Zeptus has told you people enough already! For your protection, that's why."

"I know about the empire!" Kael snapped. The king's smile was wiped from his face. His countenance turned an even deeper red.

Zeptus leaned forward and whispered something into the king's ear. King Morrindale spun around and gawked up at the man. "No, I will not! I can handle this boy's lies on my own!" The king's advisor whispered something else. "Fine," he pouted, "go ahead."

The king stepped back and Zeptus once again took the stand, a sour expression on his pale face. He placed his hands back on the railing ominously, looking like a gargoyle. He fixed a wrinkle in his robe and then addressed the crowd.

"Kael, Kael Rundown, am I right? That is your name after all, isn't it?"

Kael grimaced, but nevertheless nodded. "Aye."

"Ladies and gentlemen, this *boy* is a traitor to Vallenfend." All faces turned angrily to Kael. "We have direct sources that tell us that he was in the army, not a month ago. He, like all soldiers, left to fight the dragon. However, instead of fighting it, *he joined it* instead." The crowd was growing louder and louder, forcing Zeptus to raise his voice. "He has been working alongside the enemy of Vallenfend; the one being that is responsible for the murders of all your boys!

"Is this true, Kael Rundown?" Zeptus smirked.

Kael gritted his teeth. The situation was getting dire, fast. How did Zeptus figure all that out? "No, listen," he yelled in defence. "The dragon, she is not who you think she is! She doesn't want any part of this! She is no threat to our city whatsoever! She is the one who told me of this man's insidious plot!"

"The dragon told you what you claim to be true?" a lady screamed. "And you expected us to believe it?"

"Lies, all lies!"

"You are the true enemy here!"

"Throw him in the dungeons!"

Kael drew his sword as the crowd closed in. "Don't you see? This is what *he* wants you to do! He's trying to turn you against me! I've seen the king's treasure, what I speak is truth!"

"What was that, Kael Rundown?" Zeptus asked, cocking his eyebrow. "You say you've seen proof? And where did you find this so called truth? In the dragon's cave?" He laughed, sending chills through Kael's spine.

"Of course not! I found a room in the castle—"

"Wait, what did you just say?" Zeptus leaned farther out onto the ledge. A crooked smile was spreading across his lips. "You just admitted that you intruded into the castle. You are guilty of trespassing. This is a wanted man," Zeptus said, pointing a thin finger at Kael. "As I speak, posters depicting his face are being posted all around Vallenfend. He is wanted for various crimes. I'm only glad that we won't have to search for long."

The mob around him was thrumming angrily. They screamed and thrust their fists out at him, but Kael's sword and shield kept them at bay. He glared up at Zeptus, who wore a smug grin.

"Guards," the hubris man ordered, "seize that boy."

Kael scanned over the crowd. He sighed grimly. "If you are not willing to believe me, then you are all a lost cause." His sad declaration caused a few people around him stop, but otherwise the crowd was still wild.

Kael didn't resist as four guards appeared out of nowhere amid the crowd and tackled him to the ground. He didn't say a word or fight back as they handcuffed him and dragged him into the castle's inner wall. The crowd cheered as he was carried off.

A roar thundered from overhead and for a few seconds, the tumult of the crowd was drowned out. The king flinched from where he stood up on the wall and even Zeptus looked frightened. But Shatterbreath didn't descend. She knew if she came down now, they would kill Kael.

Zeptus was quick to shy away his fear. He must have realized that if Shatterbreath hadn't come down already, she wasn't going to at all. "That's right, *boy*. Be gone with you and your *lies,*" Zeptus called out to him as Kael was pulled out of sight. Kael caught one last look at Zeptus before he was pilled inside the gates. For whatever reason, despite his victory, Zeptus didn't seem pleased.

Either way, a new animosity was brewing deep within Kael's chest towards that man. One thing was for certain now. Zeptus was behind all this, there was no doubt about it.

Chapter 20

The dungeon, a place Kael would have preferred to stay a mystery to him. The guards had walked him through the castle from the back door, choosing a direct route to the prisons. They descended the stairs, holding Kael tight.

The granite in the hallway was dank and had mould lining the crags and spaces in between the bricks. There was a listless down here that Kael found extremely unnerving. He thought that having lived in Shatterbreath's cave for a time would get him used to something like this, but he had been very wrong.

His heart pounded in his chest. Once they reached the foot of the stairs, a fetid smell met Kael's nostrils. It reminded him strikingly of the odour that had filled Shatterbreath's cavern before she had cleaned it, except this smell was mixed with the thick stench of human filth and everlasting grime.

The cells themselves were small, only big enough to fit one bed lined with hay and a little extra room to move about. The only other things that were in the cells were the occasional set of shackles and a small chamber pot. Kael wrinkled his nose in disgust.

Weeping echoed through the dismal corridor, making Kael feel somewhat comforted that he wasn't alone. But as he passed the first prisoner, that comfort slipped away. An emaciated old lady gawked up at him, nearly all her teeth either blackened or missing. Deep wrinkles etched her gaunt face and her white skin hung on her like rags. Her eyes protruded unnaturally and her mouth stayed agape, making Kael wonder if she was even alive at all.

More people like this he passed, mostly all of them women. The majority of them seemed comatose, their vacant eyes staring into space. Those who were responsive were wailing and gnashing their teeth.

Most of the people in there should have been thieves or other lawbreakers, but there were so many of them! There surely couldn't be this many lawbreakers in one city, could there? Vallenfend was known for its low criminal activity. There was something more to this.

They kept going, passing all the cells in this block and entering another corridor. These cells were in slightly better condition, with more space, softer beds and some mild privacy between the cells. Also, the cells on the left side actually had windows too.

They shoved Kael into one of the cells. He sprawled to the ground, but picked himself back up. Before he could do anything else, the guards seized him once again. They stripped him of his armour and weapon with surprising efficiency, carrying it away and out of sight further down the hallway. Kael watched them go as they closed the door in front of him, pressing his face up against the metal bars to get a better look.

Kael noticed something purple out of the corner of his eye. Not a moment later, pain erupted in his fingers as Zeptus smacked them with a long black stick. Kael clutched his fingers and sidled away from the bars. He knelt down on the ground and breathed heavily in contempt as Zeptus's purple eyes bored into him.

"You there," the advisor said, wheeling around and jabbing the end of the black stick into the chest of a black-clad guard. Kael hadn't even realized they had been there until now. "Guard him."

"Lord Zeptus, why?" the soldier questioned, "Won't a regular guard do? Our services are required elsewhere, aren't they?"

Zeptus came face to face with the soldier, standing taller than him and looking quite imposing. "This boy is not to be trifled with. He needs a proper guard here at all times. Is clear?"

Before the soldier could reply, another black-clad guard cut in. "Sir, if I may watch over him? Trudon is right, his skills are needed elsewhere."

Zeptus transferred his scowl from the first warrior to the one who spoke. He eyed him for a moment, but at last backed off and nodded. "Fine, so be it." With that, Zeptus and his company of black-clad soldiers left Kael all alone with his guard.

Sighing loudly, Kael slumped down on his bed—which was harder than he would have preferred—and brooded over what had just happened. He thought for sure that he would be able to convince the people. He thought that they would take his side! But Zeptus...

"Hey, YOU!"

Kael slowly turned his head to the side of his cell lazily, his mouth half-open. He did a double-take as he recognized who had yelled at him. *Don Huntson?* Keeping his distance in case the boy was going to try and strangle him, Kael rose off of his bed.

"You, you're that boy I talked to, that recruit!" Don said loudly. His face screwed up as he thought for a moment. The boy was scrawny, even more so since the last time they had met. He was pressed right up against the small barred opening between cells. "Wait a minute... It was you, wasn't it! You framed me! It's your fault I'm in here!"

Kael coughed to cover a smile. "I don't know what you're talking about."

Don shook the bars. "You framed me as revenge for what I did! Curse you!"

"Framed, what do you mean? Why are you in here?"

"You bloody know why!" He shook the bars again. Kael's guard looked back to see what was wrong, then returned to his regular posture. "You're the one who stole that horse and told them that I did it, it's got to be you!" His arms went limp and he smiled through the bars. "But at least they caught you. Ha ha, serves you right, you stupid git. Now they have to let me out."

Kael shrugged. "Well, they caught me all right, but not for that. Looks like you and I are going to stay cellmates, eh?"

Don frowned. "Caught you for... What? No!" He resumed shaking the bars once again. He disappeared out of sight and Kael could hear him shaking the iron door on the front of his cell instead. "Come on, let me out! I'm telling you, I didn't steal that horse! It was this guy, this guy next door! Listen, he'll tell you!"

Kael's guard turned around, leaning on his halberd. He yawned. "So?"

Don threw a tantrum.

Lying down on his bed, Kael stared at the ceiling dismally, listening to Don's uncouth curses. What now? How could he get himself out of this situation?   He relaxed as he remembered Shatterbreath's words.   She would get him out, that's right.   He grinned as he closed his eyes. She would get him out.

A boom of thunder sounded off outside.

Kael scrambled to his feet and stood on his toes to look out the window.   Shatterbreath was flying dangerously close to the castle. So close, in fact, he could hear bells ringing in alarm.   He stuck his hand out the window to let her know he was there.

Her eyes flickered at his hand, she nodded and then she banked away from the castle.   A large ballista soared past her, missing her left wing by a hand's breadth.   With three strong beats, she was gone out of sight.

Kael lowered himself from the window.   He grimaced as he noticed his guard was turned around, staring at him. Kael was going to lie back down and try to ignore him, but he spotted the man's eyes.

He walked closer to the bars at the front.   The guard checked to see if anyone was near and then leaned in closer.   "What did you call me when we met earlier in the castle when I tried to intercept you?"

Kael hesitated.   But the man spoke with sincerity and concern, so he decided it was safe to talk back. "Korjan, I called you Korjan."

"That name," the soldier said, gripping a bar to steady himself, "it's so familiar... Why did you call me Korjan?"

Kael studied what little of his face showed through his outfit. "You have the same eyes as a man I know, a blacksmith.   The similarity is so strong, that I mistook you for him at first."

The soldier took a deep breath.   Removing his hand from the bar, he pulled the cloth away from his face.   Kael gasped, shocked by how much this man indeed looked like Korjan.   The way his hair curled, the same look of fierce concentration...   "You...you're Korjan's son, aren't you?" Kael asked carefully.

The man nodded. "Yes.   My name's Tooran." He hesitated. "I never knew my father's name until now.   All I even knew is that he had been a blacksmith before he died.   Korjan, hmm..."

Korjan's son was alive?   This...this was amazing!   Kael would have to tell him as soon as possible, assuming he would ever get out of here.

261

"Your father is still alive. He thinks you're dead," Kael said, hiding his excitement towards this new occurrence. "How is it that he doesn't know about you?"

Korjan's son, Tooran, pulled a stool over to Kael's cage. He sat down on it with a grunt. "From what I've heard, when I was very young when King Morrindale first declared war on the dragon, my father was called to join the army. He didn't want to, which is understandable. So he refused to go, preferring to stand his ground against the king's wrath rather than dying for an unjust cause. He was a strong man, and succeeded in holding off the king's soldiers when they came to take him away.

"However, he couldn't keep the soldiers from getting to his wife and to me. As he fought the soldiers around him, others slipped into his house and captured his wife and children. Without any negotiations, they took his wife and slaughtered her before his helpless eyes. And they took me. They told me he had killed himself afterwards..."

Tooran paused and ground the end of his halberd into the stone floor. "The king—or perhaps Zeptus—spared his life, knowing the pain of losing his wife and child would be punishment enough.

"But they didn't kill me. They didn't want to waste a perfectly healthy boy like me. Instead, they brought me into the castle where I learned deadly arts and superior stealth. I became a member of the King's Elite. Knowing nothing else, I grew up under harsh training and *extremely* strict discipline."

They remained quiet, except for Don, who was still cursing in the cell next door. Kael was the first to break the silence. "You said you trained in deadly arts... I fought at least a dozen of men like you. It didn't seem that hard to me."

Tooran laughed. "Of course not. If we really wanted to, we could have killed you at any moment. No, our orders were otherwise. We were meant to keep you alive, but give you a struggle. You were *supposed* to escape."

Aghast, it took some time for Kael to find his voice. He blinked several times. "Who gave you those orders?"

Tooran frowned. "I don't know. I got my orders from my superior. I don't know where he gets his."

Kael sat down on his bed, feeling defeated. *Could have killed him at any moment...* So all that...and he had been perfectly safe? He wasn't that good of a fighter after all? What was going on here? However hard he tried after that, he couldn't stop wondering who had given that merciful order, and why they would.

There came a scream from the other cellblock. Tooran turned his head to the noise. He leaned in closer to the bars, gesturing for Kael to do the same. "Listen," he whispered, barely audible, "another guard will take over in a few hours. Once I'm back on shift, I can help you escape."

"Really?" Kael asked, his hope returning. "Won't you get in trouble?"

Tooran slipped his helmet back on. "I won't get in trouble," he sighed. "Even if I'm caught, I'm too valuable. They won't execute me. The worst I could get would be fifty lashes."

Kael hesitated. "Why would you do this for me, Tooran? You barely even know me."

"I'm doing this for my father. You know him, better than I at least. When you get the chance, I want you to tell him that I'm alive."

Kael nodded. "Understand, though, I might not ever get the chance to again. I'm a criminal, remember? I'm a wanted man."

Tooran shook his head and twisted the halberd's handle in his grasp. "I know, but any chance at all is better than none. Now quiet down, before we get in trouble."

"By the way," Kael said, thrusting his hand through the bars, "my name is Kael Rundown."

Tooran stared at his hand for a moment, considering what to do. At last he gripped Kael's hand in a firm handshake. "It's a pleasure to meet a friend of my father's, Kael."

With that, he stood up briskly and kicked the stool back over to where he had fetched it. Standing erect and at the ready, he didn't talk to Kael for the rest of his shift.

Don, however, did.

"Just for conversation's sake," he said, resting up against the barred window between their cells, "do you want to know why I told you to go into the A group?"

Kael frowned on his hard bed. All he wanted to do right now was get some sleep. Just to humour him, Kael asked, "Why?"

"Well, believe it or not, I used to work for the castle." Don tapped the bars to an unknown beat. "I was hired to make as many boys join the A side as possible so that there was a higher chance they'd all die. It wasn't the best thing in the world, I know, but it kept me from having to go instead."

Leaning over to one side, Kael propped himself up. "Really?"

"Yeah," Don sighed, "if you didn't notice, they wanted to make the army as inefficient as possible. Spending their money on uniforms instead of proper armour or weapons... Harsh trainers and worthless training programs... You were never meant to succeed."

Kael made a sound that resembled a growl as he glanced at his now-dirty uniform. He had forgotten to get a new tunic. "I suspected as much, but I didn't want to get in trouble so I didn't ever say anything."

They both stayed silent for a spell. "By the way," Don said abruptly, "how *did* you manage to escape fighting the dragon?"

Kael chuckled. "I didn't." Don's expression was priceless. "She and I became...friends. That's why I'm in here now."

Their conversation was interrupted as the door to their cellblock was flung open. Two guards dressed in royal blue entered, followed by a third member to their party. Kael gawked at the man in absolute shock.

"Step away from the bars," one guard barked. "You there, get away from there." Don shied away out of sight and the third member of their party stepped forward, wearing a smug grin.

"Kael Rundown, how I loathe to see you alive," the Captain hissed.

"But—but you're supposed to be dead!" Kael stuttered.

The Captain twitched in his usual strange way. "No, I long to be, but still I am here on this earth, dishonouring my family name. I have not been granted the respect of death. Apparently my services are still needed."

"What services are those?"

The Captain gave him a deadly smile. "Identifying you, for one. I knew you went to fight the dragon, Kael. And when I heard word of you still walking around with air in your lungs, I couldn't believe it. I reasoned the only way you could have survived is if you *joined* forces with that great fire-breathing monstrosity. You seemed like the type that would do that."

Kael shook his head, still in disbelief. "How did you survive?"

The Captain twisted the cap he was wearing on his head. "The dragon knocked me aside like I was nothing more than a gutted fish. It shames me to tell you that cowardice took over and I fled from the scene, fearing for my life. I returned here and told Zeptus that everybody had died. But when you showed up, that's when I made my speculations."

Captain Terra smirked at him, leaning in dangerously close. Kael edged ever so closer. The Captain opened his mouth to say something smart, but Kael silenced him with a blow to his jaw. He hated that man.

The two guards on either side of the Captain butted Kael with the end of their spears, one striking his injured shoulder. Kael slumped in his cell, brought to his knees by the pain. He could hear Captain Terra howling in pain and outrage, which gave him some sort of satisfaction.

Another pang of pain erupted over his back. The Captain had seized a spear from one of the guards and was now striking Kael over the back with the shaft of the weapon through the bars. The guards didn't make any move to stop the enraged man as he struck Kael repeatedly. Fear lanced through Kael. Were the guards going to let the Captain beat him to death?

Finally, the guards stopped the Captain, who struggled to keep hold of the spear. Eventually the guards won over and took the spear away from him. The Captain fumed and his moustache fanned with every hot breath. All he had was a slight bruise on his jaw, whereas Kael was throbbing all over from the beating he had just received.

He touched his left eye gingerly. It was puffy and sore. His scab from the cougar slash had reopened once again. *Would it ever heal?*

"You wretched, filthy animal!" the Captain spat. A guard placed his hand on Captain Terra's shoulder and they turned to leave. He waved a finger at Kael. "You haven't seen the last of me boy. I'll be back to visit you *later*."

Kael was relieved when the Captain left. Despite the ominous warning, Kael wasn't worried. He probably *would* see the man again, just not in the same place or circumstance. When he did, Kael was going to beat him right back.

One of the guards stayed to replace Tooran, who left Kael without so much as a glance, giving no clue to how he would help Kael escape later. The new guard scowled at Kael as if he was a putrid rodent and then pulled up the stool and sat on it on the other end of the narrow hallway, his spear resting on his lap.

Kael was content to lie back down on his bed and stare up at the ceiling, reflecting and biting back the pain. Although he was bruised and ached all over because of his recent beating, he was still more hurt by the way his own people had turned on him so swiftly. Was it worth fighting for a city like that? Would all his efforts be in vain if they wouldn't appreciate or even believe him?

It was troubling, all so troubling.

Maybe they deserved what was coming for them. If they were so ignorant, then maybe being overrun by a conquering empire was a just consequence. Maybe an empire would be good for the land.

Kael laughed out loud, startling his guard. *As if an empire would ever be good for anything.* He was being too hasty to judge Vallenfend. There was something with the way Zeptus manipulated that crowd. Like putty in his hands he had weaved them and made them turn on Kael. Yes, now that he thought of it, there was something definitely strange about Zeptus. And for some reason, he could sense that Shatterbreath would know...

Thinking fiercely, Kael didn't even notice as a familiar black-clad figure entered the door several hours later. The guard didn't noticed either until the aft of a halberd had struck his temple.

Kael squinted through the darkness of his cell. Night had fallen already and he couldn't see a thing. He heard a shuffle and the rattling of keys. There was a pouring noise and then strong smell of whiskey.

Kael got to his feet and stood about a foot away from his cell door, trying to see what had happened. A dark shape rose off the limp form of his unconscious guard.

"Kael Rundown?" Tooran's deep voice whispered.

"Aye."

Without another word, Tooran unlocked the door and ushered him out. They took two steps before they were interrupted.

"Hey, hey!" Don cried, pressing up against the bars of his cell. "What're you doing?"

In a flash, Tooran had Don's scrawny neck in his thick hands, a blade pressed to the boy's neck. "Silence, fool!" he hissed.

Don sputtered. "No, wait!" he wheezed, clutching at Tooran's fingers. He espied Kael hiding off behind him. His brow furrowed. "You're letting him out? Take me with you!"

Tooran pulled the blade away and held it a foot away from Don's chest, ready to stab him through the heart. Kael intervened. "No, stop! Just let him come, what will it affect?"

Kael could sense Tooran's unease. "Everything. This boy is a threat to your survival. He will make too much noise and might cause you to get captured once again."

"Please, he doesn't have to come with us, just unlock his cell and we'll be off."

Tooran growled. He considered both choices. He released his grip and quickly unlocked the door. Saving his breath, Tooran was off at once, rushing not out the entrance to the cells, but deeper down the corridor.

As Kael followed Tooran, Don whispered something at him. "Consider our feud settled," he said, giving him a mock salute. Don exited through the door to the other cells and was gone.

"Where are we going?" Kael whispered.

"I assume you want your equipment back?" Tooran replied, just as quiet. "You did have a nice sword after all."

They reached the other end of the cellblock. A large iron door met them, bolted firmly to the wall with a heavy padlock set deep in the middle of it. Tooran protruded a key from the depths of his tunic and fit it into the key slot. With a hollow *click* the door surrendered and opened for them, swinging free with a groan.

Inside the room were many large chests, each holding another padlock to guard whatever lay inside. Tooran opened one, peaked inside, shook his head and then reclosed it. He pulled a ring of keys from his tunic and opened another. Kael was amazed by how many items he could hide in his clothing without any making any noise. Finally, Tooran reached inside a chest and pulled out Kael's armour, sword and shield. He closed the chest with his foot and fastened the padlock back on.

"What're in the rest of these, anyway?" Kael asked as he quickly girded himself with his armour.

"Confiscated items mostly, but there are also things not to be trifled within these chests."

"Such as...?"

"That doesn't matter," he said, patiently waiting as Kael pulled on a vambrace. "Just...weapons of sorts given to us. Let's just say it wasn't fully understood how they worked before they were used."

"What do you mean?"

Tooran sighed. "You ask a lot of questions, don't you?"

Kael laughed, "Your father always says the same thing."

With a smile, Tooran adjusted hood over his head. "Some of these things hold magical qualities—destructive qualities. Like I said before, some were used before it was known what they did. We locked them down here for safety."

Magic? "Who gave them to you? Was it the invading empire?"

Tooran shot Kael a look. "I don't know how you figured out about that, but yes, it was the invading empire. No more questions, I know nothing else."

So they had at least some minor control with magic. That was not good. But that also clarified another thing, what Tooran had just said—it was indeed an empire that threatened Vallenfend. Shatterbreath and Kael had been correct.

Kael wanted to ask more questions, but as soon as he finished putting on his last boot, Tooran ushered him onward. "Let us go at once. I fear at any moment we will be discovered."

As they ran through the cells, the prisoners' ghostly wails pressed on Kael from either side. They pleaded for him to free them and to help them return to their families. They cried and reached out to him with their boney fingers. Chills ran up Kael's spine, even after they left the dungeons.

They paused at the top of the stairs, allowing Kael to catch a breath. "Can't we set them free as well?" he asked between his panting.

Tooran shook his head, not even chancing to look at Kael, wary of anybody that might see them. "No, I am taking a big enough risk setting you free."

They passed through the halls, taking an unrecognizable route. At last, Tooran skidded to a halt, placing a hand out in front of Kael to signal him to do the same. As anxious as a rabbit, he turned to Kael.

"Listen, this is where we must part," he said, "I cannot take you any farther. I trust you can get out on your own?"

"Yes, I can," Kael assured him. He placed a hand on Tooran's shoulder. "Thank you, Tooran. When the situation presents itself, I will tell your father of your survival, and your bravery. I'm sure he'd be proud of you."

"Maybe, maybe not, who can say?" Tooran seemed unaffected by Kael's statement. "Can a father be proud of what I've become? No more talk, be off with you. And Kael, don't expect any sympathy from the citizens of Vallenfend, even if you are doing all this for their sake. Zeptus has twisted their minds and broken their hearts. If they get the chance, they will kill you, and so will the guards. If trouble arises, don't stay and fight, run. Got that?"

Kael nodded. "Yes. Thanks again."

"Don't mention it." Tooran waved him off. "Be gone with you now." He scurried off in the opposite direction.

Kael waited for him to gain some distance. He listened for a moment, hearing voices off in the distance somewhere in the castle. He closed his eyes and took a deep breath. *Here we go again.*

Chapter 21

Kael pumped his arms and legs. There were four guards wearing blue just behind him. He had considered fighting them and just knocking them out, but decided otherwise. He wanted to get out as fast as possible, weary that the soldiers in black would come after him instead.

Kael managed to lose one guards as he ran through the bottom floor of the castle, searching for the kitchen. When he had found the kitchen, he heaved aside the tile covering the secret tunnel and flung himself into the darkness. There, he somehow managed to find the entrance to the tunnel while at the same time, losing the remaining three guards.

This time, his short journey through the brambles was far less troublesome, for his armour protected his skin from the stinging nettles. Still, several gashes were inflicted to his face as he squeezed through.

He stopped just outside the brambles to take a breath, placing his gloved hands on his greaves. He glanced to the side as a glint of light caught his attention. He barely managed to bring up his shield as a blade attempted to decapitate him. Once again, his strange ability to slow down time saved his life.

The one who attacked him was a soldier wearing black. Kael parried each blow that was thrown at him, caught off guard by the soldier's speed and prowess. This was a much different opponent than Kael had fought before in the castle. Tooran's words echoed through his mind as the enemy's sword pounded against his shield. *We could have killed you at any moment.* He would have to be more careful now; they were no longer fighting at the same meagre level as before. This figure was fighting to kill.

They locked swords. Kael grunted as they fought to out-muscle each other. With a surge of strength, Kael knocked the soldier's sword away with his shield and followed through with a diagonal slash to the man's chest. Without hesitation, Kael was off, sprinting in the other direction.

He sprinted across the training grounds, which were silent and still. He lowered his shoulder as he approached the front gate. Kael struck the small door set in the gate, shield first. He bounced off of it and sprawled to the ground. It was more solid than he had thought. Enraged, he slashed at the door's hinges, cutting them free. The door remained in place, held by the lock on the other side. This time, when Kael tackled it, it crashed down, letting him out into the streets.

The moon watched lazily from overhead as Kael dashed through the empty, hollow streets of Vallenfend. With every shadow the moon created, with every darkened corner, nook or cranny, he imagined a black-clad figure hiding within its depths, ready to pounce and finish him off for good. He could feel his nerves fraying as his heart pounded faster than his feet could run.

Fatigue suddenly overwhelmed him and Kael stopped, mid stride, leaned over a counter of a merchant's hut and heaved. He stole a dirty rag off of a table and wiped his mouth. He glanced around with wide eyes, taking this quick opportunity to try and catch his breath. His body relaxed somewhat, sensing no immediate danger. But it was out there, he could feel it somewhere.

Something stirred from the back of the merchant's hut, so Kael set off again, this time at a slower pace. The confines of the city were close; he could see the outer wall just ahead. Sticking to the shadows, he spotted an open gate that was the perfect chance to escape from the city. He stopped himself before he dashed forward, his muscles still stiff. No, this was too perfect. It was almost certainly a trap.

Kael considered his options. He could try and outrun whatever lay just outside the wall, which had a slim chance of working. Without rope, climbing over the wall would be impossible.

His mind raced, trying to come up with a solution. He spotted a wagon and smiled, already formulating a plan. He grabbed the end of the handcart and picked it up off the ground, pushing the two-wheeled wagon out onto the road. He braced himself and gave it a push forward and then back, working up some momentum.

Then, with a mighty shove, he rolled it towards the large gate. The wagon bounced and squealed with every bump in the dirt road, but it picked up a large amount of speed before Kael let go of the handles and sent it careening out the door.

As he suspected, two swords flew out of nowhere and plunged themselves into the empty depths of the wagon. Four black-clad warriors had revealed themselves to Kael's sight, two of them trying to retrieve their swords with they had stabbed into the wagon, and two more standing confused, watching their comrades.

Kael burst from the doorway. Before the first black-clad man could even turn around, Kael plunged his sword through the soldier's back, his blade protruding out of his chest on the other side. Kael winced. They weren't wearing armour. *Of course, armour is cumbersome and noisy.* These soldiers relied on stealth and speed to accomplish their tasks.

Kael removed his sword with a pang of disgust and slashed another soldier from shoulder to hip. A twinge of pain erupted in Kael's left shoulder, stopping him from attacking the next soldier that emerged from behind the gate's large swinging door.

Kael blocked the soldier's attack and kicked him in the shin as hard as he could. The soldier faltered, reaching towards his injured shin which was most likely broken from Kael's metal boot. Taking advantage, Kael gave him an uppercut straight to his jaw, sword still in hand. The man squirmed for a moment, blood gushing from his shattered mouth, but then slumped to the ground.

An arrow bounced off Kael's armour, prompting him to move. He deflected another arrow that was aimed at his head with his shield, fired from one of the soldiers who had stabbed the wagon. Those two had given up trying to retrieve their swords and had instead aimed their bows at Kael. They notched more arrows.

Suddenly, another figure came rushing out of the gate. Kael yelped in alarm. *Don Huntson?* The boy sprinted away from the castle gates and a moment later, Kael understood why as several soldiers—both garbed in royal blue and pitch-black—rushed out of the gate after him. Kael turned away and began to sprint as well.

273

Don ignored the archers as they missed their shots, running past them. He quickly caught up to Kael and they soon were running side by side. A couple arrows flew past Kael, more burying just behind his feet. He heard and felt a *ping* across his back as a projectile glanced off his armour.

Don, however, wasn't as lucky.

Kael winced as he heard the boy scream. Don dropped out of sight, but even still, Kael did not stop. His insides burned and his legs threatened to give out at any moment. He couldn't run from this hoard of soldiers much longer!

They had nearly descended on him when they were stopped in their tracks. A giant blue form passed over Kael with a *whoosh*. The ground shook underneath Kael's feet as Shatterbreath landed directly behind him. The air reverberated around him and his eardrums nearly shattered as she gave a mighty roar. Kael fell to the ground, tumbling before he came to a complete stop, facing the battle that had erupted between his attackers and the dragon.

Shatterbreath shook her head and reared up on her hind legs as the group of soldiers tried to rally themselves against her. She flexed her great wings and roared again, making some of the regular guards trip on their own feet.

The King's Elite soldiers waved their swords at them and the two archers let their arrows fly. One projectile bounced off Shatterbreath's scale armour, but another pierce the soft membrane of her wing. The scene went suddenly quiet as Shatterbreath inspected the new wound. The soldiers remained deathly silent, fear eminent across all their faces.

Shatterbreath growled, took a deep breath and let a jet of flame escape from her toothy maw. The flame engulfed the soldiers, instantly killing almost half of them. Fire scattered in many directions as Shatterbreath closed her jaws. With a hiss, she descended on the soldiers.

They screamed and most tried to run as she began to tear their battalion apart. A few tried to stand their ground and fight. Shatterbreath whipped her great tail over the lot of them, sending a few skinnier soldiers flying through the air several yards. She

274

slammed her great clawed paw down, crushing a soldier underfoot and nearly cut another man in half with her other paw. In a matter of minutes, all the men were either dead or dying.

Blood seeping from her mouth and dripping from her claws, she turned to Kael, a snarl still on her lips. "Kael, are you alright?"

It took several seconds before Kael could overcome his awe. He finally caught his breath and blinked a few times. "Y—yes, I'm alright. Thanks for saving me."

She leaned in close to inspect him with one emerald eye as he stood back up. He patted her cheek affectionately as she sniffed him carefully and continued to look him over. "I'm fine, really!"

Still unconvinced, she backed off. "That was quite the crowd you had drawn. You seem to have a habit of getting in trouble."

Kael shrugged. "Yeah, it seems that way, doesn't it?"

"I was watching you from the sky. Who was that man you went to visit earlier, the one in the library?"

"Malaricus, an old friend. He's the one who gave me your medical supplies."

Shatterbreath grunted. "I told you not to talk to anybody. Why did you not listen to me? Do you trust this man with your life, Tiny?"

Kael hesitated. "Of course, Shatterbreath. That's why I went to see him in the first place. He's one of the smartest and most trustworthy people I know. I was seeing if he could add any more to this dilemma of ours."

"Good." She licked her wing where the archer's arrow had pierced, uttering a small growl. "And *did* he have anything else to add?"

"No, we got it spot on. I talked to a member of a secret group the king's been hiding—his elite guard force—he confirmed what we feared."

Shatterbreath's tail smashed against a lone little tree, knocking it clean out of the ground. "That bodes ill-news then, Kael. Empires are terrible things."

Kael sighed, remembering the crowd that had assembled in front of the castle and how they had turned on him so quickly. "I know. If

275

only my people will listen to me! Then we might have a chance against them! But you saw as well as I how they betrayed me. There's no use returning to Vallenfend for that purpose anymore." Suddenly, Kael felt heartbroken.

"Then, Tiny," Shatterbreath said, lowering her body, "we will have to try other cities."

Kael nearly choked. "What?"

"The only hope for your city is if we can persuade another city with a big army to join our forces to defend." She beckoned for Kael to climb up on her back. "I'm sure by the time the empire does land upon the shores; your people will believe you at last invariably."

"Yes, you're right. I was thinking the same thing earlier. I just never thought I'd have to abandon hope on my own city..." Kael's shoulders sagged as he sat on Shatterbreath's back. The sheath caps he had placed on her spines were still there thankfully. "Shatterbreath, you have no idea how it feels...to be rejected by my own people. Is there anything worse?"

The dragon didn't answer for a long time. Kael stared at her broken horn, wondering at how it got that way. "Yes, Tiny," she said morosely, "I do know how it feels. And to answer your question, yes, there are things worse than being ostracised by your own kind."

"Let's get back to the cave." Kael rubbed her neck, trying to comfort her. It was strange how easily his ill feelings could transfer to her. He had almost forgotten how hurt she was on the inside.

Kael opened the bag and rummage through, looking for the needle and thread. He found it and shoved the medical bag to the side. Threading the needle, he walked over to where Shatterbreath was waiting with her wing outstretched.

"This is going to sting," Kael warned.

"I can take it." Kael gave her a look. She rumbled playfully. "What? I can!"

The dragon growled as the needle sank into her flesh, but nevertheless remained still. Kael stitched up the fresh wound that the arrow had made when it had gone through her wing. She had many similar gashes all over her wings, but this was the only fresh wound.

He paused as she winced and then tightened up the thread around the wound, sealing the first part of it together snugly. *Yes, this will heal nicely.* As he worked, a question came to mind.

"Shatterbreath?"

"Hmm?"

"How old are you?"

The dragon huffed. "Oh, I don't know exactly. Well over a thousand years, perhaps nearing two thousand now."

He chuckled, just barely audible. "You know, you're the first female I've ever heard answer that question truthfully."

The dragon hefted her head and swivelled it over to him. She scrutinized him mischievously. "Who said I was being honest?"

Kael laughed again, surprised by Shatterbreath's humour. How had this dragon gained such a reputation of death and despair? The thought of all the men she had slain recently without hesitation shot through his mind, as well as the dreadful day when they had first met. He felt stuck between two worlds, unsure which to believe. Destruction seemed so easy for her, yet she could be so tender when she wanted.

Another question popped into his mind as he remembered what Malaricus had told him about dragons. He waited a few minutes to see if Shatterbreath would produce a question of her own to him. None came.

"Shatterbreath?" he asked over the rise and fall of her slow breathing.

"Yes, Tiny?"

"Why did you choose to spare my life? You told me you thought I was...cute, but there's got to be more to it than that."

Shatterbreath sighed, her nostrils flaring. "You're right, there is another reason. It has to do with something that happened a long time ago, something I fear is repeating."

"What do you mean?"

She checked to see if he was done, then turned to face him. "You are different, Kael. There's a power in your blood I'm sure you didn't even know about. You, Kael Rundown, are a direct descendant of one of the Favoured Ones."

277

Kael blinked. "Alright, is...is that significant?"

She clawed the ground for a moment. "A long time ago," she began, "when I was still a young dragon, there was a terrible empire that swept across this land."

"Yes, you mentioned that before. That doesn't explain why you spared my life though."

Her lip curled as she thought for a moment. "Rather than explain this to you, Kael, I'd rather *show* you, through my memories." She leaned, her muzzle hovering a few inches away from his face. She hesitated, back away, and then came in even closer. "Close your eyes and relax, Tiny. And don't panic."

His body seized as a sudden rush of energy engulfed him. Everything went white.

He opened his eyes, at once startled to find he was in Shatterbreath's rich vision. He tried to look around and move his arms, but nothing happened. Altogether, he became aware that his body didn't feel *right.*

He was also aware that he was flying.

His neck moved on its own accord. He could feel his muscles move and flex, but yet he wasn't telling them to. Slowly, the rest of his body became apparent to him. He could feel wings beating on either side of him, attached to both shoulders. His head swayed on the end of a long, sinuous neck and at the rear end of his contorted shape a tail sprouted.

If he could have, he would have gasped right then and there. *He was Shatterbreath!*

As if on cue, he turned his head and looked over his dragon body, which was green. Yes, he *was* Shatterbreath, only she was much, much smaller and a large wound was bleeding on her side. Pain filled the wound and Kael experienced it as if he was actually her.

He saw what she saw, smelled what she smelled, heard what she heard and felt what she felt. He even *thought* what she thought.

Their minds flowed together like two glasses of water poured into one.

They kept flying, despite the pain that was making the world swoon around them. Off in the near distance was a colossal mountain that rose high above the darkened world below. It had many crags and holes carved into its surface. Shatterbreath's thoughts told him that the giant tower-like mountain was the temple of the Dragon Elders.

A great sense of loss filled Shatterbreath's body and thusly Kael's as well. She kept repeating an unfamiliar name. He knew this feeling all too well, he didn't need her senses to tell him that. It was the loss of her father.

Two dragons extricated themselves from some crags and soared towards Shatterbreath. The dragons caught Shatterbreath and brought her back to the mountainside, querying where her father was. She couldn't answer them.

She was brought into the inner chambers, assisted by a smaller, lither dragon. It was rather unnerving in Kael's mind to see so many dragons as they entered a massive cavern. He was only used to one dragon, but in here there must have been at least ten, a few of them larger than Shatterbreath's true size.

All heads pivoted to catch sight of the bedraggled little dragon that was brought before them. Shatterbreath wheezed and struggled to stay upright and erect in front of the Dragon Elders.

"Young one, where is your father?" a male dragon with a large crest at the base of his skull asked.

"Dead," Shatterbreath and Kael answered sullenly, their heart dropping another notch as they confirmed what they didn't want to believe. "The humans...we had no choice but to pass over them. They—they killed him."

"Strongbeat is dead?" another brown dragon roared. "These humans have gone too far! It is good that we have called this council!"

"Calm yourself, Lizardtongue. Can't you see the young one is scared? Do not speak of her father while the pain is still fresh." The red dragon who spoke, the oldest of them all, leaned forward, staring at Shatterbreath with one large, molten eye. His movements were shaky and delayed and his size was truly daunting. It was easy to see that he was the oldest out of all the dragons there. "I'm afraid this occurrence has caused a great burden to fall upon you. However, with your father's...with him gone, we have no choice but to fill his position on this council."

"With whom?" a voice piped up. Shatterbreath didn't look that way; she was still fixed on the red dragon. "All Strongbeat had left for family was this hatchling!"

"So be it," the red one stated. "Hatchling, female, it matters not. She is the only one who can fill this spot. You are now on the council of the Dragon Elders, little one."

Lizardtongue, the brown one, growled. "This must be a jest. Her, a puny runt of a dragon? This is unheard of, Darion!"

The eldest dragon, Darion, turned his head laboriously towards Lizardtongue. "These are hardly ordinary circumstances, what is happening across this land is unheard of. Now, enough of this useless quarrelling, we must solve this dilemma."

"Indeed."

"Right, as I was saying," Lizardtongue began, pacing, "it has never been our place to meddle with human culture. The wars they wage, the disease they spread, it is none of our business.

"But this...empire they have established, it grows great and unruly and hostile towards all creatures. As well, they use rudimentary magic to force their will! If we do not intervene, the fate of the human race, as well as many others, may be in danger. Whether we like it or not, their existence affects ours."

"And what," Darion said patiently, sounding tired, "do you suggest we do?"

Lizardtongue licked his chops and swept his gaze over the dragons. "It is my suggestion that we assist the rebellious humans fighting against the empire, not directly in their battles, but in a different way entirely."

"This is foolishness," an Elder called out at the back of the room. "How can we help them without openly engaging in this war?"

"Gifts," Lizardtongue stated. "We give them gifts. Not traditional gifts, not tangible gifts. No, I mean something more."

"Are you implying we give them magic?"

"Perhaps, in a sense." Lizardtongue paused to read their reactions, cocking his head. "What I had in mind was *abilities*. We could give a group of humans the powers they would need to overcome the empire, nothing more."

A black dragon with a sinister appearance snorted. "What happens after their silly war is finished?" His voice was deep and throaty; reminding Shatterbreath of a cave she had once visited with her father. A new tear came to her eye. "What is to be done with these special humans who will hold these remarkable gifts?"

"We'll let them keep their gifts, quite simply." Murmurs ran through the dimly-lit cavern. "Imagine, for a moment. The humans will be thankful that we helped them overcome this threat of theirs. Together, we'll have peace! We will only give our power to those who deserve it. Favoured humans, the select few who won't abuse their might. We have the chance to create a utopia between our two races!"

Darion groaned as he pondered Lizardtongue's argument. "This plan of yours could hold many flaws, you realize this?"

"What's the worst that could happen?"

"Too much to say." The room was silent as Darion pondered for a moment longer. "However, this is the only feasible plan any of us has conceived so far. Ultimately, the decision is not mine. Let us vote on it."

Shatterbreath waited patiently as each and every member of the dragon council came to a vote. Most of them were in favour of the proposition, with only a few choosing against it. Darion voted for it, which persuaded many of the other dragons. It seemed as though whatever he chose, usually won.

It came time to Shatterbreath to vote. She had been hoping that it would pass right by her. It didn't. They all stared at her expectantly as she licked her wound.

"What's this?" Lizardtongue's voice rose over the silence. "What is impeding our progress?"

"The young one has not voted yet. It looks as though she might have something to say." Darion's wise eyes lingered on her. "What do you think of this, young Elder?"

Shatterbreath hesitated, and Lizardtongue scowled. She finally found her voice after a minute or so, weak and feeble. "The humans are terrible, it is in their nature to kill—I've witnessed it. What would be keeping them from using these great powers to feed their thirst for blood?"

Lizardtongue hissed. "That's enough from you. I already explained that we will give these gifts to only the most righteous and pure. This plan is foolproof."

Shatterbreath was still unconvinced, but she didn't say anything more. Darion turned his attention away from Lizardtongue and back to her. "So what will your choice be?"

She shook her head, receiving another hiss from Lizardtongue. "Nevertheless, we will follow through with our plan," the brown dragon said, his voice rising. "Her vote is not near enough to change the outcome."

Darion rose to his feet, shaking as he did. "Ah, my old bones. It is decided then. We will give some of our magic to the humans so they may overcome this obstacle. Let us organize ourselves tomorrow, and we will decide when and where this will happen."

The image of the council faded and all was black. Kael could no longer feel Shatterbreath's body enveloping him, nor did he feel any pain or any of her other senses. Her powerful voice suddenly echoed through his mind.

"They followed through with this, as planned." Her adult voice sounded so much older and stronger than moments before. "The humans that were given these amazing abilities were known thereafter as the Favoured Ones. Some received gifts that made them able to calm raging tempests with the cool of their voice; others could manipulate the very forces of nature with a simple wave of their hands. Still others had strength unmatched, speed unbridled and cunning unimaginable. With the combined strength and force of these a hundred or so, the renewed armies they amassed were able to hold off against the empire and eventually abolished it altogether." As she spoke, images passed through his mind, portraying the event where the humans were given their powers, as well as examples of their abilities and triumphant battles.

"In truth, Lizardtongue's had been correct. The Favoured Ones were indeed the most pure and noble of their race and did uphold what was expected of them." Her tone turned sad. "But alas, he did overlook one part of his plan."

A huge field suddenly spread below Kael, drenched in blood. His heart was nearly wrenched in two as he realized it was *dragon's* blood. Far below, flame and ice alike erupted all around and the corpses of dragons littered the ground. Cheering could be heard as before his eyes a group of humans slit the throat of a young dragon.

"The Favoured ones were not the ones who betrayed us, but their *children*. We had overlooked the fact that their children would not be as grateful towards us as their parents. They inherited their parents' gifts, but not their clean spirits. Instead of using their powers for good, they used their might for evil. They feared that my kind would notice their wicked deeds and soon they grew cautious and paranoid. They believed at some time the dragons would realize their mistake and take back the gifts they held.

"So, without warning, the Favoured Ones, now nearly doubled in number, turned on us. They began to kill my species by the hundreds. They aimed first for the Dragon Elders to try and eliminate all of the ones who had given them their gifts to begin

283

with. Lizardtongue, in some consolation, was the first to go. Darion, most noble of all the Elders, died of a broken heart as he witnessed the corruption of Favoured Ones, their hate towards us and the genocide of his kin. They targeted Elder's families as well, aiming to make it so that no spot on the council could ever be filled again. But they couldn't find the right families, so they decided to simply slaughter us all."

The image before Kael stayed there. So sorrowful was it, so painful, he wanted to tear his eyes away and cry, but he couldn't.

"Their action called us into action, so to speak. What was left of the council rallied together, and we managed to punish them for their crimes."

The scene changed again.

This time, Shatterbreath was perched high atop the same mountain they had met on before. But now, it was crumbling and left in ruins. Half the mountain was practically gone, leaving the other half lopsided and liable to give away at any moment. She peered down below with hate burning her eyes, down at the ones who had killed so many of her kind. Some even stared right back at her at eye level, hovering high above the ground, but they did not attack.

"Listen now, you *traitors*, you *murderers!*" she yelled, malice thick in her voice. She was much larger than in the last flashback, but Kael couldn't guess her age. Of the ten or so Elders, there were only four left now, including Shatterbreath, all of them sitting around her, wearing the same venomous expression.

"You have betrayed us and murdered our kin. *Killed* so many of my brothers and sisters with the very gifts we gave to you those sixty years ago. Your blood is tarnished with the lives of every dragon you have slain. So, with the power we still hold, I issue a curse on all of you. With each passing generation, your gifts, your abilities, will become watered down. Your children will not hold the same luxuries you have now. As your bloodline becomes diluted, so will your powers.

"It may not be imminent, but our revenge will be evident in only a few decades. With time, your lineage will be forgotten entirely, and thus the terrible crimes you have committed. I repeat, we will have our revenge, but it will be your children that will suffer."

The scene went dark again. Shatterbreath's voice echoed through his mind again. "With most of the Dragon Elders dead, that was all we could do to stop their rampage. It was impossible at that point to remove the gifts entirely all at once. Instead, as I stated, their gifts would slowly melt away, like a sand dune pummelled by the desert wind. It wasn't the severe punishment they deserved, but it was the worst we could give them.

"With no other choice, I fled to escape their wrath. It took over a century and I lost half my horn in the process, but at last the Favoured Ones stopped searching for me and their existence became but just a memory."

Kael was thrust from Shatterbreath's mind. He swayed on his feet and fell to the ground. He shook his head, placing a hand to his temple tentatively. His skin was blue and his fingers and toes were tingling, but otherwise he was fine.

His head throbbed from all the recent information. Shatterbreath shook her head as well, blinking several times as if there was something floating in front of her eyes.

"I've never done that before, that was quite odd."

Kael nodded. What a strange experience it had been to be *inside* another person's body, especially when that person was a dragon. Now he knew what it felt to be her. It was a strange new closeness, one that he wasn't sure he would have liked to experience.

"That's the reason I spared your life, Kael," Shatterbreath stated, hardly hesitating.

"What do you mean?" Kael was flabbergasted. "Are you—are you saying that I'm..."

"You are a direct descendant of the Favoured Ones, their blood runs in your veins." She began pacing around him. "It is quite clear when a dragon meets a Favoured One, there is an unspoken

285

connection which they share. That is why your father stuck out to me as well."

Kael's heart was beating faster and faster. "Really? Is that good or bad?"

Shatterbreath rolled her shoulders. "It is good because you have a power few will ever get to experience. You're ability to slow down time in your perspective when you fight—that is because of our gift. It gives you wicked reflexes and a huge advantage. Not for centuries have I seen anybody with this strong of an ability however...it is very interesting actually."

"B—but the Favoured Ones, they killed your kind! Doesn't that make me bad as well? Don't I inherit their...evilness?"

Shatterbreath laughed loudly. "Not at all, Kael! You being a Favoured One made you strike out in that silly group you were in when we met, but it was your innocence that made me spare you! There was a kindness in your heart that made you different than anybody else. You didn't want to kill me to earn respect or riches; you didn't want to kill me at all! All you wanted to do was return to your family, just like your father. There is not an ounce of wickedness in your body."

Kael was truly touched. His eyes began to water, but he pretended he had an itch on his face to hide it from Shatterbreath. "Why didn't you spare him then?" he asked, controlling his voice, "if you spared me?"

Shatterbreath cocked her head and inspected one of her glowing stones. "Fate I suppose. There was more to you than just your innocence or bloodline. I felt as though I was *meant* to not kill you. Dragons have a strong sense of destiny you know."

Kael strolled over to where she had sat down and propped himself against her leg. Emotionally and physically, he felt quite drained.

"Now that I think about it," he said, slowly nodding off to sleep, "it felt strange when I first met you as well. Maybe it was fate that made us meet, and not just coincidence."

"Perhaps. Worry about that later, I can tell you need sleep." She began to hum deeply, sending low vibrations through her body and into his.

"Hey," Kael said with a start, "do you think Zeptus might be a Favoured One as well?"

Shatterbreath stopped her humming. "I speculate that, yes. It is not uncommon for Favoured Ones to have strange physical traits as well. I was watching the way his goaded that crowd into turning on you. It would seem that his ability is persuasion over people."

"That explains a lot."

"Yes." She began to hum again. "It is quite miraculous that there are two Favoured Ones with such strong abilities as you two. Such a thing will not likely be seen ever again, especially in one city."

She remained quiet as Kael fell asleep at her side, still thinking of everything he had just learned. Quite frankly, it was a miracle he managed to any sleep at all.

Once the boy was asleep, a complacent look on his face, his arms clasped over one another, Shatterbreath gently moved him over onto his straw sleeping mat. All this recollecting had brought back pains she had never wanted to feel ever again, horrors best locked away in her mind. Now that the nightmare had returned, she couldn't stop thinking about those bloody days and the ones afterwards.

She crept to the mouth of her cave and glanced back to see if the boy was alright, and then crawled outside and up to the top of her mountain.

There, nestled in between the crystalline lake and a large tree, Shatterbreath wailed like she hadn't in years, her large tears sending ripples across the lake's surface.

The mist intensified with her sorrow, displaying her sadness.

Chapter 22

Kael usually found some comfort in the scattered chaos that was sleep. Sleep was the time where his friends would laugh with him and where the world was right and pure once again. In his dreams his mother would make him dinner with a smile and he would talk excitedly with an unscarred Faerd and Laura about trivial things that seemed important back then.

This time, there was no comfort.

Over and over, as clear as if he was replaying the moment in real life, he saw his blade plunge through a man's chest. *His blade.* Again and again, with all his might, he pushed that sword into the man's back, feeling the tissue tear and the bones break on impact to the tip. Blood was everywhere, on his face, drenching the man and staining the ground and sky.

He had *killed* a man. *Killed.* There was no chance he was going to survive a wound such as that. He shuddered in his sleep. He was a killer, he had taken a life. He thought it would have been easy; he had used that blade to slash human flesh before...but never to kill.

Each time he stabbed the man in his dreams, he heard a different sound. A grunt, a moan, a blood-curdling scream that made Kael's eardrums ache. Once he had even heard Laura's voice breaking the deadly silence.

He awoke with a start, sweat glistening on his body. He shivered and finding his shirt which he had flung off during his sleep. He covered his face within it, trying to wipe away the memory as well as his sweat. Unfortunately, the rotten thoughts remained.

He stayed where he was, sitting in an uncomfortable position, imagining the same scene once again. When Shatterbreath came over and sat opposite of him, he hardly acknowledged her presence.

"Something vexes you, Tiny," she said with a weary voice. "Are you still in shock about your lineage?"

"No, I have come to terms with that already. It makes perfect sense." He avoided her gaze. "It's just..." He struggled to find the words, his voice quavering. "I—I took a life, Shatterbreath!" he burst out.

Shatterbreath reared her head in surprise as Kael began to sob softly. She sat where she was, claws outstretched, unsure what to do. At last, she walked over and placed a warm, soft wing around him.

"There, there, Tiny," she cooed, "it is the way of things, you must learn to accept that."

"I'm not a hardened killer like you, Shatterbreath. I don't hunt for my food every day," he said through sobs, "I'm not meant to kill."

Shatterbreath grunted. "How ironic that is." Her voice startled Kael and he stopped sobbing to look up at her as she gazed into space. "I used to think all humans were meant for was just to kill."

Her scales bristled. After a minute or two, Shatterbreath shook her great head in dismissal. "Listen, it was either his life or yours. You did the right thing to kill him, that's what I told you to do, remember?"

"But—"

"Kael, these people are your enemies!" The sternness in her voice could not be ignored. "Your enemies would not hesitate to kill you. You must climb over this invisible wall you have built around you. Death is natural; death is the only luxury you should ever give your enemy. Besides, if you just injured them instead of killing them when they're in your way, aren't you only causing more agony?"

Kael shrugged, hugging closer to her warm body. "I suppose."

"Good." She folded her great wing back up. "I'm glad we've settled this, because I think I've found another task for you."

Kael wiped his eyes. "What is that?"

"Zeptus." She bared her teeth at the mention of his name. "This man is clearly a threat. He has set your city against you and has used his motivational powers to goad the king into this horrid deal to begin with. He is a threat to our success and the very sake of your city. This continent may depend on whether he lives or dies."

"I—I suppose you're right, he must be eliminated. Aside from that, he seems to have a personal grudge against me." Kael shivered.

"He is clearly the key to all this. Perhaps we can turn this all around without his influence."

"It is settled then," she said, sitting down on her haunches and thrusting out her chest in a strangely formal posture. "In a few days' time, you will make another trip back to Vallenfend, this one with the purpose to spill blood, although you are clearly reluctant to do so."

There was no more to be said, so Kael simply nodded his head.

Before Kael was ready to attempt his assassination on Zeptus, Shatterbreath decided it would be best to sharpen his swordplay first. As before, he stood in front of her and she batted at him with her paws, tail and even her head. But this time, she made it very difficult for him.

Once again, he was knocked to the ground. He didn't complain. She was training him hard now, which was the only way he would improve. He was learning how to fight well against multiple enemies, as well as honing his duelling skills. As he trained, he began to learn how to better control his strange, unique ability, sometimes startling Shatterbreath with his lightning-fast reactions.

Their training stopped when Kael's shoulder suddenly seized.

He pulled off his armour as best as he could with some help from Shatterbreath and then whipped off his tunic. He glanced over his shoulder at the reddened gauze that had been placed over the wound. Oh, he should have checked this earlier!

Tentatively, he picked at the gauze, which had become caked to his shoulder by dry blood. Inch by inch, he removed it, which left white flecks of material where it had sealed in with the wound.

The wound was swollen and miscoloured, looking somewhat like the gash that had just sealed closed on Shatterbreath's leg. It worried Kael, but he didn't say anything to the dragon, avoiding her gaze.

Shatterbreath took a step towards Kael, sniffing at his shoulder. "That's a pretty good wound," she chirped, "that will leave quite the battle-scar."

Kael frowned. "Yes it will. C'mon, let's finish my training."

Three days passed in total. Kael tightened his sword on his waist, slung his shield over his good shoulder and buckled the straps to his armour. Shatterbreath watched him with a gleam in her eye.

"Before you go," she said, trailing off slightly, "I have an idea."

Kael wheeled around. "Are you going to lend me your vision?" he asked eagerly.

"No," she replied. "Going into the castle is dangerous, even more so than it had been last time. You are going to need more help than just my vision. As much as I would like to help, I'm afraid there is only one thing I can do. Kael, I'm going to lend you my strength."

"Wh—what?"

"It is the only way you'll have a sure chance of success. With my strength, you'll be able to decimate anybody standing in your way. You'll be able to jump high and scale walls with ease."

Kael was unsure. "But when you lent me your vision, it left you with my sight as well. Won't the same thing happen?"

Shatterbreath nodded, frowning. "It will. With your strength—and no offense intended—I'll be as weak as a rabbit. Kael, I wouldn't even consider this if I didn't have absolute trust in you."

Kael nodded uncertainly. Unlike before when she had lent him her vision, Shatterbreath laid down on the ground instead of touching him with her muzzle. She pushed herself to the edge of her cave, positioning her legs, wings and tail in such a way that she appeared to meld into the rock.

"This should suffice. Tiny, come close." Kael stood just in front of her snout. "Kael Rundown, I give you the strength of my muscles, the toughness of my skin and the integrity of my bones." A rush of energy flowed between them. It lasted a long time and Kael's flesh itched all over. When the flow ceased, he didn't feel any different. "You will be nearly impossible to harm, Tiny, but be warned, you are not invincible."

Shatterbreath's head feel to the ground and her body lay limp. Cautious, Kael drew his sword. He gasped in amazement; it was as light as a feather! He laughed in glee as he bobbed up and down, hardly feeling the weight of his heavy armour. Tentatively at first, he jumped, soaring at least five feet up into the air.

Slashing his sword through the air, Kael exclaimed, "This is amazing!"

Shatterbreath was much less pleased. She growled as her neck muscles strained to try and lift her head. "Don't get comfortable with all that strength," she said through a clenched jaw, "as soon as you are done, I'm taking it all back forever. This is unbearable! I feel so...vulnerable!

Kael crouched in front of her and lifted her chin so that she could look him in the eyes—something that would have been ordinarily impossible. "Don't worry; I'll be as fast as I can." He spied her tail dancing off to the side. "How come you can still move your tail?"

"You don't have those muscles, of course. I can also move my wings. Enough talk, get going!"

Kael still didn't quite understand how this all worked, but in three joyous leaps, he was at the mouth of the cave, staring down at Vallenfend as the sun set over the sea. The castle was aglow with torches already, all the windows rooms lit up. Kael stared at it for a time, mesmerized. Somewhere in there, Zeptus was waiting.

Replicating Shatterbreath's takeoff, he propelled himself off the cliff face, flying high into the air. The wind rushed past his face, filling him with elation. Then he looked down. The forest loomed underneath and he realized how dumb he had just been to hurtle off a cliff.

Several seconds later, the trees whipped him in the face and he landed on the dirt solidly halfway down the mountain. Knees still bent, he stayed in that position, eyes shut tight. He relaxed as he realized he was still in one piece. Nothing was broken, and despite all the stinging branches, his face wasn't cut at all, only the parts of his tunic that had been unprotected.

Excitement filled Kael and he reached towards a rock that was lying nearby that was as big as his torso. As easy as lifting a fork, he picked it up and threw it at a tree. The rock struck the tree and shattered it, sending splinters flying everywhere. Kael laughed as the tree groaned and fell over.

After some more play, Kael was down the mountain faster than he would have thought possible without riding on Shatterbreath's back. He cleared the distance between the field and Vallenfend in no time at all and leapt completely over the wall, crashing into a pile of hay on the other side. Luckily, there was nobody watching.

It was nearing midnight before Kael crept up to the side of the castle that wasn't protected by the large stone wall. He loitered around for a moment to make sure nobody was watching, huddling in his armour which did little to protect him from the cold. He exhaled slowly, watching his breath with interest. Once he was sure there was no one around, he jumped up at least eight feet up the wall and plunged his dagger into the stone of the castle.

With his new strength, it was an easy task to scale the side of the castle. It didn't matter how large the cracks he grappled onto, for his fingers were more than strong enough to keep him clinging to the wall. And if there was no grip, he would plunge his knife into the brick and hoist himself up another foot until he did find one.

Kael looked down about halfway up the wall. A fit of vertigo made his vision swoon and he became dizzy for a moment. He gathered himself for a moment and shortly continued. Height no longer seemed such an obstacle, not after he had leapt halfway down Shatterbreath's mountain and survived unscathed.

Suddenly, a guard thrust his head out a window near Kael. He was probably just getting a breath of fresh air, but he turned his head and spotted the dark figure scaling the wall. His face screwed up in confusion.

"Wha—?"

Before he could say or do anything more, Kael leapt at him and grabbed him around his neck with one hand. He leaned back and pushed off the surface with his feet while at the same time twisting his body to stick his knife into the wall. The soldier flew out of the window and down into the street below, landing with a sickening *thud*. The guard let out a terrible howl as he fell.

Kael cursed, surely somebody hear that. He began to climb at an even quicker pace.

He realized that he didn't actually know where Zeptus's study even was. He could be on the completely wrong side of the castle for all he knew. The only thing he knew for certain is that he was on the top floor by now. Kael sidled over to a window, just peering over the ledge. It seemed clear, so he pushed the window open and pulled himself up and into the castle.

There was a guard standing almost directly in front of him as Kael rolled into the hallways. He tried to yell something, but Kael silenced him by stabbing his knife deep into guard's throat and removing it not a second later. Without waiting for the guard to slump to the ground, Kael sprinted away. Disgust for what he had done flashed through him. Shatterbreath's council kept him going. *Death is the only luxury you give your enemy.*

Kael rushed through the halls, desperately searching for the hallway that contained Zeptus's study. The castle's hallway weren't any less confusing than his last visit and Kael soon found himself lost.

He heard urgent voices behind him and by the sound of their worried tones, they had found the guard Kael had killed. He paused, listening. As far as he could tell there was about five of them and chances were, there would be an elite guard with them.

Rather than run away as he supposed he should have, Kael charged towards them, a strange new bravery and chilling bloodlust pushing him forwards. He slid around the corner, sword drawn, giving them full sight of him. They yelped and pointed their fingers and started to charge towards him, but Kael only smiled.

The first man made a move to strike, but Kael easily dodged his flailing attack, time slowing before his eyes. Following through with a spin, Kael slashed the man across his chest and moved on to his next attacker, easily finishing him off as well. He smashed another across his face, bone crunching under his gauntlet and then stabbed yet another. The last man stood where he was, eyes white and knees buckling. Kael leapt up and kneed the guard right in the nose and sailed past. Kael landed in a crouch, listening as the guard fell to the ground. Without further hesitation, he sprang forward into a sprint, leaving the hallway stained red.

An arrow shot past Kael's head and lodged into the wall. He yanked it free and hurled it back at the man with explosive force. When the projectile stuck, only the feathers showed poking out of his chest. The guard groaned and blood oozed from his mouth. Kael didn't wait to watch him fall. He elbowed one last guard in the head and continued forward, keeping his speed.

He turned a bend, instantly recognizing the hallway he was in. Kael slowed his pace to a crawl, crouching as low as he could. One last corner and the next hallway was the one that contained the door to Zeptus's study.

Two guards enrobed in black waited, standing still and erect. They hadn't noticed Kael so he began to creep up on them. He was about three feet away before the first guard caught sight of him. By then it was already too late. Kael jumped up and kicked the man in the chest with both feet, sending him flying through the hall.

Kael was lying on his back when the other guard bore down on him. The guard stopped, however, the tip of his sword pointing at Kael's face. Kael had his shield out already, but he relaxed once he realized it was Tooran that had him pinned.

"Kael?" he said incredulously, "what are you doing back here? I thought you were going to escape, not come back!"

"Tooran," Kael said, standing up to grip the man firmly by his arm. "I am here to kill Zeptus, please step out of the way."

Tooran winced, trying to free his arm from Kael's grip with no success. "Why are you so strong all of a sudden? What happened to you?"

"Shatterbreath, the dragon, gave me her strength." Kael itched with anticipation. He wanted to get this done and over with. He wanted to kill Zeptus. "Now, please move out of the way."

Tooran shook his head, holding Kael by his shoulders. The worried look on his face stopped Kael from brushing him off. "Listen, you must go back to her! She is in grave danger! A battalion of soldiers left two days ago to go try and slay her! I wasn't worried about it, even though a few of the King's Elite went with them. But now that you tell me this..."

Kael's eyes went wide as he realized what this meant. He sputtered for a moment, struggling to find his voice. "N—no, they were supposed to go weeks ago! Oh, why didn't I notice when they didn't come?"

"Zeptus delayed their departure for some reason. He didn't say why... Sometimes I think that man can sense things that others can't."

Extricating himself from Tooran's grip, Kael backed off, his heart pounding and his hairs standing on end. Fear wracked him and he started to tremble. Not fear for himself, but for Shatterbreath. "What have I done?! Tooran, I must go!"

He was so close! But Shatterbreath's life was more important right now than taking Zeptus's. Leaving Tooran all alone, Kael jumped out the closest window and stabbed his knife into the side of the castle. He slowed down and then pulled the blade free from the brick, falling several more feet as he did. He repeated a few more times and was down on the ground in a matter of seconds.

Pausing to get his bearing, Kael set off at a mad-dash towards the mountain where Shatterbreath's cave was. His mind was racing as he contemplated what would happen to the dragon if they reached her first. She would be nearly defenceless! With this new, sickening thought in mind, he pushed himself even harder, the ground passing underneath his feet at a dizzying rate.

He leapt over the main wall, soaring out into the middle of the field between the city and the mountain. He leapt again, travelling high up the mountainside. Speed, *speed!* He needed to go faster! But he felt no matter how fast he went he couldn't be quick enough. Despair began to creep into his chest and as he began to wheeze. The whole time, he was uttering silent prayers.

About halfway up, he spotted some broken branches and tracks, distinctly human. Tooran hadn't been lying. *Oh, please be okay!*

When Kael reached the opening to Shatterbreath's his sword was already drawn. He could hear voices from within. Struggling to listen over his haggard breath, he paused for a frantic heartbeat. Screams, roars...she was in trouble!

He dashed into the cave, the sound of turmoil growing by the second. At last he spotted them. Shatterbreath was in the same position she had been when Kael left her. An impressive battalion of men stood in front of her, trying desperately to dodge her swinging tail while attempting to attack at the same time. She was growling, flaring her wings and doing her best to fend them off, but it was only a matter of time before one of the soldiers would give a fatal strike. There were already deep gouges cut into her exposed flesh and all over her tail.

Without any more hesitation or thought, Kael thrust himself at the closest soldier shoulder first. With a yelp, the man collided into his nearest comrade, sending them both sprawling to the ground. Kael followed through with his wild attack and slashed a soldier across his legs. Bone glinted through the gash in his thighs before the man slumped to the ground, screaming.

Finishing off that soldier, Kael leapt at another, batting a sword away and stabbing the man through the shoulder. One soldier put up his shield to block Kael's onslaught, but he would not be denied. With a cry, Kael lunged and pierced right through his shield and into his neck.

Kael stepped through a growing puddle of blood to get to the next opponent. He began to hack and slash his way through the soldiers, slowly making his way towards where Shatterbreath lay defenceless.

He screamed in fury as his armour became bathed in blood and the sickening sound of metal against metal squealed in his ears. All he saw was Shatterbreath, growling at her attackers. All he felt was the need to save her.

Suddenly, a new pain interrupted his rampage. A fierce sting incapacitated his right leg, forcing him to slump to the ground. He balanced on his sword, struggling to get back on his feet, but his one leg wasn't obeying his demand.

Some soldiers moved in to try and kill him, but he still posed enough of a threat to kill the ones who were to foolish to get within reach of his sword.

Another sting erupted in his lower side and his entire body seized, forcing him to the floor. He winced at the cold touch of the cave floor and growled as a pair of boots came into view. Somewhere on his side, he could sense precious fluid leaving him, taking his strength with it. He struggled to move forward as more boots came into view.

"Well now," a snide voice said, "the strong one *can* be hurt. And if he can be hurt, he can be killed."

There was a small amount of cheering. Kael grew desperate and tried even harder to drag himself forward across the ground. He clawed at the smooth surface, inching his way ever closer to the dragon who was watching with wide, frightened eyes.

A boot struck his side and Kael yelped in pain. Shatterbreath growled, but the soldiers only laughed harder.

"Aw, look, he's trying to crawl back to the dragon. What a fool! What can your dragon do for you now, son? You're both dead, it's only a matter of time."

Kael did his best to try and shut the man's voice out of his head, focussing on using the small amount of energy he had left to pull himself ever closer. He reached out with his hand.

The snide soldier laughed once more and kicked his hand, making Kael yelp again. He could feel the anger grow inside him as the soldier mocked him. After all the trouble he had been through, after all the effort he put forth to come a rescue Shatterbreath, he would not be denied by this cocky man.

He gritted his teeth as the soldier kicked him once again with a shrill laugh. Summing up his strength, Kael forced time to move slowly. He glanced upwards as the man brought his sword up high to finish Kael off. Before he could, Kael fetched his knife from its sheath and stabbed the blade through the soldiers foot and into the ground, pinning his foot.

The soldier yelped out in pain and the rest of them moved in towards Kael with malice across their faces. With one final push, Kael reached out closer to Shatterbreath.

Ever so gently, his hand brushed up against Shatterbreath's muzzle, just above her lip.

With a surge of power of a loud growl, Shatterbreath lifted herself off of the ground, shaking her body angrily. The soldiers screamed as she bore down on them. A torrential jet of flame erupted from her mouth.

Kael, on the other hand, was instantly engulfed in pain when Shatterbreath's strength left him. His whole body ached, as if he had been working every single muscle on his body furiously. Never in his life had he been so sore. He couldn't even move. The pain was so intense.

Out of the corner of his eye, he watched with some satisfaction as Shatterbreath killed each and every one of her attackers, giving them no amount of mercy. Blood was dripping from her jowls when she returned to check on her small companion where he lay feebly on the floor.

"Kael, Kael! Are you alright?"

Kael simply groaned.

Shatterbreath kicked a body to the side and moved in close to Kael. She pointed her big blue muzzle right in his face, ruffling his tattered clothing with her deep, worried exhalations. As before, she gently touched him with the tip of her snout as she lent him some of her strength and energy. Not as much as before, but enough that he could sit upright with some effort.

"Mend yourself quickly, Kael. I don't wish to let you borrow my strength for much longer."

Kael nodded and laboriously, he fetched the medical bag from the back of the cave.

Shatterbreath watched him as he set to work, barely able to keep awake. It was almost a good thing he was so fatigued, because he barely felt it as he stitched his fresh wounds, grimacing as he closed the large gash on his right leg. Next, he moved onto the gash on his side, which was much larger and nastier-looking.

He could sense Shatterbreath's emotion, boiling within her like a cauldron, but for a long time, he didn't dare say anything. He was so tired, he didn't want to waste any more energy than necessary with talk, but mostly he couldn't think of anything to say to her.

At last, he found some words that would suffice. "I'm sorry, Shatterbreath," he whispered, wiping the blood off his hands futilely. "I should have never taken your strength, it was too risky, but I was too excited with the notion."

Shatterbreath scrutinized him for a moment, her jaw muscles working. He faltered under her sharp gaze and looked away. For a long time, she didn't say anything, which made Kael feel only worse.

He cut the excess thread off from his stitching and tore a shred off of a soldier's tunic. He patted his wounds dry with it.

"You better get some sleep, Tiny," Shatterbreath stated at last, her voice void of emotion. "As soon as I take my strength back, you're going to be very sore."

On cue, Kael felt her strength leave him once again as she touched him with a wingtip. At once, the soreness returned and he could no longer move. He slumped back over, going limp. It took him some time, but he fell asleep despite the pain that gripped him.

Chapter 23

The next day, Kael's body was feeling slightly less sore. It still burned whenever he moved, but at least he *could* move. As recompense for allowing harm to come to Shatterbreath, he began to fix her up. He gashes were large and numerous. It took Kael a long time to stitch them all.

Despite her silence as he mended her, he could sense that she had forgiven him. Perhaps she realized that he wasn't entirely to blame after all, as she had silently brooded, or it could just be that she couldn't stay angry at him. Either way, when her piercing gaze softened and her body relaxed, Kael was relieved.

As he tended to her wounds, an itching feeling crept into his chest. It grew until he couldn't ignore it and finally he blurted out, "Am I your friend, Shatterbreath?" He blushed as she looked down at him. "Or just your servant?"

Shatterbreath's features softened. She seemed very tired. She scratched lightly at a wound caused by an arrow on her check for a moment before answering. "Of course, Tiny," she said through a sigh, "you are my friend."

Kael smiled to himself.

"What makes you ask such a question?" She winced as he patted yet another wound. "Watch it!"

"Sorry," he said, backing off until her snarl subsided. "I asked that because somebody once told me that dragons were solitary creatures and would prefer to be alone. Is—is that true?"

The tip of Shatterbreath's tail danced playfully and she placed her thick head down on her paws. "Of course not," she said softly, almost to quiet for him to hear, "what a silly notion. Every creature, whether big or small, requires the company of other beings, if of their species or otherwise." She blinked slower than usual, in the way she did when she was remembering things of her past. Kael saw her do this often.

Choosing his tone delicately, he asked, "Did—did you ever have a family, Shatterbreath?"

She was taken aback and she flinched, the muscle underneath Kael's hands tightening. She lifted her head and clenched her paws uncertainly, a scraping sound protruding as she scratched the stone floor. She opened her mouth, but closed it. Her brow furrowed as if she was in pain. A tear formed in her eye.

She blinked the tear away. "I...my family..." she mumbled, taking a deep breath. "Of course I had a family. Nobody can survive for as long as I without having a family of their own. I remember them still, all too clearly..." Her voice was quavering so Kael place a hand on her leg to try and comfort her. "My mother died when I was young, and as did my father some time later. But no, I do not remember them as my family. I remember family as something else...

"My mate...my children..." She shuddered as she sobbed, great, pearly drops flowing down her muzzle and off the tip of her drooping snout, making echoing *plunking* sounds that made Kael's heart despair. He had seen her eyes water before, but he hadn't known dragons could cry. He didn't interrupt her. "I've tried hard not to remember them, but recent events have forced me to. And you, Kael, every time I look at you, it brings back the flow of memories. My son, my daughter...oh how I loved them. I would have given my life for them to live..."

"What happened to them?"

Shatterbreath's neck became taut as she recollected her past. Her jaw muscles worked as she struggled to put words to what she was thinking. "Humans," she spat, "the influence of the Favoured Ones had long passed before I decided to settle down and have a family, but still they came.

"We never did anything to harm anybody, never did anything to make them angry, but they came with swords and bows and arrows and other stinging human weapons all the same. They came for our hides; they came to kill us, just to say they were the ones who were able to. Why does the term 'Dragonslayer' appeal to you humans so much? I remember the day... I tried my very hardest, Kael, but I was too weak. *We* were too weak, my mate and I. They killed them all, my mate, my daughter, my son. And with my family, most of me died, too. I don't know how I escaped, even to this day—fate perhaps. Cruel fate.

"I ran...ran away from my past as fast as I could for a hundred years. But the pain followed me. The world was stained red with the blood of my family, and I didn't want to look at or live in it anymore. So I hid myself away from it. I found a cave where I could be alone, where the world would not look at me and laugh at this pitiful dragon. And there I stayed—here I stay for the remainder of my life.

"Then you came. Not you as a person, but you as a race. Your city, your people, *your filth.* They built that wretched city beside my lair. It was like they wanted me to attack their tantalizing fields filled with fat cattle, so I obeyed. I suppose ultimately it was my own undoing. I stopped and their anger subsided towards me. Until your current king, of course.

"All I ever wanted was to live alone, but now I can't even do that. All I wanted was to die in peace." An especially large tear rolled down her face. She smiled sadly at him. "But I no longer wish for death, because of you."

Kael listened silently and his heart sank until it felt like it was resting on the floor. Shatterbreath trembled and began to sob. He had known the sorrows that the human race had placed on her, but he had no idea of the true torment she was troubled by. She was a broken dragon, although mighty in physical form. More than ever, he felt an urge to do everything in his power to help her.

Chapter 24

Where is my favourite cloak? Malaricus wondered, scanning his study through his spectacles. *Ah, there it is! The pesky devil.* Malaricus wrapped the robe around his body, standing in front of the mirror. He fixed up his collar and proceeded to make himself appear as formal as possible. Today was a special day after all. Today he was to meet with the king! He used to do this often, but as of late, it seemed there was no time to.

He would have preferred the cause of the meeting to be for something else. Undoubtedly, the king was going to ask him about Kael Rundown. Zeptus probably organized all this.

He found his hat as well, scooped it up and slipped it over his white hair. He stared into the mirror for a moment. With a frown, he threw the floppy hat into the corner of the room. It wasn't as nice as he thought it had been when he bought it. He snatched his staff with a grumble.

Malaricus strolled out of the Royal Athenaeum, a skip in his step. His old heart was beating faster and faster. He was excited to see what the king would have to say about Kael. Last he had heard of the boy, he had escaped from prison. That was scarcely two days ago. They had sent a battalion of soldiers to go fight the dragon shortly after. They hadn't told the public why, in fact, hardly anybody knew. Malaricus suspected the battalion was sent to try and kill Kael while he was still in the dragon's lair.

By the books in his library, he hoped Kael was alright.

As he arrived at the castle's front gates, Zeptus was already waiting for him, wearing a sour scowl. "Malaricus," he said with a slight nod.

"Lord Zeptus, it has truly been a while." Malaricus dropped his fake smile. "I see you ignored my request to keep that boy out of the army."

Zeptus cocked his head, ever so slightly. "Why, Malaricus, I have no idea who you speak of."

The old scholar cleared his throat, irked by Zeptus's scratchy voice. "You know exactly who. He's been causing you no end of trouble as I understand."

Zeptus's face remained stolid, but his lip twitched. "Come," he declared, turning his back on Malaricus, "the king wants to see you, not I."

Always a pleasure to exchange words with Zeptus, Malaricus thought sarcastically, *that's for certain.* He followed Zeptus into the bowels of the maze-like castle. The old scholar could still remember the first time he had gone through there. He became hopelessly lost and to the day, he still didn't like the place. Perhaps it was the first king's intention to make his subjects get lost when he built it.

Rather than leading him to the large conference room on one of the upper floors, where they usually met, they stayed on the bottom floor and instead met in the dining hall, which was nearly as big as the conference room, although much less lavished. The room was longer than it was wide, decorated by pearly white marble. Two long tables ran the length of the room, with one shorter table at the back of the room, elevated on a higher ledge. At the middle of that elaborate table the king sat alone.

Malaricus entered to see the king pushing away a dinner plate. A servant came and took away his plate as King Morrindale patted his mouth clean with a cloth. Zeptus walked over to him, leaving Malaricus standing near the door to wait. The advisor whispered something into the king's ear and Basal Morrindale perked up.

Placing his crown back on his oily head, the king clapped his hands together. Malaricus bowed low. "Hail, King Morrindale," he said, straightening back up with help from his staff. He didn't like use a walking stick, but today his knees had been acting up.

The king waved his hand. "To you as well, Malaricus. Now, enough proprieties, I want to know of the boy, this Kael Rundown. I heard that you are friends with him."

A grin settled on Malaricus's wise face, but he brushed it away. "Yes. It seems, sire, that Kael and the dragon have become inseparable in their—I hate to call it this—friendship."

"What?" the king roared, "This is high treason, he is fraternising with our enemy!"

Malaricus hesitated for a moment, and then raised his staff slightly in a gesture to have permission to speak. The King rolled his eyes, tired of Malaricus's old ways. He waved his arm again in permission. "It would seem, sire," the old scribe said, carefully picking his words, "that Kael thinks the same thing about you."

Zeptus leaned over the king's shoulder and whispered something in his ear, shooting Malaricus an acid look. The king himself seemed to inflate like a puffer fish. He fumed in anger, leaned back in his chair and jutted his chin out threateningly in a gesture that bode ill will, but did not retort to the scribe's comment, not at first anyway.

"You watch your tongue, Malaricus," he spat, "you have been a faithful scribe for my family for years, but you are not above the law."

"Yes, King Morrindale."

"Now, in a proper way, tell me what his goals are. What does he hope to accomplish, barging into my castle these multiple times?"

Malaricus gripped his staff tighter. "Excuse me, sire, but you said multiple times... When the boy and I last spoke, he had said that he had only been inside the castle once, unless you are counting his escape from the dungeons. Though he was not *barging* in that time, considering that you put him in there to begin with."

Zeptus spoke before the king could. "Last night, there was an attempt on my life. The boy was able to infiltrate our castle, killing many of the guards in the process. He made it all the way to my door before he decided to retreat for an *unknown* reason."

Malaricus's thick eyebrows furrowed in disbelief. "Killed? I hardly believe this boy was capable of such feats. After all, don't you have sturdy defences in here?"

"And what," the king said, placing his hands up on the table threateningly, "do you mean by that?"

Malaricus bowed again. "Forgive me if I offended in any way, sire, I was, of course, referring to your military guards. Is there something else guarding this castle that I don't know about, Basal?"

The king shook his head, sitting back down in his chair. "No, of course not."

Malaricus grinned slightly.

"What else do you know of this boy?" Zeptus asked, scowling.

"He is a normal civilian, as far as I know, a simple worker and nothing more. He was sent to fight, but instead of killing the dragon, he joined sides with it."

Zeptus leaned over and whispered something into the king's ear. The king brushed him away and Zeptus walked out of the room, keeping his head straight and saying nothing more.

"Thank you for your time, Malaricus." The king dismissed him with a wave of his hand.

"It was good to see you again, Basal," Malaricus said in turn, giving a slight bow before he turned to leave. "Good day."

The doors slammed heavily closed behind him. Malaricus paused, unsure which way to go. Nobody was going to escort him out? *How rude.*

He turned around, only to come face to face with Zeptus. He gasped and placed both hands on his cane, catching his breath. "Zeptus, don't scare me like that!"

The king's advisor came up close to Malaricus. Slouching, he whispered into Malaricus's ear. "Come with me, we have to talk."

Malaricus nodded, confused, but otherwise obedient. Zeptus, with his hands tucked behind his back, strode through the halls with the scholar in tow.

Finally, Zeptus pulled Malaricus into a small, dark room tucked away at the rear part of the castle. He ushered the scholar inside and then locked the door after lighting a candle.

"Listen, Malaricus," he said with urgency. "You may think that I hold a personal vendetta against your friend, Kael. This is not the case."

"Pardon?" Malaricus wheezed, struggling to focus on Zeptus's purple eyes in the scant light. "What do you mean? Kael told me himself that you've got a grudge against him!"

Zeptus licked his chapped lips. "No," he said shamefully, "I want Kael to succeed! It may seem to you that I am behind everything that is happening. This is exactly what the king wants everybody to think!"

Malaricus sidled away from him. "No. No, I don't believe you, you're lying. The king isn't clever enough to do something like this. I know about your plot to make our city defenceless, Kael told me about all the gold you have upstairs."

"Alas, I know it's a hard thing to believe." He clenched his jaw for a moment, his stiff features softening for a moment. "But you must take my word for it. The king is behind this all! He is smarter than he lets off, which is exactly what he wants. If anything ever went wrong with his plot, he made sure that someone else would get the blame. Me. For these thirty years, he has ordered me to say and do things that would make it appear that I was the one to blame. Obviously, it has worked. As I said before, your friend tried to kill me not long ago."

Malaricus was in shock, this was all so unbelievable. "B—but...no! This cannot be! The—the *king* is doing this?"

"Yes, in fact, I've been trying to help Kael all along. I ordered my guards to let him live the first time he entered the castle, but make it look like they were doing the opposite. And I've been trying to convince Basal for all these years to stop with this terrible plot of his."

"When you whisper in his ear all the time you're really—"

"Telling him to stop."

From the look in Zeptus's eyes, Malaricus could tell he was telling the truth. If what he was saying was true, Kael was making a big mistake. When that boy set his mind on a task, he wouldn't stop until it was accomplished.

"By the books in my library," Malaricus whispered in realization, "I have to speak with Kael at once."

Voices could be heard somewhere outside. Exchanging glances, Zeptus and Morrindale left the small room. They walked down the hallway casually a short ways until they separated without so much as a second glance. Thoughts swirled in Malaricus's mind, mulling over the news he had just learnt. Zeptus was...good...

Chapter 25

"Kael, Kael?!" Shatterbreath nudged him with her muzzle, but the boy didn't move. Not more than five minutes ago, he had slumped to the ground and hadn't gotten back up. His skin was white and sweaty and when she touched his forehead with her snout, it was burning hot.

He hadn't complained about his wounds, but she could tell that they gave him discomfort. He would favour his one leg and wince if he moved in a certain way. She hadn't been very concerned because he had already patched himself up, but obviously, there was more to it.

She licked him this time, fear swallowing all other emotions and thoughts. He still didn't move. "No, no! Wake up, Kael! Please!" she pleaded, but still he remained as motionless as a tree, his mouth agape and body twitching slightly. He was breathing, but his breaths came haggard and shallow and sounded wet.

All she could do was simply stare at him, totally unsure what to do. Her brain raced, struggling to fight the chaos of fear to try and find a solution. She knew nothing about healing or human anatomy, what could she do alone?

Alone...

She perked up. That's it, she needed someone else! And she knew just who.

She flipped the boy onto his side so that he wouldn't choke on his spit or tongue and then sprang to the mouth of her cave. With a huge leap, she was airborne, tilting her leathery wings towards the dreadful city that hated her.

She circled the city a few times, staying low and close to the walls. She ignored the screams of the people, focussing on the city's library. She peered through all the windows until she found what she was looking for. Malaricus.

With a growl, she banked towards the large building. Without hesitation, she slammed into the side of the library, angling her body so that it was parallel to the walls before she did. Clinging to the side, she smashed through a window with her snout and stuck her muzzle inside. Large bookcases lay on their sides with books scattered all about the room. Furniture was pushed aside, there was rubble everywhere and the air was thick with dust. Hiding behind a desk was the frail human she sought.

"Malaricus," she said as nicely as she could manage, "please, come with me peacefully. Kael is in need of assistance, and I am hardly the one to give it to him."

The elderly man cowered still, but he poked out from behind the desk. "K—Kael is in trouble?" he said with concern. "C—can't you get somebody else to help him?"

Shatterbreath roared and the man screamed. "No! He trusts you with his life, and you are the only person I can think of to help him. There is no time to spare. You're coming with me whether you like it or not."

She readjusted her grip on the wall, sending another hail of debris falling to the streets below and thrust her tail into the building, wrapping it around the scholar's thin form. She pulled him out carefully and climbed to the top of the building. Putting him in one paw, she dodged a ballista aimed at her from the castle battlements and then launched herself into the air.

She could hear the man screaming, but at this point, she didn't care about *his* discomfort. In a matter of minutes, she had already returned to her cave. Careful not to hurt the old man, she landed heavily on the hard stone of her cave. She lost her balance and tripped, sending a tremor through the cave and making Malaricus squeak.

Shaking her head, she picked herself up, licking the blood away from her chin that she had bashed on the stone. She loped over to where Kael was still lying motionless and place Malaricus beside him.

After he had calmed down and had his full share of gawking up at her, he crouched down beside the boy, sighing loudly. Shatterbreath fetched the medical bag and put it down beside the frail man, nudging him with her snout.

She paced anxiously as Malaricus looked at Kael's wounds. He whistled when he saw the one on his shoulder and side, making Shatterbreath's throat constrict.

"This wound is infected," the man said at last, lightly touching the discoloured gash on his shoulder, "I need some herbs to make him better, otherwise he may die."

Suddenly, Shatterbreath felt very cold. She shivered. "How quickly can you get these herbs?"

Malaricus rubbed his face with a sigh. "I'm not sure if any of them are close. I could make a simple poultice that might work, but it is very weak, it probably wouldn't do the trick."

"Is that it then? What else can you do?"

"Well, there is one herb that when mixed properly, can cure almost any disease or ailment. But it is hard to find and comes in limited numbers, plus it shares its home with the Icecrows, at the very top of their mountain, where they roost."

Shatterbreath jumped onto all fours. "We must get it at once!"

"No, it's far too risky," Malaricus said, also rising to his feet. "The Icecrows will most certainly kill you. They're not the friendliest of birds, not to mention they hate dragons."

"That matters not," Shatterbreath said, baring her teeth, "all that matters to me is Kael's life. Tell me what this herb looks like and how to find it."

"The herb is a small blue flower that grows in clumps," the feeble scribe described, holding out his hands as if it were actually in his fingers. "It has unique rough-edged leaves and a short stalk. When you see it, you'll know."

"Thank you, Malaricus. I shall leave at once."

"Wait, mighty dragon, there is something you must know first, about the king and Zeptus!"

311

But Shatterbreath was already at the mouth of her cave, head pointed out into the cool sky. "It must wait for now, old scribe," she said as he scrambled to reach her side. "There is no time for this."

"But Zeptus, he's..."

Malaricus's voice cut out as the *whoosh* of wind rang through her ears. Her heart thrummed in her chest. *Icecrows,* the most dastardly of animals. Besides humans, these creatures were the only real threat to dragons. She directed her flight northward, towards Icecrow Island, named due to its sole inhabitants.

The flight was a long one, far longer than she would have liked. The ground passed effortlessly below her as she beat her wings harder and harder, picking up speed with each wing stroke. Pretty soon, she left land altogether and the huge expanse of ocean stretched before her.

Shatterbreath didn't like the ocean. It made her feel small and weak in comparison to its unbridled strength and size. Why she had chosen to make her home scarcely a fifteen minute's flight away from the ocean, she couldn't recall.

It didn't take long until an island appeared not far in the distance. It was a small island, mostly covered by mountains and smattering of sullen trees. A shroud of coldness enveloped the island, either from geographical location or from the influence of the islands inhabitants. She set her sights on the tallest peak, which flattened into a plateau at the top. She slowed her pace as she saw the first of the Icecrows.

The Icecrows were just as their name implied. They were large, each one about the size of her small companion, Kael, and covered in sharp, ice-like feathers. Their beaks where crooked, their claws where sharp and overall they had a piercing appearance. They had broad wingspans and long tail feathers to keep them in the air. Still, Shatterbreath would have preferred to be dealing with normal crows over these brutes.

She hovered for a moment, scouring the surface of the tall mountain with her clever eyes. There were very few of the Icecrows in the air right now for they hated daylight.   However, this expedition would be no less risky.

The Icecrows' haggard caws echoed through the air, sending a shiver over her scales. Oh how she hated these creatures. Icecrows and dragons shared an ineffable rivalry between them. Icecrows hated dragons because they breathed fire and they hated anything warm. Dragons hated Icecrows because they were simply nasty creatures. *At least the feeling was mutual.*

Shatterbreath took a deep breath, pushing all useless thoughts aside. Her wounds still hurt, but she pushed that pain aside. Kael's safety was more important than her comfort.

She flapped closer to the mountain, giving it a wide berth to begin with. Like a wolf circling its prey, she continued to grope the mountain with her sight from afar, trying to find the flower the scribe had spoken of. Even with her remarkable vision, she was still too far away to pick out the flower from among the sparse vegetation.   Plus, Icecrows kept most of the ground hidden underneath their bodies. With *her* luck, she was guessing the flower would most likely be located right in the middle of their central congregation spot.

A shriek interrupted her thoughts and she turned sharply to find an Icecrow lunging at her. The creature was much smaller than her, and faster, but it was still no match against her alone and soon she had the little thing in her claws. With a tug, and a squawk, the two halves of the crow fell down into the frigid water far below.

Shatterbreath growled as she inspected her claws, which were now covered in ice. The blood of the Icecrows froze nearly instantaneously—she would have to refrain from killing any with her mouth, otherwise she would get a stuck jaw.

More screeches erupted from the top of the mountain plateau and several forms extricated themselves from wiry, tangled nests. She groaned as dozens of Icecrows flew at her.

This was going to sting.

She waited until the crows were nearly colliding with her, and then dipped sharply. She felt a sting in her already-injured tail as an Icecrow sank its freezing talons into it. She batted her tail, making the crow collide with another, sending them both careening away in a squawking heap.

She stayed in her dangerous dive, wings folded in close to her side and eyes partially close. The Icecrows couldn't keep up and she could hear them lagging behind. She came out of the dive, pulling up so sharply, that many of the Icecrows plunged into the water below because they weren't able to mimic her. She kept pulling up and into a back loop. She spun around to make herself right-side up and bore down on the tail end of the group of Icecrows that had been following her.

She slashed as furiously as she could at every dark body that passed by her, sending a waterfall of frozen blue blood behind her. Her claws were caked with ice, but she slashed with such fury, it didn't matter how dull they were. At least two dozen bodies littered the water by the time she passed completely through the wave of Icecrows.

Struggling to gain some altitude, Shatterbreath chanced a look behind. The Icecrows and their crooked beaks were catching up now as she tried to climb. The ice on her claws was weighing her down and her wings had a layer of frozen blood lining the frontal edge.

The Icecrows caught up to her, clawing and biting at her ferociously. She roared and spun around through the air, slashing at them as best she could. When one latched onto her shoulder, she was forced to clamp her jaws down on it before it damaged her wing. Her tongue went numb and her jaw froze slightly open. At least she had managed to get the crow off.

More and more crows were clinging to her, so she did the only thing she could think of. She angled herself towards the mountain plateau in a collision course. She slammed into the surface of the plateau, crushing nearly all the crows that were on her. She bounced off the ground and hit it again, tumbling until she came to a complete stop some distance later.

Blackness fringed her vision for a moment as she got up to her feet. She inspected the area around her. Just behind her was a large gash in the earth where she had dug up the ground in her crash, as well as a trail of injured or dead Icecrows.

A screech sounded from above, forcing her to shake off her dizziness. A crow slammed into her, at the frontal base of her neck. She roared through her frozen mouth and fell over backwards, kicked off the crow with her hind claws and then rolled back onto her feet. More crows came at her so she quickly spun around, killing a good portion with one swing from her tail.

She rose on her hind legs, using her tail to help her balance. The throng of Icecrows that had been following her earlier was coming, in less than five seconds, they would overwhelm her. Shatterbreath took a deep breath through her nostrils.

She released a jet of flame which melted the ice in her mouth. The fire struck the group of Icecrows and killed almost all of them at once. The few lucky ones that survived met Shatterbreath's claws moments later as burning bodies struck the ground.

The throng of Icecrows was gone, but she melted the rest of the ice on her claws, just in case, and then turned her attention towards finding the flower. What Icecrows were left were either still sitting in their icicle nests, or now avoiding her.

A few of the remaining crows cawed at her and scrutinized her large form angrily with their beady little blue eyes. To warn them off, she roared as mightily as she could, flexing her wings, swinging her tail and letting a conflagration of flame escape from her jaws.

The crows kept their distance, but nevertheless kept watch.

Dragging her tail, Shatterbreath made her way through across the plateau, weaving in between the icicle nests. These she left completely alone. She didn't want to bother the mothers sitting on their nests.

315

Finally, in the rough middle of the patch of nests, right where she assumed it would be was the flower she was looking for. It looked exactly as Malaricus had described, with tight, coarse leaves and a bough of small blue flowers sprouting from the top. The flowers grew on a thick, wide mound of what she assumed would be feces from the Icecrows. Interesting, the Icecrows feces acted as manure for the flowers. If it wasn't for the crows, this flower wouldn't even be there to begin with. That was annoying.

She gingerly collected an ample amount, holding them in her right paw. This would be more than enough to help Kael. With a wince, Shatterbreath crouched low and propelled herself into the air where she hovered for a moment, eye level with the flock of Icecrows.

Without incident, she flew away from Icecrow Island. The crows didn't attack her, probably sensing that she had gotten what she came for and didn't mean them any harm. That or they were wary that she could incinerate them in a heartbeat.

By then, all the ice had melted from her wings, and flying was once again an easy task. Her body was tingly all over from the cold and she had yet more cuts all over her body, but at least she had survived, and if she hurried, so would Kael. A sense of serenity befell her, knowing that all would be well soon. More than anything, she felt overwhelming joy that her tiny companion would be saved, *all thanks to her*.

Chapter 26

The scholar took two of the small blue flowers and ground them into a poultice, along with some water from the lake on top of the mountain and a few other local herbs.

She watched closely as Malaricus applied the poultice to Kael's wounds, making sure he didn't do anything he wasn't supposed to. After he was done with Kael's wounds, he put one of the flowers in his mouth so he could chew on it as well, which would cure any infection or disease he had.

Shatterbreath took the rest of the flowers and ate them herself. They tasted like field berries mixed with tree bark. It was an interesting flavour, but not one that she preferred. As soon as she swallowed them, she could already feel warmth in her belly and a tickle in her cuts.

"Thank you, Sir Malaricus," she said once he was all done, "I shall take you home at once."

Malaricus patted his hands clean on his robe. "Wait! There is something I must tell Kael when he wakes up!"

Shatterbreath shook her head. "No, if he no longer requires any medical attention, I would like to be alone with him, understand?"

Malaricus was about to disagree, but she snorted, sending a tendril of smoke curling towards the ceiling. He changed his mind. "Alright fine, take me home."

As nicely as she could, she picked him up by the scruff of his robe and placed him in between her shoulders. Before he could say anything else, she had already launched off the mountainside, picking a direct path back to the city. She didn't want to give him the luxury of flight any longer than was necessary. He tried to say something to her about Zeptus, but she couldn't quite hear his weak voice over the whistle of the air. She simply grunted once and a while as he spoke.

She dropped him off just outside the city gates, receiving frightened looks from the nearby guards and barks from dogs. Without any delay, she flew back up to where Kael was still sleeping. Already she could see that he wounds were healing nicely.

The first thing he was aware of was the pain. Oh, how his body ached! It felt as though every single muscle in his body was screaming angrily at him. There was a warm tingling in his stomach, on his leg and side, but otherwise he felt pretty lousy. He moaned and tried to turn onto his side, but his body wouldn't obey.

He was aware of a recurring volley of warm air and a large presence near him. He heard Shatterbreath's voice talk to him, but he couldn't understand what she said at first.

"Say that again?" he mumbled.

"How are you feeling?" she asked.

He opened his eyes, just a crack to see Shatterbreath's great muzzle floating overhead. "Sore," he said balefully.

She chuckled and there was a sliding noise as she wrapped her tail loosely around him. "That's to be expected, I was trying to use your strength to move myself when I was attacked. It doesn't help that you haven't moved for a while."

Kael groaned again and twitched his fingers. Slowly, he worked up enough willpower to lift an arm to rub his groggy face. He opened his eyes and with a deal of effort, sat up.

"Wh—what happened? How long was I out for?"

Shatterbreath rolled her shoulders. "Perhaps three days. Your wounds became infected because you spent too much time on me instead of looking out for yourself. When you fainted, I fetched your scholar friend, Malaricus, and had him heal you."

"Really?" Kael said, impressed, "I bet he didn't like that."

"No, he didn't. But with his advice, I was able to get you an herb that has healed you, by going through no small amount of danger I might add."

"Thanks." Tentatively, Kael tried to stand up, but fell back down. With Shatterbreath's help, he eventually stood up, wobbling on his stiff-as-wood legs. "You can't imagine what this feels like," he said with a groan.

"I might have an idea." She grinned at him, but her face grew became serious again. "Tiny, I don't mean to rush you, but this problem with Zeptus still hasn't been fixed."

Kael nodded. "I know. Give me a few days, and I'll take care of it once and for all."

Chapter 27

Kael stood in the middle of a large crowd, listening with growing anger as Zeptus spoke with a sardonic tone about him, with the king smiling sinisterly behind him. The advisor was feeding the crowd lies that Kael was Vallenfend's enemy and that he should be destroyed and hated. To Kael's dismay, the crowd was cheering in agreement. The city seemed have turned their hatred from the king towards him instead.

His wounds were completely healed and his energy returned, all thanks to Shatterbreath, Malaricus and those strange blue flowers. Shatterbreath's wounds had fully healed as well. After he was feeling better, he was an easy task to sneak back into Vallenfend. The same female guard had let him through once again. Kael had been lucky she hadn't seen any of the wanted posters depicting his face.

Clearing his mind from everything else, Kael reflected everything he had learned about archery, fingering the wood of the bow in his grip. He took a deep breath and fetched an arrow discreetly from his quiver, notching it onto his bowstring. With his hood up, he slunk through the crowd, sticking close to the outside of the throng.

He paused for a moment to hear what the purple-eyed devil was saying atop his perch up on the wall. That was enough. *Time to end this.*

Kael, his body tense, raised his bow and arrow. Time slowed to a standstill as he looked down the shaft of his arrow, past the metal tip and onto his target. His breath echoed loudly in his ears until he held it. His muscles strained as he pulled the string back, the world around him melting away as his concentration peaked. All was still, all was silent. A snarl fixed on his lips, Kael let go of the bowstring.

Everything was still slow as the arrow left the bow. The string made a *twang* and vibrated long after the projectile was loosed, moving as slow as molasses. Leisurely, the arrow flew towards Zeptus, straight as a sunbeam.

320

The king's advisor stopped talking suddenly, his mouth slightly askew. His brow furrowed and the finger he had raised to corroborate what he was saying curled into his fist. The arrow was halfway to its target. *Please,* Kael pleaded, *please!*

Zeptus turned his head.

Everything returned to normal as Zeptus noticed the arrow. He sidestepped, just before the arrow struck. Suddenly, everybody was screaming. Kael flung himself into the chaos that had arisen, hoping to become lost in the crowd.

"Stop!" Zeptus yelled. The crowd obeyed at once, all turning to look at him—all except Kael, who was trying to shove his way through. "Seize that boy!"

Guards sprang out of nowhere and grabbed Kael around his shoulders, pinning him in a way that he was forced to look up at where Zeptus stood, leaning over the ledge.

"This is the second time you've made an attempt on my life," he spat, "but now we've caught you. I promise you, *boy,*" he faltered for a moment, "that you will rot in jail for the rest of your life." There was something more in his voice.

King Morrindale was standing just beside Zeptus, a satisfied grin spread across his aloof face. Kael squirmed for a moment, racking his brain for a solution. An idea jumped into his mind.

"It's good to see you today," he called out, thrusting out his chin with a cocky smile, "King *Murderdale.*"

The king winced as if he had been struck. "What?!"

The guards on either side of him loosened their grip, unsure what to do. All eyes averted to the king, who had stepped forward as Zeptus stepped back. For a moment, just a second, Kael swore he saw Zeptus beaming. That couldn't be, he must have been wrong.

The king blinked and slapped the stone he was leaning against. "No, no! You won't get away from me this time!"

"I'm sorry, King," Zeptus announced, "the law is the law. The consequence for uttering that name is irreversible, with no exceptions, no matter who said it."

"I am above the law!" the king shouted in his face. Zeptus's calm expression didn't falter.

"Apologies, King, but it seems you made that law unbreakable, even for you."

The king shouted in anger, but otherwise, couldn't do anything else. As much as he didn't like it, he had been beaten this time.

Zeptus took the stand once again. "Hear this, Kael Rundown; your penalty takes place immediately. You are to leave the city at once to confront the dragon by yourself without any assistance or weapons."

Kael caught his breath. It was a good thing he had decided not to bring his sword along with him. The guards hesitated, but when Zeptus nodded, they him go. Kael gladly surrendered his bow, aware of the alternative.

He took a step to leave, but the king stopped him. "But know this, boy," he hissed, the malice as thick as honey in his voice, "henceforth you are hereby banished from the city of Vallenfend. If I or anybody else ever sees you in my kingdom again, I don't care what you say nor do, I *will* have you killed on the spot."

Kael nodded morosely and turned around, avoiding the people's eyes. He could physically feel how they detested him right then. He felt disgraced, dishonoured and alone. He had failed once again, and now he would have to suffer an even greater consequence than ever before—*banishment*. He shivered and hugged his stolen robe tighter around his body as he hurried away. All he wanted to do was get back to Shatterbreath.

Zeptus watched him go the whole way, until Kael had disappeared from the advisor's chilling purple eyes. He had...helped Kael. It if wasn't for him, the king would have most likely carried through with his original penalty. What was happening?

When Shatterbreath picked him out in the field some time later, she could already tell he had failed. A whiff of smoke escaped her jaws, but she didn't say anything. He stood in front of her for an awkward moment, trying to decipher what she was thinking about him.

"What happened?" she said at last.

"I missed," he stated, wincing. "They were going to lock me up, but I called the king *Murderdale.*"

"And?"

"They let me go. The punishment for calling him that is that going to you, alone and without a weapon. Usually, it means death."

"That was very clever."

Kael shook his head. "Maybe, but the king banished me! If I ever return, they'll kill me."

Shatterbreath cocked her head. "I guess it is time we move on then. There is truly no hope for your city. We have to turn to the other neighbouring kingdoms and plead for their help. That is," she raised her brow, "if you still want to help your ungrateful city."

Kael thought that he would have answered without hesitation if he was ever asked that. It disturbed him that he didn't right away. He mulled over it for a second, considering if the city was still worth all his trouble. Then he remembered all the good times he had in Vallenfend, and all the good people that lived inside that loved and cared for him, despite the hate the general public had displayed towards him.

But then again, Zeptus had been affecting them, twisting their minds to what he wanted them to think. Perhaps it wasn't their fault after all. Perhaps they were simply...misguided. Whether or not they hated him, he could not let Vallenfend fall. There was no other option.

"I will do whatever it takes to save Vallenfend," Kael said proudly.

Shatterbreath beamed. She lowered her shoulders so Kael could climb aboard. "Good. Let us delay no longer, hop on, Tiny. Let us be off at once."

Kael obeyed and as Shatterbreath lifted off into the sky, he could only wonder what new adventures would await him in a different kingdom.

Shatterbreath tilted her wings towards her cave. The mist around the mountain was weak and the sunlight poured overtop like water from a pitcher. But instead of gazing down at Vallenfend, or towards the awaiting mountain, Kael was looking out *over* the mountain range, towards unknown lands, unsure whether to be eager for what awaited him, or afraid.

323

End of Book One.

Made in the USA
Lexington, KY
08 March 2014